REPRISAL

KERRY KAYA

Boldwood

First published in 2020. This edition first published in Great Britain in 2022 by Boldwood Books Ltd.

Copyright © Kerry Kaya, 2020

Cover Design by Colin Thomas

Cover Photography: shutterstock

A CIP catalogue record for this book is available from the British Library.

Paperback ISBN 978-1-80280-005-0

Large Print ISBN 978-1-80280-007-4

Hardback ISBN 978-1-80280-006-7

Ebook ISBN 978-1-80280-008-1

Kindle ISBN 978-1-80280-009-8

Audio CD ISBN 978-1-80280-000-5

MP3 CD ISBN 978-1-80280-001-2

Digital audio download ISBN 978-1-80280-003-6

Boldwood Books Ltd
23 Bowerdean Street
London SW6 3TN
www.boldwoodbooks.com

For Shannon.

1

In a cloud of sickly-sweet cheap perfume, Angie Townsend tottered through the front door of her daughter Cathy's maisonette in a pair of dangerously high-heeled open-toed white stilettos. Talk about mutton dressed up as lamb. Completing the look, she wore a short black leather mini-skirt, an off-the-shoulder red woollen sweater, and an ever-present Rothman cigarette dangled precariously from the corner of her scarlet painted lips. She rolled her heavily mascaraed eyes up to the ceiling.

'He'll be the bleedin' death of you one day.' Clasping her daughter's jaw, she squinted through the curling cigarette smoke to take a good look at her girl. She none too gently tilted her face from side to side. 'Look at the state of you. He's battered you to within an inch of your life.'

'Leave it out, Mum.' Cathy wrenched her face free and tucked a strand of blonde hair behind her ear. Trust her mum to overex-aggerate. Other than a bruised cheek bone, there was barely a mark on her. 'You know what he's like when he's had a drink,' she said, referring to her husband, Terrance. 'He just gets heavy handed, that's all, doesn't know his own strength.'

'Doesn't know his own strength?' Angie exclaimed. 'Look at the state of this place and look at the state of your boat race. You need to take a good, long, hard look in the mirror, my girl.' She set about righting the kitchen table and chairs that had been knocked over in her daughter and son-in-law's latest fight. 'And you should be thinking about that baby you're carrying,' she said, stabbing her finger towards her daughter's prominent bump. 'You'll end up with social services breathing down your neck. You mark my words, girl, they'll end up taking that baby away from you.'

Cathy rolled her eyes and with great difficulty, clambered off the sofa. Still able to fit into her skinny jeans, she pulled her baggy T-shirt down over her bump. 'Just don't start if he comes back. That's all we bleeding well need, you two at each other's throats again.'

Angie opened her mouth to answer and quickly snapped it closed again. She watched her daughter's face contort with pain. ''Ere, he hasn't hurt the baby, has he?'

'No.' Cathy shook her head. 'He might be a lot of things, but he wouldn't do that.' She crossed over the kitchen to switch on the kettle. 'It's this little bugger,' she said, pointing down at her bump. 'Been playing football with my bladder all day, it has.'

'Well, you know what that means, don't you?' Sitting down at the table, Angie took out another cigarette and, using the butt of the previous one, she puffed on the fresh cigarette greedily until it sparked to life. 'It's bound to be a boy.'

Cathy grinned. She hoped so. She'd always wanted a son. She made her way back to the table and took a seat. 'If it's a boy, we're going to call him Terry. You know, short for Terrance.'

Puffing on her cigarette, Angie rolled her eyes. 'Leave it out,

Cath. You don't want to name the poor little sod after that ponce.'
She tilted her head to one side and studied her daughter. 'I've
heard that he's got some little tart on the go. That no-good
scrubber Donna Cassidy from across the estate. Been seeing her
for a good few months, he has, by all accounts.' She screwed up
her face. 'It's disgusting. The girl is barely even legal, and have
you seen the bloody state of her? She looks like she could do with
a good wash, right soapy looking cow, she is.' She reached out to
clasp her daughter's hand and her voice became gentle. 'You
know as well as I do that if she's a permanent fixture, then it's got
to be serious between them.'

The smile slid from Cathy's face and her heart lurched. She
wasn't stupid, or deaf, come to that. She'd heard the gossipmon-
gers whispering behind her back as she passed them by in the
street. 'Leave it out, Mum. They're just rumours, that's all. Of
course he isn't seeing someone else.' She rolled her eyes up to the
ceiling. 'And as for Donna Cassidy, bleeding hell, that little tart
has seen more helmets than the entire army did during the war,
and she isn't even eighteen yet.'

Angie leaned across the table. 'I know it isn't what you want to
hear, Cath, but it's been going on for a few months they reckon.'
She shrugged. 'I'm only repeating back what everyone else is
saying, darling, and if it is true, then it's not like all the other
times. This is different, this is serious.'

Hearing a key turn in the lock, Cathy stood up. 'Just don't
start,' she hissed, 'and don't mention Donna bloody Cassidy to
him, whatever you bleeding well do.'

'Ain't gonna say a word.' Watching as her daughter re-boiled
the kettle, Angie held her finger to her lips, her expression the
epitome of innocence.

Walking through to the kitchen, Terrance Matlock lifted his
eyebrows in mock annoyance. He was a tall man, well built. With

thick dark brown hair and brown eyes, he also had a rugged handsome face. 'Should have known you'd be here, Ange. Next time me and her' – he pointed across to his wife – 'have a ding-dong, we'll give you a bell, so you can have a front-row seat.' He crouched down to speak jovially in her ear. 'Wouldn't want you to miss out now, would we?'

'Ding-dong? Is that what you call battering the girl half to death?' Angie pursed her lips and looked up at her son-in-law through hooded eyes.

'Yeah, like I said, a ding-dong.' He placed a paper bag filled with fish and chips and a bottle of cheap wine down on the table. 'Go on, girl, get your laughing gear around that.'

The argument forgotten about, Angie rubbed her hands together with glee. She'd already had her dinner, but wouldn't say no, especially not when her son-in-law was buying. It was about time he put his own hands into his pockets, instead of poncing off her all the time.

Rolling her eyes, Cathy grinned. Angie could so easily be bought. She'd do anything for a drop of wine, and for as far back as she could remember, her old mum had always been the same.

'Come on, Cath.' Pulling out a chair, Terrance gestured for his wife to sit down with them. 'As you keep on telling me, the baby needs nourishment.'

'Yeah and it'd do you well to remember that,' Angie piped up. 'The baby needs nourishment not punishment,' she added, grinning at her own wit.

Cathy smiled. She loved it when her man was like this, caring and attentive. Only it never seemed to last for long. She pushed the dark thoughts to the back of her mind and popped a greasy chip into her mouth. Still, once the baby arrived, he was bound to change his ways, he just had to. It was what she was counting on.

2

Sitting alone at a corner table in their local public house, The Jolly Fisherman, Cathy sipped at a glass of lemonade as she watched her husband across the bar. As always, he was the life and soul of the party, and even from where she was sitting, she could hear his booming voice laughing and cracking jokes. Pity he wasn't always so jovial, she thought to herself bitterly.

'You all right, Cath?'

Cathy looked up at the woman standing beside her and nodded.

'Shove over then.' Stella Mooney's voice was loud.

Cathy shuffled along the seat. Sitting beside the tall and slim woman, she couldn't help but feel like a frump, and self-consciously, she pushed her blonde hair away from her face, then straightened out the baggy top that strained across her swollen stomach. She'd known Stella for most of her life and had always thought of her as one of the most beautiful women she had ever seen. Even as a child, Stella had been exquisite. With a heart-shaped face, poker straight deep red hair and vivid green eyes, men fell over themselves to be near her. She couldn't help but compare herself, and not for the first time did she wish that she had been blessed with Stella's looks, rather than the dull wavy blonde hair and ordinary features that she had been lumbered with.

'You know people are talking,' Stella said between mouthfuls of white wine.

Cathy looked up; a flush of shame fell across her face and she let out a long sigh. 'If you're referring to Donna Cassidy, then it isn't true. My Terrance might be a bit of a ladies' man, but that's as far as it goes.'

Stella gave her a pitying glance. 'I'm not talking about the local bike,' she said, nodding towards the entrance doors that Donna had flounced through just moments earlier. 'I'm talking about that baby of yours.'

'What about my baby?' Cathy's eyes widened, and stealing a glance towards her husband, she placed her hand protectively across her bump.

Stella bit down on her lip.

'No, come on, out with it,' Cathy implored. She turned in her seat to get a better view of the woman. 'What are people saying about my baby?'

'Well' – Stella leaned in closer – 'people are saying that that baby in there is my brother's.' She nodded across the pub to where her brother, Paul, was standing at the bar.

Cathy's mouth fell open. Not only was Paul Mooney fast on his way to becoming a known face, but he was also rich, handsome, and could have his pick of women. Why on earth would he want anything to do with her?

She laughed off Stella's words. 'Don't be ridiculous.'

Stella raised her eyebrows. 'I'm only repeating back what everyone else is saying, and well, you did have a bit of a thing for him once upon a time, didn't you? It's common knowledge that the two of you were as thick as thieves.'

'And he had a bit of a thing for me, too, if you remember rightly.' Cathy picked up her lemonade and, as she studied Paul, her heart skipped a beat. Even after all this time apart he still had an effect on her. She'd loved him once and supposed that a part of her still did. After all, what wasn't there to love about Paul Mooney? With a mop of dark brown hair and deep blue eyes that reminded her of sapphires, she often thought of him as a lovable rogue, albeit a dangerous rogue if crossed. But still, that ship had sailed a long time ago. 'But anyway, we're just friends.' She lifted her wedding finger in the air, indicating to the gold band. 'As you can see, I'm married now.'

'That's what I told them, and the thing is, Cath, I like you and wouldn't want there to be any bad blood between us, but' – she jerked her head towards her brother – 'if this causes us any problems, it'll be your head that rolls.' She gave Cathy a wide smile, showing off a set of even white teeth. 'Am I making myself clear?'

'Crystal.' Cathy hid her face behind her glass, her cheeks flaming bright red. For the life of her, she couldn't believe what she'd just heard. She turned to look at her husband. The last thing she needed was for him to hear the gossip. She walked a tight rope with him as it was and didn't want to add fuel to the fire.

'Well, I'm glad we cleared that up.' Stella's smile widened as her brother made his way over to the table. It was the kind of smile that stopped men in their tracks. 'Cathy here was just saying that she doesn't have long to go,' she told her brother as she glanced down at Cathy's bump.

Paul Mooney nodded thoughtfully. 'How are you keeping, Cath?' There was a gentleness to his voice, a side of him that so few people saw.

'Good, really good, actually.' Of course it was a lie, and as Cathy smiled up at him, she was more than thankful that she had had the hindsight to plaster on a thick layer of foundation to cover up the bruise across her cheekbone before coming out for the evening. Paul had a short temper at the best of times and would have gone mental if he'd known that Terrance took his fists to her. It was in his nature to look out for those he cared about.

'Good, I'm pleased.' He tilted his head to one side to look at her. 'You look well.'

'Of course she looks well. She's blooming, that's what pregnant women do.' Stella rolled her eyes at her brother's obvious stupidity.

'Yeah, I know,' Paul barked back. Cathy was not only blooming, but she also looked beautiful. Pregnancy obviously suited her.

He heard Terrance's booming voice come from behind him and turned his head. Personally, he'd never liked the man. Not to mention, he was one of Mad Dougie Ward's boys. Matlock may have been a face on their estate, but in Paul's eyes Matlock was nothing other than a prick. Still to this day, he believed that Cathy could have done so much better for herself. He told himself it wasn't jealousy. He and Cathy had had their chance when they were kids and it hadn't worked out between them. However, she still owned a piece of his heart and he had a feeling that she always would.

'Well, it was nice to see you, Cath.' He leant forward, dropped a kiss on her cheek, and had to resist the urge not to take her in his arms, and never let go. 'Take care of yourself, darling.'

'I will do.' Cathy gave him a wide smile, forcing herself not to look in her husband's direction. She could feel Terrance's glare on them and knew that as soon as they were alone, he would question her about the interaction. 'And you, you take care of yourself, too.'

'You know me, Cath.' He grinned, lifting his shoulders in a shrug. 'Trouble seems to follow me around.'

Underneath her husband's watchful eyes, Cathy squirmed in her seat. Just go, she silently begged of Paul. Couldn't he see how much trouble he was getting her into by just talking to her? 'Well, you take care,' she repeated.

'Yeah, I will do.' Narrowing his eyes, Paul turned to look over his shoulder a second time. 'Do you want me to have a word?' he asked, referring to the fact that Donna Cassidy had practically draped herself across Terrance's lap.

'No, of course not.' Cathy smiled to hide her blush. Inside of her though, humiliation burned. Of all the people to witness Terrance's indiscretion, it had to be Paul, her first love.

Paul gritted his teeth. 'Well, you know where I am if you want him sorted out.'

'Thanks,' she mumbled.

'Right, well' – he leaned forward and gently gripped her shoulder – 'see you around then, Cath, and take care of yourself, sweetheart.'

'Will do.' Cathy forced her voice to sound a lot chirpier than she actually felt. As Paul left the pub, her cheeks flamed bright red. She couldn't help but wish a big hole would appear out of nowhere and swallow her up.

* * *

'What did that prick want with you?'

Just as Cathy had predicted, as soon as they had closed the front door behind them, the mask Terrance put on when they were out in public slipped.

'Who?' She shrugged, pretending not to have a clue what he was talking about.

'Paul fucking Mooney. I saw him, he was all over you like a fucking rash.'

'Don't be daft.' Cathy laughed off his comment. 'Me and Paul are just mates; we've known each other for years. He was just asking about the baby, that was all.'

'Are you trying to imply that I don't know what I saw?'

The tone of her husband's voice caused the hairs on the back of Cathy's neck to stand up on end. 'I'm not implying anything.' She took off her coat and draped it across the arm of the artificial leather-covered sofa. 'Why would I do that?'

'Yeah, why would you do that?' Terrance's eyes were hard. 'Why would you call me a liar?'

Cathy's mouth dropped open. 'I didn't call you a liar.' She stumbled back, bumping the back of her legs against the sofa. 'I would never call you that.'

'But you just did.' He cocked his head to one side and gave her a quizzical stare.

'No... no I didn't.' Cathy screwed up her face as she tried to think back. Had she called him a liar and maybe not realised?

'Yeah, you did.' There was an edge to Terrance's voice. 'That's what you blatantly said.'

The first slap that connected with the side of Cathy's face was as loud as a gunshot, followed in quick succession by a second and third slap around the back of her head.

'Stop,' she cried. Still, the blows kept on coming. Falling back onto the sofa, Cathy held her arms protectively across her bump. 'You're going to hurt the baby.'

'Mine or his?' Terrance's face burned bright red, and between each slap and punch, he roared at her. 'Is that what this is all about? You want to protect his kid?'

'It's your baby,' she cried.

Still the slaps rained down on top of her.

* * *

Not only was Paul Mooney fast on his way to becoming a known face, but his reputation preceded him.

'So, what do you reckon?' Jason Milner, Paul's business partner and sidekick, asked.

'I reckon he's taking the piss out of us.'

They paused inside the entrance of a snooker hall, and as they looked around, they spotted the man in question hunched over a snooker table towards the back of the premises. With a cue stick in hand, he gave a carefree laugh as he stood poised to take a shot.

In unison, they moved forward and, snatching up a cue stick of his own, there was a purpose to Paul's swagger. 'Oi,' he shouted out.

Seeing Paul Mooney charge towards him, Michael Nicholls made a run for it in the opposite direction.

'Oh no you don't, you slimy little fucker.' With ease, Paul caught up with him and, grasping a handful of Michael's hair in his fist, he dragged him towards the fire escape. Outside in a narrow alleyway, he slammed Michael up against the brick wall. 'You owe me money.'

'And I said I'd get it to you; I gave you my word, didn't I?' Michael looked between Paul and Jason. They were big men, huge in fact. Both were tall with wide shoulders and athletic builds to match their height. The fear Michael felt came off him in waves. Beads of sweat broke out across his upper lip and he snaked his tongue across it. 'I'm just having one or two cash-flow problems,' he stammered. 'As soon as I'm back on my feet, I'll get you your dough.'

Paul thought this through. 'So you're telling me you haven't got my cash?' he asked with a smile.

Michael relaxed slightly, hoping more than anything that Paul was in a good mood. 'Nah, not yet, but I will, honest to God I will. I swear to you on my kids' lives that I'll get you your money.'

The smile slid from Paul's face. 'So, you haven't got my dough, but you've got the money to come in here, have a game of snooker and shove chisel up your fucking hooter?'

'What?' Michael's face paled and he wiped the back of his hand underneath his nose, giving away the fact that just as Paul had predicted, he'd recently snorted a line of cocaine.

'You heard me, you fucking degenerate.' Taking the cue stick, Paul smashed it into the man's gut. The fact that Michael worked for Samson Ivers, a serious face, meant absolutely nothing to him, and why should it? Paul was on the up; he was about to make his presence known, and more fool anyone who got in his way.

Groaning in pain, Michael slumped forward and, using the cue stick, Paul repeatedly crashed it down across the back of the man's skull. 'No one,' he spat, 'takes the piss out of me and gets away with it, and that includes fucking you.' For good measure, he drew back his steel toe-capped boot and executed a sickening kick to Michael's ribs. 'You've got twenty-four hours to get me my money, and if you don't' – he kicked out once more, taking great delight in the crunch of a bone snapping in two – 'you're a dead man fucking walking.'

Barely even breaking out in a sweat, Paul pulled back his shoulders, flung the cue stick on top of Michael's semi-conscious body, then walked out of the snooker hall as though he didn't have a single care in the world.

* * *

Lifting the back of her hand, Cathy pressed it against her cheek, which was still smarting from the stinging back hander her husband had dished out. 'Why do you always do this?' she cried. 'Why do you always have to do this to me? I'm your wife.'

'Wife?' Terrance roared back. 'That's right, you're my wife. You're my property to do with as I please, as I see fit.' His brown eyes darkened, and as he screwed up his face, he clenched his fists into tight balls. Launching himself forward, he backed his wife up against the kitchen counter. 'You're mine,' he screamed in her face. 'Mine, not Paul fucking Mooney's.'

Recoiling, Cathy turned her face away. She could smell alcohol and stale tobacco on his breath. The fumes were enough to make her want to gag. 'And what about Donna Cassidy?' She stuck her chin in the air and there was a steely glint in her eyes as she confronted her husband. 'I've heard the rumours; I know what you've been getting up to behind my back.'

'What are you talking about?' Terrance swallowed deeply and as his Adam's apple bobbed up and down, he narrowed his eyes. 'Has your mother been putting ideas into your head again?'

'Everyone is talking about the two of you.' She pointed out of the kitchen window. 'You and her, that Donna,' she spat, 'you're the talk of the estate.'

'Nah.' He took a step backwards and gave a nervous chuckle. 'Don't be daft, Cath.' He looked around the open plan lounge and kitchenette. It might not have been much, but it was his, or more to the point, it was Cathy's, seeing as the tenancy was in her name. If she was to throw him out on his arse, he'd have nowhere to go, and he knew for a fact that he didn't fancy kipping at Donna's place, what with her mum, dad, and half a dozen siblings all squashed together in a two-bedroomed flat. 'They're jealous, that's all. Jealous of what me and you have got.'

'Jealous?' Cathy scoffed. 'Jealous of this?' She swept her hand around the small, outdated kitchen. 'Why the hell would anyone be jealous of this?'

'I dunno, babe.' Thinking fast, he pulled her roughly into his arms. 'They're jealous of us. Jealous that we've got a bright future ahead of us. Me and you, we're going places, ain't we?'

'Going places?' Cathy shook her head from side to side as she eased herself out of his embrace. The fact that he hadn't denied the affair hung heavy in the air. 'And where the fuck are we supposed to be going exactly?'

'Come on, Cath.' He gave her a beaming grin, showing even white teeth. 'It's me and you, ain't it? You know what I'm like. She doesn't mean anything to me. You're the only woman I want. We're married, ain't we? That's gotta tell you something.'

Cathy's blood ran cold. So, the rumours were true after all. Closing her eyes, she inwardly sighed. He'd sworn the last time she'd caught him cheating that he would never do it again, and she, like a silly fool, had believed his every word. Inside her the baby kicked and she rested her hand upon her bump. She couldn't do this any more. For the baby's sake she couldn't continue to allow Terrance to treat her like a doormat, nor could she let him dish out punches and slaps whenever she dared step out of line. What kind of a role model was that for their child? No, enough was enough. If she didn't stand up to him, tell him that she wanted him to leave then he would continue using and abusing her. She'd been strong once; she took after her mum in that department and Angie would never have allowed a man to treat her with disregard. No, whether he liked it or not, Terrance was out on his ear, not only for her own sanity but also for her unborn child's.

* * *

Leaving the snooker hall, Paul climbed back into his car. It was a brand-new Range Rover with tinted windows, alloy wheels, and cream leather seats. He turned to look at Jason. 'Twenty-four hours,' he reminded him. He was in half a mind to drag Michael back out of the hall by the scruff of his scummy drug-infested neck and to the nearest cash point. 'That's all we're giving him, and if the slimy bastard doesn't pay up, I'll cut his fucking bollocks off and give 'em to his missus as an early Christmas present.'

Jason chuckled. Paul was hot-headed all right, and although it had been said in a jocular manner, he knew for a fact that Paul meant every word he said. It was at times like this that he was reminded just how dangerous his best mate actually was.

'So, where to next?' Tearing his gaze away from the snooker hall, Paul leaned back in his seat and lit a cigarette.

From his jacket pocket, Jason pulled out a small black leather-bound notebook. As he flicked through the worn pages, he ignored the snigger that came from his mate. The little notebook contained every debt owed to them. Unlike his business partner, for the life of him, he was unable to remember who owed them what. The bottom line was that this little book was his only way of keeping track. In fact, the notebook was more than worth its weight in gold, as far as he was concerned. 'Head towards Tilbury.'

'Are you sure?' It was said tongue-in-cheek.

Snapping the notebook closed, Jason held it aloft in the air. 'Say's so right here in black and white.'

Paul rolled his eyes and started the ignition. At the side of his jaw, a nerve twitched. 'Did you see that ponce Terrance Matlock in the boozer tonight?' His arms were taut as he turned the steering wheel. 'What the fuck Cathy sees in him, I'll never know.' He gave Jason a sideways glance and shook his head. 'That slapper Donna Cassidy was all over him like a fucking rash and right in front of Cath an' all.' His fists tightened around the steering wheel. It was only the fact that he had bigger fish to fry that was stopping him from going back to The Jolly Fisherman and smashing his fists into Terrance's face.

Jason nodded. As always, he was amazed at just how quickly Paul's mood could change. He was also one of only a few people who knew the extent of Paul's true feelings towards Cathy Townsend, as she'd been known before she'd married. He knew for a fact that her waster of a husband had been given more than one swerve over the years all because Paul still loved her. 'He'll get his comeuppance, mate.'

'Yeah, and you'd better believe it.'

As the car sped through the streets, Jason snatched the seat belt and snapped it into place. The bottom line was that he wouldn't want to be in Terrance Matlock's shoes when Paul finally caught up with him and showed him the full force of his wrath.

* * *

Cathy breathed heavily through flared nostrils, and as she swallowed down a mouthful of bile, the acrid bitter acid burned the back of her throat. Terrance may as well have thrust a steel blade into her heart, so intense was the pain his latest betrayal had caused her. She watched her husband begin to right the furniture that had been knocked over during their fight and fought the urge not to scream out loud.

'No,' she spat. 'No, no, no.' Her voice became louder, bordering on hysterical.

With the dining chair poised in his hand, Terrance looked up. 'What the fuck is wrong with you now?'

'You and her!' Cathy screamed from the kitchen doorway. She reached behind her for a bread knife and sliced it through the air. 'I want you out! I want you out of my home! I want you out of my life!'

Terrance narrowed his eyes. With her hair sticking up all over the place, his wife looked deranged, and he burst out laughing. 'Leave it fucking out, Cath.'

'I want you out.' With the knife still firmly clutched in her fist, Cathy took a step forward. 'I mean it,' she screamed, 'I want you out!'

'Tough fucking shit.' Flopping down on the sofa, Terrance opened up a newspaper and pretended to read through the headlines. 'This is my gaff,' he said, not bothering to even look up. 'My fucking gaff.'

'I said that I want you out.' When her husband still made no attempt to move, Cathy darted across the room, spread open her handbag, and fished out a small address book. Her hands shook, so intense was the rage that pumped through her veins. Every fibre of her being threatened to be consumed by the grief his infidelity, his betrayal, had caused.

Over and over again, he had hurt her, and not just physically. She'd lost count of the number of times that he had climbed into bed beside her in the early hours of the morning, reeking of an unfamiliar perfume. Not to mention the number of times she had scrubbed lipstick marks from the collars of his shirts, a shade of lipstick she would never have been seen dead wearing. He had no shame in parading Donna around. He hadn't even tried to hide the affair. How many times did he expect her to stand by and watch as he cheated on her with other women?

'If you don't get out,' she growled, 'then I'll call Paul Mooney and tell him to come and drag you out.' Stony-faced, she began frantically flipping through the address book.

Terrance looked up. He swallowed deeply, watching as her fingers flew through the pages of the small book. 'Leave it out, you stupid mare.' A coward through and through, a shiver of fear ran down the length of his spine. The last thing he wanted or needed was Paul Mooney on his case, and despite Terrance's reputation as a hard man, when it came to Mooney there was no contest. Mooney was more than just a little bit unhinged, he was crazy. 'You want me out, eh?' He slammed down the newspaper and jumped up from the sofa. 'I'm gone and trust me darling this'll be the biggest mistake of your life.'

'Nah, I don't think so.' Cathy yanked off her wedding ring and threw it in his face. 'Marrying you was the biggest mistake of my life.'

Ducking down to dodge the ring, Terrance straightened up. 'You'll regret this,' he spat.

'Never.' Cathy watched as her husband headed for the front door, and when she heard it slam behind him, she promptly fell to her knees and sobbed her heart out.

3

Two weeks later, after a hard days' graft, Paul and Jason headed for the local café for a well-earned spot of lunch.

Jason studied the menu; he leaned back in his chair and rubbed his stomach. 'I'm so fucking hungry I could eat a scabby horse.'

Paul chuckled and, giving over his order, he leaned back in the chair and looked to Jason expectedly.

'I'll have the sirloin steak, medium, with chips and tomatoes.' He snapped the menu closed and looked up at the waitress. 'And can you take the seeds out of the tomatoes?'

Shaking his head, Paul burst out laughing. 'Take the seeds out? What the fuck is wrong with you, Jay?'

'What?' Jason protested. 'I don't like them.'

'And I don't like looking at your boat every day, but I don't have any other choice, do I?' With a smile upon his face, he shook his head a second time and looked up at the flustered waitress. 'He'll have the tomatoes as they come, love.'

The waitress smiled her gratitude and walked away.

'Take the fucking seeds out.' Paul continued to chuckle.

His cheeks turning red, Jason shrugged. Lifting his mug, he took a deep gulp of tea as he studied Paul over the rim of the cup. 'Did you hear that your Cathy threw that waste of space Matlock out?'

Leaning back in the chair, Paul drummed his fingers on the table. It had been a long time since Cathy had been referred to as his. 'Yeah,' he finally answered, 'I did hear something along those lines.'

'And what about him, Matlock?' Jason asked, raising his eyebrows.

'Matlock.' Paul gritted his teeth. 'Let's just say, now that Cathy has seen sense, he's fair game as far as I'm concerned, and trust me, when I get my hands on the no-good ponce, he's gonna wish he'd never been born.'

Jason nodded. Paul's reply came as no surprise to him. Even as he'd asked the question, he'd already known what his best mate was going to say.

* * *

Terrance had just about had enough. With nowhere else to go, he'd reluctantly found himself at Donna's home, and after initially placing his size-ten feet firmly underneath the table, the situation he now found himself to be in was starting to wear thin.

He rubbed wearily at his temples as the start of a blinding headache made him feel as though his head was in a vice.

'And so I said to her, keep your nose out of mine and my Tel's business.'

'What?' Terrance looked up. Half the time, he drowned out Donna's incessant chatter. He leaned to one side as one of her younger siblings chased the family dog around the kitchen table, and he swallowed down his irritation. At times, it felt as though he was living in a zoo, and he wasn't only referring to the stale stench that permeated the property.

Donna took a long drag on her cigarette. 'Cathy's bloody mother,' she snapped. 'She was talking shit about me and you.' She blew out a long stream of smoke, then stubbed out the cigarette in an overflowing glass ashtray. 'And I won't put up with that, Tel. What me and you have is special.'

'You spoke to Angie?' He could feel his temper begin to rise and he resisted the urge to lash out. Shacking up with Donna because he had nowhere else to go was one thing, but she certainly wasn't about to become a permanent fixture in his life.

'Yeah I did, and I put the old bat straight an' all.' With a smug expression across her face, Donna leaned back in the chair and spread open her arms. 'Going on and on, she was, about that kid your ex is about to drop, as if it's something special. I mean, anyone would think she's the only woman in the world to ever get pregnant, the way she was carrying on. And like I told her, it's only a matter of time until me and you have a baby of our own, ain't it?'

'A baby?' Terrance choked on his words, and as he began to cough uncontrollably, he glanced down at her belly, hoping more than anything that she wasn't hinting she was already pregnant. He could think of nothing worse. Just the very thought of having a child with Donna was enough to bring him out in a cold sweat.

'Well, it's gonna happen one day, ain't it?' She picked up her cigarette packet, plucked out a fresh cigarette, and brought it to her lips. 'Let's face it,' she said, sitting forward in the chair, 'it's the only way the council will give us our own place.' As she lit her cigarette, she turned her head. 'Ain't that right, Mum?'

Yvonne Cassidy nodded. 'That's right, Don'. That's how me and your dad got this place.' She rolled her tongue across her decaying teeth and lounged back against the kitchen counter. Her stained T-shirt with the slogan 'bite me' in big red letters strained against her bulging gut.

In that instant, it was almost like looking into the future. What was that saying? Like mother like daughter? At least Angie had a bit of nous about her and knew how to look after herself. He glanced down at his watch and, noting the time, he scraped back his chair and abruptly stood up.

'Where are you going, Tel?'

'Out.' Terrance looked down at the woman he had risked his marriage for and felt genuinely sick to his stomach. Even if she did find herself pregnant, how could he be certain that it was even his kid? Let's face it, she'd been around the block more than once, had Donna.

As he made his way out of the kitchen, he shook the dog away from his leg. All the bastard thing had done since he'd turned up on Donna's doorstep was try and hump him. He reached for the front door handle and resisted the urge to boot the randy little fucker up its arse. Instead, he bared his teeth and growled loudly, until the mutt ran back down the hallway with his tail between his legs.

'When will you be back?' As she scooped up the dog, there was a whine to Donna's voice that he had never noticed before.

He watched as the dog licked her face and felt sick to his stomach. What was the betting the dirty cow didn't even bother to wash the mutt's saliva off her face before climbing into bed later that night? Swallowing down his repulsion, he flashed a smile, the kind of smile that he knew women couldn't resist, including Donna and her skank of a mother.

'How long is a piece of sting darling,' he answered with a wink.

'Oh, one more thing, Tel.' Yvonne joined her daughter in the hallway. On her hip, she jiggled the youngest of the Cassidy clan. The child's constant screams went right through his head.

With his smile still firmly in place Terrance raised his eyebrows. He had places to go and people to see and was already running late.

Yvonne's yellow nicotine-stained fingers plucked a fresh cigarette out from the packet, and she gave him a gap-toothed grin as she lit up.

'Don't forget to hand over your half of the rent money when you get back.' She gave him a sly grin. 'You're as good as family now, and if this is going to be yours and our Donna's home, your little love nest,' she chuckled, 'then it's only right that you pay your way. After all, every little bit helps. Here, I'll tell you what. I could even put a few quid away for yous each week. That way, you and our Don will have some cash to fall back on once she's up the duff.'

'That's a good idea. What do you reckon, Tel?' Standing beside her mother, Donna beamed with delight.

Terrance stared at the two women. He opened his mouth to speak but was rendered speechless. Fuck that. He gave a shudder and, screwing up his face without bothering to answer, he stepped out of the flat and slammed the front door closed, leaving Donna and her mother firmly behind him.

* * *

With a rolled up twenty-pound note held between his thumb and forefinger, Lucas Vaughn lifted his head and glanced in the rear-view mirror. He watched as a car pulled into the car park and swallowed down his irritation. After all, it wasn't the first time that Terrance Matlock had kept him waiting. Shaking his head, he

returned to the task in hand. Holding a compact disk case towards
his chest, in quick procession, he expertly snorted two fat lines of
cocaine from it. Sniffing loudly, he wrinkled his nose and pinched
his nostrils, wiping away any excess powder in the process. Then
licking his index finger, he gathered up the remaining remnants
of white powder and rubbed them furiously across his gums.
Glancing up at the mirror for a second time, he rolled his eyes,
threw the case back into the glove box, and climbed out of the car.

'You're late.' Leaning casually against the car, Lucas crossed
his arms over his chest, then glanced around the otherwise empty
car park. 'In fact' – he fixed his glare back on Terrance and
squared his shoulders – 'you're starting to seriously piss me off.'

Ignoring the remark, a wide grin spread across Terrance's face
and he rubbed his hands together as he strolled casually towards
the car. 'What have we got this time then?'

Lucas gritted his teeth. There was something about Matlock
that grated on his nerves. He was too cocksure of himself for a
start. Without answering, he pushed himself away from the car
and made his way around to the boot. Springing open the lock,
he gestured towards several large cardboard boxes.

'Same as last time.' He gave Terrance a sidelong glance, his
tone sounding bored. 'Dougie said to pop them out for a tenner
each, okay?'

Terrance pulled the nearest sealed box towards him and
ripped apart the brown parcel tape. Filled to the brim, each box
contained a selection of men's designer shirts that were still
encased in individual clear plastic wrappers with the price tags
attached. He'd make a fair few bob selling the shirts, and the
money was already burning a hole in his pocket.

The transaction complete, Lucas slammed down the boot and
made his way back around the car. It didn't escape his notice that
he was driving a brand-new Audi, whereas Terrance drove a

clapped-out Mercedes that would look more at home on the fore-court of a scrap yard than on the road.

'Hey Matlock,' he called out, 'about time you scrapped that shit tip, ain't it?' He grinned as he watched Terrance's eyebrows knit together and knew his words had the man's back up. 'You should try your luck and run it over to the Carters' scrap yard over on the view. You never know' – he grinned – 'if they're feeling generous, you might even get a couple of quid for it.' He paused and scratched his chin as though thinking it over. 'What is the going rate for scrap metal these days?' He chuckled out loud and, climbing behind the wheel, he slammed the car door closed behind him. In the rear-view mirror, he watched the flurry of anger crease Terrance's face and, turning the key in the ignition, he laughed even harder, before screeching out of the car park.

* * *

'Fucking prick,' Terrance growled. With a scowl spread across his face, he watched as the Audi sped out of the car park and slammed the car boot shut with as much force as he could physi-cally muster. The Carters, the fucking Carters. He screwed up his face. He'd heard all about Jimmy Carter's antics. Rumour had it that he had a liking for the one-eyed snake, the fucking Nancy boy. Why Tommy Carter hadn't put his dirty cunt of a brother into the ground he had no idea. By all accounts, the brothers were as close as ever. The very thought sickened him and he gave an involuntary shiver. 'Dirty fucking bastard,' he muttered out loud.

As for Lucas fucking Vaughn, who exactly was he, and where the fuck had he even come from? All he knew was that the younger man had turned up out of nowhere and quickly climbed the ladder, barging his way into Dougie Ward's firm, and making himself indispensable in the process. Now look at him. By all accounts, he was one of Dougie's right-hand men and was apparently well respected by the big man himself.

His scowl deepened and he climbed inside the car. Digging his fingers inside his denim pocket, he pulled out a wad of cash, recalling Yvonne's demand for rent money. Why the fuck should he pay anything? It wasn't even his flat, and the last thing he planned to do was stick around. His thoughts turned to his wife and the little maisonette that she kept spick and span. A slow smile spread across his face; opposite where he'd parked the car was a florist shop, and as he started the ignition, an idea formed in his mind and his grin grew even wider.

* * *

Balancing a cup of tea on the arm of the sofa, Cathy leaned back against the cushions and closed her eyes. Two weeks her Terrance had been gone and she was finally coming to terms with her new life as a single soon-to-be mother. She felt her baby kick inside her and she automatically placed her hand upon her bump and caressed it lovingly. She could do this, she told herself. She could bring her baby up alone, just like her mother had done before her. She had never met her father and her mum had only ever been vague about him. Sometimes she wondered if Angie even knew herself who he was.

A knocking at the front door made her groan out loud. Talk of the devil. Ever since her husband had left, Angie had become a constant visitor. She placed the cup on the floor, pushed herself up from the sofa, and waddled towards the front door. The sight in front of her almost made her stagger backwards. Of all the people she was expecting, her husband was not one of them. Quickly, she composed herself, and with a stony expression, she leaned against the door frame with her arms folded across her chest. 'What do you want?'

Terrance spread open his arms. 'I'm back, love.' He gave her a wink. 'Did you miss me?'

Cathy raised her eyebrows. 'Miss you?' she exclaimed.

'Well, I missed you.' He gave her a beaming smile. 'And I want to come back home. This is where I belong, love. Just you, me, and our kid – one big happy family.'

'Has Donna thrown you out?' She took a moment of satisfaction in seeing him grovel. 'What did you do?' She tilted her chin upwards as though thinking the question over. 'No, wait, don't tell me' – she placed her finger in the air – 'let me guess, you gave her a clump for having the audacity to answer you back?'

'No, love, nothing like that. Honest to God, me and her were nothing serious.' He shrugged and a sly grin spread across his face. 'It's different to what me and you have got. What we have is special.'

'She did throw you out then.' Having heard just about enough, Cathy made to close the door.

'C'mon, Cath.' He jammed his foot inside the door frame in a bid to stop the door from being closed in his face, and his voice took on a desperate measure. 'I'm back, love. You always knew I would be. This is where I belong, home, here with you.' Taking the bundle of cash from his pocket, he waved the money underneath Cathy's nose. 'You can even go out and buy that pram you've had your eye on.' It was a lie of course; he had no intention of handing over his hard earned dosh, especially not for some pram when she could buy a cheaper version out of her own money that did the exact same job.

'You're like a bad penny,' Cathy groaned. Despite herself, she couldn't help but smile; he could charm the birds from the trees when he wanted to and call her a fool but to know that she'd got one over on Donna Cassidy made her smile just that little bit wider.

'Can I come in?' Terrance put on his best grin. 'I promise that I'll be on my best behaviour. Look, I bought you these.' From behind his back, he produced a bunch of pink carnations, the petals already drooping.

Looking from the flowers to her husband, Cathy rolled her eyes and pulled the door open wider. As much as she hated to admit it, the truth was, she was struggling without him. The rent needed paying, and with only enough money in her purse to pay for the gas, electric, and some food, she didn't know how she was going to cope, and that was without the baby things she still needed to buy; the poor little bugger still didn't even have anywhere to sleep, let alone clothes and nappies. 'Best behaviour,' she warned.

'On my life, Cath.' He stepped around her, walked through to the lounge and plopped himself down on the sofa. 'How about making a cuppa for your old man?' He rubbed his hand over his stomach. 'Oh and I wouldn't say no to a bacon sandwich either, if you've got one going.' He winked.

Cathy sighed. So much for him changing his ways, she thought. She flicked the switch on the kettle, opened the fridge door, and took out four rashers of bacon. Dropping them into a pan of sizzling oil, she stood back against the kitchen worktop, and watched her husband. She couldn't help but wonder if she'd just made a big mistake by letting him back into her life.

4

'Oh Mum, look at this, isn't it lovely?' Cathy and Angie were at the Dagenham Sunday market and pointing to a wicker Moses basket adorned in ivory satin and cream-coloured lace. Cathy's face lit up.

'If it's what you want, then get it,' Angie answered as she ran her hand across the smooth satin and smiled her approval. The basket was beautiful, even she had to admit that.

'I don't know. What do you think? It is lovely though, isn't it?' Tightly clutching her purse, Cathy was in two minds. She lifted the price tag and felt her heart sink. She was at least fifteen pounds short.

'Is it what you want?' In a moment of tenderness, Angie placed her arm around her daughter's shoulders. It wasn't often she openly displayed affection to her only child and, pushing a lock of blonde hair out of Cathy's face, her voice was gentle. 'If it's what you want then get it, Cath.'

'I can't. I don't have enough money.' Cathy flicked the price tag. 'I've only got twenty pounds on me.'

Slipping her hand inside her handbag, Angie pulled out her

purse. 'That husband of yours should try getting a job. It wouldn't hurt him to put his hand in his pocket. That baby you're carrying is his responsibility, too, you know.'

'He has got a job,' Cathy sighed.

'Selling a bit of knocked off gear isn't a job, Cath.' Angie pursed her lips. 'The lazy bastard should try getting out of bed before lunchtime once in a while.'

'Mum!'

'All right.' Angie held up her hand. 'I was only saying, so stop being so bloody touchy.' She unzipped her purse and took out a ten-pound note, then fished around in the bottom of her handbag for a few pound coins. 'You can pay me back when you've got the money, or better still, Terrance can pay me back.' She winked.

Cathy rolled her eyes. 'Thanks, Mum.' She reached out to touch the cream lace. She could just imagine her baby asleep in the basket, lovely and warm, and as snug as a bug, as her Nanna Pat used to say.

'We'll take this one.' Lifting her hand, Angie caught the stall holder's attention and, passing across the money, she smiled as she watched him place the basket into a large see-through plastic bag. 'There you go.' She handed the package to her daughter. 'Can you manage, darling?'

With the basket tucked underneath her arm Cathy nodded. It wasn't too heavy and she couldn't help but feel proud. Nothing but the very best would do for her baby.

'Look who it is.' Looking through the crowd of shoppers, Angie sucked her teeth. 'She's got a nerve showing her face around here.'

Cathy looked up. Walking towards them was Donna Cassidy, surrounded by several of her mates. 'Just ignore her, Mum,' Cathy groaned. 'I don't want to cause a scene, not here, in the middle of the bloody market of all places.'

As they passed by one another, Cathy lifted her chin in the air and kept her back ramrod straight. Oh, how she hated Donna Cassidy. Just being in close proximity to her husband's mistress was enough to make her blood boil.

'Oh, by the way' – Donna stopped, and with the backing of her sniggering friends, she placed her hands on her hips, thrust out her chest and smirked – 'he only went back to you out of pity.'

'What?' Slowly turning around, the fine hairs on the back of Cathy's neck stood up on end. Finally, she was face-to-face with the young woman her husband had been sleeping with. And she was young, too, a lot younger than Cathy could have ever imagined. Beyond the makeup and hair extensions, Donna looked exactly what she was, a kid. Only just out of school, her skin was still smooth, youthful, and fresh, even if the image she was trying to portray was not.

As she looked the girl over, Cathy felt nothing but repulsion. Her mum was right, Donna was a soapy looking cow, and in a way, she supposed that wasn't Donna's fault. It was probably all she'd ever known, and it was common knowledge that the rest of the Cassidy family was just as grimy. Just one glance at the girl's parents was enough to tell her that. How her Terrance could even think about putting his hands on this child, let alone actually carrying it through, she would never understand. And to know that he had crawled into bed beside her after touching Donna was enough to make her want to vomit. 'What did you just say to me?'

Despite the cold weather, Donna was dressed in skin-tight light grey tracksuit bottoms and a white T-shirt with a plunging neckline that showed off her ample cleavage, all thanks to the push-up bra she had put on that morning.

She gestured towards her body. 'You heard me.' She smirked. 'My Tel, he couldn't keep his hands off me and he told me himself that he was only going back to you, because he felt sorry for you. I mean' – she looked around at her friends and gave a cocky grin – 'as soon as you've dropped that kid, he'll come running back to me. He even told me that he couldn't wait to see the back of you, once and for all.'

'Ignore her, Cath.' Tugging on her daughter's arm, Angie spat out the words. 'She's just some dirty little slapper.'

Donna threw her head back and laughed. 'Me a dirty slapper?' She looked Angie dead in the eyes. 'From what I've heard, you'd do anything for a bit of free meat. Shagging the local butcher for a while, weren't you?'

* * *

Kid or no kid, Donna's words were like a red rag to a bull and, throwing the Moses basket to the floor, Cathy charged forward, grabbed a handful of Donna's dark hair extensions in her fist, and dragged the girl to her knees. 'You dirty, vindictive, nasty whore,' she roared, emphasising the words as she slapped Donna around the back of her head. 'You dirty, filthy little slapper. That's my mum you're talking about.'

Not wanting to lose face in front of her friends, Donna tugged at Cathy's wrists. The older woman was stronger, a lot stronger, and her fingers held on in a vice-like grip. 'Let me fucking go,' she roared. Twisting her body this way and that, she managed to get to her feet. Much to her dismay, Cathy still held a handful of dark hair in her fist, the very same luxurious dark brown hair that she had saved up for weeks to pay for. She threw her head back and glared. 'You just wait until I tell my Tel about this,' she growled, 'then maybe you'll see just how serious he is about me.'

Cathy charged forward a second time. 'Stay away from my husband,' she warned. As she turned to look at the crowd that had gathered around them, Cathy's heart was racing. 'Be careful of this one,' she declared, her voice loud, 'she's got a dirty little habit of trying to steal other women's husbands.'

'You should smack her one,' a female voice piped up from the crowd of onlookers.

'She's nothing but jailbait,' another shouted in disgust.

It was at that moment Angie intervened. As much as she had wanted to see Donna get her comeuppance, she was also reminded that her daughter was heavily pregnant. 'Enough now, Cath. Leave the little whore to play her games.' Pulling on her daughter's arm, she dragged her to where the Moses basket had been dropped onto the mud-splattered floor.

'You'll see,' Donna called out from behind them, 'he'll come back to me, you just wait and see.'

'Piss off, little girl,' Cathy spat back.

'Ignore her,' Angie hissed as she bent down to retrieve the Moses basket.

In the struggle, the plastic bag had been split open and the ivory satin had been trodden into the mud.

'No,' Cathy cried. She pulled the basket out of her mother's arms and swiped away the dirt. Left in its place was a dark stain. 'It's ruined,' she cried.

'No, it's not.' Angie rolled her lips together as she inspected the damage. 'It'll come out if I put it in to soak.' Even as she said the words, she wasn't so sure she would be able to shift the stain.

'It's an omen, Mum.' Glaring after Donna, Cathy was close to tears.

Angie sighed. She didn't like to admit it out loud, but she couldn't help but feel the same way. The spoiled satin could well be a sign of what was to come.

5

Later that evening, Yvonne Cassidy nodded in an approving manner as she gave her eldest daughter the once over. 'You look the bollocks, Don, a right little stunner.'

Preening herself in front of the bathroom mirror, Donna grinned. She turned to the side and sucked in her stomach, revelling in the way the short black skin-tight dress skimmed across her curves, showing off her long legs and ample double-D breasts. She already knew that she looked good, but still she basked in the compliments her mother gave her.

'He won't be able to keep his hands off me.' She applied a thick sticky layer of lip gloss across her lips and then turned her head to the side. 'Look at me,' she said, 'I'm ten times better than that bitch he's married to will ever be.' Her lips curled down at the corners and her forehead furrowed, making her features turn ugly. 'Cathy needs to fuck off out of it. Terrance is mine, and the quicker she gets that through her thick skull, the better.'

'That's right, Don.' Yvonne nodded in agreement. 'You go and get your man back, sweetheart.'

'Oh, I will do, Mum, don't you worry about that.' She sprayed a generous amount of sickly-sweet perfume up and down the length of her dress, fluffed out her long dark hair extensions, slipped on her high heels, and then spread open her arms. 'Well, how do I look?'

'Stunning.' Yvonne's chest swelled with pride. Her girl was a looker all right. The fact that Donna had only just turned seventeen and was already on to her fifth man in as many months was wiped from her mind. She followed her daughter towards the front door. 'Keep the noise down when you get home,' she said, lowering her voice. 'I don't want your dad to wake up. You know what a miserable old bugger he is.'

Donna rolled her eyes. From day one, her dad had shown his disapproval at her choice of boyfriend. He hadn't liked the fact that Terrance was a face, that he had a reputation as a hard man. As far as Donna was concerned that was half the attraction; she loved Terrance's notoriety, loved the fact people gave her respect whenever she was with him, and if that wasn't enough, Terrance wasn't only handsome, but he was loaded too. He took her to fancy restaurants and had even paid for a hotel for the night when they'd first begun courting. 'Don't worry,' she groaned, 'we'll be as quiet as we can be.' She slung the strap of her handbag across her shoulder and then opened the front door. 'See you later, Mum. Wish me luck.'

Standing on the doorstep, Yvonne grinned. 'Good luck, babe, not that you're going to need it. One look at you and he'll be putty in your hands.' She grinned.

'Tell me something I don't already know.' Throwing a cocky wink over her shoulder, Donna sauntered off towards the pub.

* * *

Swallowing down a mouthful of dry white wine, Angie crossed one shapely leg over the other. She picked up her cigarette box and plucked out a cigarette. Lighting up, she inhaled deeply, then slowly blew out a long thin stream of smoke. She loved nothing better than to be in the pub. Over the years, the boozer had become more like a second home to her. Well known and well liked on the estate, she had an endless supply of friends or acquaintances who she could sit with, and if her luck was on the up, then more often than not, she didn't even need to take her purse out of her handbag the entire night. It was a win-win situation as far as she was concerned.

She glanced across to Samson Ivers and felt her heart swell with affection for him. Over the years, he had hardly changed at all, and even though his dark hair was more salt and pepper these days, she still thought of him as one of the most attractive men she had ever laid her eyes upon.

Despite being in his late fifties, Samson ran the estate with an iron fist. Every drug sold on the streets went through him first, and woe betide anyone who had the audacity to try and take him on. There was an air about him, a confidence that only someone who had spent many years at the top of his game could carry off. He stood up from his seat, his physique still strong and muscular, and led Paul Mooney and his sidekick, Jason, towards the men's toilets. She shook her head; it was about time the silly old bugger slowed down a bit and left the running of the estate to someone half his age.

'I see your Cathy took him back then. He'll never change; his type never do, do they?'

Her best friend, Irene, nudged her in the side, breaking her thoughts. Lifting her head, Angie watched as her son-in-law entered the premises and made a beeline for the bar. He was a

cocky bastard; it was obvious in his swagger and the smug smirk
spread across his face.

Pursing her lips, Angie narrowed her eyes. As much as she
hated to admit it, Irene had made a point. After all, a leopard
never changed its spots, as the saying went. 'She's a fool, Rene,'
she sighed. 'Always will be when it comes to him.'

She picked up her wine glass and chugged back the contents,
quashing down the familiar ripple of heartache that burned
through her. Turning her head in time, she watched as the door
Samson had slipped through moments earlier swung closed
behind him. Like many a woman before her, her girl was a fool all
right.

'Were there any problems?' Leaning back against one of the white
enamelled sinks, Samson cast his eyes between the two young
men standing before him.

'Nah.' As he passed across a small black holdall, Paul shook
his head. If truth were told, a part of him was glad to be shot of
the contents. He had no intentions of becoming one of Samson's
many drug runners, not when he could earn at least three times
as much working for himself.

He watched as Samson pulled across the zip. Drug taking had
never been his scene, and as far as he was concerned, it was a
mug's game. However, dealing drugs, now that was something
that did interest him. He pushed his hands into his denim
pockets and held his breath while Samson inspected the
contents. Deep down, he knew he was being irrational. Neither
he nor Jason had even opened the bag, let alone dipped their
hands inside. Still, it was a nerve-wracking moment.

Despite Samson's lovable character, he could be a right nasty bastard when the mood took him, and he certainly wouldn't think twice about stabbing a blade into one of their necks, if the need arose. Paul glanced towards Jason before nodding down at the bag. 'It's all there.'

'Of course it is,' Samson answered. Not many people had the fortitude to try and take him on and he chuckled out loud at the fact that the idea had even crossed young Paul's mind. From inside his jacket pocket, he pulled out a bundle of notes and paused before passing it across. 'I want you to go and see someone, an acquaintance of mine.'

Paul and Jason looked at one another. This hadn't been part of the deal. The only thing they had agreed to do was collect the holdall, and that had been for a considerable price. 'Who?' Paul asked.

'Dougie Ward.'

'Mad Dougie?' Jason's eyebrows shot up and he gave Paul a warning glance.

'Why do you want us to go and see him?' Returning Jason's glance, Paul hastily composed himself.

'I want to know if the slimy fucker is trying to get one over on me.'

'And how would we know that?' Paul narrowed his eyes. 'He's hardly gonna tell us, is he?'

Samson grinned. There were no flies on the young man before him and he had a feeling that he would go far, much to his displeasure. There was only room for one major player on the estate and that was him. 'Of course he ain't gonna tell you. Why the fuck would he tell you pair of lairy little fuckers anything?'

Screwing up his face, Paul crossed his arms over his chest. 'What's the point of us seeing him then?'

Samson ignored the question. 'I've arranged for you to do a couple of jobs for him, nothing too heavy, just enough to see what's going on.' He gave a knowing wink, as though he was letting them in on a great big secret. 'And then I want you to report everything back to me.'

'How about you go fuck yourself.' Paul's forehead furrowed. He had his own reputation to think about and becoming a grass, an informer, wasn't a part of his plan.

'I'll pretend I didn't hear that.' Samson grinned. He stabbed his finger forward in a warning, his expression becoming stony. 'But only the once.' Walking forward, he tapped his knuckles on the wooden door, then passed the holdall through the open gap. He turned around and gave them a chilling grin. The fact that they hadn't agreed to his request meant absolutely nothing to him, and why should it? As far as he was concerned, he had given an order and he expected his order to be carried through. 'Just keep your eyes peeled, that's all I'm asking. Don't let me down, lads.' He made for the door. 'Oh, one more thing.'

Paul looked to him expectantly.

'A little dickie bird told me you touched one of my boys. Michael Nicholls, to be precise.' He stabbed his finger forward. 'Now I can't have that.' He gave a grin, a jovial smile that didn't quite reach his eyes. 'It looks bad for business. So think of this as a warning, your first and only warning. Do you get my drift, lads?'

As Samson exited the toilet and the door swung closed behind him, Paul leaned against the sink and his nostrils flared. 'Who the fuck does he think he is?' he growled. 'We ain't his fucking lads.'

Jason nodded. 'What do you reckon?' he asked.

Deep in thought, Paul chewed on the inside of his cheek and nodded. As far as he was concerned, they owed Old Samson nothing. They didn't work for him and certainly weren't one of his many foot soldiers. 'You know what?' he finally answered. 'This could actually work in our favour.' Pushing himself away from the sink, he slapped Jason on the shoulder and gave him a wink. 'I'll make the phone call.'

'This wasn't the plan,' Jason reminded him.

'I know, but like I said' – he raised his eyebrows and smiled – 'it could go in our favour.'

'And what about—'

'I'll sort everything out,' Paul cut him off. 'Don't worry. I'll make the phone call. If the worst comes to the worst, we're just going to have to shake things up a lot faster than we originally planned.' He was thoughtful for a moment, then gave a light chuckle. 'The slippery old bastard is trying to set us up. Let's face it, if everything goes tits up, nothing will come back to him, will it?'

Jason screwed up his face. 'Bastard,' he spat.

'Nah.' Paul's tone became serious. 'Smart, but not smart enough to pull the wool over my eyes. Old Samson and Mad Dougie have had their day, they just don't know it yet.'

Jason was thoughtful. 'What about Matlock?' He watched as Paul's expression clouded over and held up his hand. 'I know you've got beef with him, that you blame Matlock for stealing Cathy away from you, but he's still a face mate and with Samson and Dougie out of the picture, you know as well as I do that he's going to throw his weight around and try to take over the estate.'

His back ramrod straight, the muscles across Paul's shoulders tensed. 'Matlock's mine,' he growled. 'And believe me, I will have the fucker.' In fact, he'd more than have him; he planned to decimate the bastard. If Matlock hadn't come on to the scene, him and Cathy could have been happy, they'd have still been together, and he blamed both Angie and Matlock for taking away the only good thing in his life.

A few moments later Paul entered the bar. Across from him, Samson was sitting at a table. They locked eyes and Paul gave a

42   KERRY KAYA

nod of his head. For all intents and purposes, the action came
across as respectful, as if he was paying Samson his dues. In
truth, it was nothing of the sort. Hiding the scowl that threatened
to spill across his face, Paul pushed open the side door, stepped
out into the car park, and marched across the tarmacked ground
towards his car. They may have been new to the game and a bit
wet behind the ears, but the old man had made a big mistake in
thinking that they would take the fall for him – a very big
mistake.

* * *

Angie was on the war path. Not only was she livid that her
daughter had allowed her waste-of-space husband to come back
home, but over the past few weeks, she had heard more than
one rumour that he was up to his old tricks and carrying on
with Donna Cassidy. As much as she loved being known as
Terrance's mother-in-law she wished to God that she'd never
pushed Cathy into his arms. Her daughter had been through
hell and back all thanks to her husband, and underneath the
charm Terrance was nothing but a bully boy who got a kick out
of terrorising women.

Marching towards the block of flats where her daughter lived,
Angie yanked open the entrance door, and with a face like thunder, she practically ran up the concrete staircase.

Barely even pausing to catch her breath, she thumped her fist
on the front door.

'Mum.' Opening the door, Cathy stared at her mother. 'What
are you doing here?'

'Get your coat on.' Pushing her way into the lounge, Angie
stood with her hands on her hips. 'I knew it,' she spat. 'I knew it
wouldn't take him long, but you wouldn't listen to me, would you?

Thought you knew best? Well, guess what, Cath? You knew didly fucking squat.'

'What?' Pushing her hair off her face, Cathy blinked rapidly as she tried to get her head around what her mother was saying. 'Who are you talking about?'

'Him. Terrance.' Angie shoved her daughter's coat into her hands. 'Put your coat on, Cath. That waster you're married to is in the boozer right now with that little tart Donna draped all over him. They're making a mockery of you.' She blew out her red cheeks. Never before had she felt so angry. 'I knew he couldn't be trusted. Didn't I tell you not to give him a second chance, that a leopard can't change its spots?'

Cathy's heart lurched, her mind reeling. Lost for words, she slipped her arms into her coat and nodded. All the while, she wanted to kick herself. How could she have been so stupid, so naïve, to believe his lies. The promises he'd made meant nothing. He'd even sworn on their unborn child's life that he was going to change his womanising ways. 'But he swore to me that he would change.'

Angie shook her head. 'You're too naïve, Cath, that's your trouble. Of course he said he would change his ways. The bastard wanted an in, didn't he?'

Her cheeks flushing bright pink, Cathy nodded again. 'I suppose so,' she answered, blinking away tears.

'Enough of that.' As she wiped away her daughter's tears, Angie's expression was stern. 'There'll be plenty of time for crying, but right now isn't one of them. Are you going to let them make a fool of you like this? Are you gonna let them make you the laughing stock of the estate?'

Cathy shook her head. Of course she wasn't. Despite what Angie thought, she did still have some pride left inside of her. 'The no-good bastard,' she spat.

'You said it, Cath,' Angie answered through gritted teeth. 'He'll never change. His type never do. You should have got shot of him the first time he cheated on you. That should have been your warning, my girl, right there.'

Silently, Cathy bowed her head. She should have known that Terrance wouldn't be able to keep his promise, that given the chance he'd still sleep with anything with a pulse. Raising her head, there was a defiant gleam in her eyes. 'Come on, Mum,' she growled, 'I'm going to sort that little scrubber out, once and for fucking all.'

* * *

As usual for a Sunday evening, The Jolly Fisherman public house was heaving with customers, all of them in a joyous mood as they crammed in a few more drinking hours before they returned to work the following morning.

Storming through the pub door, the scent of cheap perfume and cigarette smoke hit Cathy full on. Tears threatened to sting her eyes and her skin became ashen as she spotted her husband sat brazenly on a barstool with his little tart's arm draped around his neck as she whispered sweet nothings in his ear.

'See, what did I tell you?' Angie spat. 'He's making a mockery of you, and that's putting it mildly.'

'I'm not putting up with it any more, Mum,' Cathy growled over her shoulder. Pushing her way through the crowd Cathy came to a halt just a few feet away from her husband and crossed her arms over her chest.

'Well, this looks fucking cosy,' she spat.

Caught in the act, Terrance and Donna sprang apart. The action brought her no comfort and she glared at each of them in turn. 'Well?' she demanded. 'What the fuck is going on here?'

The smirk that snaked its way across Donna's face only angered Cathy even further and, reaching for the nearest glass, she threw the contents into her adversary's face.

'Oi.' Terrance jumped to his feet, and as he shoved Donna from his lap, she landed on the floor with a scream. 'What the fuck do you think you're playing at?' he bellowed. Taking the cuff of his shirt, he wiped traces of claret-coloured wine away from his face, all the while, cursing his wife.

'What am I playing at?' Cathy screeched back. 'What the fuck are you doing with her?' Lunging forward, she screamed in his face. 'I trusted you, you even swore on our baby's life.'

'It's not what it looks like.' A hushed silence fell across the bar, and as Terrance looked around him, he inwardly groaned. The stupid mare had made him look a fool in front of the entire pub. 'Do yourself a favour, shut your trap, and go fucking home.'

Cathy glared and, looking up at her husband, she took in his bloated face and sly, beady eyes. For the first time since he had walked into her life, she saw him, really saw him, just as everyone else around her did. In that moment, it hit her. What exactly was it that she was fighting so hard for? Her mum was right. Beneath the act he liked to put on for his cronies, he was a liar, a waster, and a ponce. It was a lightbulb moment and rage at her own stupidity began to burn through her. Enough was enough, as far as she was concerned. Donna was welcome to him.

'Tell her, Tel. Tell her that you're gonna leave her as soon as she's dropped that kid.'

'Shut up.' Glancing behind him, Terrance hissed out the words.

Getting to her feet, Donna thrust her chest in Cathy's direction. 'He's my man, and you need to get that through your thick skull.' She spread open her arms and smirked. 'Always has been, always will be.'

A giggle that began in Cathy's belly edged its way up through her chest and out of her throat, and throwing her head back, she roared with laughter.

'Cathy.' As she looked around her at the stunned faces in the crowd, Angie tugged on her daughter's arm. 'This isn't the time to be laughing, darling. This isn't a joke.'

Wiping the tears of laughter from her eyes, Cathy glanced behind her. 'Oh, but it is, Mum. He is the fucking joke.' She turned her attention to Donna. 'And as for you, little girl, you're welcome to him, darling. He's all yours and good luck to you, because you're going to fucking need it.'

'What?' Donna's jaw dropped.

'I said that he's all yours.' Lunging forward, Cathy grabbed a handful of her dark hair and pulled her across the small round wooden table that separated them. 'You're welcome to him,' she spat, 'but this' – her free hand formed a fist and she swung it forward – 'is for trying to treat me like I'm some kind of fucking mug.'

'She's crazy.' Falling to the floor, Donna threw her arms across her head and whelped out loud. 'Help me, Tel,' she cried. 'For fuck's sake, do something and help me.'

A blind mist fell across Cathy and even as she was being dragged away from the terrified girl, her feet continued to kick out.

Grabbing his wife's elbow, Terrance snarled, 'I told you to go fucking home.'

'Get off me.' Still breathing heavily through her flared nostrils, Cathy wrenched her arm free. 'I meant what I said. She's welcome to you. Me and you are done.' She yanked her wedding ring off her finger and flung it across the pub. The clang of the metal as it hit the floor and rolled into an unused dusty corner was as loud as a gunshot. 'We are done,' she screamed.

The punch to the side of her face silenced not only Cathy, but the entire pub, and as they looked at one another, not one person attempted to pull the big man off his wife.

'Get off her.' It took a moment for Angie to comprehend what had just taken place and, coming to her senses, she grasped a handful of Terrance's collar, and using all of her strength, she tried to pull him away from her daughter.

Terrance batted Angie away from him and dragged Cathy towards the exit. He snarled at his mother-in-law, 'Do yourself a favour and fuck off, before I do you some damage. And as for you,' he hissed, tightening his fist around Cathy's arm, 'I told you to go fucking home.'

* * *

'What the fuck happened in here?' Entering through the side entrance, Paul had arrived just minutes too late. He took in the scene before him and his eyes widened. Broken glass was in the process of being swept up, and as he made his way towards the bar area, he sidestepped around the damage.

Stella joined her brother at the bar and raised her eyebrows. 'She shocked me, that's for sure. I didn't even know she had it in her.'

'Who?' Leaning casually against the bar, Paul looked down at his sister. 'Has old Maud been up to her usual tricks again?' He smiled as he looked across at the elderly woman in question. Sitting at a corner table in a world of her own, Maud sipped at a glass of port and lemon. Mad Maud they called her, and many a time, she'd screamed the pub down, just because someone had looked at her the wrong way.

'No,' Stella sighed cautiously, 'and how I answer that question depends on what sort of mood you're in.'

'What sort of mood I'm in?' Straightening up, Paul screwed up his face. 'What are you talking about?' He glanced around him, a bewildered expression on his face. 'What happened in here?'

Stella bit down on her lip. She knew her brother inside out, and knew he was about to go absolutely ape-shit when he found out what had just gone down. She smoothed down her hair, stalling for time. 'It was your Cathy.'

'Cathy?' Paul's eyes widened, and as he looked around him for a second time, a slither of panic slid down his spine, making the tiny hairs on the back of his neck stand up on end. Across the bar, his gaze found Angie. The expression of worry etched across her face only heightened his concern. 'Is she okay? Has she been hurt?'

'Is she okay?' Stella laughed. 'It was Cathy who caused all of this. Donna Cassidy, the silly little cow, took the brunt of her rage, and as for Matlock, well, he copped a face full of red wine for his trouble, and that was just the start of it.'

'Matlock,' Paul snarled. He pushed himself away from the bar and clenched his fists. 'What did the no-good ponce do this time?'

'What do you think?' Stella sighed. 'What he always does... paraded that little tart Donna around. He gave Cathy a pretty hefty backhander as well, before dragging her out, and from the look of it, it wasn't the first time either.' She paused and reached out to touch her brother's forearm. 'Don't get involved, Paul,' she begged of him. 'Stay out of it. Cathy's a fool for staying with the man, you know that as well as I do. She had her chance to get away from him, and well' – she raised her eyebrows, her beautiful face looking forlorn – 'she took him back, didn't she? That's got to tell you something.' She studied her brother's handsome face, forcing him to look at her. 'This thing you've got for her needs to end and fast, before she makes a mug of you. She made her choice, made her bed so to speak, now leave her to lie in it.'

Backhander... that was the only word that resonated inside Paul's brain, and as he shook his sister's arm away from him, he snarled, 'Keep your nose out of my business, Stell. In fact, sister or no sister, I'm warning you now, keep your opinions about Cathy to yourself.'

Stella's mouth dropped open. 'I was only—'

'I said, keep out of it.' Paul stabbed his finger forward. At times, Stella reminded him of a jealous girlfriend rather than his sister, his own flesh and blood. 'I don't want to hear it, all right?' He began to walk away, paused, then retraced his steps. 'You might keep Jay,' he said, referring to his best friend, 'on a short leash, but don't you dare try to do the same with me. You are not my fucking keeper.'

As her brother stormed back out of the pub, Stella chewed on her bottom lip. 'I was only trying to help,' she called after him, and when she received no reply, she threw her arms up into the air. There was trouble brewing, she could feel it in her bones. Reaching inside her handbag, she took out her purse and made her way across to the far side of the pub where a public payphone was attached to the wall. 'Jay,' she sighed, pushing more coins into the slot, 'I need you to go and find that idiot brother of mine, before he goes and does something stupid.'

From a split eyebrow, blood trickled down the side of Cathy's face. She kicked out her feet in a desperate attempt to get away from her husband's heavy fists.

He grabbed her by the ankle and dragged her roughly off the sofa. Landing on the thin carpet with a loud thud, her hands and feet flayed around her, and resembling a wild cat, she fought even harder. Not only was she fighting for her own life, but also for the life of her unborn child. Out of breath, her cheeks were bright red and her hair that had been pulled up into a neat ponytail stuck out in all directions.

'Leave me alone.' As she screamed out the words, she managed to scramble to her feet and escape his clutches. Red marks that would soon turn to bruises littered her face and her beaten body ached with each and every breath she took.

'Leave you alone?' Terrance roared. 'After what you've just done to me?' He jerked his thumb towards the front door and his voice rose even further. 'You've just made a show of me, made me look like a mug in front of the entire fucking boozer.' He stalked forward until she was backed up against the kitchen sink. His eyes bulged, his face had turned bright red, and spittle gathered at the corners of his snarled lips as he lifted his large, clenched fist in the air.

Cathy's heart raced; she could taste her fear, it was that strong. Inside her womb, her baby kicked out furiously, almost as though he or she somehow sensed the danger they were both in. She reached out behind her and her fingers curled around a metal object. In her panic, she was unable to tell if it was a knife or a spoon. At that moment in time, she didn't care what it was, as long as it stopped him and gave her enough time to free herself from his grasp. She brought the object around and jabbed at the side of his neck. It wasn't hard enough to seriously harm, just startle him, or so she thought.

The sharp nick to the side of his neck stopped Terrance dead in his tracks. He brought his hand up to touch the wound and the second he took it away again blood began to squirt upwards.

'What have you done?' He staggered backwards and still the blood squirted, spraying over himself, his wife, and the kitchen. In the distance, he could hear his wife's screams and he dropped to his knees, still clutching at his neck.

Cathy's eyes were wide and filled with disbelief. Tearing them away from her husband, she looked down at the object in her hand. It was a small kitchen knife, the one she used to peel the vegetables on a Sunday morning. She dropped the knife to the floor and almost slipped on the blood in her haste to recoil away from him.

'I thought it was a spoon,' she whimpered.

Terrance's eyes bulged and as blood covered his hands, face, and shirt. He began to groan. 'Phone for an ambulance, you dozy mare,' he croaked out.

Rooted to the spot, Cathy could only stare at her husband with wide frightened eyes.

'The... phone...' Slumping onto his side, Terrance's eyes rolled to the back of his head and his voice trailed off.

'Tel?' Before taking a tentative step forward, Cathy placed her hand upon her chest as though the action would somehow steady her racing heart. There was no response. 'Tel?' She stooped down as far as her swollen belly would allow her to and gingerly reached out her arm. 'Tel?' She prodded him with a shaking finger. There was no response and, placing her hand on his shoulder blade, she shook him harder. 'Tel, wake up.'

Still, he didn't respond.

6

Paul was incensed; he almost snapped the car key in half as he attempted to turn it in the ignition. Finally, the car purred to life and, pushing his foot down on the gas, he sped towards the edge of the car park, leaving behind him a plume of exhaust fumes and dust.

'Bollocks.' He slammed his foot on the brake, lurching forward and almost crashing head-first through the windscreen before being thrown back in the seat. What the hell was he thinking? He didn't even know where Cathy was. He knew she lived on the estate, but let's face it, that didn't mean she had left the pub and gone back to the home she shared with Matlock. For all he knew, she could have gone to her mother's home, and if she hadn't gone there, well, Harts Lane was a big estate and she could be absolutely anywhere. It would be the equivalent of searching for a needle in a haystack. He dragged his hand across his face, turned to look across at the pub, then reluctantly switched off the ignition, and threw open the car door.

As he entered the pub, from the corner of his eye, Paul took note of his sister and shot her a warning glare to stay out of his way.

'Where is she?'

'Who?' Turning her head, Angie's eyes were hard.

'Cathy, who do you think I'm talking about?' He watched her squint up at him, the crow's feet around her eyes becoming even more prominent. 'I'm warning you, Angie, don't fuck me about. Where is she?'

'Piss off,' she slurred. 'I ain't gotta tell you fuck all.' Sitting back in her seat, she crossed her arms over her chest and licked at her dry lips. 'Who the fuck do you think you are, coming in here and speaking to me like that?' She pointed a red painted talon towards his chest. 'I've known you since you were a kid, you little shit, and you don't scare me.' She gave a nasty chuckle. 'In fact, it would take someone a lot bigger than you to scare me, sweetheart.'

He leaned closer to her ear, his voice dripping with menace. 'Then I'm going to tear this estate apart looking for her. The choice is yours, Ange. We can do this the easy way or the hard way, but I can promise you now, I will find her.'

He watched her pick up her wine glass and stifled down the urge to knock it out of her hand and shake her roughly by the shoulders. Despite her bravado, he could see her mentally weighing up her options. It was so typical of Angie. She never did anything unless she was going to benefit from it.

'Angie,' he roared, 'I'm this close to tearing the estate apart, starting with this fucking boozer.'

Without looking up at him, Angie gave a nonchalant shrug. As much as she didn't want to see Cathy harmed, Paul was the last person she wanted around her daughter. When they'd been teenagers, her Cathy had been besotted with Paul; she'd hung off his every word and Angie hadn't liked it one little bit. It was jealousy she supposed; why should her Cathy have a man on her arm when all she herself had ever had were one night stands or quick flings? The longest relationship she'd been involved in only lasted a matter of months and even then it had been her who'd done all the running. 'He said he was taking her home. There, are you happy now?' she spat.

Paul shook his head. 'Do you know something, you are one selfish fucking cunt, Ange. She's your daughter, your own flesh and blood. Why the fuck are you still sitting here, eh? Why ain't you banging down her front door?' He clenched his fists into tight balls. 'So help me God, if anything has happened to her, then you'd best start running as fast and as far away from me as you can, am I making myself clear? Because I will end you for this, if it's the last thing I ever fucking do.' He glared around the pub, and his voice rose as he now addressed the regulars who sat nursing their pints, the same regulars who had sat and watched Matlock raise his fists to a woman, the very same woman whom he just so happened to love. 'I'm gonna end all of you for this.'

This time, Angie looked up. Despite the alcohol she'd sunk, the stark warning brought ice cold fear to her heart. She'd always known that he was dangerous. Even when he'd been a kid, there had been an underlying hint of menace about him. Another reason why she'd put her foot down and put an end to his and her daughter's budding romance, before he'd had the chance to become more than a permanent fixture in Cathy's life.

'In fact, Ange, you've just earned yourself a place on my shit list.' He stabbed a stiff finger dangerously close to her face. 'And I'm telling you now that you'd better pray to God or whoever the fuck you want that that bastard hasn't harmed a single hair on her head, because if he has, I will be coming back for you, and that ain't no threat, sweetheart,' he said, emphasising the words, 'it's a fucking promise.' With those parting words, he stormed out of the pub and made his way back to his car, all the while, cursing everyone and everything around him.

From day one, he'd known that Terrance Matlock was bad news, and in a way, he blamed himself. He should have done more to warn Cathy off him. In fact, he should have taken his fists to Matlock and beat the living daylights out of him, and God only knew he'd wanted to. He should have fought harder, should have scared the bastard off from touching what was his, right from the very first moment he'd even had an inkling that Matlock was sniffing around and showing an interest. Instead, he'd swallowed his knob and skulked in the shadows, like the jealous, pathetic fool that he was.

It was Angie he blamed for his and Cathy's break up; she'd poisoned Cathy against him, and had done everything in her power to tear them apart. It had worked too; all she'd needed to do was drip feed doubts into Cathy's mind and before he knew it Cathy had begun distancing herself from him. When Matlock had come onto the scene, Angie had driven the final nail in the coffin and all but pushed Cathy into his arms, severing Paul and Cathy's romance.

As he turned the steering wheel, his muscular forearms strained against the soft cotton of his shirt and his thoughts turned to Cathy. Just the very thought of her being in danger spurred him on and, pushing his foot down on the gas, he sped through the streets towards the south side of the estate.

* * *

Fear caught in the back of Cathy's throat. Her husband was dead. She'd actually killed him. Nestled safely inside her womb, her baby kicked out, this time a lot softer than it had previously, and absentmindedly, she placed her blood-stained palm upon her swollen tummy. The gentle kicks were somewhat soothing to her.

Surprisingly, she found that her husband's actual death didn't bother her as much as she'd always imagined it would. In fact, if she was being really honest with herself, the moment she had come face to face with his young lover, his little slut, something had changed inside her, and her feelings had shifted. She couldn't say that she loathed him, but in the same breath, she couldn't say with a certainty that she loved him either.

She walked sedately to the sink, twisted open the tap and began to methodically wash away the blood that stained her hands. No, if she was being really honest, what bothered her more, much more, were the consequences of her actions. What would become of her now? What would happen to her child? She couldn't go to prison; she knew that as well as she knew her own name.

She dragged her hand across her cheek, her skin as pale as the white porcelain cups that somehow sat unscathed on the kitchen sideboard. It was self-defence, wasn't it? That's what she would tell the police. She'd killed him before he had the chance to kill her and their unborn child, and he would have done, she was certain of it. Her bruised face and battered, aching body were proof of that.

She looked down and watched with fascination as the dark copper-coloured liquid that had been her husband's blood swirled down the plug hole. At that moment, the iron scent that was as alien to her as it was distinctive, hit her nostrils.

Suddenly, her stomach lurched, making bitter acrid bile rise up in her throat and, hanging onto the stainless-steel sink, she began to retch. She glanced over her shoulder. Terrance lay still in a pool of blood, his deathly pale bloated face was already beginning to turn grey, and his unblinking, unseeing, lifeless eyes stared up at the ceiling. There and then, Cathy retched even harder.

7

Downing her wine, Angie made her excuses and left the pub. Out on the street, she pulled her thick coat around her slim frame and began the short walk across the estate.

As her high-heeled shoes clip-clopped across the pavement, she told herself she was only doing what she should have done a long time ago, the first time she'd ever had an inkling that her son-in-law had taken his fists to her daughter.

It had taken young Paul Mooney to make her realise that she'd let her only child down, and as much as she hated to admit it, Paul was right. What sort of a mother was she? She screwed up her face as she recalled Paul's words. Just who the fuck did the little bastard think he was talking to? So what if she liked a drink? That was her prerogative, her choice, and she was a big girl, she could do whatever the fuck she liked.

She lit a cigarette and puffed on it absentmindedly. Paul Mooney knew nothing about the sacrifices she'd made, nor the hardships that she had suffered as a single mother. She'd scrimped and scraped to put a roof over her child's head, to make sure she had food in her belly and clothes on her back. No, Paul knew fuck all, all right. She'd even sacrificed her teenage years for her daughter and had gone without many a time to raise her.

Burdened with a small child, no man had wanted to stay with her long-term. Oh, they would charm her all right, and sweet talk their way into her bed, but after the deed was done and they had pulled their trousers back on, they couldn't wait to get away from her. It was as if she was tainted somehow. Some of the men she had encountered over the years would even leave her with promises to call the next day, but they never did, and in the end, she never even expected them to.

Flicking the cigarette butt to the kerb, Angie sighed. She would have given anything and everything to have a man love her as much as Paul so obviously loved her daughter. Not that she was jealous of her girl, mind. Why would she be? It was something she often asked herself, and as the question entered her mind, waves of guilt washed over her. For a brief moment, she squeezed her eyes shut tight. Deep down, she knew she was jealous and that was half the problem. If she was being even more truthful with herself, she knew it had been envy that had made her tear the two youngsters apart. Her own spite had been the only reason she had poisoned Cathy's mind against him. Why should her girl have a man like Paul, who was so obviously in love with her, when she herself had nothing, no one?

For so long, for so many years, she had blamed her daughter for the way of life she had lived, but she knew Cathy wasn't the real problem, not really. After all, her girl was good, both inside and out, a real little stunner. God only knew that she should have been proud of her, yet she wasn't. She couldn't help but resent her daughter, and even when she had been a small child, her Cathy had been nothing other than a burden to her.

As Paul had not-so-kindly pointed out, she was hardly mother of the year material. She could count on one hand the number of times she had actually taken her to the park or baked fairy cakes with her. Wasn't that what normal, real mothers did? The truth was, she was a selfish woman and she had never put Cathy's needs before her own. All she'd ever done was put her own wants and her own happiness first, not that it had ever got her very far, mind.

Before she knew it, she had reached her destination, and as usual, nerves began to get the better of her. For all these years, she'd kept her mouth shut. It had been expected of her. He'd expected it, but no more, and unless he took action, she was going to scream her daughter's parentage from the rooftops.

Lifting the brass door knocker, she let it drop back down with a loud clatter. It seemed to take an eternity for the door to open and she forced herself not to fidget. After all, there was only so many times she could wipe her clammy palms down the length of her denim skirt.

'Angie.'

She could hear the surprise in his deep voice. After all, it wasn't every day that she turned up on his doorstep, and as he arched an eyebrow towards her, she almost lost her nerve, but only almost. Young Paul had put the fear of Christ into her, and as she thought back on his threats, she gave an involuntary shiver.

'It's Cathy.' She looked down at her feet and took a deep breath. 'In all these years, I've never asked for anything.' She lifted her head and looked him in the eyes. 'I've never asked anything of you. I've never asked you to declare her as yours. I never expected you to do that, and I never pushed you to either.'

His eyebrow inched up higher and his forehead furrowed, revealing deep-set lines. 'I can sense a but coming?'

Angie nodded. 'But... but I think she needs your help now.' As soon as the words had left her mouth, Angie looked away. Even now, she wasn't thinking of her daughter, not really. All she was doing was trying to save her own skin. After all, wasn't Cathy's father as much to blame as she was? He'd let her down, too, hadn't he?

'Then I think you'd better come in.' Pulling open the door, Samson Ivers moved his large frame to one side and gestured for her to enter his home.

Swallowing deeply, Angie gave a weak smile before stepping across the threshold.

Screeching to a halt outside a block of maisonettes, Paul yanked his key out of the ignition and flung open the car door. He took a moment to glance up at the building before slamming the door closed and jogging across the small courtyard. The area was in near darkness, and with just one dimly lit streetlight illuminating the way, he pulled open the entrance door and ran up the concrete staircase, taking the steps two at a time until he reached the upper walkway.

Briskly, he made his way along the landing and, reaching the front door, he took note of the quietness. The eerie silence made his heart lurch. Maybe he'd been wrong after all. Perhaps he'd overreacted and Cathy wasn't in danger as he'd first feared. Perhaps she and Matlock were already in bed making up? He pushed the sickening thought from his mind, rubbed his hand across his face, and cursed himself. His overreaction was going to make him the laughing stock of the pub, and as he began to walk away, his cheeks flamed pink. After the way he'd attacked her, his sister would never let him live it down, of that he was certain. In a way, he didn't blame her. The way he'd spoken to her was not only out of character, but also bang out of order.

He reached the concrete staircase, and with his hand on the

banister rail, he glanced back across to Cathy's front door. He'd already made a fool of himself, why not go the whole hog? His strides were long as he retraced his steps, and without missing a beat, he thumped his fist on the wooden door.

Angie had never been inside Samson's home before, and as she stepped inside the lounge, she resisted the urge to look around her. In fact, it took all of her strength to not look up at the framed portrait above the fireplace. Instinctively, she knew who it would be: Harriet, his late wife, and she would prefer not to see a picture of the woman he had chosen over her and their daughter, still taking pride of place in the lounge, thank you very much.

'So...' Taking a seat on an overstuffed armchair, Samson lit a cigarette and stretched out his long legs. 'What's this all about?' Two thick plumes of grey smoke snaked down from each of his nostrils as he studied her.

Gesturing towards the equally overstuffed sofa, Angie waited for him to answer before placing her handbag on the polished floorboard and perching her backside on the edge of the obviously expensive piece of furniture. Despite not wanting to, she found her gaze traveling upwards until she found Harriet's face staring back down at her. The curve of her smile looked almost triumphant, just like the cat who'd got the cream. In a way, she supposed that she had. After all, she had won Samson's heart, hadn't she?

'Well?'

She tore her gaze away from the portrait, swallowing down the ripple of jealousy she felt. Why should Harriet have lived the high life when she was the one who had birthed his child? She swallowed down a second wave of jealousy, knowing full well she wasn't the only woman to have borne him children. If the rumours were true, then her Samson, as she always privately thought of him, had fathered enough children to make a football team.

'Angie.'

There was more than a hint of impatience in his tone and she resisted the urge to snap at him, to tell him to shut up and let her think.

'It's Cathy,' she finally answered.

'So you said.' He shrugged as though bored, as though her turning up out of the blue and wanting to talk about their daughter was an everyday occurrence.

'Actually no, this isn't about Cathy at all.' She sat up straighter, and her blue eyes flashed dangerously. 'This is about Paul, Paul Mooney.'

'What about him?' Samson narrowed his eyes and there was an edge to his voice that pleased Angie to no end.

Angie allowed herself to smile. She could see that she had his full attention. 'I want you to get rid of him. He's causing problems for our daughter; he even had the gall to threaten me. He's dangerous and he needs disposing of.' Which wasn't entirely the truth, no. The main reason she wanted Paul out of the way was because she didn't want Cathy anywhere near him; she didn't want to sit back and watch their little love story unfold. From day one she'd loathed Paul Mooney, and if she wasn't careful he'd take Cathy away from her. At least with Terrance, he was a womaniser, not to mention a wife beater, and for as long as Cathy was with Terrance then she would still want her mother around. The problem was, Cathy had been a teenager when Angie had torn her and Paul apart; now she was a grown woman, she knew her own mind, and no matter how many times Angie put on the waterworks or begged her daughter not to get involved with Paul,

Angie knew her pleas would fall on deaf ears. Cathy wanted Paul and there was nothing she or anyone else could say to stop that.

She watched as Samson stood up, walked across the room and opened a polished walnut sideboard. It wasn't until he took out two crystal glasses that she realised it was a drinks cabinet. He poured out a generous measure of whiskey into each glass, then passed one across to her. She took a sip, grimacing as the gold-coloured liquid burned the back of her throat.

Samson drained his drink in one go and, pouring out a second one, he held out the filled glass in a celebratory manner. 'Don't worry about Mooney. I've got my own plans for that little upstart, and let's just say that his days on this earth are well and truly fucking numbered.'

Angie took a sharp intake of breath. She hadn't expected her request to be met so easily. Sipping at her whiskey, she swallowed the liquid down and a slow smile spread across her face. 'That, Samson,' she said, 'is one of the greatest things you have ever said to me.'

Still hanging onto the sink, Cathy jerked her head towards the front door. Fear grasped at her heart and icy shards of blind terror ran down the length of her spine. She let out a strangled sob. It had to be the police, it just had to be. Someone must have heard her screaming and called them. Any other day, she would have been grateful, but that was before, before she had stabbed her husband and ended his life.

In a daze, she began to walk forward. The thumping on the front door grew louder, and for a brief moment, she slammed her eyes shut tight. No one was going to believe it was self-defence. Just one glance at the blood-soaked padded coat she was still wearing was enough to tell her that. What had she even done to help save her husband's life? Nothing, that's what. She hadn't even called for an ambulance.

With shaking hands, she reached out for the door handle. All she wanted to do was run away, but even she wasn't daft enough to know that was an option.

'Cathy, it's me, Paul. Open up.'

Her shoulders slumped and she exhaled loudly. In that moment, she didn't know whether to laugh or cry. All she felt was relief wash over her. Tentatively, she moved closer, her fingers curling around the metal door handle.

'Cathy, open the door.'

His voice made her pause. As ridiculous as it seemed, once he'd found out what she'd done, what was to stop Paul from calling the police? After all, he wouldn't want to incriminate himself, would he? At the same time, it would hardly be good for business if he suddenly became an informer, a grass. Oh, she was so confused and she rubbed her hand across her face, wishing that the action would somehow make everything all right.

'Cathy.'

She positioned herself in front of the door, took a deep breath, pulled down the handle, and inched it open a crack, just enough so she could peer through the tiny gap.

'Go away, Paul.'

Paul gave her a bright smile, the kind of smile that would have made her tummy flip over once upon a time.

'I'm just checking that you're okay.' He jerked his thumb behind him. 'I heard about what happened, you know, back in the pub,' he said, trying to peer past her into the flat.

Instinctively, Cathy closed the gap. 'Just go away, please,' she begged of him. 'Now isn't a good time.'

'Come on, Cath.' He placed his hand on the wooden door and

the action almost made Cathy's heart stop beating. All he had to do was gently push and she would go flying backwards. She felt drained, as though the energy had been zapped right out of her. 'I only wanted to check up on you. Is he here? Terrance, I mean.'

The sound of her husband's name was enough to make her bottom lip quiver. 'No... no he's not. Please, Paul, just go away.'

Her words seemed to have the desired effect and, nodding, he made to walk away. It was only as her fingers relaxed their grip that the door flew wide open and smashed against the wall with a loud crash and then, much to Cathy's horror, he was stepping over the threshold.

* * *

With a spring in her step, Angie made her way back to The Jolly Fisherman. If luck was on her side, she would make it in time to have a couple of drinks before last orders were called. Hugging her arms across her chest, she grinned happily to herself. It was about time Samson had come in useful. After all, the bugger had done sod all to help her out over the years. Not a single penny had he given her while her Cathy had been growing up, and all the while, he and the bitch he'd been married to had lived the life of Riley. He had a beautiful home, did Samson. The best house on the estate by far, it boasted a paved driveway that in itself was larger than her two-bedroomed flat. As for the house, well, the bay windows with the thickly lined swag curtains were just gorgeous.

She thought of her daughter then and the smile slid from her face. In a rare moment of motherly concern, she wondered if she was okay. Her son-in-law had really whacked her one. She pushed the thought to the back of her mind. Of course her girl would be okay. She was tough, just like she herself was, and let's face it, with the upbringing she'd had, her Cathy had had no other choice but to be strong.

Looking up and down the street, she waited for a car to pass, then quickly crossed the road. The pub was like a beacon to her. The brightly-lit lights that shone through the window, and the faint sound of music called to her, it always had done. As she reached the saloon bar entrance, she paused and looked around her. Paul Mooney's threat was at the forefront of her mind and, noting that he wasn't in close proximity, she nodded and plastered a wide smile across her face. Like Samson had said, his days were numbered, and she held the knowledge to her, as if it were a great big secret. In fact, it was one of the best secrets she could have ever been told, and keep it to herself she most certainly would.

8

As a wave of nausea forced its way through Cathy's body, her heart plummeted. The situation had now become real, as though Paul's very presence inside the maisonette had brought her back to reality. The reality being that her husband was laid out on the kitchen floor in a pool of his own blood, as dead as a dodo.

She watched Paul bring his arms up to his head. His elbows were tucked in as he held onto the back of his neck. 'What the fuck?' He turned to look at her, his eyes wide and disbelieving. Within moments, he was upon her, his gaze trawling over her face, inspecting the injuries Terrance's meaty fists had inflicted. 'What the fuck has he done to you?'

The tone in his voice alone made her want to cry. It was so typical of Paul. Her own safety, just as it always had been, was his only concern. She opened her mouth to speak, only nothing came out.

He put his hands on her limp arms and moved his head from side to side, forcing her to look up at him. 'What the fuck has he done to you, Cath?' He inspected the slit above her eyebrow. 'I think you might even need a couple of stiches, babe.'

Reaching up to tentatively touch the cut, Cathy's throat felt as though it was filled with sandpaper and she swallowed deeply, biting back the tears. Her fingertips were slick with blood and when she finally spoke, her voice was husky. 'He... he... was...'

Paul nodded. She watched him glance over his shoulder and saw him swallow just as deeply as she herself had done moments earlier. 'I know,' he whispered, 'and you don't have to say it, darling. I already know. He would have killed you given half the chance, wouldn't he?'

'I have to phone the police.' She wrenched herself out of his arms and took a deep breath. She wasn't thinking straight. In fact, she wasn't thinking at all. Her mind and body were numb, as if she was in a daze. Looking down at herself, she rubbed at her arms furiously, wanting to bring some life into them, wanting more than anything to actually feel something, anything. 'I have to call them. They have to come and...' She nodded down at her husband's body, leaving the sentence unsaid.

'Like fuck you are,' Paul barked out. He grabbed her forcibly by her forearms and gently shook her. 'No police. You'll go down for this. Is that what you want, Cath? To rot away in a prison cell and for who, eh? For that piece of shit?' He glanced behind him and screwed up his face. 'He deserved everything he had coming to him; you know that as well as I do. I need you to think clearly, Cath.' His voice was a lot gentler now, almost pleading. 'Who's gonna look after your kid if you go down, eh? Angie, social services, foster care? Or how about children's home after fucking children's home? Is that what you want for your kid, to be passed around, used, and abused by all and fucking sundry? Because if it is, then tell me and I'll call the filth myself, right fucking now.'

She shook her head, tears blinding her vision. Of course it wasn't what she wanted. Angie's threat that she would have her baby taken away from her suddenly became more real, but what was the alternative? 'I killed him,' she whispered. 'I killed my own husband.' The tears came then, great big sobs that shuddered throughout her body and threatened to take her breath away. 'I'm scared, Paul, so scared.'

'Come here.' Paul gently pulled her shaking frame into his arms. 'It's going to be all right, Cath.' He stroked her hair. 'I'm going to help you sort this out, okay?' He took a step backwards and, holding her at arm's length, his sapphire blue eyes that had always mesmerised her in the past were filled with concern and something else she noted: love. 'I'm going to fix this.'

He released her then and, as he rubbed at his temples, she could sense his mind ticking over, thinking of a way, any way that he could help her. However, even she could see there was nothing he could do to help. He may have been a lot of things, but he wasn't a miracle worker. He couldn't turn back time, could he?

Finally, he looked up at her. 'I need you to go and shower.' His fingers reached out to touch the hardened strands of her hair that had been splattered with blood. 'I need you to shower. You need to wash off the blood, sweetheart.' He spoke to her as though she was a child, and she numbly nodded at his words, implicitly trusting him. 'You need to get dressed and then I need you to go back to the pub. You have to be seen in there.'

'No.' Cathy's eyes flew wide open and she gulped loudly. Returning to the pub was the last thing she wanted to do. 'I can't, I can't do that.'

'Yes you can and you will.'

There was an urgency to his voice, and absentmindedly, she nodded, if for no other reason but to placate him. As she walked from the room, her movements were both sluggish and slow, as though the energy had been zapped right out of her. Reaching the door, she stopped and looked over her shoulder.

'What will you do with him?' she asked quietly.

Paul looked up. He still hadn't thought of a solution as of yet, and he resisted the urge to shrug his shoulders. 'I'll think of something, Cath. Don't worry about it, okay? Just go and get yourself cleaned up, sweetheart.'

She nodded a second time, then walked towards the bathroom.

* * *

Lucas Vaughn watched his boss Dougie Ward warily. They were at Dougie's home. He'd nicknamed the property the Manor and the word conjured up an image of a long sweeping tree-lined driveway that led to a large, grand dwelling, boasting a thick blanket of dark green ivy weaving its way up the intricate outer brickwork. In actual fact, the property was nothing of the sort. No, the Manor was actually a disused morgue that Dougie had bought at auction. He'd bought the remote property, lock, stock and barrel, for a steal, and much to his delight, that had included the contents, too. The property boasted not only a cold room containing several working fridges, but also a shiny black private ambulance, pine coffins for viewing purposes, and a stainless-steel embalming table that sat proudly in the middle of the sterile room. And it was sterile, Dougie made sure of that. The pungent unmistakable cloying scent of disinfectant permeated the air.

As he'd entered the cold room, Lucas swept his gaze over the table. The action had almost become a habit of his and he knew for a fact that he wouldn't rest easy until he had seen the face of the unconscious man laid out before him.

Methodically, Dougie began polishing a series of instruments and, taking a cloth, he lovingly wiped it across the steel handle of a scalpel. Why? Lucas had no idea. Within seconds, the instrument would be bloody. Still, it wasn't his place to ask questions, and as a result, he didn't. After all, he wasn't daft, and more importantly, he didn't have a death wish.

With the scalpel held between his thumb and forefinger, Dougie looked up. He was a medium-set man of average height with mousey brown hair that was beginning to turn grey at the temples. At first glance, there was nothing about him that screamed out dangerous. More importantly, there was nothing to alert an innocent bystander that they should steer clear of him. It was only after being in his presence for a few moments that it became clear something wasn't quite right. He was unhinged – that was the first thing people usually noticed. There was an arrogance about him and a complete loss of human emotion that set him apart from others.

'I've got a couple of men coming in.' He tore his stare away from Lucas to look at Ernest Bright, a man of equal age and build. With a nod of his head, he motioned for him to throw the bucket of icy cold water over the unconscious man.

Lucas watched the man gasp and splutter as the water roused him, and he kept his face neutral. Despite being a hard man and being more than capable of looking after himself, this was the part Lucas loathed. Any moment now, the man would begin screaming. His high-pitched wails would resound off the walls, and he would thrash his arms and legs around, powerless to escape the bindings that tied him to the table. He silently willed the man to stay quiet. It was the fear that Dougie craved – the paralysing fear that his latest victim was being subjected to – that, coupled with the knowledge that his life was now completely and utterly at Dougie's will. There was fuck all he could do about it. The screams Lucas duly noted only seemed to spur Dougie's viciousness on.

'It wasn't me, Mr Ward, I swear on my life it wasn't.'

Dougie began to laugh maniacally. He lifted the scalpel in the air, as if inspecting it for any finger marks. 'That's what they all say,' he answered, with a long theatrical sigh. Satisfied that the instrument had been polished to perfection, he took a step towards the table.

'Please, Mr Ward, whatever you think it is I've done, I swear to you it wasn't me.'

'It wasn't me.' In a sing-song tone, Dougie mimicked the man's voice. His eyes held a steely glint to them, as he glared down at the table. 'I have it on very good authority that you've been telling all and sundry that I'm mad, that I'm some kind of fucking nut job.' He held the scalpel in the air and his voice took on an incredulous tone. 'I'm not mad, am I Ern?'

Ernest shook his head from side to side. His lips opened to reveal a set of crooked teeth and he gave a soundless cackle. Minus his tongue, he could only grunt out incomprehensible sounds that only Dougie seemed to understand.

'Honest to God, it wasn't me.' The man's eyes widened. As the enormity of the situation sank in, he thrashed his head from side to side, as if he believed the action would somehow save him – even though Lucas knew from experience that it wouldn't, nothing would.

Dougie chuckled once more and he shook his head as though disappointed. 'As I've already stated, that's what they all say.'

Behind them, Lucas cleared his throat. All he wanted to do was get out of the room, and more importantly, get away from the barbaric torture that he knew for a certainty would come. Drugs may have been Dougie's main game, a living that he obviously profited from greatly, if the wealth that surrounded them was anything to go by, but it was torture that the mad man thrived on. He took delight from it with a pleasure that for the life of him, Lucas was unable to get his head around. As far as he was concerned, the murders were senseless. There was no reasoning behind them. There was nothing for the mad man to gain by murdering those he believed had slighted him. 'You were saying, Mr Ward, that you've got some men coming in?' he asked impatiently.

Dougie paused. He had totally forgotten that Vaughn was even in the room. 'That's right. That sly bastard, Samson, has arranged for them to do a couple of jobs for me.' He pointed the scalpel forward and his voice had a steely tone to it. 'Now, I don't trust them, I don't trust anyone.' This was said as a barbed threat that Lucas duly took on board. 'Maybe other than Ern over there, but that's only because the cunt can't fucking talk.' He nodded towards Ernest, almost apologetically, and the man grinned back at him maniacally in return. He turned back to face Lucas. 'Watch them. Watch their every fucking move, and report everything back to me,' he instructed.

Lucas nodded. 'Was there anything else?'

'Nah.' Dougie shook his head and turned back to the table. He squinted down at the shackled man as though trying to figure out which part of his body he should slice away first. 'Oh, one more thing.'

'Boss?' About to walk from the room, Lucas came to a halt. He closed his eyes in irritation and gritted his teeth before turning back around, his expression once again neutral.

'Arrange a meet with Matlock and make sure the bastard hasn't tried to tuck me up.' He looked into the distance and shook his head disapprovingly. 'I swear that little fucker was dropped on his head as a child.' He sighed dramatically. 'Still' – he grinned, opening up his arms – 'who am I to judge?'

Lucas gave him a weak smile. He wasn't sure if Dougie actually expected an answer from him or not, and so he kept his mouth firmly closed. After all, the man had said it himself, who was he to judge? And let's face it, if anyone had been dropped on their head as a child, then surely it had to be Dougie. The man was a different breed altogether. He was stark raving mad for a start.

Lucas turned on his heels and walked from the room, thankful to be able to gulp in lungsful of fresh air. Behind him, he heard Dougie begin to whistle. It was a cheerful little tune, and he knew instinctively that that was when the real screaming would begin. The knowledge was enough to make him feel depressed.

* * *

Cathy walked out of the bathroom wearing a fresh set of clothes, and rubbed the damp towel over her head.

She could see Paul in the kitchen area and deliberately avoided looking down at her husband's body that was still laid out on the tiled floor where she had left him. She studied Paul's muscular back. His movements were easy and carefree, and she stifled the urge to cry at his involvement. She should never have involved him in her problem. Briefly, she pondered the word. The murder of her husband was a little bit more than just a problem, and that was saying something.

Her detachment from the situation and lack of emotion startled her. It had to be the shock, she told herself, it just had to be. Once upon a time, she would have moved heaven and earth for her husband, until that was, he had betrayed her over and over again. His infidelity and careless disregard of her feelings had finally taken its toll, and as a result, his death made her feel nothing. It was almost as though she was an empty vessel. Her entire body felt numb.

Paul turned to face her then, and she could see that he had emptied out the small cupboard underneath the sink. Every single bottle of bleach and floor cleaner she owned was now sitting on the worktop. She also noted that he had dragged the large rug that she kept in the lounge closer to the kitchen.

She gave him a small smile and he gestured towards the worktop.

'This was all I could find.'

Cathy nodded; it was all she had.

He looked down at his watch. 'You need to get a move on, Cath. You have to get to the boozer.' He cleared his throat. 'You need an alibi, darling.'

'What are you...' She glanced down at her husband and shuddered. She had already asked the question once, and he hadn't been able to give her a straight answer, but she had to know. For her own sanity, she needed an answer from him, even if it was one that she didn't like very much. 'What will you do with him?'

Paul shrugged. 'Don't you worry about that.' He moved towards her and rested his hands on her shoulders. 'All you need to think about is getting to the pub, and when you get there, you're going to tell them that Terrance has fucked off. Tell them that he left you.' He looked down at the body, his usual handsome face now hard and twisted with hatred. 'Tell them that he went to live with one of his many slags.'

She swallowed deeply and a flood of panic washed over her. 'No one will believe that.'

'Then make them fucking believe it.'

It was said a lot harsher than he'd intended, but she had to know the score. This wasn't some lovers tiff, it was murder, and if anyone was to catch so much as a whiff as to what had gone down, then she could say goodbye to her freedom. More importantly, she could say goodbye to her kid. It stood to reason that she would have the book thrown at her, and even if by some miracle she found herself some shit hot lawyer and pleaded self-defence, there was no guarantee that she would get off with the crime. Well, at least not before spending some considerable time locked up on remand.

'Okay, Paul.' It was said quietly and his heart went out to her.

'I'm sorry, Cath. I didn't mean to...'

Cathy put up her hand, cutting him off. 'No, you're right. I need an alibi.' She gently rubbed her bump. 'And I have to put this little one first, don't I?'

She walked away from him then and, closing his eyes, he rubbed his large palm across them wearily. She would thank him one day. After all, he was only looking out for her best interests, something her husband had never done. He looked down at the rug and chewed on the inside of his cheek. After thinking the situation through, the only solution he could come up with was to use the rug to transport the body out of the flat. From the size of Matlock, he was guessing the task in hand would be no mean feat. He was a lump, was Cathy's husband, and he was going to need some help in moving him, there was no question about that.

'Come on.' His voice sounded a lot more cheerful than he actually felt. 'Get yourself off to the boozer, sweetheart.'

The front door closed quietly behind her and Paul sighed. Fucking Matlock. His only regret was not taking the man out himself. In fact, nothing would have given him greater pleasure, not that he could tell Cathy that, of course. He had a feeling that she was fragile enough as it was.

* * *

Angie was astonished. The last person she'd expected to see waltz through the pub doors was her daughter.

'What are you doing back here?' Angie narrowed her eyes, until they were two mere slits in her drawn face. 'Let me look at you.' She roughly grasped her daughter's jaw and tilted her face from side to side, as she inspected the latest damage her son-in-law had inflicted. 'He's a vicious bugger, a fucking animal. Whatever the fuck you see in him, Cath, I can't for the life of me understand.' She shook her head, a smug expression across her face. 'I would never have put up with it. You don't take after me in that respect, do you, darling?'

Cathy wrenched her face free. 'I must take after my dad then, eh?' she replied angrily. 'Not that I would know. I've never had the privilege of meeting him, have I?'

There was an edge to her daughter's voice that Angie had never heard before, and immediately, the grin was wiped from her face. She held up her hand, feeling both contrite and thoroughly ashamed of herself. 'You're right. I'm sorry, Cath. It was a cheap shot, and well, quite rightly, you've put me back in my fucking place.'

Cathy nodded; it was her way of accepting the apology. She swallowed deeply at the lie she was about to tell, and it was no white lie. She, better than anyone, knew that. No, the words she was about to utter were huge, colossal, and off the scale when it came to telling a porky pie. She glanced down at the glass of wine sitting in front of her mother. She would do anything for a shot of something right now, to take the edge off how she was feeling.

'Yeah well, he won't be bothering me any more.' She recalled Paul's warning. She had to make them believe her. 'He's left me, Mum.'

'Left you?' Angie's mouth dropped open and, picking up her wine glass, she chugged back the contents. 'I see,' she spat, 'so even after everything that went down, he still left you for that little slapper, did he?'

Avoiding her mother's gaze, Cathy nodded. 'I expect so, but let's face it, Donna – the bitch that she is – wasn't the only woman he was carrying on with, was she?' At the back of her throat, she could feel a sob waiting to release itself, and she swallowed quickly, willing herself to calm down. 'I really don't want to talk about it any more,' she continued. 'I just want to forget all about Terrance Matlock.' She touched her swollen tummy. 'I've got enough on my plate, what with this little one. He or she doesn't need a father like him. He was a useless bastard anyway, a proper wanker.' She gave a chuckle that bordered on hysteria. 'At least you were right about that, Mum. He was one useless fucking ponce, wasn't he?'

Angie narrowed her eyes. It didn't escape her notice that her daughter spoke in the past tense when referring to her husband. Still, perhaps that was a good thing. Her girl was finally putting Terrance firmly behind her. She sighed. All along, she'd known that this would happen. Her son-in-law was typical of the men where they came from – shag a bird, get her in the club, and then fuck off, that was their motto. She better than anyone, knew that to be true. Just look at Samson; he'd not only walked but had ran as fast as his feet could carry him when she'd told him all those years ago that she was expecting.

She tilted her head to one side. 'Did you see Paul?'

Cathy's heart thundered in her chest. 'Paul?' she repeated back.

'Paul Mooney.'

'No.' Cathy shook her head from side to side. She could feel her cheeks blush pink and was sure that her mother would be able to see right through her lies. 'Why would I have seen Paul?'

Angie shrugged. 'He came looking for you, that's all. Thought you might have seen him.'

'No.' She glanced once more at the wine. Her throat felt so dry.

'I don't suppose that husband of yours left you any money either?'

Cathy shook her head; money was the last thing on her mind.

'No, I didn't think so.' Pursing her lips, Angie took a crisp ten-pound note out of her purse. Oh, she knew Matlock's type, all right. 'First thing Monday morning, you need to get on to the social, darling. You're gonna need money to pay the rent and what not.'

'I thought I could get a job, nothing too heavy. The bookies are always looking to take people on, and I've always been good at maths.'

Angie threw her head back and roared with laughter. 'And you know full well the only reason the bookies are always looking for new staff is because of how many times it gets turned over.' She shook her head. 'The poor buggers are left traumatised by all accounts.' She gave a nonchalant shrug. 'I suppose having a sawn off shoved in your face would do that to you though. Anyway,' she said, her voice rising, 'you can't work. You're about to have a bloody baby.'

'I've still got two months to go.' Cathy chewed on the inside of her cheek, thinking it over. 'It could fit in nicely with my little cleaning job.'

Angie shrugged. 'You'll think of something, Cath. Here, take this.' She passed across the ten-pound note. 'Go and get us both a drink, dry white wine for me, oh, and you can keep the change.'

Cathy did as her mother bade and, standing at the bar, she took a moment to close her eyes and take a deep breath. She could do this, she told herself, as she pushed away the familiar sense of panic that threatened to envelop her. She could keep up the pretence that Terrance had upped and left her for another woman.

Her thoughts turned to Paul and tears filled her eyes. Had he already disposed of her husband's body? She spotted Stella Mooney staring towards her and inwardly shuddered. Stella could be a hard bitch when she needed to be. She took after her brother in that respect, and if the look she gave her now was anything to go by, then by rights, Cathy should have dropped down dead.

There and then, Cathy decided that she was done playing the victim. She lifted her chin in the air, blinked away the tears, and then returned the stare. Stella was the first to look away, she noted, and although it may have been a small feat, it felt as though it was somewhat of a victory. She mentally chalked one up for herself.

* * *

'I still can't believe it. Little Cathy, eh?' Jason gave his best mate a sideways glance. He watched Paul's shoulders tense and knew instinctively that his back was up, as it always was whenever Cathy's name was mentioned. He swiftly changed the subject. 'I think I'm going to ask Stell to marry me.'

'What?' With the shovel raised in mid-air, Paul turned his head.

'I'm thinking of asking your Stella to marry me.' Jason gave a slight shrug of his shoulders.

Wiping the sweat from his forehead, Paul slumped down on the muddy bank, and with the shovel held between his legs, he cocked his eyebrows. 'Seriously?' He flicked his gaze over the grave they were digging. 'You choose now to bring up the fact you're going to ask my sister to marry you?'

Jason gave a light chuckle and, leaning on the shovel, he nodded down at the deep hole. 'Seems as good a time as any. I mean, the grave has already been dug, you know, just in case you fancy tipping me in on top of Matlock.'

'Leave it out.' Paul shook his head and snorted with laughter. His sister was like a firecracker and she had a wild side to her. She was afraid of no one and she had a smart mouth on her, too. It was a dangerous combination. Their old mum had often remarked that Stella could never be tamed, but somehow, his best mate had managed to do just that. Well, to a certain degree anyway. He stood up and resumed digging for a moment, and his eyes twinkled mischievously as he looked across at Jason. 'But you so much as even think about hurting her, and I won't think twice about digging a second grave.'

Jason threw his head back and roared with laughter. 'It ain't you that scares me. Let's face it, Stella is more than capable of digging the grave herself.'

Paul grinned; his mate had made a valid point. 'You'd best stay on her good side then, eh?'

'That's the general plan, mate.' Jason winked back.

9

SIX MONTHS LATER

Stella angrily swiped a lock of loose red hair out of her face. Dressed in her fluffy pink dressing gown, she should have felt like a princess. After months of meticulous planning, today was her wedding day, and as she had her makeup expertly applied, she growled at the nervous woman who stood over her with a makeup brush in hand.

'For fuck's sake, will you just give me two minutes to breathe?' she yelled.

'Stella,' her mother, Cynthia Mooney, snapped. 'What the fuck is wrong with you today?' She turned to look at the woman who had been paid a hefty sum of money to apply her daughter's makeup. 'I'm sorry, love. She isn't usually as bad tempered as this. Just give her a few minutes to calm down. Why don't you go and help yourself to a cup of tea, and then come back and try again?'

The girl all but raced out of the room, all the while wishing that she hadn't agreed to do Stella Mooney's makeup. However, it was too late to back out now, wasn't it?

'Now, what has got into you?' Cynthia asked, once the girl was out of ear shot. 'If it's last minute nerves, well, that's perfectly normal, darling, and it'll soon pass.'

Without answering, Stella threw her head back against the head rest and puffed out her cheeks. If only it was last minute nerves, if only that was the root of her troubles. She bit down on her lip. She could feel the first set of tears fill her eyes, and she wiped them away, smudging her makeup in the process.

'It's not that, Mum,' she finally answered.

'So what is it then?' Cynthia crouched down beside her daughter and looked up into her beautiful face. To this day, she still wondered how on earth she had managed to produce such stunningly beautiful kids. 'Come on, darling, you can tell me anything, you know that.'

'Where is he, Mum?'

Taken aback, Cynthia pushed herself to her feet. 'Who?'

Stella rolled her eyes. 'Jason, of course.'

'Well' – confused by her daughter's question Cynthia waved her hand in the air – 'with our Paul most probably. He is the best man, after all.'

'Yeah, and that's what worries me.' She stood and snatched up the telephone receiver, then pressed redial for the umpteenth time that morning. 'It just keeps ringing and ringing.'

Cynthia shook her head. 'Stop your worrying, Stell,' she said, 'you're going to ruin your makeup if you're not careful.'

Stella rolled her eyes for a second time; her makeup was the least of her worries. Her Jason told her everything and the fact he and her brother Paul were paying Dougie Ward a visit terrified her. She'd heard more than one rumour about the man to know that he was a nutcase, a complete and utter mad man. Who knew if Jason and Paul would even make it out of his home in one piece?

* * *

Cathy admired her reflection in the bathroom mirror, and letting out a long sigh, her shoulders drooped. She wished now that she hadn't agreed to accompany Paul to his sister's wedding as his guest. It wasn't as though Stella even liked her that much. In fact, she was pretty certain that Stella positively loathed her. Oh, she had never said as much, of course, but she'd seen the glares the red-headed woman shot in her direction whenever she was in close proximity.

A tiny cry from the bedroom caught her attention and she smiled as she made her way towards her son's screams. 'Mummy's coming,' she called out.

He was a handsome little baby, was her Kieran, and she loved every single inch of him. The only downfall was that he also happened to be Terrance's double, but the love she felt for her own flesh and blood made her ignore that little fact.

'Hey, what's all this?' She scooped her son up into her arms and pushed her face closer to his, peppering his little face with butterfly kisses. He smelled of his own special little scent, mixed with traces of talcum powder. Her heart melted all over again. 'Come on now,' she said, 'let's get you dressed.' On a tiny plastic hanger that hung on the wardrobe door was a little blue and white satin sailor suit that Paul had bought especially for the occasion. 'Oh, you are going to look like a little smasher.' She grinned happily.

As she began to dress her baby, she thought back to the weeks and months after his birth. She'd cried bucket-loads, and once the tears had started, they hadn't seemed to want to stop. Her mum and the health visitor had seemed to think that she was suffering from the baby blues, but she wasn't, not really. She'd cried for Terrance, and as much as he'd been a liar, a womaniser,

and a ponce, he'd still been her husband and she'd loved him
once. He could be a right charmer when the mood took him, and
as much as he'd made her life a living hell he'd had his good
points too: he could be attentive, caring, and kind; there were
times when he'd even made her laugh. Of course it had never
lasted for long, and once she'd forgiven his latest beating or infidelity then he went back to his old ways and she was once again
walking on egg shells, living in fear of the next time she said the
wrong thing and he gave her a good hiding. Still, she carried the
guilt of his death around with her. It was always there, hanging
over her like a thick black cloud, and she supposed in a way it
always would.

Her thoughts wandered now towards Paul. He had been her
rock since her husband's death. He had even helped her to
acquire the little job in the book makers. She had a feeling that it
was all thanks to him putting out the hard word that, for the first
time in years, there was never so much as a whiff of trouble in
there. Well, at least not on the days that she worked anyway. The
little toe rags had even stopped stealing the pens.

She glanced in the direction of the lounge and frowned. She
would have thought that she would have heard from him by now.
He usually telephoned her several times a day, checking up on
her, as he called it. The thought made her smile. Oh, he had been
her rock all right. They were indebted to one another. Terrance's
death and his subsequent removal would always be proof of that.

* * *

Ten miles away, Paul and Jason were at Dougie Ward's home: the
Manor. Unlike their previous visits when they had been
instructed to wait in the hallway to complete the exchange,
today they had been ushered inside what could only be

described as some sort of cold room. At least, that was what it looked like if the floor to ceiling stainless-steel fridges were anything to go by.

'Stella will have my guts if we're late.' Jason glanced down at his watch, then raised his eyebrows expectantly towards his best friend. 'Where the fuck is Mad—' He stopped himself just in time and began again. 'Where the fuck is Dougie?'

Just like Jason, Paul wasn't happy. They were supposed to have been in and out within minutes, and now, thirty minutes after they'd arrived, Dougie still hadn't made an appearance. He knew it was a mind game on Dougie's part, and as a result, he was livid.

'Where is he?' he snapped.

The hint of a smile played out across Lucas's lips. He opened his mouth to speak, but quickly snapped it closed again when he heard Dougie's booming voice come from behind him.

'Hello boys.' Dougie's voice dripped with sarcasm as he peered out from behind his heavy. 'Sorry I kept you so long.' He moved forward and opened out his arms theatrically. 'But as you can see, I was a bit busy.'

Paul stared at the man in front of him and was positively taken aback. Dressed in what could only be described as cotton theatre scrubs with a long, thick, red rubber apron tied around his waist, Dougie looked like a mad scientist. He suppressed the urge to laugh, even if it was more out of shock than anything else.

Twisting on the tap, Dougie began to methodically wash his hands. 'Cleanliness,' he said, 'is very important.' He looked down at his fingernails and, taking a small hard-bristled brush, he set to work, dragging the brush backwards and forwards. 'You'd be surprised at just how much blood gets underneath these.' He let out a long sigh as he held out his hand to show them exactly what he meant.

Dumbstruck, Paul nodded. He caught Lucas's eye and gave a

nervous cough. 'I don't mean to rush you, Mr Ward, but it's my sister's wedding day.'

'Is it now?' Dougie was all smiles, but still he didn't hurry himself. Once he'd patted his manicured hands dry, he held his arm out towards Ernest and took from him a large holdall. 'Excuse Ernest,' he said. 'He would offer his congratulations, but as you well know he's minus a tongue, and therefore is unable to speak. Poor bugger is a mute.' He shook his head and the smile left his face as he raised his eyes heavenwards in mock sadness. 'You see, Ernest here, well, let's just say that he annoyed me one day, and well' – he mimicked a slicing action – 'as a result, Ern lost his tongue. Ain't that right, Ern?'

Ernest nodded maniacally and opened his mouth wide, showing that he was indeed minus a tongue.

Beside him, Jason blanched and Paul gave a slight shake of his head to erase his fears. He had heard the rumours of how Ernest had lost his tongue, and it had happened years before he had even met Dougie. 'I'll bear that in mind, Mr Ward.' Paul smiled, warily.

Dougie smiled in return. 'Wise choice.' He looked down at the leather holdall in his hand as though weighing up the contents before passing it across.

Paul reached out his hand.

Tutting loudly, Dougie shook his head from side to side, causing the tiny hairs on the back of Paul's neck to stand up on end. It was common knowledge that Dougie Ward was more than just a little bit cuckoo. In fact, to put it mildly, he was a fucking lunatic and would make the inmates of Broadmoor look relatively sane. 'Not so fucking fast, sunshine. I think I'll take that one first.'

Paul looked down at the holdall on the floor beside his feet. He stooped down to pick it up when he heard Dougie tut a second time.

'Ernest will take care of that.' He grinned then, a slow maniacal grin. 'The mute bastard has to earn his keep somehow, doesn't he?'

Straightening up, Paul glanced towards Lucas. Throughout the entire exchange, the heavy's expression had remained impassive and he wondered briefly how the hell he managed to spend a considerable amount of time in Dougie's company without going crazy himself. Taking a step away from the bag, he watched as Ernest snatched it up with large claw-like fingers. Talk about surreal. Just moments in Dougie's presence, and he was beginning to question his own sanity.

The exchange finally complete, Paul and Jason practically fell over themselves to get away from the mad bastard.

'Fuck me.' Once they were outside, Jason took a sharp intake of breath. 'The bloke is a fucking nutcase.'

'I know.' Looking over his shoulder, Paul chewed on the inside of his cheek. He was clearly rattled and it showed.

'Do you reckon there were bodies in that fridge?'

Paul shrugged. He didn't have a clue. The only thing he knew for certain was that he had to finish what he'd started, and a lot sooner than he'd intended. 'Come on,' he sighed. 'We'll drop this lot off with that old fucker Samson, then shoot off home. Like you said, Stella will have your guts if you're late.'

They climbed into Paul's car, and on the drive back to Barking, they were both quiet, both lost in their own thoughts.

* * *

Stella had never felt so relieved. She collapsed into the chair with the phone glued to her ear. 'Where the fuck have you been?' She listened to Jason's reply and clicked her fingers towards the makeup artist. Setting the phone down beside her, she smiled widely. 'Looks like I'm still getting married after all.'

Cynthia rolled her eyes. As if there had ever been any doubt about that. Jason loved the bones of her daughter and she knew instinctively that there was no way on earth that he would have disappeared on their wedding day. Her Paul would have made sure that that never happened.

* * *

Cathy smiled shyly as she opened the front door to Paul. Her hair was loose and the blonde locks tumbled down her back in cascading waves. She wore a sleeveless pale-blue dress with an embroidered sweetheart neckline. Around her waist, accentuating her figure, she had secured a thin silver belt.

'Will I do?' She grinned.

Nodding, Paul let out a soft whistle. 'You look the business, Cath.'

As her cheeks blushed a bright shade of red, Cathy averted her gaze. She passed across her son to him and smiled to herself as Paul made a great fuss of the baby. He would make a fantastic father one day. The very thought made her heart lurch. She wondered then about the woman who would one day ensnare Paul's heart. Whoever she was, she knew for a fact that she was going to be one very lucky woman.

'Are you ready then?' Paul glanced at his watch. He intended to drop Cathy off at the church, then quickly come back and collect Jason.

'I'm ready, and how about you? Have you got the rings?'

Paul made a show of patting down his pockets and she tilted her head towards him. 'Paul?' she warned.

A slow smile crept across his face. 'Of course I've got them.'

Shaking her head, Cathy grinned. Yes, the woman who finally kept Paul's attention long enough to make him want to settle down was definitely one very lucky woman.

* * *

The wedding ceremony that had taken place at St Margaret's Church in Barking had gone off without a hitch, much to Cynthia's relief. She really didn't think she could take much more of her daughter's hysterics for one day.

Seated at the reception, she smiled as she watched her daughter and new son-in-law take to the floor for the first dance. The haunting voice of Gregory Abbott belting out 'Shake You Down' filled the air and she smiled. The song was one of Stella's favourites, and even though Jason hadn't wanted that particular song for the first dance, Stella had got her own way, as she always did wherever her son-in-law was concerned.

She turned to look at her son. He was a handsome devil all right. He took after his late father in that department. She watched as he whispered something into Cathy's ear and smiled softly as she watched the young woman throw her head back and laugh. He was besotted with the little blonde and her son, and quite rightly so. Little Kieran was a lovely baby.

Cynthia continued to watch them. She had always liked Cathy. She was a good girl, the type of girl any mother would be delighted to have as a daughter. She had often thought that her and Paul made a wonderful couple. Even when they had been young teenagers, she had believed they were a match made in heaven. How the girl didn't realise that her Paul was in love with her, she had no idea, but Cathy seemed oblivious to his thoughts and feelings. Perhaps that was half the attraction? Or perhaps Paul was too scared to wear his heart on his sleeve in case she turned him down. When Cathy had ended their relationship all those years ago, it hadn't only broken Paul but it had also changed him; he'd become harder, less tolerant, reckless. Oh she wasn't daft; she'd heard the rumours on the estate that her son was considered a law unto himself, dangerous. But he wasn't really, not deep down, he'd just never got over losing Cathy.

* * *

Not one to usually drink alcohol, the champagne bubbles had gone straight to Cathy's head and she felt a little tipsy. Excusing herself, she made her way to the ladies' toilets and as she pushed open the door and walked through, she recoiled slightly. She hadn't expected to see Stella. She plastered a wide smile across her face and headed straight for the toilet cubicle. When she came back out moments later, Stella was waiting for her.

'It's been a lovely wedding, Stell,' Cathy said, beaming, 'and you look stunning, truly beautiful.' She looked into the mirror and admired Stella's dress. It was ivory, fitted, and the bodice was covered with thousands of twinkling diamantes. She truly did look beautiful. As she washed her hands, she caught Stella's eyes and noticed that, much to her dismay, the other woman didn't return her smile.

'What are you doing here, Cathy?'

Cathy's stomach dropped and, after she switched off the tap, she turned around. 'Paul invited me,' she said as she dried her hands on a paper towel.

Stella thought this over. 'Tell me. What really happened to Terrance?' Her expression was hard as she asked the question. 'What exactly did you rope my brother in to doing for you? Did you ask him to kill your husband? Is that what you did?'

'No.' Stunned, Cathy swallowed hard and shook her head vigorously. 'Of course I didn't.'

Stella screwed up her face. 'I was there in the pub that night. I watched him tear out, and the mood he was in, he was ready to commit fucking murder. He killed for you, didn't he?'

'Don't be ridic—'

Yanking on Cathy's arm, Stella snarled, 'I saw him.' She tightened her grip and her long French manicured fingernails dug into the soft flesh. 'And let's face it, he's so obsessed with you that he would do just about anything you ask.'

'No.' Cathy wrenched her arm free and shook her head sadly. She could sense the anger coming off the other woman in waves. She'd always had a temper, had Stella, even grown men were wary of her. 'You don't own him, Stella.' Her voice was quiet and composed. 'The way you carry on isn't natural. Why do you see me as such a threat?' She tilted her head to one side. 'And despite what you might think, he is his own man. I didn't ask him to kill anyone. Why would I even do that?'

'Because,' Stella snarled, 'you wanted to get rid of your husband so you could ensnare my brother. That's what you've always wanted. I've watched you hanging onto his every word. You don't take your eyes off him.' She screwed up her face. 'It's sickening to watch. You know that he's worth a bob or two, that he's going places, and you want a share of it. You want to be the big I Am.'

Cathy pulled herself up to her full height, all five feet, two inches of it. She knew that if she didn't put Stella in her place and fast then she would never know a day's peace again. Stella would do anything in her power to wrench Paul away from her, even if all they were ever going to share was a friendship.

'You're right.' Cathy sucked her teeth. She couldn't show her fear. 'Terrance is dead, but it wasn't Paul who killed him.' She watched

Stella's beautiful face pale underneath the brightly lit fluorescent bulb. She spread open her arms. 'It was me, and let me tell you now, lady, before you even think about spouting my business to anyone else or informing the Old Bill, you should know this. Your brother, oh, and also your new husband, let's not forget his part in all of this, well, they are up to their pretty little necks in this, almost as much as I am. You see, they disposed of the body. Buried him, in fact.'

Stella gasped.

'So' – Cathy pointed her finger towards Stella's chest – 'stop with the little digs, Stell, because from where I'm standing, it's me that holds all of the cards, not you. I mean, just what would happen to your precious brother and your wonderful new husband if I should suddenly grow a conscience and find a need to confess my wrongdoings to the police?'

'You wouldn't.'

Cathy raised her eyebrows to the ceiling. 'Wouldn't I?' she asked innocently. 'Do us both a favour, Stella, and leave me and Paul alone.' She shook her head and gave Stella a pitying look. 'You know, I used to like you. I even thought we could have been friends once, but now' – she looked the woman up and down with distaste – 'now you are nothing but an irritation to me.'

With those parting words, she held her head high and exited the ladies' toilets. She had a sneaky suspicion that Stella wouldn't cause her any more problems, not if she knew what was best for her. Within moments, she was back at the table and, seeing Paul hold her son in his arms, she smiled down at him.

'Are you okay, sweetheart?'

'Yes.' Cathy's smile grew even wider, and for the first time in months, she genuinely did feel okay. She sat down and, catching Stella's eye, raised her glass in the air in a toast. She then turned towards Paul. Perhaps it was the champagne giving her more confidence, she didn't know, but she pointed the glass towards him. 'To us,' she said.

Paul mirrored the action and lifted his own glass in the air. 'To us,' he repeated back.

* * *

Once the wedding reception had ended and Paul had escorted her home, Cathy invited him in for a coffee. Somehow she felt that something between them had shifted. Whether that was her imagination or not, she didn't know, but she took a wild guess that only time would tell. If she was about to make a fool of herself, then so be it.

Taking a sip of her coffee, Cathy gave a shy giggle. 'I was just thinking back to when we were kids.' She sucked on her bottom lip and gave him a coy grin. 'Do you remember when...'

Paul's cheeks flamed. He had a good idea as to what she was referring to and he put his head into his hands and groaned. 'Don't fucking remind me.' He looked up then and smiled. 'Not that it wasn't good,' he was quick to point out, 'because it was. In fact, it was better than good. It was out of this fucking world, but fuck me, Cath, I don't think I even knew what I was doing.'

Cathy giggled and she gave him a wink. 'We were just kids,' she said, grinning, 'how could either of us have known what we were doing?'

'Well, let me just say that I've improved my game a great fucking deal since then.' He groaned as soon as the words had left his mouth and momentarily closed his eyes, feeling mortified. 'I shouldn't have said that. I'm sorry.'

Cathy smiled. She watched him set his mug on the floor and give an embarrassed cough.

'I think that maybe I should get going. You're probably tired, right?'

Cathy nodded. He gave her a smile and made to walk past her. When she reached out to take his hand, she felt his body stiffen.

'Don't leave,' she said, looking up at him, 'not yet. Stay the night.' It was said quietly, surprising both her and Paul.

'Are you sure that's what you want?'

'I've never been surer.' Getting up from the sofa, Cathy gripped his hand even tighter. 'Now take me to bed and show me just how much you've improved.'

Paul didn't need asking twice and, leading the way, he practically ran up the staircase, much to Cathy's delight.

10

Angie was angry and it showed.

'You told me he was taken care of,' she spat, 'that his days on this earth were numbered. So, answer me this, why the fuck is Mooney still walking, talking, and more importantly still fucking breathing?'

Samson let out a long sigh. 'These things take time,' he answered.

'Take time?' Angie's shrill voice filled the air. 'I don't have time.' She had seen just how close her daughter and Paul Mooney had become and she didn't like it one little bit. Her daughter was beginning to rely on him a little too much, in her opinion, and that could never be a good thing. Mooney had well and truly crawled his way into her daughter's life and as a result, she was livid. If she wasn't careful Paul was going to steal Cathy away from her, and then what would happen? She would be completely alone, she would have no one, Paul wouldn't stand for her using Cathy as a stop gap when she was down on her luck, or when she had no one else to go to the pub with.

'I've already told you that the situation is in hand.' Samson spread open his arms. 'And it is. Like I said, his days are fucking numbered.' He smiled to himself. As far as he was concerned, his little plan to dispose of both Mooney and the mad bastard Dougie Ward was on track. As he'd already stated, these things took time.

Slumping back on the sofa, Angie sighed angrily. 'They had better be,' she snapped.

'They are,' Samson placated her. A slow grin spread across his face. At this very moment in time, Jerry Dolan, his right-hand man, was lifting out a package of cocaine from the bag that Paul Mooney had dropped off earlier that afternoon and replacing it with an identical bag filled to the brim with baking powder. Just as he had done, in fact, every time Mooney had dropped off.

He steepled his fingers across his chest and stifled a laugh. When the shit hit the fan and he confronted Dougie about the snidey bags of coke, he was bound to put two and two together and believe that Mooney was on the take. Samson grinned even wider. Paul Mooney wasn't going to know what had hit him, and as for Dougie, well, the mad bastard's head was going to roll when, even after Mooney's demise, coke would still be replaced. The plan was a masterpiece and it would give him the perfect excuse to take Ward out without any repercussions coming back on himself. After all, everyone in their world would see that he'd had no other choice but to end the thieving mad bastard. As far as he was concerned, he would be killing two birds with one stone, much to his pleasure.

* * *

Two weeks later, Cathy sat at Angie's kitchen table. In front of her was a mug of tea. Taking a sip, she grimaced at the taste.

Angie raised her eyebrows. 'Something wrong with my tea?' she asked. 'Is it not good enough now for her ladyship?'

Cathy laughed heartily and she pushed the mug across the table and away from her. 'The tea is fine, Mum. It's me, I just can't stomach it.'

Angie frowned and as she sat back in her seat, she lit a cigarette and angrily blew out a thin stream of smoke. 'How long?' she barked out.

'Six weeks,' Cathy replied happily.

Shaking her head from side to side, Angie glared at her only daughter. 'Oh, Cathy, you stupid, stupid mare. Are you not content with raising one fatherless child? You want to add a second one to the mix?'

'How will my baby be fatherless?' Taken aback, Cathy frowned. Admittedly, she hadn't expected Angie to be truly over-joyed at the prospect of a second grandchild, but at the same time, she'd expected a bit more support than this.

'What is wrong with you, Cathy?' Angie banged her fist down on the table. 'Didn't I teach you anything? To not open your legs for all and fucking sundry for starters? And as for Paul Mooney' – she stabbed her finger forward – 'he's bad news and you know that as well as I do.' She gave a bitter laugh. 'And you thought that you had problems with Terrance? Well, let me tell you now, lady, they were nothing compared to being stuck with him, Paul, for the remainder of your life.' She was thoughtful for a moment. 'It's not too late to get rid of it. We could nip to the doctor's in the morning and get you an appointment with the abortion clinic. By tomorrow afternoon, it will all be over with.'

'Get rid of it?' Tears sprang to Cathy's eyes and she blinked them away furiously. 'I'm not getting rid of my baby.' Her hand automatically travelled to her tummy. 'You don't know anything about Paul. You haven't seen how good he is with me and Kieran. He loves this little boy like his own.'

'But he ain't his, is he?' Angie answered. 'One day that boy's dad will be back and then what, eh? Are you going to go for round two, make it a hat-trick and have yet another fatherless child?' She laughed nastily, a high pitched cackle that rang loud in Cathy's ears. 'At least two of them would share the same DNA.'

Scraping back her chair, Cathy got to her feet. She placed little Kieran on her hip and his podgy little legs kicked out excitedly as she stared down at her mother. 'You're a fine one to talk, Mum. Let's face it, you would know all about fatherless children, wouldn't you? Where is my dad exactly, and more to the point, who is he?' She looked down her nose at her mother. 'To be honest, it really wouldn't surprise me if you didn't even know yourself who he is. Like Donna Cassidy said, you'd do anything for a bit of free meat. So what exactly was my father offering you? I'm guessing it was a bit more than just money?'

Angie jumped up from her seat. The slap across her daughter's face was both hard and loud. Immediately, the baby began to scream and she instantly regretted what she had done.

'Oh my God, Cath, I didn't mean to do that, honest to God, I didn't.' She went to make a fuss of the baby, checking that he was okay when her daughter backed away from her.

'Yes you did, Mum, and it isn't the first time either, is it?' Pressing the back of her hand to her cheek, Cathy spat out the words. 'But I can tell you now, it is the last time. My Paul has never raised his fists to me and you have the cheek to stand there and look down your nose at him?' She shook her head sadly. 'I'm not a child any more, Mum. Nothing you say will turn me against him this time.'

Angie had the grace to look away. Her daughter had just hit the proverbial nail on the head, and it was true. In the past, she had torn the two apart. Lie after lie, she had told her daughter, all in the hope that Cathy would turn against him, and after a lot of perseverance, her plan had eventually worked.

'If you can't be happy for me then just stay away. I mean it, Mum. Paul is my life now. I'm having his baby, and the quicker you get that into your head, the better.'

As her daughter raced from the room, Angie pressed her hand across her mouth and slumped down onto the nearest chair. She really could cut out her own tongue at times. Oh, she better than anyone knew that she had a wicked streak inside her, but to lash out at her daughter... She stared down at her hand as if the limb were suddenly alien to her. Oh God, she had sworn the last time she'd slapped her daughter that she would never do it again, and now look at her. She'd not only gone and done it, but had done it when Cathy had been holding little Kieran, her grandson.

* * *

Paul kissed the top of Cathy's head and, as he pulled her underneath his arm, he whispered in her ear, 'I love you, you know that, right?' He meant every word, really meant it. Whenever he was with her, she made him feel level-headed. She had a calming influence about her that made him want to reign in his formidable temper, and it was formidable. The reputation that preceded him was proof of that. Even when they had been kids, she'd had always known exactly what to say to calm him down. It was just what she did, and for that fact alone, he loved her.

Cathy grinned. 'I've got a good idea.' And it was true, she did know that he loved her, loved both her and her young son. Her hand reached down to softly rub her still flat tummy. He would love this little one when he or she was born just as fiercely, she was certain of it.

'Will you put the girl down?' Cynthia's voice was stern, but her eyes twinkled with joy. 'My first grandchild, eh?' She looked down at Kieran and quickly corrected herself. 'My second grandchild,' she said, rubbing his podgy little hand.

'You're not going to start crying again, are you?' Paul rolled his eyes before winking across to Cathy.

'I will if I want to.' Cynthia reached out her arms to take the child from his mother. 'And less of your cheek, you,' she playfully scolded.

Cathy grinned. She had always loved Cynthia. She was the very epitome of what a mother should be, and after growing up with Angie, Cynthia was like a breath of fresh air. She loved her children with a ferociousness that Cathy was determined to one day aspire to.

From the hallway, the telephone began to ring and, turning her head, she watched as Paul lifted up the receiver. Within a split second, his whole countenance had changed.

'Problem?' she enquired.

He looked up at her and gave a forced smile that didn't quite reach his dark blue eyes.

'No problem.' He placed the receiver back on the cradle, hardly even saying two words to the caller. 'I have to shoot off for a bit though. You don't mind staying here with my mum for a while, do you?'

'Of course she doesn't.' Cynthia spoke for her son's girlfriend. 'We can have a good natter and talk babies.'

Cathy laughed softly. 'Sounds perfect to me.' She turned to look at Paul. 'Are you sure that you're okay?'

'Course I am.' He kissed the top of her head. 'As I keep on telling you, you don't have to worry about me.'

Cathy watched him go, and as the front door slammed closed behind him, she narrowed her eyes. She knew Paul inside and out, and she knew when something was troubling him. Oh, he could tell her otherwise until he was blue in the face, but she wasn't daft. She knew the truth; she always did when it came to him.

* * *

Slamming his foot on the brake, Paul brought the Range Rover to a screeching halt. He yanked the key out of the ignition and jumped out of the car. 'What the fuck is going on?' he yelled.

Jason shook his head in a warning. His fingers held the struggling young man beside him in a vice-like grip, and as the boy tried to flee from the scene, he jabbed his elbow into the side of the terrified boy's face.

With a groan, the boy dropped heavily to the concrete floor.

'Well?' Reaching into the backseat of the car, Paul brought out a baseball bat. He vaguely recognised the boy as being one of Samson's young foot soldiers.

'Tell him. Tell him what you just told me.' Jason spat out the words and he breathed heavily through his flared nostrils. 'You need to hear this,' he told Paul. He turned his head back to the boy. 'Oi, you little fucker' – he kicked out his heavy boot – 'tell him. Tell him everything.'

Devan Barkley placed his hands protectively over his head. He'd only just turned seventeen, and with light brown skin and startling blue eyes, he was a skinny kid and small for his age. Fear caught in the back of his throat and, looking between the two men, he tried to weigh up his options. Samson Ivers may have been his biological father, but between him and Mooney, he didn't know which one out of the two scared him more.

His gaze settled on Paul. He saw the anger spread across the older man's face and knew for a fact that he was capable of violence, real violence. Mooney's temper was legendary on their estate, and they were not made-up tales. No, they were real-life accounts told by people who had seen first-hand the extreme violence Mooney had dished out. As the man in question stood over him with a baseball bat held in his fist, he looked not only scary, but downright terrifying.

'Is that your car?' Paul surveyed the area around him. It was in near darkness and he knew for a fact that there were no CCTV cameras in operation, despite what the sign on the nearby dimly lit lamppost stated.

As the colour drained from his face, Devan warily nodded.

Taking the bat, Paul walked around the car. It was a decent motor, an XR3I – the dream car of any boy racer – and for a short second, he felt a moment of pity for what he was about to do. However, only for a moment. He then proceeded to smash each window to smithereens.

With each loud crash, Devan winced. He'd saved up for months to buy the car and knew for a fact that his wheels were the envy of his peers. For the first time in his life, he actually had some street cred.

'Now that,' Paul said, pointing the weapon towards Devan, 'is me just warming up.' He stalked forward, crouched down and grasped the boy's jaw tightly in his fist. 'Now, you are going to tell me exactly what the fuck is going down, and if you don't, then I'm going to break every single bone in your fucking body until you start talking, because let me tell you now, you are seriously beginning to fuck me off.'

Devan's body shook. He looked up at the two men and physically cowered away from them. With each passing second, their large frames seemed to grow even larger. It was at that moment, he regretted smoking the joint he had happily shared with his friends. The sweet pungent scent of the grass lingered, and that laced with the fear he felt, was enough to make him want to empty his bowels. 'It's the coke,' he finally stuttered.

Paul glanced up at Jason and narrowed his eyes. 'What's he talking about? What fucking coke?'

Devan swallowed deeply. 'The coke, man,' he stated. 'The coke you got from Mad Dougie. Well, some of it was snide, see, and Samson is going off his fucking trolley. He's on the warpath, ready and waiting to maim anyone who gets in his way.'

'How do you know this?' Paul tightened his grip on the boy's jaw. 'Who told you this?'

Fright got the better of Devan. A wet patch appeared between his legs, and as the steaming urine seeped onto the cold concrete beneath him, he squirmed even harder. 'It was Samson,' he cried. 'I heard Samson tell Jerry Dolan. He's going mental, reckons you replaced one of the bags with baking powder or something like that. He reckons you've tucked him up.'

Paul threw the boy away from him, straightened up, then glanced across to Jason and slowly shook his head. This wasn't good and that was an understatement. 'Is this a joke?'

Jason shrugged. His expression told Paul everything he needed to know. It was no joke. In actual fact, it was a nightmare, a nightmare of epic proportions.

'Get out of here.' Paul raised the bat in a warning and watched the boy scramble to his feet before running away as if his life depended on it. The kid looked positively terrified, not that he gave one iota about the boy and his feelings.

'What the fuck?' Jason's eyes were wide. 'What the actual fuck, Paul?' he growled.

Paul looked into the distance and rubbed at his temples as he tried to think the situation through. He knew for a fact that they hadn't touched the contents of the bag, so who exactly had replaced the coke, if indeed anyone even had? And more to the point, why was this the first time he was hearing about it? Why had none of the men in his employment given him a heads up on the situation? It was a fuckup of epic proportions, and as a result, heads would roll. He'd make sure of that, if it was the last thing he ever did.

'You know that this puts us in the firing line, right? We collected that coke; we were the ones who dropped it off.'

Paul didn't answer. He wasn't stupid and knew exactly what this sudden change of events meant. Instantly, he regretted letting the boy go. He needed to vent his anger out on someone and could think of nothing he would like better than to take the bat and smash it across the boy's body until he was a broken and bloodied mess on the floor.

'Michael Nicholls,' he finally growled. 'He took the bag from us, and it's no secret that he likes a bit of Charlie.' He slammed his fist against the palm of his hand. 'Get in the motor. I'm gonna kill that fucking ponce once and for all when I get my hands on him.'

11

Talk about Oscar winning performance. Samson was pleasantly surprised by his theatrics. He screamed and hollered down the phone at Dougie Ward, barely even letting the nutcase get a word in edgeways.

'Where is my coke?' he screamed. 'Think you can get one over on me, do you? Me, fucking me?' Adding to his performance, he poked a stiff finger into his chest. 'You think you can treat me like I'm a first-class fucking cunt? I pay you,' he continued, barely even pausing to take a breath, 'a great deal of fucking wedge for my merchandise. I've stayed loyal. I could have gone elsewhere. I could have gone to the fucking Turks, who, let me tell you now, were more than willing to make a deal, but I didn't. I stayed loyal to you, to fucking you, and this is how you repay me?'

He allowed Dougie the opportunity to answer him and could hear the shock in the madman's voice. He actually sounded contrite and he had to stifle down the urge to laugh once more.

'This,' he continued, 'will be all over the smoke by the end of the night and you, you thieving bastard, will rue the day you ever tried to tuck me up – to treat me, me,' he spat, 'like a fucking cunt.'

He slammed the phone down with a ferociousness that almost split the plastic receiver in two. Oh, he was good all right, better than good. He was a fucking mastermind. He slowly turned around to face the group of heavies in his employment who had gathered in the lounge waiting for instruction from him. Taking direction from his number two, Jerry Dolan, they were big men, as tall as they were broad shouldered, and more than capable of taking care of his business. 'Get out there now and find that fucking cunt Mooney.' He threw Jerry a sly grin. 'I want the bastard brought to me.' He paused momentarily to light a cigarette. 'And make sure he's alive.' He stared at each of the men in turn. 'You got that?'

Jerry and the crowd of heavies nodded, their bull necks virtually disappearing as they did so. 'Got it, boss.' They grinned back happily.

* * *

Bringing his car to a halt outside The Jolly Fisherman, Paul threw open the door and jumped out with Jason swiftly following behind him.

'He's got to be in here,' Paul stated.

Jason nodded. They had already searched all over the estate looking for Michael Nicholls, and still they had come up empty-handed.

They pushed their way into the public house and bustled through the crowd of revellers. As usual for a Saturday evening, it was noisy and crammed to the rafters with punters. The familiar scent of cheap perfume and stale cigarette smoke clouded the air and filled their nostrils.

'Over there,' Jason shouted to be heard above the music and, with a flick of his head, he indicated towards the back of the premises where the pool table was housed.

Without missing a beat, Paul stormed forward. His hand shot out and he grabbed Michael around the throat. 'You and me are gonna have a little chat.'

'What?' Michael's eyes bulged and the colour drained from his face. Even though he'd been expecting this visit, he was once again reminded of just how powerful, how dangerous, Mooney was. 'I gave you your dough back. You know I fucking did, and with a hefty amount of fucking interest, might I add.'

Paul ignored Michael's protests and dragged him bodily towards the exit, all the while, he had to stop himself from laying his fists into the terrified man.

Outside on the pavement, Paul could no longer control himself and he swung his fist full pelt into Michael's face. The man staggered backwards from the force of the blow.

'Where is it? Where is the coke?' Paul's words came out in a low, menacing growl.

'How would I know?' Regaining his balance, Michael wiped the back of his hand across his mouth, smearing blood across his cheek. Looking up and down the near empty street, he was stalling for time. 'How the fuck would I know where it is?' Unusually, he was now full of bravado, his tone bordering on mocking. 'Why don't you ask Samson where it is?' He smirked.

'Because you, you cunt, were the one who took the fucking bag from us.' Slamming his fist into Michael's gut, Paul's breath streamed out ahead of him, and as Michael dropped to his knees, he grasped a handful of his hair in his fist and roughly snapped his head backwards. 'Where is it?' he demanded. 'And I'm warning you now, don't even try to fuck me over on this. I know it was fucking you. It's no secret that you hoover that fucking shit up your nose. So, where the fuck is it?'

Michael groaned out an inaudible reply. Blood trickled down his chin and onto the front of his shirt from a deep split at the corner of his mouth, and hawking deep into his throat, he spat out a mouthful of blood. 'It wasn't me.' Gone was the bravado; he was clearly terrified. 'I swear to God, Paul, it wasn't me.'

Paul was so incensed he could practically taste the anger he felt. He was no mug and as such, wouldn't be treated as one. Grasping Michael's head, he repeatedly slammed it against the wheel arch. Each loud crash spurred him on. The fact that he could so easily kill meant absolutely nothing to him. He had gone past the point of no return. No amount of reasoning would lift the red mist that had descended over him.

Michael slid unconscious to the ground and Paul proceeded to punch and kick out his heavy boots with as much strength as he could physically muster. As far as he was concerned, the hammering he was dishing out was long overdue.

'Paul.'

The warning in Jason's voice immediately made Paul look up. His chest heaved from the exertion. He heard the screech of tyres grinding to a halt on either side of where they were standing, and was hastily brought back to his senses. He looked around him as four of Samson's most loyal men, all built like the proverbial brick shithouse, jumped out of their cars and advanced upon them. Not for the first time did he want to curse his temper. Not only should he have waited until he was thinking straight, he should have put the feelers out and played clever instead of jumping in head first.

'You piece of shit.' He kicked out at Michael's unconscious body one final time, hoping more than anything that he had actually killed the man. As far as he was concerned, he was nothing but a sly, sneaky, useless fucking ponce who more than deserved death.

'Mr Ivers wants a word with you.' There was a hint of delight in Jerry Dolan's gruff voice as he dragged him towards the waiting car. Paul noted that he and Jason had been separated, and as he made himself comfortable on the back seat, he watched with irritation as Michael Nicholls's prostrate body was peeled from the pavement and unceremoniously dragged towards the rear of the car.

'Let's get this over with, shall we? Leave the no-good treacherous bastard where he is.'

The unexpected punch to the side of his head not only made Paul see stars, but also made him inwardly groan a second time. He'd been right all along; it was definitely a nightmare all right.

As he threw open the front door, Samson's expression was a mask of pure anger.

'Get in here, boy.' For a brief moment, he was impressed with his men. He hadn't expected to see Paul Mooney on his doorstep so quickly, and there and then, decided to give Jerry a pay rise. The big man was a diamond as far as he was concerned.

He walked through to the lounge, knowing full well that the two boys would be dragged in behind him. In front of the patio doors, he came to a halt, and as he slowly turned around, his eyes flashed dangerously.

'You thieving bastards,' he spat. 'Do you take me for a fucking mug? Who was it that gave you the wink that you could steal my' – he stabbed a stiff finger into his chest and his gravelly voice rose even further – 'my fucking coke?'

Paul opened his mouth to speak but, taking a menacing step

forward, Samson cut him off. He clenched his meaty fists into tight balls and noted that much to his annoyance, the boy didn't flinch. In fact, he didn't even bat an eyelid. Samson pointed down at the overstuffed sealed polythene bag on the glass coffee table; a split down the centre of the bag was clearly visible and spilling out of it were traces of white powder. 'This' – he snatched up the package and waved it underneath the younger man's nose – 'is not what I sent you to collect. It isn't what I paid a considerable amount of money for.' He threw the bag across the room. It landed on the floor with a soft thud and a cloud of white powder filtered up into the air. 'That,' he hollered, 'is not the fucking coke I paid for.'

Both Paul and Jason watched the cloud of white powder settle on the furniture as though it was the most fascinating thing they had ever seen.

Tearing his eyes away from the scene before him, Paul shook his head. 'I don't know what you want me to say...' he began.

'You don't know what I want you to say?' Samson roared out the words. For the life of him, he couldn't understand the front this kid had. He'd known from the start that the lairy little fucker was a danger to him, that the little runt had the intelligence to take over the estate. Not only that, he had the nerve to see his threats through. The quicker the kid was out of his eye line, the better. 'I want to know who gave you the wink to switch my merchandise.' His voice rose a decibel with each and every word he spat out. 'Who gave you the fucking nod?'

Paul was perplexed. 'I don't know. We did what you paid us to do. We collected and dropped off, that was it.' He opened out his arms. 'Why the fuck would we switch the bags?'

Spittle gathered at the corners of Samson's lips and his eyes bulged. Was this kid for fucking real? 'Because, you little bastard, you want what's mine, and let me tell you now, I've erased men from this earth for doing far fucking less. So what makes you think that I'll turn a blind eye now, that I'll let you, either of you,' he spat, flicking his eyes between the two men, 'off with this fucking piss take?'

Paul was genuinely confused. He was more than aware that both he and Jason were outnumbered, and if they wanted to get out of the situation alive, then he needed to use his brain, to think the situation through. He knew that as well as his own name.

'Well?' Samson's voice rose even further and he screamed out the words. 'Who gave you the fucking nod?'

Paul tried to think back. They had collected the holdall from Dougie. No, that was wrong. It had been Lucas Vaughn who had handed over the merchandise. He had then slung the bag into the boot of the car, just as he had done many times before. Then he had driven the car straight to Samson and dropped it off. Neither he nor Jason had opened the bag, so just what exactly had gone so very wrong?

'It had to be Dougie.' Paul looked around him. He was talking fast and hated himself for that fact. 'He must have switched the bags. It has to be him.'

Samson narrowed his eyes. He wondered how long it would take for the penny to drop, for the boy to connect the dots. 'Dougie you say?' He lifted his eyebrows in mock surprise and glanced towards his heavies. 'You mean to tell me that my old pal Dougie had the front, the audacity, to do this to me?'

Paul nodded, and as he continued to look around him, the first stirring of rage began to flow through his veins. The mad bastard had been happy to use him, to put his name in the frame.

'Well?' Samson was suddenly all smiles and there was a craftiness in his eyes as he opened out his arms. 'The fucking audacity of the man, and to think all along, he was prepared to let me think that it was you. You that had stolen from me.'

Paul shook his head. He was barely even listening. Despite the anger he felt, none of it made any sense to him.

'Well, boys' – Samson was full of camaraderie – 'you're not going to let him get away with that, are you?'

Paul looked up and shook his head a second time. His eyes narrowed. Of course he wasn't going to let the mad bastard get away with it.

It was the exact reaction Samson was hoping for. He lit a cigarette and took a deep drag before blowing out a cloud of smoke. 'Well?' He gestured towards the front door. 'Off you go then, lads. Make the mad fucker pay.'

The heavies created a pathway and, taking one long last look around him, Paul flicked his head towards the front door, indicating for Jason to follow. Still, he didn't understand what had just taken place.

Outside on the street, Jason exhaled loudly. He lifted his hand to show the slight tremor there. 'Fuck me, I thought our days were numbered.'

Paul didn't answer. He glanced back towards the house. He had to admit that he felt just as relieved as his brother-in-law did, but why did the whole situation feel so very wrong? Why had Samson even let them leave? If the boot had been on the other foot, he knew for a fact that he wouldn't have.

'Stella would have had my guts if Samson had topped us.'

Rolling his eyes with irritation, Paul began to walk away. 'Defeats the object a bit that, don't you think?' He shook his head. 'You need to grow a backbone, mate.'

Jason sighed. Easier said than done when it came to his wife. 'So, what's the plan now?'

Paul came to an abrupt halt. He blew out his cheeks and looked up and down the empty street. 'I don't know about you, but I'm going home.'

'Home? But what about...' Jason jerked his thumb behind him. 'Are we just going to leave it like that?'

'Nah.' Paul followed his friend's eye line. 'Of course we're not, but I need to think. None of this is right. Something is off.'

'Are you going to make the call?' He fell into step with Paul as they walked down the street.

Paul lifted his shoulders in a shrug. 'Right now, I need to collect my car and then go home, shower and change.' He gestured to his shirt and grazed knuckles. The last thing he needed was to end up getting his collar felt while still covered in Michael Nicholls's blood. It was bound to be one situation he wouldn't be able to easily talk himself out of.

* * *

Cathy settled herself on the sofa with a cup of hot chocolate. She had finally given up on Paul coming back to collect her from Cynthia's house, so had made the short walk back home with little Kieran in his pushchair. As much as she hated to admit it, she was worried. It wasn't like him to let her down. Even the excuses Cynthia gave for her son's absence had brought her no comfort. Just where the hell was he?

She drank her drink, set the mug on the floor, and then gently rubbed her tummy. 'Where's your daddy, eh?' She spoke softly. Already, she loved this new tiny life growing inside her.

At that moment, the front door opened and she quickly glanced at her watch. It was nearing midnight. Heavy footsteps ascending the staircase made her jump up from the sofa and race out into the hallway.

'Paul?'

She saw his body freeze and narrowed her eyes. Surely he would have known that she would wait up for him.

'I'm just going to shower.'

Cathy's heart sank. Where had she heard those words before? It had been one of Terrance's favourite phrases after he had spent the evening with one of his many women.

'Paul?'

She watched him bow his head and her heart sank even further. No, please God, not again.

'I can't do this right now, darling. I really need to shower.'

Prickles of fear ran down the length of Cathy's spine. She'd thought that her Paul was different, that he would never betray her trust. Oh, she wasn't stupid. She knew he would look at other women. What man didn't? But to go that one step further and actually touch, she would never have believed him capable of it, until now that was. Tears pricked her eyes. No matter how much she loved this man, she wasn't prepared to idly sit by and do nothing whilst another man used and abused her. She chased up the staircase after him and tugged on his arm, pulling him bodily towards her.

The sight which met her made her gasp out loud. Paul's shirt was dotted with red splotches of blood. She pressed her hand to her mouth and her eyes opened wide with fear. All thoughts of him spending the night with another woman were gone from her mind. 'Oh my God,' she cried. She reached out to touch the shirt and he gently pushed her hand away. 'What happened to you?'

'It's not mine.' His voice was quiet and he couldn't look her in the eyes. 'It's not mine, darling.'

Cathy gripped onto the banister rail. She felt as though her legs would buckle underneath her. 'Who?' she began.

'It doesn't matter whose.' He put his finger to her lips, silencing her, and without a backwards glance, he carried on up the staircase, knowing full well that she would follow.

In the bathroom, he kicked off his boots and stripped off his blood-stained clothes.

'Please, Paul.' She glanced down at his grazed knuckles and fear caught in the back of her throat as her body shuddered. 'What have you done?'

Paul sighed. Still, he couldn't look her in the eyes and Cathy resisted the urge to shake the truth out of him.

'I did what I had to do, Cath. You wouldn't understand, darling.'

'Is he...?' She swallowed deeply, not wanting to finish the sentence. A part of her wasn't even sure she wanted to know what it was he'd done.

Paul shrugged. It was a nonchalant shrug that caused her heart to sink even further and she closed her eyes tight. Seeing him like this scared her and reminded her of exactly what he was capable of. Not that he would ever hurt her or Kieran, that was one thing she was certain of.

As he stepped underneath the steaming water, she instinctively bent down and gathered up the stained shirt and denim jeans and held them to her chest. How could he be so calm? It didn't take a genius to suss out the fact that he had seriously maimed someone, and yet, he didn't seem to have a care in the world. He was completely and utterly unnerved by his own actions. Her heart beat faster as she continued to watch him. A part of her wanted to berate this man for what he had done, but how could she? She herself had killed her own husband, and he had been there for her, by her side, without question.

'I'll put these in to soak.' It was said quietly and when he didn't answer, she walked from the bathroom. She knew then that she had inadvertently embroiled herself into his world, a world that she had sworn she would never have a place in. It was at that moment that she felt the first stirring of the child embedded within her womb – a child who would one day follow on in their father's footsteps. A wave of dread swept over her. She'd known right from the very start that he didn't hold down a nine-to-five job, that he wasn't a plumber or a white collar worker. No, she'd known exactly who her Paul was, and she had welcomed him and the life he led with open arms. It was a sobering thought.

* * *

Cathy was still scrubbing away the blood from Paul's shirt when she heard him walk into the kitchen.

'I'm sorry, darling.'

She could hear the sincerity in his voice and, taking a deep breath, she gently placed the scrubbing brush down onto the draining board and turned to face him.

'There is nothing to apologise for.' She wiped her hands dry, joined him at the table and wearily sat down on a wooden high-backed chair. 'I knew from day one that this was your life.' She gave him a gentle smile. Oh, he was so handsome. It was hard to believe that there was another side to him, a side that was both violent and ruthless. 'But promise me that you will not embroil our babies into the same way of life.' She reached out to clasp his hand tightly. 'I can't bear the thought of spending my days and nights worrying about them, too. I want more for them. I want them to get away from all of this.' She looked around her. Despite the recent lick of paint and new flooring, the kitchen still felt as though it was tainted. 'I want more for them, Paul.'

Paul nodded. 'I want the same, darling.' He sighed heavily and as he looked down at the spot where Terrance's body had laid, he gave her a small smile. 'I promise, Cath, I won't bring our kids into any of this.'

* * *

Paul barely slept through the night, and as he shifted onto his back, he stared up at the ceiling. The events of the previous evening ran through his mind on a loop. Why did nothing make sense? Why had Samson sent them on their way unscathed? The old bastard had his own reputation to think of, and if he had really believed they were responsible for stealing his merchandise, then shouldn't they be dead by now? Their bodies should be buried in the woods or supporting a flyover somewhere. As the man himself had stated, he had murdered men for doing far less.

Gently easing the duvet away from him, Paul swung his legs over the side of the bed and, sitting up, he rubbed his palm across his face.

'You're awake early.'

He turned his head to look at his Cathy and a rush of love fell over him. Even with her hair sticking up all over the place and traces of mascara smudged underneath her eyes, she was beautiful to him. 'Go back to sleep, sweetheart.'

'Where are you going?' Glancing down at her watch, Cathy groaned. 'It's only just turned six.'

For a brief moment, Paul considered lying and he sucked in his bottom lip, contemplating what he could say. Finally, he decided to tell her the truth. After all, she wasn't daft and had already seen the worst of him. She had seen what he was capable of. 'I've got some business to sort out, darling.'

'The same business as yesterday?' She sat up, suddenly alert, her beautiful face etched with worry.

Paul raised his eyebrows but didn't answer and, standing up, he pulled on his boxer shorts.

'It is, isn't it?' Her hand flew to her still flat tummy and he watched with fascination. Even now, she was only thinking of their child. She was a blinding mother, was his Cathy.

'I have to. I have to sort this out, Cath. Some bad shit went down, and well, it's down to me to sort it all out.'

'How bad are we talking?' Cathy was up and out of bed. She stood in front of the door, as if she could somehow stop him from leaving the bedroom.

'Bodies in the boot of a car type of bad shit.' As he continued to dress, he gave her a smile to take the edge off his words. 'Listen, darling, it's under control, I promise.' The lie easily tripped off his tongue. He only wished it was true. Mad Dougie made Samson look like a pussy cat, but he knew he had to front the man out. He had to know the score, and more than anything, he had to get to the bottom of the missing coke. He had a horrible feeling that there was a lot more to the sorry story than met the eye.

Cathy began to cry and as he moved towards her, she flapped her hand dismissively. 'Ignore me, it's my hormones,' she said half-laughing, half-crying.

Despite the laughter in her voice, he could hear the fear there and he pulled her into his embrace, his strong arms wrapping around her tiny frame. 'It'll be okay. I'm going to sort this out,' he soothed. 'I promise you, Cath.'

With her head against his chest, he held her to him and gently kissed the top of her head before stepping out of her arms and leaving the room. Making his way towards the bathroom, he paused and, retracing his steps, he made his way into Kieran's bedroom. Looking down at the child he'd grown to love as his own, he smiled softly. Little Kieran was fast asleep. His chubby little arm was positioned above his head and the faint snores alerted Paul to the fact that the child was in a deep sleep. He was a handsome little boy and he wondered then what the child snuggled inside his Cathy would look like.

Another handsome little fucker, no doubt. Of course the unborn child could be a girl, a daughter who would look like her mother. The thought made him smile even wider. From behind him, he could hear Cathy sigh. He turned his head and grinned at her.

'Everything will be okay, Cath. You just wait and see, darling.'

As she leaned against the door frame, she smiled at him. It was a sad smile tinged with fear, and his heart went out to her.

'Just be careful, please,' she begged of him. Her hand wandered towards her tummy. 'I need you to come back home safe. We all need you.'

'You know me, Cath,' he answered, but the smile had left him. He was no fool and knew for a fact that if he managed to leave the Manor still in one piece, then it would be nothing short of a miracle.

Dougie Ward's fury knew no bounds. Even the screams that came from the man chained to the steel table were unable to bring him comfort. Already, his latest victim was minus his fingernails and several teeth. He dragged the scalpel viciously across the man's skin. His hands were slick with blood and it took all of his concentration to keep his grip on the steel handle.

On the other side of the table, Ernest grunted loudly, his mouth open wide. The remainder of his stubby little tongue jutted up and down.

'Calm fucking down, Ern.' Dougie looked up. He had no qualms with Ernest and knew for a fact that the man was as loyal as they came. In fact, his old friend was of the same mind as him. He loved the torture and violence almost as much as he did. In a way, they were kindred spirits.

Ernest grunted once more, and as Dougie threw the scalpel into a metal tray, the clash of metal against metal was loud.

'Lucas.' He screamed out the name of his heavy, his minder. Minder – the word had always amused him in the past. He had no need for such a man to watch over him. He was more than capable of taking care of himself. It was the people around him who needed minding, and more often than not, they were just as aware of that fact as he was.

'Boss.'

Dougie grinned, showing an uneven row of white teeth. He untied his leather apron and passed it across to Ernest. On the table, the man's screams had quietened down to pain-filled whimpers. The fact that he had been left on the table to bleed out, slowly and painfully, was not lost on anyone, least of all the victim himself.

'We're expecting company.' Dougie grinned even wider and he had to stop himself from rubbing his hands together with glee. After his telephone call with Samson Ivers, he knew for a fact that he would have fun with this pair of thieving bastards. Already, he could hear their screams echoing around the room. It was a heady thought.

'Anyone I know?' Lucas's voice sounded bored, as though they had company every day of the week, which of course they didn't. Dougie didn't have friends, per se.

Lucas's voice brought Dougie back to reality and he looked up. 'A couple of Samson's men.' He glanced nonchalantly at the victim on the table. He was bored of hearing the man's terrified screams. 'Let's give the thieving cunts a good welcome, eh?' He picked up the scalpel, walked back around the table and, grasping a handful of his latest victim's hair, he roughly pulled back his head, exposing the neck area. The pale exposed skin was stark underneath the fluorescent lighting. 'A real Manor welcome,' he said, expertly gliding the scalpel across the bared throat.

Dodging the blood spray, Lucas nodded and abruptly left the room.

Washing the blood away from his hands, Dougie began to whistle. From the corner of his eye, he took note of Ernest's movements. He was fickle when it came to his instruments. They had to be both clean and sterile, and he had bought an autoclave at auction for that very purpose. It had cost him a small fortune, but at the end of the day, money was irrelevant when it came to cleanliness. He watched the man rinse the instruments underneath hot water before loading them into the metal bucket and he sighed happily. Good old Ernest. He was like a Godsend to him, and he thanked his lucky stars every day that he had this man in his life.

Lucas was worried. He walked outside into the courtyard area and took in deep lungsful of air. He'd overheard the one-sided telephone conversation between Dougie and Samson Ivers, and was genuinely perplexed. Underneath his feet, the uneven patio slabs shifted. They had had problems with the drains in the past and the courtyard had flooded over on numerous occasions. It was the blood clots and body matter clogging up the drains that caused the problems, and it didn't escape his notice that as he stepped on the slabs, he was walking upon the remains of Dougie's victims. The underlying stench of rotting flesh that permeated the air alerted him to that fact and he inwardly shuddered. Turning back towards the property, he checked that the coast was clear, then hastily pushed his hand into his denim pocket and brought out a handful of loose change. He needed to get to a telephone box, and fast.

'Lucas.' Dougie's sing-song booming voice was loud.

Lucas closed his eyes tightly and as he rubbed wearily at his temples, irritation spread throughout his body. He took a deep breath before shoving the coins back into his pocket and reluctantly returning inside the premises.

12

'Are you okay?' As he drove through the streets towards Dougie's home, Paul gave Jason a sidelong glance.

'Yeah.' Jason gave a slight shrug of his shoulders.

Paul nodded. They continued on in silence, and after a few beats, he cleared his throat. 'You're a bit quiet. Has that sister of mine been giving you grief?'

'Nah.' Jason shook his head and, lighting a cigarette, he slumped back in the seat. 'She's worried.' He turned his head, shrugging for a second time. 'She thinks we've gone too far, that we're in over our heads.'

Paul didn't answer. He flicked the indicator and turned onto the lane where Dougie Ward's morgue was set. 'We've come this far.' He pulled over to the kerb, observing the impending property before them. 'And like fuck are we gonna give up now.'

* * *

Anger rippled through Dougie. He may have loved torture and violence, the thrill of the chase, but underneath the lunacy, he was a businessman first and foremost. Acting as a middle man, the drugs that he bought in considerable quantities then sold on, brought him ludicrous amounts of money. A rather large fortune to be precise and, coming from a council slum, dragged up by alcoholic parents who had barely acknowledged his existence, he had no desire to return to his grass roots.

The intercom at the front gate buzzed throughout the property and he turned his head to watch on the CCTV monitors a vehicle drive into view.

He was at the front door with Ernest and Lucas behind him before the two men had even exited the car. He grinned widely, the type of smile that hid the psychotic tendencies at his very core.

'What is this all about, eh?' Paul slammed the door shut behind him. 'Who the fuck switched that coke?'

The tone in the younger man's voice rankled, and as the smile slid from Dougie's face, the muscles in his back stiffened. Just who the fuck did this little fucker think he was talking to? Behind him, Ernest grunted out a series of incomprehensible groans, and he held up his hand to quieten the man down. 'It's all right, Ern.' He reassured him in his sing-song voice. 'I'll take care of this.'

'Well?' Paul stormed across the paved driveway. 'What the fuck is going on?'

'That, my son, is exactly what I would like to know.' Dougie smiled brightly, a beaming grin that resembled a predatory shark as he showed off a row of white teeth. 'Come.' He swept his arm towards the entrance hall. 'It's bad for business to discuss matters on the doorstep.'

'I don't give a fuck.' Paul looked around him. There was no one in close proximity to hear the exchange. The property was a safe distance away from the road and any prying eyes, hence how the mad bastard had got away with his murderous deeds for so long.

'And like I said, it's bad for business to air our dirty laundry in public. Come.' He made off towards the hallway, leaving the two men on the doorstep. He knew they would follow. He had a knack of knowing such things and prided himself on his intuition. After all, it had kept him at the top of his game for many years.

* * *

As they entered the property, Paul's body was on red alert. He didn't trust the nutcase. It was common knowledge that he was a fruit loop and Paul wouldn't put anything past him. They passed an antique hallway table. Placed on the top in a neat pile were several unopened letters and laid beside them was a cowhide leather handled letter knife. The silver blade was long, thin, polished and extremely sharp. He shook his head. Who the fuck owned a letter opener in this day and age? About to walk past the table, he caught Jason's eyes and, jerking his head towards the makeshift weapon, he indicated for him to pick it up. As far as he was concerned, the more weapons they had to defend themselves, the better.

Inside the sterile cold room, the familiar stainless-steel mortuary table, wash basin and instrument cabinet were laid out before them. Unusually, at the head of the table, a smear of rust-coloured blood trailed from the table to the floor. Paul guessed that it had been left there for his and Jason's sole benefit – to unnerve them, to warn them that they were in for the same torturous treatment as the previous victim.

Tearing his eyes away from the blood, Paul looked Dougie in the eyes. 'Did you set me up?'

'Me?' Dougie began to laugh maniacally and his eyes glazed

over. Beside him, Ernest grunted out a series of groans, each new grunt louder than the last.

'Yeah, you.' Paul stood his ground. To show any form of fear would have been his undoing. Out of the corner of his eye, he clocked Lucas Vaughn's movements and braced himself, ready to attack or defend, whichever one came first.

Ernest continued to grunt loudly, the screeching seemingly spurring Dougie's madness on.

'Did I set you up?' Dougie looked from Ernest and then to Lucas, as though he could barely believe what he had just heard. He rubbed at his temples, his expression incredulous. 'Are you having some kind of fucking laugh with me?'

Paul swallowed deeply. With one eye still on Vaughn, he clenched his fists into tight balls, poised and ready.

'I can't believe this lairy little fucker has just accused me of setting him up.' Staring straight ahead of him, Dougie spoke to no one in particular. 'Did I set you up?' He turned back to face Paul, as if only just remembering he was in the room. Spittle began to gather at the corners of his snarled lips. 'Did I set you' – he took a step closer, his face poised just inches away from Paul's – 'fucking up?'

'It's a fair question.' Paul swallowed once more. The atmosphere sizzled with anticipation. Up and close with the maniac, he could feel the man's rancid breath on his face, could sense the madness. It radiated out of his pores. He might as well have been holding a neon sign above his head with the word 'nutcase' emblazoned across it.

'Did you hear that, Ern?' Dougie began to laugh, a high-pitched cackle that matched Ernest's grunts. 'He reckons it was a fair question.'

Ernest's screeching had reached a crescendo and he motioned with his hands for Dougie to attack.

'All in good time, Ern, all in good time.' He was smiling now, as if he was actually beginning to enjoy himself.

Paul looked around him. The very thought that this man was able to walk the streets freely amongst the innocent joe public was insane. 'You mad fucker.' Before he could stop himself, he'd spat out the words.

The tension in the room reached breaking point. For a few short moments, there was nothing but an eerie silence.

'What did you just say?' The smile left Dougie's face. Behind him, Ernest opened his mouth and roared, his stubby little tongue jabbing up and down.

'You mad fucker.' Paul didn't hesitate in repeating back the words. 'You mad fucking fuck.'

The words were enough to send Dougie over the edge. His meaty fist shot out, connecting with Paul's jaw, and that was when pandemonium well and truly broke out.

In a thick hot gush, rivets of crimson-coloured blood squirted up into the air, and Ernest, whose throat had been unceremoniously cut from ear to ear, dropped heavily to the floor.

Seeing the blood-stained letter opener in Jason's fist, shock resonated across Paul's face. He'd barely had the time to think the situation through before Dougie's hands were wrapped around his throat and he'd been slammed across the mortuary table. All the while, Dougie continued to laugh maniacally, the high-pitched cackle deafening to Paul's ears.

Despite his best efforts, Paul was unable to push the madman away. He had a strength about him, the likes of which Paul had never come across before. He pulled at Dougie's fingers, desperate to breathe. His lungs were beginning to scream for air. His throat felt as though it was on fire, and no matter how much he kicked out, he was unable to shift the weight on top of him. In the distance, he could hear Jason, could hear him trying to drag

Dougie away, could hear the punches landing and the futile kicks that Dougie batted away from himself, as though he was swatting away a mere fly.

With Dougie's laughter still ringing loudly in his ears, Paul's life flashed before his eyes. An image of Cathy, the love of his life, entered his mind, followed by little Kieran, whom he loved as his own child, and then the unborn infant nestled safely inside Cathy's womb. He would never see his own child's face. The notion was enough to destroy him.

From the corner of his eye, he saw Lucas advance towards them. In his fist, he held a blade – a long thin boning knife. This was it, Paul decided. This was the moment his life was about to be taken away from him. With trepidation, he turned his face away and slammed his eyes shut tight. For the first time in his life, he wasn't afraid to admit that he was terrified.

Still laughing his maniacal laugh, Dougie froze before he toppled forward. His lifeless body, the equivalent of a ten-ton truck, trapped Paul to the table. After gasping for breath, Paul used whatever strength he had left inside of him to push the madman's body to the floor.

Breathing heavily from the exertion, Paul clambered off the table and rubbed at the indentations Dougie's fingernails had left around his throat.

Warily, the three remaining men stared at one another.

'You took your fucking time,' Paul growled.

'What?' Lifting his shoulders in a shrug, a slow grin spread across Lucas's face. As he threw the bloodied knife that still contained traces of Dougie's brain matter to the floor, the tension left the room. 'I was waiting to see how you handled the situation.'

'You fucking dickhead.' Stepping over Dougie's body, he

pulled Lucas into his arms and laughed. 'You fucker. I was starting to think you'd switched sides.'

'Leave it out.' Moving on to embrace Jason, Lucas grinned. 'As if, mate.' He glanced down at Dougie's motionless body. From a deep head wound, bright crimson-coloured blood seeped out onto the tiled floor. 'Trust me, I've been waiting months to take that fucking nutcase out.'

Paul nodded and looked around him. The clinical room gave him the creeps. It had done so since the very first moment he'd stepped foot inside it. 'What the fuck is this all about, eh? Who switched that coke?'

Lucas shrugged. 'Your guess is as good as mine, mate, but one thing I do know is that the mad bastard may have been a looney tune, but he wasn't in the habit of switching merchandise.' He stepped over Dougie's body and motioned for them to follow him.

They came to halt outside a door at the far end of the corridor, and from his pocket, Lucas took out a brass key. 'You wouldn't believe how long it took me to get hold of this,' he stated with a grin. 'Dougie wasn't one to trust easily.' Twisting the key in the lock, he pushed open the door to reveal a wood-panelled room that was both small and dimly lit. 'This is what you came for, right?'

Holding just a worn wooden desk and a captain's chair with bottle green upholstered arms, the sterile room was otherwise devoid of any furniture.

'It's empty.' There was more than a hint of disappointment in Paul's voice and he looked towards Lucas expectantly. 'Where the fuck are the goods?'

Lucas gave a smug grin and pressed on the light switch, instantly bathing the room in light. Then he reached up to press a button above the door frame. Walking into the room, he pulled open one of the large panels to reveal behind the wooden slats a hidden room that in itself was at least four times the size of the study.

Paul's eyes widened. Talk about an Aladdin's cave. It was the ultimate drug dealer's lair. Every available surface held weighing scales, and bags and bags of narcotics. Everything from cannabis to heroin to amphetamines were laid out before them in all their glory, ready for the taking.

'Fuck me.'

Lucas chuckled. 'I told you,' he said. 'In the desk drawer is his phone book. All we have to do is go through his contacts and we're gonna be fucking raking it in.'

Dragging his gaze from the desk, Paul looked around the room and rubbed his hands together. 'Let's get a move on and shift this lot.' He paused for a moment to allow himself the time to think the situation through. 'Are there any coffins on the premises?'

Lucas snorted with laughter. 'Yeah, I can remember seeing a few in the storage room. They're a bit basic and battered around the edges, but still in pretty much good nick.'

'Good.' Sweeping his arm around the room there was a twinkle in Paul's eyes. No one, not even the Old Bill would want to look inside a coffin should they be stopped transporting the haul. 'Let's fill 'em up then.'

Thirty minutes later, they had cleaned out the room. Three pine coffins were filled to the brim with narcotics and a fourth was filled with the contents of Dougie's safe. At a wild guess, there had to be at least a hundred thousand pounds in cash and jewellery.

With the lids firmly in place, they stood back to inspect their handiwork.

'All we need to do now is shift this lot over to the lockup and job done.' Paul grinned.

Lucas returned the smile. 'I'll bring the van around to the back doors.' He winked.

'And what about this place?' Jason asked.

Paul looked up and sneered. 'Torch it.'

Lucas smiled even wider. He could think of nothing better. 'I'll chuck the jerry cans in the van while I'm at it then.'

* * *

With the private ambulance reversed into the lockup, Lucas switched off the ignition and jumped out of the van. Positioned in a remote location, it was perfect and out of the way, therefore, there was less chance of any busybodies observing their comings and goings.

'I'll run this over to the Carters'.' Once they had finished unloading the coffins, Lucas patted the side of the van. 'They'll get rid of it for a drink.'

Paul nodded. 'We'll follow on behind.'

'Nah' – Lucas shook his head – 'no point in us all going there. I'll get one of the brothers to drop me back afterwards.'

Shrugging, Paul glanced down at the coffins. Stacked up against the bare brickwork, they looked out of place. 'Right then. You go and get rid of the van; we'll lock up and then meet you at the boozer. Oh, and tell Tommy I owe him one.'

Lucas nodded and, watching his two friends exit the lockup, he climbed into the van, started the ignition and then eased out of the entrance. In the rear-view mirror, he watched as they locked up behind him and, switching on the radio, he began to hum along to the song playing. Before long, he was singing at the top of his voice and drumming his fingers on the steering wheel. He felt as though the weight on top of his shoulders had finally lifted. Never again would he have to answer to Mad Dougie's demands, nor would he have to look over his shoulder, expecting to find the equally crazy mute watching his every move. All in all, it had been a good day. In fact, it had been better than good. It had been fucking fantastic.

* * *

'Do you think he's all right? I mean, up here?' Paul tapped the side of his head.

'Who, Lucas?' Setting down his pint glass, Jason frowned. They were in The Jolly Fisherman and he kept his voice low as he answered.

Paul nodded. 'I think he's losing it.' He tapped once again at his head. 'Something's not right up here.'

'Course he's all right.' Jason raised his eyebrows, dismissing the question. 'Why wouldn't he be? We fucking did it, mate. We pulled it off.'

The fact their friend had taken so long to finish Dougie off was playing on Paul's mind, and as he chewed on the inside of his cheek, he replayed the events that had taken place. If he hadn't known better, he would have fully believed that Lucas had been waiting for Dougie to take them out first.

He picked up his glass and gulped at the amber-coloured liquid. From the corner of his eye, he spotted the man in question enter the bar and without even giving them a second glance, he headed straight for the men's toilets.

Narrowing his eyes, Paul set the glass back down on the wooden bar top. 'I'll be back in a minute.' He slapped Jason on the shoulder and followed on behind their friend.

* * *

Lucas opened the cubicle door and immediately came to an abrupt halt.

Leaning against the sink with his arms crossed over his chest, Paul raised his eyebrows. 'That's a nasty little habit you've got there, mate.'

'I don't know what you're talking about.' Beads of cold sweat broke out across Lucas's forehead and he resisted the urge to wipe them away. He made his way to the sink, twisted open the tap and briskly washed his hands. All the while, he could sense Paul's eyes boring into the back of his skull, and he avoided glancing up into the mirror.

'You know exactly what I'm talking about.' Clenching his teeth, Paul moved forward. 'That fucking shit that you're shovelling up your nose. I knew it. I knew there was something off with you.'

Lucas lifted his shoulders a second time. 'Nah, like I said, I don't—'

Before he could finish the sentence, Paul had swung him around and slammed him up against the wall. 'Tell me something. Why did you really wait so long to end Dougie? Were you hoping that he would take us out first? Is that what happened? Was that your plan, all so you could hide the fact that it was you who switched the coke from underneath that mad cunt's nose?'

Lucas's eyes widened and he pushed Paul roughly away from him. 'Is that what you think of me?' He glared at him.

'It's how it comes across,' Paul spat back.

'How it comes across?' Lucas snarled, repeating back the words. He shook his head slowly, barely able to get his head around what he had just been accused of. 'What, you think I just spent the last year of my fucking life sucking up to that mad cunt just to watch my pals die? Have you got any idea of how it was for me? How sick I felt every single time he called me into that fucking morgue of his, that fucking abattoir, because that's exactly what it was, let's make no fucking mistake about that? Did it not occur to you to wonder how I felt, wondering if I'd walk in and find one of my best mates laid out on that gurney?' His face turned red and spittle gathered at the corner of his lips. 'Have you got any idea of how that was for me?' He stabbed his finger into Paul's chest. 'Or how about wondering if every time he summoned me, I was walking into a trap, that the mad bastard had sussed out this plan that you fucking devised, and that it was me who was going to be sliced wide open like a pig?'

'Point taken.' Paul had the grace to look down at the floor.

'No,' Lucas hissed, 'you put me in there. You were the one who wanted to know how he ran his business. You were the one who wanted to be privy to his contact list, and you don't know the hell I had to go through to get it.'

'You're wrong,' Paul sympathised. 'I do get it. You needed something to get you through the day and the coke—'

'Fuck the coke.' Lucas screwed up his face. 'The day was only the half of it. What about the nights, eh?' He took a menacing step closer, their noses almost touching. 'What about when he had me ferrying about body parts, or when he had me swilling buckets of blood and body matter down the drain?' His face screwed up even tighter. 'But that was only after I'd sifted through the buckets first. I was up to my elbows in blood and clots as big as fucking dinner plates most nights. The mad fuck was paranoid he'd be caught bang to rights like that serial killer Dennis Nilsen was. And then there were the screams, let's not forget about the fucking screams. Every time I close my eyes, I hear them, they're up here.' He pointed angrily to his forehead. 'They're up here and they never go away.'

'I'm sorry, mate, I didn't know.' As he took a step backwards, Paul was apologetic.

'That's right, you didn't know. You didn't know fucking shit, but I still did that for you, for us. I could have walked, but I didn't. I stuck to the plan, and as for you and Jay, well, your lives didn't seem to change much, did they?' He gave a bitter laugh. 'Nah, in fact, they only seemed to get better, didn't they? Jay got married and as for you, you shacked up with Cathy, and now look at you, you're gonna have a kid. Must have been fucking rosy for you, but what about me, eh? I was the one left behind.'

It was said bitterly and shame flooded through Paul. Everything Lucas had said was true. Their lives really had seemed to go from strength to strength. He had a horrible feeling then that the friend he had sent into Dougie Ward's firm was very different to the friend who had walked back out.

'I'm sorry, mate,' Paul told him with sincerity. 'Maybe I should have pulled you out sooner.'

'What, just maybe?' Laughing bitterly, Lucas shook his head. 'You've got the front to stand there and tell me you're sorry. Well, trust me, mate,' he spat, 'you're not as sorry as I fucking am.'

With those parting words, Lucas stormed out of the toilets, leaving Paul to stare after his back. Leaning against the ceramic sink, he sighed deeply. All along, he should have known that Lucas wasn't responsible for the snidey coke, which in his eyes, left only one other person. Samson fucking Ivers.

* * *

Samson had spent the evening celebrating the upcoming demise of both Mad Dougie and Paul Mooney. In high spirits, he had sunk brandy after brandy, and as a result, he was well and truly over the drink driving limit. Not that that deterred him. As long as he could walk in a fairly straight line, then as far as he was concerned, he was all right to drive. Exiting The Jolly Fisherman, he stumbled across the car park and, belching loudly, he leaned up against the side of the car and took out a bunch of keys from his jacket pocket. It took him three attempts to align the key with the lock and as he turned the key, the door sprung open with ease. In hindsight, far too easily, but that was the funny thing about hindsight – it only ever became obvious once it was already too late to turn back time.

He grinned to himself as he ducked his head down to climb inside the vehicle. Once seated, he lit himself a cigar, taking great satisfaction as he took three short sharp puffs, before winding down the window half an inch to help clear the fog.

The sudden sensation of cold steel against the side of his neck caused him to freeze, the cigar hovering just centimetres from his open lips.

'Hello, Samson.' Despite the knife he held up to the older man's neck, Paul's voice was amiable.

'What the fuck are you doing here? You're meant to be—' The tip of the knife dug into his flesh and, snapping his mouth closed, Samson swallowed deeply.

'Dead?' Paul finished off the sentence. He dug the knife in a little deeper, watching with fascination as deep red rivets of blood seeped onto Samson's starched white collar. 'Sorry to disappoint, but as you can see, I'm still very much alive and kicking. Now fucking drive.' He pulled one arm around Samson's neck, restraining him, whilst using the other hand to keep the knife in place. 'You and me are gonna have a very long overdue chat.'

* * *

Thirty minutes later, Samson eyed the young man before him warily. 'Come on, son.' Despite the fact that he had been bundled out of the car, then subsequently trussed up like a chicken in his own home of all places, he grinned widely, showing a row of nicotine-stained teeth. 'We're practically family now.'

Paul narrowed his eyes.

'Cathy,' Samson nodded. 'She's my daughter. I'm surprised her mother never mentioned it, but that' – he sighed theatrically – 'is Angie all over, isn't it?'

Paul's eyes narrowed even further. The revelation was news to him and he wondered briefly if his Cathy knew who her father was. If she did, then she'd never mentioned it. She'd always thought of herself as a Heinz fifty-seven, a whodunnit. They had even laughed about it in the past.

'So you see – that baby my daughter is carrying is my grandchild. My blood will run through that child's veins, and that, son, whether you like it or not, makes us family.'

Paul snarled. The contempt he felt for this man was clearly evident. 'Do you really think I would let you' – he took a menacing step closer – 'anywhere near my kid?'

Samson swallowed deeply. He could barely feel his hands and feet, the bindings were so tight. He'd underestimated Mooney, of that he knew with a certainty. He'd been a fool. He should have taken him out himself when he'd had the chance. Only just like hindsight, it was too late to amend what was already done.

'You set me up.' Paul's expression became murderous and he stabbed a rigid finger towards the front door. 'You sent me to my fucking death,' he spat.

Samson didn't answer. He contemplated lying, but what was the point? And more importantly, what could he even say? It was true. He had wanted to get rid of him, both him and Mad Dougie, and until the very moment he had set foot inside his car, he'd fully believed his plan had been successful.

'And now this?' Paul allowed himself to grin as he gestured around him. 'The drugs, the estate – it's all fucking mine.'

'You're forgetting something,' Samson sneered. 'This estate belongs to me.'

'Did.' Taking a seat on the overstuffed armchair, Paul kicked his legs out in front of him and made himself comfortable. '*Did* is the operative word here. It *did* belong to you, but now' – he glanced around him for effect, as though he was sizing up his new empire – 'now it's all mine.'

'And you think you'll get away with this? That my demise won't cause ructions?'

Paul shrugged and gave a smile that chilled Samson to the very core. 'I can handle it.' It was said with a cockiness that Paul fully believed. 'Trust me' – he gave a nod of his head – 'I've handled far worse.'

Samson returned Paul's steely glint. 'You won't get far, not once that mad bastard Dougie gets his hands on you...'

'Dougie's dead. Did I forget to mention that?' Paul laughed at the obvious shock that fell across Samson's face. 'Yep.' He gave a slight shake of his head and sighed with mock sadness. 'Dead as a fucking dodo in fact. So you see, there really isn't anyone to stop me, is there? And should anyone come around asking questions' – he paused – 'well, it was a turf war, wasn't it? Dealer killing dealer. I doubt the Old Bill will even take much notice. As far as they're concerned, I did them a favour taking the two of you out. And as for me, well, my name won't even come into the equation. Why should it? I'm not on your payroll. I'm not one of your soldiers, no' – he cracked his knuckles and grinned – 'there ain't jack shit to connect me to either of you.'

Samson's heart sank and as beads of cold sweat broke out

across his forehead and underneath his armpits, he knew his days on earth were numbered. He glanced up at the portrait of his late wife and took in the curve of her lips, the faint smile. She appeared to be mocking him. She'd warned him that he would never make old bones, that his way of life and ultimately his chosen career would one day be his undoing, and how right the stuck-up, sanctimonious old bitch had been. 'And you think my men will accept you into the fold? That they'll take orders from you?' Samson sneered. 'You're nothing but a fucking kid.'

Paul laughed. It was a hard laugh that made Samson's stomach sink even further. 'The majority of them have been taking orders from me for the past year.' He shrugged in a blasé fashion. 'You see, Samson, they had a lot more nous than you ever gave them credit for. They knew you were on the out, just like that mad fucker Dougie. Only you were too far up your own arse to see what was going on right in front of your own eyes, and as for the ones who didn't want to play ball, the ones who stayed loyal to you like your pal, Jerry, and our good friend, Michael Nicholls...' He glanced at his watch. 'Well, right about now' – he made a slicing action across his throat and winked – 'I don't think much of their chances. It's curtains for them.'

Resigned to his fate, Samson momentarily closed his eyes and his voice was hard. 'Just do me one final favour and make it quick.'

Paul gave a carefree shrug of his shoulders before slowly rising to his feet. 'No final words? Or how about any last words of wisdom I can pass on to your daughter?'

'Just get it over with,' Samson barked out. Why the fuck would he want to give his daughter any last words of wisdom? He didn't even know her, not that he voiced this out loud, of course. His expression remained hard and he looked up at Paul with pure hatred in his eyes. He was in no mood for pleasantries. The anticipation alone for what was about to come was enough to make his heart race and his bowels loosen. He averted his gaze. They both knew what was going to take place; they both knew that at the end of the night, there would only be one victor, and it sure as hell wasn't going to be him.

Moments later, the cold steel blade plunged into his chest with such strength that he gasped out loud. It took a few seconds for him to feel the pain, but when it came, it was a deep piercing, pulsating, burning pain, the likes of which he had never experienced before. In that instant, he wished for death to take him quickly, just to put an end to the agony.

As his life's blood seeped out of his body, Samson slumped forward onto the carpet. The end was near. His last thoughts before he sunk into unconsciousness and then inevitable death, was that he had clearly, clearly, underestimated Paul Mooney.

13

The funeral of Samson Ivers was a large grand affair and the chapel at Ripple Road Cemetery was standing room only. Anyone who was anyone was in attendance, and although he would have never said it out loud, Paul was somewhat impressed. He'd had no idea that Samson had had so much clout in the underworld.

Sitting in the front pew, as was his given right, considering he was now the new kingpin of the estate, Paul glanced towards the wooden casket. The spray of lilies that adorned the lid had cost him a small fortune, but under the circumstances, he saw the elaborate gesture as money well spent.

As the vicar's voice droned on, Paul resisted the urge to roll his eyes and shift his weight. His head remained pointing forward, his expression neutral. Cathy's hand slipped into his and, turning his head, he gave her a gentle smile. She had no idea she was attending her own father's funeral and he intended to keep it that way. He glanced towards Angie and, feeling his gaze upon her, she turned her head. The look she gave him told him everything he needed to know. She suspected his part in Samson's demise, he was certain of it. He stuck his chin out, returning her glare, silently daring her to outwardly accuse him of murder.

He hadn't forgotten his threat to end her life, and if it wasn't for the fact that he loved Cathy and wanted her by his side, nothing would give him greater pleasure than to wrap his hands around Angie's throat and squeeze the life out of her; it wasn't as though anyone would miss her, other than Cathy of course. But he wouldn't lay a hand on the old bat, not unless she gave him a further reason to.

Twenty minutes later, the mourners were trailing out of the chapel and following the coffin to where it was to be interred into the ground. As they came to a halt in front of the chosen plot, Paul caught Jason's eyes and raised his eyebrows. It took all of his willpower to keep the smug smirk from his face. They were on the up. The plan he had so painstakingly devised had finally, all these months later, paid off.

* * *

Standing towards the back of the crowd, Devan Barkley used the grubby cuff of his sleeve to wipe his red-rimmed eyes. He still couldn't believe that Samson was gone, dead, murdered in his own home. His poor mother had screamed and hollered the house down when she'd been told the news. In the days afterward, she had sat in her favourite armchair, just rocking backwards and forwards. In her arms, crushed to her ample bosom, she'd held a gilt-framed portrait of the big man himself.

'Your daddy's gone now,' Cristiana told him in her soft Jamaican accent, her big brown eyes glistening with tears. 'You have to make him proud, Devan.' She gripped his hand in hers, the raw grief she exhibited frightening him. 'Make your daddy proud, boy.'

He watched the mourners begin to disperse and moved back even farther, hiding his skinny frame behind a large oak tree. From his viewpoint, he observed Paul Mooney. The man really thought he was something special. The way he swanned around, holding court, grated on Devan's nerves and, screwing up his face, his forehead furrowed at the sight before him.

Samson Ivers had been his father, not Mooney's. It should have been him shaking hands with the mourners. It should have been his mother sitting in the front pew, having her shoulder sympathetically patted. Instead, she had been relegated to the back of the chapel, silently weeping, as if she was nothing, as though she had never meant anything to his father. She had borne the man a son, and had pretty much raised him alone ever since, a fact that Devan conveniently pushed to the back of his mind.

He watched Mooney move off towards the pathway to where the black limousines were waiting, and from his hiding place, he continued to observe him. As far as he was concerned, it was no coincidence that Mooney had gone searching for his father, and it was no coincidence that his father was now dead. He stored the information away. The anger he felt lodged deep inside of him. He was convinced the man had killed his dad. It had to be him. Who else, other than Paul Mooney, would have had the gall to commit such a heinous act?

One day, Devan would make Mooney pay for murdering his father, even if it was the last thing he ever did.

14
———

With just one year between them in age, Kieran and Jonah were not only brothers, but also best friends. They shared a close bond, were protective of one another, and woe betide anyone who dared overstep the line with either one of them.

Both were tall, handsome young men, and with strong muscular physiques, they were what was commonly referred to as the spit out of their father's mouths. With dark brown hair and chocolate brown eyes, Kieran took after his father, Terrance, in looks – a fact which secretly annoyed their mother. As for Jonah, he had brown hair a shade lighter than his brother's and sapphire blue eyes. There was no mistaking who his father was. The resemblance between Paul and Jonah was uncanny and often remarked upon by more than one person who came into their orbit.

'Oi.' Seated in a local café, Jonah kicked his brother underneath the table. 'Looks like you've pulled. That bird can't keep her eyes off you.'

'Who?' Kieran looked up from his cooked breakfast and glanced around him.

Jonah flicked his gaze to the right of where he was sitting. 'Fuck me, bruv. She looks like she could eat you for breakfast and spit you out again for lunch.'

Kieran grinned. It was a heart-stopping smile that looked so similar to his father's. 'Nah' – he flexed his fingers – 'there hasn't been a woman born yet who could do that.'

Jonah smiled and shook his head in disbelief. His brother's womanising ways were legendary. Love 'em and leave 'em, that was Kieran's motto.

They continued eating and Jonah had to stifle a laugh. He could see his brother eyeing the woman up and he raised his eyebrows towards him. The woman was old enough to be their mother, and not only that, but she also looked dog rough. With a face full of makeup and a mop of dark brown hair piled on top of her head that resembled a bird's nest, Jonah wouldn't have touched her with a bargepole. No, he liked his women to be the epitome of what an Essex girl should look like. Give him a bird with blonde hair, fake tan and fake tits, and he was as happy as a pig in shit. But as for Kieran, well, if he knew his brother as well as he thought he did, then he knew for a fact that the cogs were already turning inside his head. Not only would he contemplate giving her the time of day, he would also contemplate actually taking her to bed. The very thought was enough to make him shudder.

Their meal eaten, they stood up to leave, and as they reached the door, Kieran turned back to face the woman. He flashed her a wide smile. 'Are you all right, sweetheart? You look as though you've seen a ghost.'

Donna Cassidy smiled. It was a shy smile, and considering the way she was dressed, it looked out of place. Beside her, a small child sat in a stroller eating a sticky bun, the white icing smeared across his chubby cheeks. 'Sorry,' she said, 'it's just, well, you look like someone I used to know.'

Jonah laughed out loud and clapped his brother on the back. He knew instinctively that Kieran's rather large ego was about to rapidly deflate. So much for his brother's belief that he was God's gift to women.

'Right.' Kieran was clearly embarrassed, but he hastily composed himself. 'Well, I can assure you, there is only one of me, darling.' He grinned back.

Donna laughed lightly. She took a cigarette out of its packet and placed it between her lips. 'Well, you're his double,' she said, lighting up and blowing a thin stream of smoke up into the air. 'Maybe you know of him: Terrance Matlock?'

Kieran pretended to think it over. 'Nah, never heard of him, sorry.'

She shrugged. The action caused Donna's ample breasts to rise and fall, and it took all of Kieran's strength to keep his gaze focused on her face. 'Like I said, you're his double.'

'Right.' With his brother's laughter still ringing in his ears, Kieran none too gently pushed Jonah out of the café.

'You're losing your touch, bruv.'

'Yeah, all right.' Kieran screwed up his face. It was no skin off his nose. The woman was a dog and he hadn't even been that interested, even if his cock had told him otherwise.

Jonah continued to laugh and, turning his head, he noted the woman was still watching them intently through the café window. 'So who's this geezer you're supposed to look like?'

'Fucked if I know.' Kieran glanced at his watch. 'Come on, if we don't show our faces and sharpish, then Dad will end up blowing his fucking top.'

Jonah sighed. Their dad was a hard taskmaster and the fact

that they were his sons, his own flesh and blood, made absolutely no difference when it came to business matters.

* * *

Seated behind the desk in the office suite above The Jolly Fisherman public house that he now owned, Paul glanced at his watch and sighed with irritation. Where the fuck were his boys?

As the minutes passed by, he tapped his fingers impatiently on the chrome and glass desk. 'Where are they?' he barked out.

Seated on one of the velvet couches scattered around the office that looked far too small for his large frame, Jason shrugged. They were good lads, and as fond as he was of his nephews, he knew for a fact that they took what they had for granted. They had never had to graft like the elder generation had. Everything they had ever desired had been handed to them on a plate. Even their positions within the firm hadn't been earned. As Paul's sons, it was a given right that they should sit at the very top of the ladder.

'Fuck knows,' he sighed. He glanced towards Darren Mitchell, one of their trusted firm members who sat on a second sofa, and raised his eyebrows. 'But I can tell you this now, mate, they're not pulling their weight.' He held up his hands, knowing for a fact that his best friend and brother-in-law wouldn't like being told the truth. 'They should be out grafting, not chasing after every piece of skirt who dares to look in their direction. It's like they've got a radar on top of their fucking heads. Just one whiff of a bird on the horizon and fuck work. All they can think about is dipping their fucking wicks.'

Paul closed his eyes in irritation. The way his boys, especially Kieran, chased after women was alien to him. What was so wrong with finding a good woman and settling down like he had done with his Cathy? All these years later, and still, she was the only woman he would ever want.

'Jay's right.' Taking his cue from Jason, Darren cleared his throat, feeling more than a little bit uncomfortable to be discussing his boss's sons. 'They're good kids, you don't need me to tell you that, but they've got the attention span of a fucking gnat, and if I'm being honest, I'm sick and tired of cleaning up after them. They're becoming a liability. Three times last week alone, I had to chase after them, and when they did finally put in an appearance, they were as high as a fucking kite.'

'I'll have a word.' Paul swallowed down his embarrassment. In fact, he would do more than have a word. The boys were taking the piss and that was the understatement of the century.

Just moments later, the boys burst into the office and he glared at both of them in turn.

'Where the fuck have you been?'

'What?'

It was his youngest son who answered and the nonchalant tone in Jonah's voice was enough to make Paul charge out of his seat. The scrape of the chair on the polished wooden floor as he jumped up was loud in the otherwise quiet room. About ready to commit murder, Paul grasped a handful of his son's shirt in his fist and pulled him bodily towards him.

'What?' he growled. 'You lairy little fucker. You've got the audacity to stand there and say what? What the fuck am I paying you for, eh? You earn a good fucking wedge and for doing what?' he roared. 'For doing fuck all, that's fucking what.'

'All right, Dad.' Always ready to defend his brother, Kieran's back stiffened. 'We get the picture; you've made your point.'

It was said in such a carefree manner that Paul snapped his head towards his eldest son. God only knew how much he loved this boy, and even though he hadn't sired him from day one, he'd treated Kieran as his own. He had even given him his surname. The fact that he wasn't his real father, his own flesh and blood, had always remained a closed family secret. He would be as devastated as the boy would be if the truth was to ever come out. 'Don't you all right, Dad, me,' he growled. 'What the fuck do I pay you for, eh?' He shoved his youngest son away from him and bellowed in the elder boy's face.

Kieran sucked in his bottom lip. His cheeks flamed bright red and he was thankful there and then that their uncle Jason and Darren were the only witnesses to the long overdue bollocking their dad was giving them. They took the piss and he was the first to hold his hand up and admit that fact. 'Sorry, Dad.'

Paul walked back around the desk and, taking a seat, he shook his head. He had built his business up with nothing but a reputation and hard work, and he would be fucked if his sons were going to bring them all down, because, as both Jason and Darren had rightly pointed out, they couldn't keep their minds on the job in hand.

'It was his fault.' Jonah jerked his thumb towards Kieran and smirked. 'He was chatting up some old dog.'

Raising his eyebrows in a warning, Kieran thumped his brother on the arm.

'Do fucking what?' Paul was up and out of his seat once more. The tone in his voice was enough to alert any bystanders with half a brain cell that he was about to erupt with fury. As he stalked forward, out of the corner of his eye, he saw Jason throw up his arms. Wasn't this exactly what he had been trying to warn him about? 'What did you just say?'

Jonah had the sense to look down at the floor. 'Nothing,' he mumbled, 'it was a joke, that's all.'

'A joke?' Paul bellowed. 'Do I look like I'm fucking laughing? Are you taking the piss out of me?'

'No, of course not.' Resembling a naughty child in the head-master's office, Jonah kept his head firmly down.

'Am I paying you to chat up women?' He stabbed his finger none too gently into the side of his son's head. 'Is that what I'm fucking doing?'

'It wasn't like that, Dad.' Despite the fact that he could happily throttle Jonah, Kieran would protect his brother to the hilt. It had been ingrained in them as children to always look out for one another and have each other's backs, no matter what. 'What happened was, we were in the café, you know, having a bit of grub like, and there was this bird, right old fucking dog she was, and well, she said I reminded her of someone she knew and' – he gave his brother a death stare – 'we just lost track of time, that was all.'

'Oh, that's all fucking right then, is it? You pair of lairy little fuckers lose track of time and leave me, your uncle, and Darren to do all the donkey work, which I might add, is nothing fucking new, is it?'

The two boys looked contrite and as he looked at each of his sons in turn, Paul shook his head. For the life of him, he couldn't understand what went on inside their heads. They'd had it too easy, he rightly guessed. When he had been of the same age, he'd been a grafter and had had to fight his way to the top. He'd beaten some real hard men to get to where he was today, whereas all the boys had had to fight for was the surname he'd given them. There was always some muppet somewhere who wanted to take them on, because of who they were, all so they could boast they had taken down one of Paul Mooney's sons.

'Buck your ideas up.' He stabbed a stiff finger into each of their chests, then returned to his desk. Wearily, he rubbed at his temples and, snatching up his cigarette packet, he took one out and placed it between his lips. 'Barkley' – he cupped his hand around the flame from the lighter and took a deep drag before noisily blowing out a cloud of smoke – 'the bastard, is causing us aggro.'

Kieran glanced towards his brother. Personally, he couldn't stand the man. He swanned around with long swinging dreadlocks and spoke with a mockney Jamaican accent. 'I've never liked Barkley,' he piped up.

'No one likes Barkley,' Jason quickly answered, screwing up his face. 'He was a ponce back in the day and is still a ponce now. It's all that mockney Jamaican talk I can't stand. The prick thinks it makes him look like a bad man. I highly doubt he's even been to Jamaica.' As if reading his nephew's mind, Jason pondered over the enigma that was Devan Barkley.

'Been to Jamaica?' Paul chuckled. 'I doubt he's even stepped foot outside of London.'

Together, the men laughed.

'So what's his problem with us then?' Taking a seat, Jonah looked between his father and uncle.

Paul glanced towards Jason before answering. 'Lucas.' He heard the boys groan and held up his hand. 'Seems that Luke has got himself into some trouble with Barkley, a gambling debt or something, and well, he used this place' – he gestured around the room – 'used all of the boozers, in fact, as a commodity.'

'Do what?' Jonah was up and out of his chair, his fists clenched at his sides. 'You ain't gonna let him get away with that, Dad, are you?'

Paul held up his hand a second time and glanced across to Darren.

Taking that as his cue to leave, Darren got to his feet. He didn't take his dismissal personally. He wasn't family, and the way he saw it, the less he knew the less he could repeat should he ever find himself on the wrong side of a capture. 'I'd best be off,' he said, grinning.

Paul waited for the door to close before turning back to his sons. 'With this place,' he said, 'just like all the other pubs, I'm the majority stakeholder.' He held out his hand towards Jason. 'With a second and third share belonging to your uncle and Luke.'

The boys nodded. They already knew this.

'The thing is, Luke's share' – he gave an embarrassed shrug and wagged his finger between his sons – 'this stays strictly inside this room, do you understand what I'm saying?'

The two boys leant forward in their seats, more than intrigued as to what their father was about to say.

'Well, Luke, in principle, is a joint owner, but' – he took another drag of his cigarette – 'it was never put through the legal system.'

'And thank fuck for that,' Jason interrupted.

'So' – Paul gave the boys a wry smile – 'as far as Luke knows, he has a stake in the pubs. He gets paid, same as we do' – he gestured once more to Jason – 'but legally, his name isn't stated anywhere on any documentation where the businesses are concerned.'

Both Kieran and Jonah sighed with relief.

'What's the problem then? What's Barkley causing hag for? Just tell him Luke has nothing to do with the pubs. It's nothing to do with us.'

Paul turned to look at his eldest son. 'I wish it was that simple, son.' He rubbed at his temples. 'Barkley is demanding for the debt to be repaid. He wants the pubs and he doesn't give a fuck how he gets his hands on them. That makes it personal – personal to me and your uncle.' He gestured to where Jason sat across the room. 'The fucker has already been in here this morning, throwing his weight around. Scared the shit out of poor old Sue, he did, and that's something I can't and won't swallow.'

'Fuck Barkley.' A mental image of the barmaid Sue entered Jonah's mind. She had to be in her mid-sixties, if not even older. She was part of the furniture and had worked behind the bar for years. 'And fuck Lucas. He ain't your problem, Dad, the low-life fucking junkie.'

'Oi.' Paul stabbed his finger towards his youngest son and shook his head in a warning. 'That's enough of that.' A familiar flurry of guilt spread through his veins. The boys would never know just how much he owed to Lucas. To them, he was just some junkie, someone not to be trusted. They didn't know the truth of the matter, didn't know that Lucas had only started out on the wrong path, because of him and his plan to take control of Mad Dougie Ward's assets.

'What about Barkley's firm though?' Kieran asked. 'I've heard they can be a bit tasty.'

'What firm? If you're referring to that bunch of cowboys he runs with, then they are fuck all for us to worry about. Fuck me, if they had half a brain cell between them they'd be fucking dangerous.'

'I'll tell you what...' Jason dug inside his trousers pockets and, pulling out his car keys, he threw them towards his nephews. 'Go and find Lucas. One of you can take my car, just make sure you look after it.' He grinned. 'You know the usual places to look for him.'

The boys nodded and silently left the office.

As he watched his sons leave, Paul cocked his head to one side. 'You're sending them on a wild goose chase.'

'I know.' Sitting forward, Jason spread open his arms. 'It's pay day, mate, and you know as well as I do that there is only one place he's gonna be, where he always fucking is on pay day – the Fiddlers.'

Leaning back in the chair, Paul rubbed at his temples. Everything Jason had said was true. The Merry Fiddlers, in Dagenham, was one of the larger boozers they owned, and after taking over, gutting the place out, and giving the décor a modern twist, not to mention a blinding deejay, it seemed to pull in the younger clientele. With the younger crowd, came the drugs, hence why Lucas always put in an appearance on pay day. The fact that the drugs he bought in large copious amounts were being supplied to the dealers by Paul himself seemed to be a big part of Lucas's attraction to the pub. It was done as a fuck you, and both men were more than aware of that fact.

'Come on.' Paul slowly rose to his feet. All of a sudden, he felt his age and, twirling the keyring around his index finger, he pondered over the idea of retiring. As quickly as the idea came into his mind, he pushed it away. How could he pass the reins over to the boys? They were nowhere near ready to take over, and in a way, he supposed that was his fault. He'd never given them anything remotely heavy to deal with, just the odd debt that was owed to them, debts he knew would be repaid with the minimum of fuss. 'Round up some of the lads. We'll take him mob-handed if need be.'

They headed for the door and, reaching for the door handle, Jason looked over his shoulder.

'Do you want me to whack him one?'

Paul laughed. It was a long-standing joke between them. Over the years, and on more than one occasion, they had wanted to smash their fists into Lucas's face, if for no other reason than to knock some sense into him, to make him see the error of his ways, and to make him kick his coke habit, once and for all. But of course they wouldn't. Lucas was like family, and just like family, they remained loyal to one another through both the good and bad times. Although, Paul had to admit, that when it came to Lucas, there were more bad times than good.

Leaning back against his car, Jaden Collins was smoking a cigarette as he waited for his two best friends. When he saw them emerge from the pub that their father owned with faces like thunder, he sighed heavily and crushed the cigarette out underneath his heavy boot.

'I know that look,' he grumbled. 'Problem?'

'Problem?' Kieran growled. He lit a cigarette and took a deep drag before blowing the smoke out noisily. 'Lucas is on the missing list, as per fucking usual,' he said, leaning his body against the car. 'The waster has been causing aggro with that snidey fucker Barkley.'

'Nothing new there then,' Jaden answered. It was no secret that Lucas had had a very expensive coke habit. The coke Paul had been able deal with, but in recent years, Lucas had progressed to crack. The hard man was a shadow of himself, a dangerous shadow at that, who wouldn't think twice about selling out his own granny for the price of a hit.

'Fucking Luke,' Jonah joined in. 'Why the fuck Dad puts up with him, beats me, and look at the amount of shit he causes. He's toxic like a fucking cancer.'

'So where does Barkley fit into this?'

'Oh, that's the best part,' Kieran spat. He inhaled a lungful of smoke. 'Seems our good friend Luke has used his share of the pubs as a commodity for a gambling debt.'

'But,' Jonah carried on from where his brother left off, 'the lowlife junkie had no way of ever paying it back.' He gritted his teeth. 'What sort of a fucking imbecile would do a deal with a crack addict anyway?'

Jaden looked up at the pub. 'A smart one,' he answered wearily.

The two brothers followed their friend's gaze. As much as they hated to admit it, Jaden had made a valid point.

'Come on.' Kieran flicked the cigarette butt to the kerb. 'It's time to go and find that fucker before my dad ends up blowing a fucking gasket.'

Jaden didn't even bother to ask where they should head to. It wasn't the first time they had had to go searching for Lucas, and luckily for them, he was a creature of habit and stuck to the same usual crack dens.

* * *

Devan Barkley considered himself to be a bad man. Gone was the skinny, scruffy kid of yesterday. With a little bit of help from steroids, his body was now broad-shouldered and muscular, something he took great pleasure in showing off, but it was his business acumen that he really prided himself on. He owned a string of brothels, and on the side, amongst his other business interests, he sold anything and everything he could get his hands on – from women, to stolen goods, to speed, to crack, to heroin, and of course more than a little bit of puff in between. He was the type of man who never forgot a slight made against him and that included the murder of his father Samson Ivers. Twenty years he'd waited to exact his revenge on Paul Mooney, and now that time had come he couldn't have been happier. In fact, he was as happy as a pig in shit.

Lounging back on a leather sofa, he scratched at the stubble across his chin as he watched the scene unfolding before him. On a large rug in the centre of the room two women were in various stages of undress as they auditioned for his latest parlour. As music from a state-of-the-art sound system blared out, they gyrated seductively in time to the music.

'Devan.'

The shrill voice of his live-in girlfriend, Keisha, broke his reverie.

'What?' Barely even taking his eyes away from the two women on the bed, Devan barked out his reply.

Standing in the doorway with a young child on her hip, Keisha was blonde, blue-eyed, petite, and as Devan often remarked, had the personality of a pit bull. She eyed the two women with disgust and screeched at the top of her lungs, 'Get those fucking slags out of my home.'

Devan jumped up from the sofa, his long swinging dreadlocks slapping against the side of his face from the force of the action. Within seconds, he was in her face, his features contorting with rage. On the bed, the two women immediately ceased their lewd act and were in the process of pulling the sheet around their scantily clothed bodies.

'Keep fucking dancing,' he growled and, backing his girlfriend out of the room, he bellowed into her face, spraying her with spittle in the process. 'Get the fuck outta my face.' He grasped a handful of her hair in his fist and dragged her towards the rear of the property. As a final gesture, he kicked her in the small of her back and sent her flying through to the lounge area. Oblivious to the fact that she was holding their child in her arms, he raised his fist in the air as she came to a shuddering halt. 'You stay in here.' He breathed heavily through his flared nostrils, so acute was his anger. 'Have you fucking got that?'

Keisha rubbed at the small of her back. It was on the tip of her tongue to answer him back. She loved it when they argued, loved to see just how far she could push this big, strapping, hand-some man of hers. It was the making up she loved the most. She craved it and believed with all her heart that it kept their relation-ship alive.

As far as she was concerned, they had a connection, a chem-istry that sizzled beyond anything she had ever known before. So what if they argued like cat and dog? It was what they did. They could fight and fuck for England, and it was as exhilarating as it was exhausting. As he turned his back on her, she glared at him. However, to physically lash out whilst she was still holding their young daughter in her arms, that was low, even for him.

She looked down at little Chanel's face. Her daughter's big blue eyes were so much like her daddy's as she stared up at her.

'Oi.' As her man stormed back to the two whores laid out on the bed, she screamed after his retreating back, 'You could have hurt the fucking baby.'

'Fuck off, Keish.' He pointed towards the front door noncha-lantly. 'If you don't like it then there's the fucking door, so why don't you do us both a favour and fuck off.'

Screwing up her face, Keisha slumped down on the sofa. 'Fucking bastard,' she muttered under her breath. Picking up the remote control, she pointed it towards the television. Once her daughter was settled and engrossed in watching a children's cartoon, she glanced down the hallway and shook her head. The heavy beat from the sound system pounded through the walls and, kicking the door closed, she turned up the volume on the television. He'd better make it up to her, she decided. It didn't even occur to her to take his advice and leave. Why should it? She loved this man and like fuck was she going to sit idly by and let another woman get her claws into him.

* * *

As he returned to the lounge and resumed his position on the sofa, Devan shook his head. 'Fucking women,' he grumbled.

Marty Hanratty nodded and, taking his eyes off the two women who lay out on the rug, he returned to the task of building a joint. Once done, he placed it between his lips, and lighting up, he took a deep toke. 'They're only good for one fucking thing.' He grinned, flicking remnants of ash and glowing embers from his T-shirt.

Devan raised his eyebrows. Taking the joint from his friend, he drew on it, deeply filling his lungs with smoke. As he savoured the taste of the grass, the sweet pungent scent filled the room. He was in a bad mood now, all thanks to Keisha and her big fucking trap. She knew exactly how to push his buttons and was able to get his back up within nanoseconds. It was a particular skill of hers.

His gaze lingered on the two women. They were coming to the end of their routine and were virtually naked, a sight he could never tire of. Nah, if Keisha didn't learn to keep her big mouth shut, he'd end up outing her. He licked his fleshy lips and beckoned for one of the girls to join him. With long blonde hair piled loosely up on top of her head, big tits, and a tight little arse, she was just his type. He pulled down the zip on his jeans, then pulled the giggling naked girl onto his lap. In fact, fuck Keisha; she and her big mouth were already out the door, as far as he was concerned.

15

Over the years, Cathy and Stella had come to somewhat of a truce. They may not have been the best of friends, but they shared a mutual respect. The love they had for Paul was enough to make sure it stayed that way.

Years earlier, Paul had moved them into a large four-bedroomed property in Chigwell, and sitting at the granite table in her spacious, modern kitchen, which was her pride and joy, Cathy watched her niece, Katelyn. With long strawberry blonde hair and green eyes, little Katie, as they called her, was absolutely stunning. The only child of Stella and Jason, Katie was the sweetheart of the family. Just a year younger than Jonah, she was her cousins' greatest ally, as they were hers.

'Have you seen the boys?' Taking a sip of her coffee, Cathy eyed her niece over the rim of the mug. Even as she asked the question, she already knew the answer. Katie and the boys were as thick as thieves and often joined at the hip. Both Kieran and Jonah were protective over her and she knew for a fact that they had gotten into numerous scrapes over the years, all because someone had had the audacity to try and chat up their little cousin.

Katie's face lit up and she nodded. 'We went to a club last night on Southend seafront. Oh, we had such a good time...' Her voice trailed off and she gave her auntie a shy smile.

'What?' Cathy cocked her head to one side. It wasn't like Katie to act so coy. In any normal circumstance, there were no secrets between them, unless it involved her sons' antics, of course.

'Oh, nothing.' Reaching for her mug, Katie took a sip of the scalding liquid. She could practically squeal with delight, she was so happy, but she wouldn't, not here and definitely not in front of her auntie. After all, she wasn't daft, or stupid, come to that.

The cause of her happiness was a man named Jaden Collins, with brown skin and turquoise blue eyes, he was beautiful, absolutely gorgeous, and it had been a case of love at first sight, at least on Katie's behalf, anyway. Jaden also happened to be the best friend of her cousins. Not only did he match them in physique, but in looks, too. They made an intimidating trio, and sandwiched between them when they went out for an evening, she often felt like a princess.

Cathy laughed lightly. 'Don't,' she said, pointing a manicured finger towards her niece, 'give me all of that old fanny.' She watched the girl blush and leaned across the table. 'Come on, out with it. What is making our little Katie turn a bright shade of red?'

Katie grimaced at the words. Once upon a time, she had loved being known as little Katie, but she was a woman now and wanted to be treated as such. How on earth was she ever going to embrace womanhood if everyone still thought of her as a child, including her cousins?

'Have you met someone?' Standing up from the table, Cathy opened the cupboard and took out the biscuit tin. 'Well?' She placed the tin on the table and pushed it in front of her niece. She knew that Katie had a sweet tooth and she smiled to herself as she watched the girl hesitate. Her hand hovered over the tin before she shook her head and replaced the lid.

'I'm watching my figure.'

Cathy laughed. Watching her weight, that was a new one. Any other day, Katie would have devoured the biscuits. After all, custard creams were her weakness.

'So who is he?' Sitting back down at the table, Cathy picked up her mug. 'Do the boys know him?' she asked innocently.

'Oh, Auntie Cath,' Katie gushed, 'he is so lovely, and he treats me right, you know, looks out for me.'

'I knew it.' Cathy sat back in her seat, pleased with herself for sussing out her niece's secret. 'Well, who is he then?'

Katie hesitated for a second time. The problem was they were keeping their relationship a secret and she knew for a fact that her cousins wouldn't take well to the news. They would see it as an affront, a stain on their friendship. They could be funny like that; they saw her as theirs, their property, so to speak. She sighed. She knew Jaden loved her, at least that's what he told her every time he climbed into bed beside her.

'Do I know him?' There was concern in Cathy's eyes.

Katie nodded. 'But you have to promise me, Auntie Cath, that you won't tell the boys. They can't know, not yet anyway. We will tell them, but in our own time, when the time is right.'

Cathy sat back in her seat. An uneasy feeling washed over her and a part of her regretted starting the conversation. 'Who is he, darling?'

Katie took a deep breath. 'It's Jaden. Jaden Collins.'

Closing her eyes tight, Cathy sighed. She'd known Jaden since he was a little boy. He'd been a nice, polite kid and had grown into an equally nice young man. He also happened to be her sons' best friend and she knew for a fact that this news wouldn't go down too well. 'Oh darling,' she sighed, 'anyone but Jaden, and the boys would have accepted it.'

Katie bit down on her lip and tears sprang to her eyes. 'Well, they are going to have to get used to the idea, Auntie Cath,' she cried. 'You see, I'm...' She looked away and lowered her voice until it was a mere whisper. 'I'm pregnant.'

'Oh, Katie.' Cathy shook her head sadly. The silly girl really couldn't see the trouble her bombshell was about to bring them. She reached out and clasped her niece's slender hand in hers. 'I think maybe we should ring your mum, darling.'

As the tears blinded her vision, Katie solemnly nodded. Instinctively, she knew it was going to be a long, long day.

* * *

Darren Mitchell parked his car beside Paul's and, leaning back in the seat, he waited for his boss to climb out of his own car before following suit.

It was a well-known fact that dealing with Lucas was the equivalent of skating on thin ice, extremely thin ice. He was a hard fucker at the best of times, with fists the size of shovels. Not only was he difficult to manage, but once narcotics were brought into the equation and the coke was raging through his bloodstream, he became virtually unmanageable, hence why, in any normal circumstance, they were more than happy to leave either Paul or Jason the unfortunate task of dealing with him. No, Lucas wasn't the usual type of junkie they were used to dealing with. He was, in fact, the bane of their lives, not to mention a ticking time bomb.

'You know, if it was me...' Charlie Wilson nodded towards the pub. He was a good looking man with dark brown hair, brown eyes and a naturally cocky, aggressive nature. 'I'd plant a bullet between his eyes and just be done with it. The man is a fucking joke and that's an understatement.'

Darren sighed. He could see Charlie's point, not that he would ever voice his opinion out loud, of course. He knew when to keep schtum, and when it came to Lucas, that was exactly what he did. He knew for a fact that both Paul and Jason loved Lucas like a brother. He still remembered the old days before Lucas's habit had become his only driving force, before he'd become out of control. He had liked the big man once. He'd been astute, reliable – a man you were more than happy to have by your side when faced with trouble. Now, though, there was virtually nothing left of the person he'd once been.

In silence, Darren opened the car door, stepped outside and, leaning his forearms on the open door, he turned back to look at Charlie. In his late twenties, Charlie had only been on Paul's payroll for a couple of years. In Darren's eyes, he was still a kid. He hadn't lived through the good old days like he had, nor the bad days, he surmised. He hadn't been there while Paul had taken over Samson Ivers' drug empire. He hadn't been there to witness the murders, the bloodshed. They were all the same. These young kids, they were bloodthirsty, but when faced with an actual turf war, they shit themselves and went running back to their mothers for protection.

'Let me tell you something, Charlie, that kind of talk will be your undoing. Let me give you a heads up, son. When it comes to Lucas, Mooney would rather see a bullet lodged inside your brain than ever willingly harm a hair on that man's head.'

Charlie rolled his eyes and climbed out of the car. He wanted to tell Darren to shove his warning up his arse, but he wouldn't. He wasn't daft, and more importantly, as Darren had so poetically pointed out, he didn't want to end up on the wrong side of Paul. Now that was one man he didn't want any bad blood with.

In silence, both Paul and Jason, with their firm behind them, walked across the car park of The Merry Fiddlers. Situated on the corner of a cross roads in Dagenham, it was, in their opinion, in the perfect position to attract punters. Before they had even reached the heavy entrance door to the public bar, they could hear music pumping out and guessed correctly that it was going to be a busy evening, much to their pleasure. There was nothing worse than a boozer whose main clientele were just half a dozen or so of the same usual regulars sat at the bar, nursing a pint of bitter, night after night.

Just as Paul had predicted, the public bar was busy, and making his way through the throng of customers, he caught the bar manager's eye.

Big Bernie was as his name suggested, big. Standing well over six foot four, he was as wide as he was tall. Not to mention, he was handy with his fists, which was always a good attribute when it came to running a public house. Beckoning them over, he was already filling two glasses with whiskey as they approached.

'Is he here?' Paul picked up the glass and took a large gulp, savouring the burn as the liquid slid down his throat.

'He's here all right.' Bernie flicked his head towards a door with the words Staff Only emblazoned across it in large gold lettering. 'He's been up there for hours. He was out of his nut before he even got here, so fuck knows what sort of state he's in now.'

Paul groaned and rubbed his palm wearily over his face. They were the words he'd been dreading.

'Listen, Paul.' Bernie leaned his large forearms across the bar and lowered his voice. 'I may be out of line here, but someone needs to say it. Lucas needs sorting out, mate, and fast. Now I swallow his antics, because of who he is, but' – he opened up his arms apologetically – 'when he's like this, when he's buzzing off his nut, it isn't good for business, mate, and as for those fucking degenerates he brings in with him' – he raised his eyes to the ceiling – 'they stink the fucking pub out.' He reached underneath the bar top and brought out a can of lavender air freshener. 'I have to spray this every time one of them walks past the fucking bar.'

Raising his eyebrows, Paul shook his head sadly. He'd never felt so ashamed. As far as Lucas was concerned, enough was enough. He needed sorting out and the sooner the better. He would even pay for him to have a stint in rehab if he thought it would do any good. However, knowing Lucas, he would probably kick off and do a disappearing act before the word rehab had even left his mouth.

'Don't worry, Bern, we'll sort him out.' Gulping down his whiskey, Jason motioned towards the staff entrance that led up to a large two-bedroomed apartment. 'Let's get this over and done with, shall we?'

Paul followed suit and, downing his drink, he moved forward, his heart already heavy at the thought of what could be waiting for them at the top of the stairs.

As they ascended the staircase, the foul stench Bernie had warned them about hit them full on.

'Fuck me.' Placing his hand over his mouth and nose, it took all of Paul's strength not to gag. He could see now why Bernie was complaining so much. The smell, in his opinion, wasn't just the usual stale scent of body odour. No, it was much more than that and could only be described as an unhealthy mixture of ground in dirt, stale sweat and vomit, with a cloying underlying scent of chemicals added into the mix.

They made their way through the flat and, entering the lounge, they found Lucas slumped on the floor, his back against a sofa, his head on his chest, and his arms limp. Beside him on the polished floorboards was a used hypodermic syringe.

'What the fuck is this?' Paul stared down at the needle as though it was alien to him, then looked to Lucas. Kicking the offending syringe across the floor, his expression became murderous. 'Who the fuck supplied him with this?' He turned his head to look at Jason, his eyes mere slits, and his tone accusing. 'Did you know about this? Did you know he was jacking up?'

'Of course I fucking didn't.' Jason's face was hard. 'What do you take me for, eh?'

Grasping the T-shirt of the nearest person he could physically lay his hands on, Paul bellowed into the face of a skinny man whose rodent-like features reminded him of a ferret. 'Who supplied the fucking brown?'

'He's out of it, mate,' Jason said, his voice flat. 'You're not going to get any answers from him.'

Paul looked down at the ferret-faced man. He could feel his blood begin to boil, and with it his temper escalated to terrifying heights. He may have earned a living, a very good living to be precise, selling narcotics, but heroin was where he drew the line. Only the lowest of the low would touch the shit, and for most users, it was the end of the line. There was no coming back once the brown was running throughout their bloodstream. 'Nah, these low-life fucking junkies brought skag into my boozer.' He began punching his fist into the man's face, using as much force as he could physically muster. Before long, his knuckles were grazed and bloodied and the man's face was a swollen, bleeding mess.

He'd barely even broken out in a sweat when he dropped the unconscious man unceremoniously to the floor and proceeded to drag him by his greasy hair through the apartment. At the top of the staircase, he roared out Bernie's name.

It took just seconds for the big man to make an appearance in the hallway, with Darren and Charlie following closely behind.

'Clear the pub out. We're closed.' He kicked the first of Lucas's acquaintances down the stairs. 'And get these fucking degenerates out of my sight, before I end up committing fucking murders tonight.'

Bernie didn't need to be told twice and knew for a fact that it was more than his life was worth to argue the case. They would lose a fortune closing down the pub for the night, but what was the alternative? The full force of Paul Mooney's wrath? No, he may have been a big man and more than capable of taking care of himself, but even he didn't fancy his chances where Mooney was concerned.

Once the room had been cleared, Paul sank into a chair and held his head in his hands. Heroin, fucking heroin. How the fuck had it come to this? He looked up and, locking eyes with Jason, shook his head sadly. 'He's going into rehab. I don't care if the bastard shouts, hollers or screams the fucking place down. He is going. It's either that, or I'll make him go cold turkey myself. I'll lock him in the fucking cellar if need be.'

Jason nodded in agreement. He continued to study Lucas. How they hadn't noticed how far down he'd slipped before now was beyond him. The tell-tale signs were not only there, but they were glaringly obvious – from the dark rings underneath his eyes, to his hollow cheeks and sallow skin. It was all there, only they had been too wrapped up in the businesses and their own lives to even notice just how low their friend had sunk.

Opening his eyes, Lucas took one look at his two friends stood

over him and scooted across the wooden floorboards, his fingertips reaching out desperately to clasp the dirty syringe.

Jason watched him in disgust. 'Looks like the cellar it is then,'
he said dryly.

* * *

Tears of frustration slipped down Keisha's cheeks and, bending
down to scoop up both her and her daughter's belongings from
the pavement, she continued to scream out a tirade of obscenities.

'You no good bastard!' She heaved her daughter up onto her
hip. 'You no good fucking ponce. All you're good for is the slags
you have to pay for, that's about your fucking limit, ain't it? You're
nothing other than a low-life pimp and you've got the front, the
fucking audacity, to call yourself a bad man?' She snorted out a
derisive laugh. 'You jumped up prick. I know you, you just
remember that, boy.' She pointed a red painted talon towards him
and her chest heaved from the exertion of their latest fight. 'I
know the real you. I still remember that skinny kid from the
estate, the same kid everyone used as a joey, the one who was
picked on and bullied by all and fucking sundry.'

Her words brought Devan charging back out of the house. 'I
don't pay for no woman,' he sneered, 'and that includes fucking
you.' He kicked the clothes she had gathered up across the pavement and, stooping down, he grasped her jaw tightly in his fist.
Gone was the mockney Jamaican accent. His voice was now pure
cockney. 'Now fuck off, before I kick you up and down this
bastard street.' His grip tightened. 'Don't test me, Keish, because
you are walking a thin line with me, a very thin fucking line.'

Keisha swallowed hard. Without his money, she would have
nothing. Surely, he didn't expect his own daughter to go without
food or a roof over her head? 'Is that so?' Pulling herself away

from him, she spat out the words and, placing little Chanel on the floor, she began to throw into a black bin liner the clothes, makeup and toys he had thrown out of the house they'd once shared.

Well, two could play at this game, and with nowhere else to go, she decided that she would pay his mother a visit. Cristiana had never been able to resist a sob story, and that, coupled with the fact that she was actually the mother of her only grandchild, was enough to guarantee a roof over her and her daughter's heads, despite what Devan might have to say about the situation.

With as much dignity as she could physically muster, Keisha swung her daughter up onto her hip, then curled her fist around the neck of the bin bag. 'See you around,' she said, grinning. 'Oh, and if I were you, I'd get yourself checked into the nearest clinic. It's common knowledge that those two slags are riddled. Why do you think the last parlour they worked at slung them out on their ear?' She paused as if thinking the situation over. 'Gonorrhoea I think the rumour was. Still' – she shrugged – 'it could be worse. It could have been fucking AIDS.' She paused once more for effect. 'Or maybe it was the other way around, anyway' – she grinned innocently and glanced down at his nether regions – 'you take care of yourself, Dev, and don't forget to get yourself checked out.' Of course it wasn't true, not that Devan was to know that, and let's face it, he was so obsessed with his cock that with a little bit of luck, even if it was for just a few short moments, she really hoped that the bastard fully believed his dick was about to turn green and drop off. It served him right, as far as she was concerned.

* * *

Devan slammed the front door closed. His throat felt dry and he automatically slid his hand down the front of his unbuttoned jeans and had a quick feel around. He was no quack, but nothing, much to his relief, felt off or out of place.

Fucking Keisha. All she ever did was cause him hag and the fact that he had fathered her child meant he was stuck with her for the considerable future. Still, he told himself, he didn't have to pander to her every want and need. He grinned nastily. In fact, if he so wished, he could make the next eighteen years of her life as miserable as sin. After all, he was Devan fucking Barkley and he wasn't widely known for his sunny disposition. No, it was the violence and the sheer lack of human concern that he was notorious for, and other than his mother, women meant fuck all to him. They were ten a penny, as far as he was concerned.

Walking through to the main lounge that housed three large black leather sofas, a rug and a sound system that he liked to blast out day and night, he took one look at the two scantily clad women in question and jerked his thumb towards the door. 'Get the fuck out of my yard,' he sneered.

Their mouths dropping open, the two women practically ran from the room, so intense was their fear of the big man.

'What's that all about?' As he watched the retreating woman who had just moments earlier been sitting across his lap, legs akimbo, Marty Hanratty raised his eyebrow quizzically.

'Fucking slags,' Devan growled. Keisha had been right about one thing. He was spending far too much time thinking about his cock of late. 'Did you drop off the brown?'

'Course I did.'

'And?'

Marty cocked his head to one side, his expression suddenly serious. 'That fucking Alek Symanski. I don't trust the fat cunt; he's a squealer.' He placed a joint between his lips and lit up. 'You mark my words,' he said, his voice thick from the smoke he'd inhaled, 'he's going to bring us trouble.'

Snatching the joint from Marty's fingers, Devan took a deep toke. Alek Symanski was a trader, or to be more precise, he was what was known on the street as a middle man. He had a vast network and could get his hands on virtually anything. Nothing was out of his reach. It had been Alek he'd gone to for the heroin. Naturally wary, he didn't trust the man as far as he could throw him, and considering Alek's considerable bulk, it was fair to say that he wouldn't be able to throw him very far. Still, Alek had his uses and as long as he toed the line, Devan was happy to deal with him.

'Forget that fat cunt, did you drop off?'

Marty grinned. 'Yeah, it was a piece of cake. Fucking skag heads, they'll inject any old shit into their bodies.'

Devan nodded happily. It was common knowledge that junkies would sell out their own grannies for the price of a fix and he knew there and then that his plan to use Lucas Vaughn as a way of getting Paul Mooney's attention was well under way.

With Paul's words still echoing inside his mind, Lucas shook his head nonchalantly from side to side. Across his face was the familiar sneer that he saved for whenever his two friends were in close proximity.

'Did you hear what I said?' Paul growled.

Noting the clenched fist at Paul's side, Lucas was still shaking his head as he scrambled unsteadily to his feet. 'Fuck you.'

The punch to his face was both sudden and unexpected, and, dropping to the floor like a sack of potatoes, he held his arm protectively across his head and face. It was all he could do to ward off the blows. It was a first for Paul to physically lash out at him, and he was reminded once more of the man's strength.

That and the fact that he had finally pushed his old friend too far.

'Did you hear what I said?' Paul breathed heavily through his flared nostrils and his fists remained firmly clenched into tight balls. 'Has it finally sunk into that drug-addled bastard brain of yours that you are done, that you are going into rehab, even if I have to drag you there myself?' He stabbed his finger forward in a menacing fashion. 'And believe me when I say this,' he spat, 'you are staying there for the duration until I' – he poked his thumb into his chest – 'deem otherwise.'

It took all of Lucas's strength to not scream out a tirade of obscenities. They couldn't do this to him. They couldn't have him locked away, even though a little voice at the back of his head told him they could. As Paul had already stated, he would use his money and his reputation to see to it that he was locked up for the duration. His name alone would be enough to employ a team of heavies to stand guard over him, day and night, and with the fear of Paul's wrath ringing loudly in their ears, it would be more than their life was worth to not see to it that he remained locked up.

'Fuck you!' He couldn't stop himself from screaming out the words. Just one last hit, that was all he needed, and then they could take him wherever the fuck they wanted. As he was hauled up from the floor and dragged from the room, all the while kicking and screaming, his last thoughts were of the dirty syringe and the fix he so desperately craved.

* * *

Stella was on the war path and as she paced the length of her sister-in-law's kitchen, she glared at her daughter. One moment, she wanted to hug her and the next, she wanted to fell her to the ground. The stupid, stupid girl had no idea just how much having a baby would change her life. She was only young, a baby herself, and here she was talking about bringing a new life into the world. She wanted to wipe the smile off her daughter's face. The dreamy expression was beginning to royally piss her off.

'But he loves me, Mum.'

'Loves you?' Stella rounded on her daughter. 'He loved getting you into bed, you mean. You just wait until that baby is screaming the house down. Is he going to love you then? Is he going to love you when he realises that he is stuck with you for the remainder of his life, because let's all be honest here, that's exactly what having a baby means.' She took a deep breath. Inside her chest, her heart thundered and she placed her hand upon it. 'Loves you?' she spat. 'His life ain't gonna change, is it? He can still go out when the need takes him. He can still go out and shag his way through half of bastard London if he so wishes, but you' – she pointed a red talon in her daughter's direction – 'you, my girl, will be the one left behind. You will be the one going out of your mind with worry, wondering what it is he's getting up to when he says he's out, supposedly working all hours of the bastard day.'

Cathy raised her eyebrows. Instinctively, she knew that Stella was only saying out loud how she really felt deep down. It was no secret that she had never trusted her husband, even though he had never given her cause not to. It was in her nature to be suspicious and it was just one of the traits from her brother that she had inherited.

'Stell,' she began.

'No.' Stella screamed the word. 'You know what I'm saying is true.' She shook her head from side to side, her eyes flashing dangerously. 'For all you know, Paul could have taken more than one flyer over the years. How do you know that he hasn't been warming some little slag's bed while he was supposedly working?'

Spitting out the words, she lifted her fingers in the air, using them as quotation marks.

Cathy rolled her eyes. To sleep around behind her back wasn't in her Paul's nature. He was as loyal as they came and she trusted him implicitly.

'And what about your father?' Stella's voice rose even further as she glared at her daughter. 'Have you stopped for one moment and thought about what he is going to say about all of this?' She laughed bitterly. 'No, of course you fucking haven't. As long as little Katie is okay, then fuck everyone else, that's your motto these days, isn't it?'

'Stella, that's enough.' Cathy's voice was sharp. She could see that her warning had the desired effect, and as her sister-in-law slumped down into a chair, she stood up and walked towards the large American fridge. Taking out a bottle of wine, she collected three glasses from the overhead cupboard. 'Have a drink and calm the fuck down. She's not the first girl to be caught out, and certainly won't be the last.' She poured them each a large glass of wine and sat down once more.

Swallowing down a mouthful of wine, Stella shook her head sadly. 'All that education wasted,' she said with disappointment. 'All your life, Katie, you've wanted for nothing – private schools, skiing lessons, horse riding lessons – and for what? To end up pregnant at eighteen?'

Katie wiped the tears from her eyes. She might have been a fuck up in her mother's eyes, but already she loved her baby. It had happened, and her parents were just going to have to get over that fact. She pushed the glass of wine across the table and away from her. 'I'm keeping it, Mum.'

'Of course you are,' Stella answered bitterly. She chugged back her wine and started on her daughter's. 'Well, what are you waiting for? Let's get the boy wonder himself here and see what he has to say about all of this.'

Cathy rolled her eyes. She patted her niece's hand and reached for her mobile phone. Her Paul may have a temper on him, but tonight she was going to need him to play the role of peacemaker. He may well be the only one who could save young Jaden's life.

* * *

Katie could barely look her cousins in the eyes, and as they ranted and raved, the first hand of fear gripped at her heart. Why wasn't Jaden sticking up for her? Why wasn't he telling them all that he was her man and that he would stand by her? It had to be the shock, she told herself, the shock her news had brought. She should have told him first, should have let him know the score before telling anyone else her secret. It was unfair of her to let him find out he was about to become a father in front of her entire family.

'Who is he?' Kieran's voice was loud, and as he clenched his fists into tight balls, he roared even louder. 'Because I'm gonna fucking kill him when I get my hands on him.'

Licking at her dry lips, tears pricked the back of Katie's eyes and she shook her head from side to side. She'd known all along that her family wouldn't take the news well, that they wouldn't roll out the red carpet and celebrate the fact that she had a life growing inside of her. In their eyes, she was still little Katie, a child not a woman, but to see them hell-bent on wanting to string her child's father up by his nether regions made her feel positively terrified.

'Who is he?' As Kieran bellowed in her face a second time, his breath was hot on her face. She could smell the faint scent of alcohol and peppermint and guessed correctly that he had been out for the evening before being summoned home.

Once again, Katie shook her head. Her cheeks were already wet; the tears she silently wept were stinging her eyes. Out of her line of sight, her auntie Cathy was trying to calm the situation down, and she loved the woman even more for it. Her own mother, on the other hand, had said nothing. It was as though she was happy to stand by and let the men of the family scream and shout at her.

'I'm saying nothing, and you can't make me.' With defiance in her eyes, she choked out the words. From the corner of her eye she looked to Jaden, silently beseeching him to help her out. When he wouldn't meet her gaze, her heart broke all over again. Why was he saying nothing? He loved her, didn't he? He'd told her so enough times. With a sudden clarity, and much to her horror, she realised that her mother had been right all along. He'd only loved getting her into bed. He'd only wanted her because she was by rights untouchable. She had been the ultimate forbidden fruit. It was a sobering thought.

* * *

For well over an hour, Katie had kept her mouth firmly closed, despite her cousins' best efforts to try and make her spill the beans. As her father and uncle entered the kitchen, she turned her head towards them, her eyes wide with fear. She could see the worry etched across her dad's face and guessed correctly that her mother's phone call had put the fear of Christ into him.

'What's happened?' He pulled her tentatively towards him, then held her at arm's length and, studying her face, his voice was full of concern. 'Are you hurt?'

'What's happened?' Stella screeched out the words. 'This one,' she spat, her face twisted with contempt, 'has only gone and got herself fucking pregnant.'

'Do what?' Jason's face paled at the words.

A new wave of tears washed over Katie. Her daddy looked terrible, as if her revelation had somehow broken him. His skin was ashen and his eyes were both wide and disbelieving.

'Pregnant? What are you talking about?' He searched her face, begging her to tell him that Stella was wrong, that she'd made a terrible mistake.

'Exactly what I said,' Stella spat, 'she's pregnant. You know, got a bun in the oven, as in, she's in the fucking club.'

'I know what pregnant means,' Jason snapped at his wife. Then, looking back to his daughter his voice became gentle. 'Is this true, Katie?'

'Dad.' Katie reached out to touch his arm. He had only ever been kind to her, had only ever been her rock. Her mother, on the other hand, had always been demanding. She'd had plans for her daughter, big plans, and was hell-bent on her becoming someone she wasn't. If she had had her way, she would have ended up becoming a doctor or a barrister. It was laughable really. She was of the same blood as the rest of the family and there was more chance of the pope having a wank than her going to medical school.

'Answer the question. Is this true?' Jason's expression became thunderous and he snatched his arm away.

Katie nodded and her voice croaked as she spoke. 'I'm sorry, Dad...'

Her father shook his head and it took all of her strength to not run from the room. The disappointment spread across his face was enough to break her heart in two. She would never have willingly hurt him, never.

'Tell me who he is, Katie. Tell me who the dirty bastard is.' It was said in such a calm manner that his words frightened her, much more than her cousins' shouting and screaming had done. At this very moment in time, her daddy, her lovely kind-hearted father, looked positively capable of murder.

It was then that she ran from the room, and as the hot salty tears blinded her vision, she vowed there and then that for as long as she still lived and breathed, she would never reveal who the father of her unborn child was. Not one single word would she ever mutter. It was her baby and her business, and hers alone.

That evening, when the house was once again empty, Paul watched as his Cathy tidied the kitchen and he had to keep the smile from his face, a smile he would never have believed he even had inside of him. It had been a day, all right, what with Lucas and then little Katie dropping her bombshell.

'Come on, out with it.' He cleared his throat and puffed out his chest. 'Who's the fucking culprit? And I know that you know who he is. It's written all over your face.'

Cathy didn't answer him. She knew exactly just how much trouble the revelation was about to bring and, thinking of her niece, she wanted to spare her the upset. She had seen little Katie's face, seen how heartbroken she had looked when Jaden hadn't declared the child as his. The boy had disappointed her. She had always been fond of her sons' friend, but this she wasn't so sure she would ever forgive. The boy had literally left the poor girl out to dry, left her to face the consequences alone.

'Come on, babe' – Paul opened out his arms – 'since when did we have secrets between us, eh?'

Thinking deeply, Cathy poured herself a fresh glass of wine. He was right, of course he was. They had no secrets between them, at least none that involved family anyway. She swallowed down a large mouthful of wine before answering. 'The boys' – she shook her head – 'are going to go mental.'

Paul raised his eyebrows. 'Why the fuck would the boys go ape-shit?' He took a step away, his handsome face hard. 'Unless of course they know the bloke responsible?'

'It's Jaden.' She was out of her seat and clutching at his fore-arms, forcing him to look at her. 'Please, my darling, don't say anything, don't tell the boys, not yet anyway. Let the dust settle first and once everything has calmed down...' She trailed off.

'Jaden?' There was incredulity in Paul's voice and, stepping out of Cathy's embrace, he leaned his weight on the back of the dining chair for support. The muscles across his broad shoulders and forearms were rigid. 'Jaden? You mean that kid who just stood in my kitchen and said nothing, said fuck all?' There was more than a hint of anger in his voice. It was an anger mixed with disbelief. 'That same kid who spent every waking second he could in my' – he stabbed his thumb into his chest, as though the boy had personally affronted him – 'my fucking home?'

'The one and same,' she answered dryly.

'The fucking bastard. I'll kill him for this.'

'Oh, no you will not.' There was a strength to Cathy's voice that shocked both her and Paul, and as she wagged her finger towards him, two pink spots appeared on her cheeks. 'You will say nothing. It's Katie's choice and she will decide if and when she wants to reveal who the father is, not you.'

'That fucking kid. I always knew he was a wrong'un, didn't I always say that?' He walked across the kitchen, threw open the patio doors and gulped down lungsful of air, as if doing so would erase the anger that had spread throughout his body. 'And to think he has sat at my table. I've fed the fucker.' He turned his head. 'We even took the bastard away on holiday with us when the boys were younger.'

Cathy laughed. It came out as a sarcastic cackle and after shaking her head at him, she quickly downed her wine in two large gulps. 'You thought he was a wrong'un.' It was more of a statement than a question. 'Well, he wasn't a wrong'un when you saw fit to put him on your payroll, was he?'

Paul averted his gaze. He hated to admit it, but his Cathy had him there. He'd been more than happy to employ the boy to do his dirty work.

'Or how about when you sent him trawling halfway across the country doing business for you? A wrong'un,' she exclaimed, stabbing a stiff finger towards him, 'don't make me fucking laugh. Oh, I know everything. I know all of your dirty little secrets. It's me you're talking to, remember? So don't give me all of that old bollocks. He's only a wrong'un when it suits you.'

Paul sighed. 'I have to give him a dig, you know that, don't you, babe?'

Cathy tilted her head to one side. 'A dig for what? For doing something your own sons do on a nightly basis?'

Paul screwed up his face. 'That's different and you know it is.'

'Is it?' Cathy laughed lightly. 'The only difference is that Katie was caught out and thank the heavens' – she looked up at the ceiling – 'the boys haven't been yet.' She paused. 'Well, at least that we know of anyway.'

Paul continued to scowl. 'Nah, my boys have got more fucking sense than that,' he spat out.

'Do they?' Cathy tilted her head to one side. Deep down, she hoped he was right, not that she would tell him that, of course. 'Had the talk with them then, did you?'

'What talk?' He narrowed his eyes.

'The talk. I take it you sat them down and had the talk with them? You know, the father and son talk? The one about them using protection? The one about them not getting some poor innocent girl in the club?'

'Leave it out, Cath.' He looked away and Cathy could see the faint blush to his cheeks. It took all of her strength to not laugh in his face. He'd always been the same, had her Paul. He may have been a hard man out on the street, but the moment sex was mentioned, he suddenly became shy. It would have been endearing if it wasn't so comical.

'I'll take that as a no then.' She topped up her wine glass and took a long sip, all the while, basking in his discomfort. 'Oh well, here's hoping for the best then. We are still a bit too young to become grandparents, though, so let's just hope and pray the boys, as you said, have got more sense and are being careful.'

His face screwed up even tighter at her words. 'Enough now, Cath, you've made your point, darling.'

Setting her glass down, Cathy went to him and, curling her fingers around his forearm, she looked up into his face. He was still a handsome man and he'd aged well over the years, just like a fine wine. Only the slight greying at his temples portrayed his true age. 'These things happen, Paul. Look at our Jonah, he wasn't planned, was he? But that didn't make us love him any less.'

'I suppose so.' Paul was thoughtful for a moment. 'But that boy had better own up to his responsibilities, and if he doesn't...' He gave a slight shake of his head, leaving the rest of the sentence unsaid.

Cathy nodded. Of that, she could agree on and she hoped to God that Jaden came through for her niece, for both his sake as well as Katie's.

16

Two weeks later, Jonah eyed his friend above the rim of his pint glass. 'So who do you reckon this bloke is?'

Gulping at his drink, Jaden shrugged. The fact that he couldn't look his best friend in the eye wasn't lost on either of them.

'I mean' – stuffing his hand into his jeans pocket, Jonah continued – 'it's not like she even goes out very often, is it?' He paused for effect. 'Let me reword that. What I mean is, she doesn't go out without us being present, does she? And I've never even seen her talk to a bloke, let alone go off and do anything with one.'

'I dunno.' Jaden looked around him for an escape route. He knew he should have declined coming out for the evening, and ever since Katie's bombshell, he'd avoided his two best friends like the plague. He was only grateful that Kieran hadn't decided to join them for the night. One brother was bad enough, but two, well, let's put it this way, he didn't think much of his chances, should they guess the truth and the situation get out of hand. They were hard little bastards, the Mooney brothers, and being their best mate, he knew that to be a fact, considering the number of scraps they had got into over the years. Unless they ended up having a tear up of some sort, the brothers actually considered it to be a quiet night out.

'Yeah, but surely you've thought of someone it could be?'

'I said, I don't fucking know. Can we just drop it now?' Jaden snapped out the words. They sounded a lot harsher than he'd intended, and to his ears, the outburst made him sound even guiltier.

As Jonah shrugged, Jaden hastily averted his gaze. He didn't like the way his mate was eyeing him. He'd always been the same, had Jonah. He was a shrewd fucker, and out of the two brothers, he was the thinker, the one who was suspicious of everything and everyone around them. Those dark blue eyes of his had a knack of being able to look into your very soul, something that had always amused him in the past. Until now that was, when he himself was on the receiving end of Jonah's scepticism.

On the stereo system 'Hot in Herre' by Nelly began to blare out, and he could feel his cheeks redden. He'd danced to that song with Katie, right underneath the watchful eye of her cousins, and the memory of that night, coupled with Jonah's stare, was enough to make him want to squirm.

'Is there anything you need to tell me?' It was said in a carefree manner, too carefree, if he knew Jonah as well as he thought he did.

'What the fuck are you talking about?' Jaden snapped his head towards his friend.

Jonah lifted his eyebrows. His silence told Jaden everything he needed to know, and he momentarily closed his eyes. He should have known that Jonah would be the one to suss everything out.

The sudden punch to his face felt like the equivalent of a car crashing into him, and he staggered backwards, feeling somewhat dazed.

'I knew it,' Jonah snarled. 'I knew from the moment she dropped the bombshell that it was you.' His fists flew out a second, third and fourth time. The actions were so fast that Jaden could barely block the blows, and as blood poured from a slit eyebrow, he knew for a fact that if he didn't get to his feet and fast, then Jonah would finish him off. It was as simple as that.

'It weren't like that,' he hollered above the music. 'It was all her doing. She chased after me. She wouldn't leave me the fuck alone, kept putting it on me. How was I supposed to turn her away?'

It was the worst thing he could have said, and as Jonah's fists swung towards him even faster, he resigned himself to the fact he was in for a well-deserved hammering.

There was something about Donna Cassidy that Kieran liked, really liked, and after their chance meeting in the café, he had actively sought her out. Much to his pleasure, he had actually found her just days later, sitting at the exact same table where he had first seen her. It was her easy manner that he liked, he decided. That and the way she didn't demand anything from him. She was more than happy to spend the night in his company as and when she could. She didn't demand his attention like many of the girls before her had. In his eyes, there was no greater turn off than a woman who believed that he belonged to her, that he was her property, that he should come running at her beck and call.

As he lay back in her double bed with the pillows behind his head, he looked around the small bedroom. It was nothing fancy and certainly nothing like his own bedroom at his parents' house, which was filled with the latest gadgets on the market. Whatever his little heart desired he had in abundance, but Donna's home, on the other hand, was what his mother would describe as shabby. The furniture, including the bed where he now lay, had seen better days, but it was clean and more than comfortable, and he loved it. In fact, he loved everything about the little set up she had going on. From the sound of her children laughing and squealing, and more often than not, arguing over a favourite toy, to the washing machine that seemed to be in constant use, to the scent of a cooked breakfast sizzling away in the big frying pan in the kitchen.

He lit a cigarette and smiled down at the woman in question as she began to stir beside him. He'd needed this, really needed it. After the past couple of weeks he'd had, a night of sex had been the perfect way for him to forget the trouble that had been brought to his family's door. Anger rippled through him once more. When he got his hands on the bastard who had touched his little cousin, he would happily throttle the life out of him.

Opening her eyes, Donna gave him a wide smile then proceeded to stretch out lazily across the bed. As she did so the sheet slid from her body, exposing her large breasts. Just the mere sight of her dark nipples was enough to make him begin to harden.

He continued to watch her and as she sat up, she took the cigarette from his fingers, took a deep drag, then blew out a thin stream of bluish-grey smoke.

'Will I see you tonight?'

'Maybe.' He could hear the hope in her voice and, taking the cigarette back from her, he shrugged. Beside him on the bedside cabinet his mobile phone vibrated. He casually glanced towards it and, seeing his brother's name flash up on the screen, he hastily switched the phone off. Donna snuggled in even closer and he smiled softly. After spending the past two weeks thinking it over, curiosity had finally got the better of him and he cleared his throat. 'Do you remember that day in the café?'

Donna cocked her head to one side. 'Which day?' she asked innocently. 'The first time, or when you came back looking for me?'

Pulling her underneath his arm, Kieran kissed the top of her head. 'The first time.'

'Of course, what about it?'

'You said that I reminded you of someone. I think you said I was his double?'

Donna giggled. Despite the age difference between them, her girlish laughter made her seem a lot younger than she actually was. 'Don't tell me you're jealous?' she scoffed.

He shook his head. Although he had to admit, he didn't like the fact that she had been with other men before him.

'That's right, I did say that.' She looked up at him. 'And you do look like Terrance, a lot like him actually. There are a few differences though.' She reached up to touch the cleft on his chin. 'But only subtle differences.'

'So, who is he?' He kept his voice light. He needed to know exactly who this Terrance bloke was, and more importantly, what he had meant to her, but he decided to play it safe. He didn't want to sound any more jealous than he already did.

'Terrance...' She turned onto her side and curled herself around him. He could feel the warmth of her body as she slid her arm around his waist. 'Terrance Matlock. It was all a long time ago, but I thought I loved him. I was just a kid really. I didn't even know what love was, and then one day he just upped and left. He disappeared into thin air.' She laughed lightly. 'And broke my heart in the process.'

Kieran thought this through, somewhat pleased that he didn't have competition, and that the man was no longer on the scene. His relief made him realise how much he'd come to have feelings for this woman. She made him feel something other than a need to just get her into bed. He didn't know how she'd done it. He didn't even care how she'd done it, but somehow, his Donna as he began to think of her, had managed to do what dozens of women before her could have only dreamed of doing.

'They say he ran off with another woman, but I don't believe that.' She shook her head from side to side and looked into the distance. 'I think...' She was quiet for a moment, almost afraid to say the words out loud. 'I think that she killed him, her and her new fella.'

'What?' Taken aback, Kieran looked down at her.

'Yep,' Donna sighed deeply, 'he was married you see, and well' – she shrugged as if embarrassed by her past – 'I think she, the wife I mean, I think she killed him, or at least her new bloke did. He's a face, a serious face.' She sat up and reached for her own pack of cigarettes. 'I think together they killed him.'

'A face?' Kieran thought this over. He knew most of the London and Essex faces, all thanks to his dad. 'So, what's the name of this bloke?'

Donna shook her head. It was more than her life was worth than to accuse Paul Mooney of murder. 'It doesn't matter,' she said, dropping the cigarette packet onto the bedside cabinet and sliding her hand underneath the sheet. 'Forget I even said anything.'

Kieran shrugged, but as he flipped her onto her back, he couldn't ignore the fact that she had more than piqued his interest. He would do some digging around of his own, he decided.

* * *

Not one to let a grudge weigh him down, Jonah had already somewhat forgiven his best mate for his wrongdoings, and as he studied Jaden's battered face, he grinned at him amicably.

Jaden, on the other hand, knew that at any moment now, he was in for round two – one brother down, another one to go – that was how it worked with the Mooney brothers. They were like a tag team. Their viciousness spurred one another on, and he could only hope that Kieran would put in an appearance, and pretty sharpish. Resigned to his fate, all he could do was pray that the deed would be over and done with as quickly as possible.

'Chill out, for fuck's sake.' Jonah puffed on his cigarette as though he didn't have a care in the world. 'I'll square it with my brother, don't worry about it.'

'Don't worry about it?' Jaden would have laughed, if his face didn't hurt so much. As it was, he was worried that the slit across his eyebrow needed a stich or two, or maybe even three. Every time he moved his forehead, he could feel the pulsating, swollen skin flap open. He studied his friend. It was all right for Jonah to say don't worry. It wasn't him who was about to get battered for the second time in less than twenty-four hours.

'Yeah.' As he lounged back in the chair, Jonah grinned. 'Like I said, don't worry about it.'

Just moments later, Kieran entered the small Portakabin. The land the cabin sat on was owned by their father, with the hope to one day build apartments upon it. Until that time, they used the cabin as an unofficial office, a place to meet up to drink and smoke a bit of green in relative peace. They had even been known to bring women back there on the odd occasion after a night out.

'What the fuck happened to you?' Looking from his brother to his best friend, Kieran's eyes were wide.

Sheepishly, Jaden looked to Jonah, and as Kieran stepped closer, he braced himself for what was about to come.

'Funny story,' Jonah said, 'while you were shagging that ropey-looking bird of yours, I' – he poked himself in the chest – 'was trying to suss out who exactly had got their hands on our Katie.'

'She ain't ropey.' It came across as a little dig, and as such, Kieran screwed his face up at his brother's words.

'If you say so.' Jonah flicked his hand dismissively, then jerked his head towards Jaden. 'As you can see, I sorted the problem out.'

'Well?' Staring at his friend, Kieran shook his head, a bewildered expression across his face. 'Who is it then?'

Jonah flicked his hand a second time, and as the realisation finally settled across his brother's face, he stood up, ready to jump in if need be.

'You wanker.' Kieran lunged forward, only to be forcibly dragged back by Jonah.

'I said, I've sorted it,' Jonah bellowed in his face.

'Nah.' Kieran pulled himself free and his fists were clenched into tight balls, ready to attack. 'You might have sorted it, but I fucking haven't, and he ain't getting away with this, the dirty bastard. You're meant to be our mate, our fucking pal. We trusted you; I fucking trusted you.'

'Like I said, I've sorted it.' Jonah easily restrained his brother and with his arm firmly placed across Kieran's shoulders, he swept his free arm towards their friend. 'Jaden here is going to do the honourable thing and ask our Katie to marry him.'

'What?' Jaden staggered backwards, as though the wind had been punched right out of him and his face paled. 'I never agreed to that.' He looked to Kieran, his eyes beseeching him. 'I never said I would marry her, I'm too young to get married.'

The smile left Jonah's face. 'You should have thought of that.' Stalking forward, he gave a little wink, snaked his free arm around Jaden's shoulders, and squeezed him tight. 'Welcome to the family, mate.'

* * *

Katie was over the moon. On her wedding finger was the biggest diamond she had ever seen, and as she turned her hand this way and that, the diamond twinkled underneath the fluorescent lights.

Sipping at her orange juice, she caught her auntie's gaze and giggled. 'Oh, Auntie Cath, I'm so happy. I could literally scream the house down.'

Cathy laughed heartily. It was good to see her niece looking so happy, and as she sipped at her wine, she glanced towards her two sons and Jaden. It was a shame that the groom-to-be didn't look as happy. She had a niggling feeling that the engagement and upcoming nuptials weren't quite what he'd had planned out for his future. Still, she reasoned, it had been the right thing to do. A new life was soon going to be brought into the world, and the child would need both a mother and father.

'Are you okay, sweetheart?' She felt Paul's arms wrap around her waist and looked up at him. 'Everything's going well, eh?' He nodded towards the guests who had been invited to the engagement party. Even Stella and Jason seemed to be in good spirits.

'Everything's going to plan.' She patted his arm, turned around and, reaching up on her tip toes, she kissed his cheek, savouring the familiar scent of him.

'You know' – he pulled her tight and whispered in her ear – 'maybe we should think about getting married. What do you say?'

Cathy gave a soft smile, but it was tinged somewhat with sadness. How could they marry? She was already married to Terrance and that was one can of worms they didn't want to open up. Her gaze darted towards their sons. The boys had always believed they were married, as did everyone else for that matter. The fact that she used Paul's surname and behaved as his common law wife was enough to erase any suspicions they or anyone else may have had. She heard him sigh and cuddled into him. It broke her heart that she couldn't give him the one thing he wanted, but what was the alternative?

'You didn't hear me right, Cath.' He cuddled into her even further. 'Marry me.'

'What?' Pulling herself back slightly, Cathy looked up at the man she had loved for so many years. 'Say that again.'

'Marry me.' Pulling her close once more, he cocked his eyebrow and smiled a cheeky grin. 'What do you say?'

'But...'

'I've already looked into it.' Paul cut her off, guessing what she was about to say. 'And getting a divorce will be a doddle.' Well, at least it should be if he forged Terrance's signature on the forms. 'So what do you say?'

'I say yes.' Tears glistened Cathy's eyes as she half-laughed and half-cried.

Behind them, the loud clatter of a glass smashing from the lounge area broke the moment, and seeing the culprit responsible, Paul groaned out loud.

'For fuck's sake,' he growled. 'I'll end up murdering this fucker.'

Staggering towards them was Lucas. The glazed look in his eyes was enough to tell Paul that he was buzzing off his head. So much for getting himself clean. Two weeks in rehab had obviously done nothing. He only hoped it wasn't the brown he was on tonight, although he had a sneaky suspicion it most probably was.

'Sorry, mate, sorry, Cath. Had a little accident there.' Lucas opened up his arms apologetically. 'I'll pay for any damage caused,' he said, sloshing the remaining alcohol he was holding over the tiled floor.

Paul closed his eyes. At times like this, he could happily throttle the life out of Lucas. He watched with a mixture of sadness and embarrassment as the guests moved out of harm's way. He saw the way they wrinkled their noses and he didn't blame them. He could smell the man from at least twelve feet away.

'You take care of him.' Cathy smiled up at him gently. In her hand, she held a cloth and he smiled his appreciation.

'I'm sorry, babe,' he mouthed to her.

Flapping her hand, she gestured towards the garden. 'Get him some fresh air and I'll stick the kettle on.' Even as she said the words, she knew it would take a bit more than a bit of fresh air and a strong black coffee to sober Lucas up.

As Paul half-dragged, half-guided Lucas towards the patio doors, she failed to notice her eldest son watching the scene unfolding before him with more than a healthy hint of interest.

17

Luckily for Kieran, Lucas was a creature of habit, and when he forced his way into the squat, he found the man in question's prostate form slumped out on a worn and stained rickety sofa that looked as though it would collapse underneath his weight at any moment. He looked around him and wrinkled his nose. Not only could he smell vomit, but it actually smelled as if something had crawled inside the squat and died. He looked around him half expecting to find a body hidden underneath the pile of moth-eaten stained blankets that had been thrown into the corner of the room.

He shook his head in disbelief. He knew for a fact that Lucas was in possession of an upmarket flat in the up and coming Docklands area. He knew that, because it was his father who actually paid for the lease. However, Lucas, being the useless junkie he was, preferred to spend his days and nights high on whatever shit he could get his hands on, surrounded by what could only be described as the scum of the earth.

'Oi.' Kieran prodded Lucas with his shoe, and when he

received no answer, he kicked out even harder. 'Oi,' he shouted, 'rise and fucking shine.'

Lucas opened one eye and, seeing Paul's eldest son before him, flapped his hand dismissively. 'Fuck off.'

'Nah, I don't think so.' Kieran grinned. It was a heart-stopping smile that was lost on Lucas.

'I said—'

Kieran yanked the big man up by the arm. With his face poised just inches away from Lucas's, Kieran made a mental note not to breathe in too deeply. 'And like I just said, I don't fucking think so.' He released his grip and watched with annoyance as Lucas slumped backwards, his limbs appearing both heavy and sluggish. 'Me and you are gonna go and have a little chat. So sober yourself up and quick. I'll even make it worth your trouble.' He winked.

* * *

Settled inside a pub on the outskirts of London, far away from prying eyes, Kieran and Lucas made an odd couple. Wearing dark denim jeans, a crisp white shirt and expensive shoes, in appearance, Kieran was poles apart from his father's friend, who looked exactly what he was: a junkie. The T-shirt he wore was filthy and he stank to boot. It was a mixture of ground-in dirt, stale sweat, and chemicals. The stench was so strong that Kieran could smell him from across the table, despite the expensive aftershave he had splashed on earlier that morning.

'So, what's this all about? A bit cloak and dagger, ain't it?' Lucas greedily gulped down his whiskey and immediately picked up the second filled glass that Kieran had placed before him. When the boy had collected him that afternoon, he had fully expected to be hauled in front of Paul. That's what they usually did whenever he was summoned. Why couldn't they just leave him be? For the life of him, he couldn't understand. He had no interest in the businesses and had more than made that clear over the years. Being a part owner in the pubs made him feel as though he had more than one albatross hanging around his neck, and not for the first time did he wish that they would just cut him loose and let him live his life how he wanted. And more importantly, how he deemed fit.

Kieran sipped at his drink. He placed the glass down on the table, then sat up a little straighter.

'You've been around for years, been in the same circles as my dad.' He watched the older man closely. Lucas was still a large man, and despite the amount of drugs he had sunk over the years, his dark brown eyes were still sharp and alert.

'Yeah, and?' It was said with suspicion and, lounging back in his chair, Lucas raised his eyebrows.

Leaning across the table, Kieran glanced around him before answering. 'I want to know about a face.' He sat back in his seat and opened out his arms slightly. 'I don't have a name, but I do have the name of the geezer he may or may not have topped.'

Lucas narrowed his eyes. 'What you asking me for? Ask your old man.' He shrugged. 'I haven't exactly been keeping track of who's done what over the years, have I?'

'No' – Kieran shook his head – 'I can't do that. You know what he's like. He would ask too many questions. He's like a fucking blood hound. Once he gets started, he doesn't let things lie, if you know what I mean.'

'You hiding something from your old man, boy?' Lucas raised his eyebrows and sat up straighter. 'What are you digging around for?' he asked, his mood now sombre. 'Let the past rest; it has no place in the present. I, better than anyone, know for a fact that no good comes from dragging up what's already been done.'

Kieran sighed heavily and slumped back in the seat. He knew that Lucas tried to blot out his demons, whatever the fuck they were, and that over the years, his dad had tried to overcompensate by buying the man all and sundry. Take the Docklands flat for example; his dad splashed out thousands of pounds each month, just to try and keep a roof over Lucas's head, and still he wasn't happy. No, within days of acquiring the flat, he had sublet it out to a young city couple. His preference was to doss down in squalid rat-infested squats with the rest of the low-life junkies he liked to surround himself with. 'I just want a name, that's all.'

Lucas gulped down his whiskey, then gestured towards the bar. 'Get me another drink, boy, and then I'll see what I can remember.'

Eagerly, Kieran jumped up. He had to know everything there was to know about this Terrance bloke, and more than anything, he had to know who his competition was, even if that meant dragging up the past, as Lucas had so pleasantly put it.

Alek Symanski was sweating profusely, and as a pool of warm cloying sweat settled underneath his armpits, he resisted the urge to squirm. It didn't help matters that he was still wearing his trademark long, thick leather coat that felt far too warm and heavy for the confines of the vehicle he was being driven in. He was a big man with a prominent beer belly, shoulder-length wavy mousey brown hair, and piercing blue eyes that he had inherited from his grandfather, a Polish immigrant who'd had a penchant for women, boozing, brawling and skulduggery.

As a child growing up, Alek had looked up to the old man and wanted nothing more than to emulate him, which he subsequently did with vigour. As a result, Alek had a penchant for dipping his greedy little fingers into a lot of pies, and was well known on the streets as a middle man. For a considerable price, he could get his hands on just about anything from Uzi machine guns to large quantities of narcotics.

Thirty minutes earlier, he had been snatched off the streets outside one of his favourite cafés in Forest Gate, East London. It was from there that he ran his business, like a king holding court. He could usually be found sitting at a table towards the back of the property, barking out his orders to the unfortunate minions who worked for him.

When a rough hessian sack that stank of petrol had been yanked down over his head, and he'd been roughly bundled into a van so fast that his feet had barely touched the ground, he'd had little chance to comprehend what was going on, let alone take a look at his abductors. Whoever they were, they were professionals, and that fact alone frightened him much more than anything else he had ever known.

The rumble of the engine was the only sound in the otherwise quiet vehicle. Sandwiched between two lumps on the uncomfortable van floor, he felt his heart hammering wildly in his chest. He wasn't afraid to admit that the eerie silence unnerved him. It was a clever tactic on their part, and he, better than anyone, knew that this was his capturer's intention. It was used as a strategy to both disorientate and perturb him, a fact that he had to admit was working.

For what felt like hours, he had been driven at speed. His backside was numb from the hard metal floor and he yearned to stretch out his legs and have a drink. His throat felt so dry and the cloying petrol fumes stung his eyes and made his chest wheeze with every breath he took. Instinct told him that they were on the motorway somewhere. For all he knew, they could be driving him to the ends of the earth, someplace remote, somewhere no one would be able to hear his screams. A sense of panic set in. Were they planning to burn him alive? Was that the reason he could smell petrol? It was both a heady and terrifying thought.

Despite his best efforts to get some kind of acknowledgement out of the men, they remained silent. Who were they, and more importantly, what did they want from him? He tried to wrack his brains, thinking back over the previous weeks and months of who exactly he could have upset. The list, much to his chagrin, was long. Even his own mother had often proudly remarked that he could cause a row in an empty room, such was his mindset.

* * *

Pulling out a wooden chair, Paul sat down. They were in a disused public house on the border of Suffolk and Essex that he and Jason had recently purchased. They were still in two minds whether or not to pull the premises down and then rebuild to their own specification.

He lit a cigarette, took a deep drag, then blowing out a cloud of smoke, nodded towards Darren and Charlie.

As the hessian sack was pulled from his head, Alek screwed his eyes shut tight, the sudden onset of light momentarily blinding his vision. It took a few moments for him to acclimatise to his surroundings, and when he finally realised exactly who it was that had captured him, fear flickered across his face.

'For fuck's sake, Paul, was this really necessary?' He nodded down at the thick chains that bound him to the chair, his voice a decibel higher than usual. 'Haven't you heard of a fucking telephone?'

In silence, Paul continued to smoke his cigarette. The atmosphere sizzled with anticipation, the occupants of the room awaiting his next move.

Alek looked around him. He was beginning to perspire again and wished they would have at least let him take off the coat. The thick leather was sticking to him like a second skin. 'Paul...'

'I want the names of every dealer who shifts brown on my manor.' Paul's voice was loud and strong.

'Don't tell me someone has stepped on your toes.' Alek looked around him a second time and took note of Darren and Charlie hovering in the background. They were commonly referred to as the clean-up team and they were good at their job. He had even used their services himself on occasion. 'Is that what all of this old bollocks is about? You haven't been paid your fucking dues, and now you want to collect?'

'I'm going to ask you one more time, and trust me, Alek, it is in your best interests not to fuck me about. You're the middle man. You make it your business to know what is going down, who is buying, who is selling, et cetera, et cetera, so' – his voice became a low rumble – 'who is selling brown without my specific say so?'

'I can't divulge something like that.' There was a hint of shock in Alek's voice. 'Have you lost your fucking mind? If I started spouting my mouth off, it'd be the end of me. Come on, Paul.' He smiled lightly to take the edge off his words. 'You know I can't divulge information, not even to you. What are you trying to do, man, have me topped?'

Paul stood up and returned the smile. It was a smile that didn't quite reach his eyes, a fact that was duly noted by those in the room. 'I don't think you quite understood what I said.' His voice held a note of menace. 'Let me make this clear; it wasn't a request. So I'll say it again. I want to know who is supplying, and you, Alek, had best start fucking talking.'

'Come on, Paul, we're mates, ain't we?'

The sudden punch to Alek's face silenced him and, as he stood over the man, Paul's face darkened. 'I asked you a question.'

He executed a second and third punch with such force that the chair holding Alek's large frame swayed from side to side precariously. 'Who is supplying brown?'

'You know I can't...' Blood poured from Alek's mouth. Already, his left eye was beginning to swell. He was terrified and it showed. Despite his huge bulk, he wasn't a natural born fighter, and deep down, he was well aware of that fact. If truth were told, without backup, he wouldn't be able to punch his way out of a paper bag. He didn't have a bona fide reputation as a hard man like the man in front of him did. He'd only gained his rep by a natural cunning, and ordering others to do his dirty work for him. 'If I open my trap, I'm dead, you know that.'

'We can stay here for as long as it takes.' Paul walked the length of the bar. From a small round wooden table, he picked up a claw hammer and a six inch nail. 'But you are going to talk, and then I'm going to kill you. It's as simple as that.'

Alek's eyes widened and he flicked them between Paul, Jason, and then finally to Darren and Charlie. 'Come on, Paul,' he shouted, 'you don't have to do this.'

'Oh, but I do.' Paul grinned in return.

'Come on, Paul.' Clearly terrified, Alek struggled against Darren and Charlie as they held his hand flat down on a table. 'Don't do this,' he cried.

As the nail was hammered through his flesh and muscle, Alek let out his first bloodcurdling scream of the day.

* * *

Lucas sipped at his drink and looked around him. A creature of habit, he could sniff out a dealer from ten miles away, and his gaze settled on a man sitting in a corner booth at the far side of the pub. He needed a fix and fast. His skin was already beginning to crawl, and as he scratched at his arm unconsciously, his grimy fingernails dragged across the soft flesh, leaving angry red welts. The dealer was like a beacon to him, and he could barely drag his eyes away.

'Lucas.' Glancing over his shoulder, Kieran knew that he had to keep the older man's attention, and he opened out his arms, hoping more than anything to block out Lucas's view. 'You were going to tell me what you could remember.'

'Yeah.' Barely acknowledging the boy, Lucas's gaze remained focused on the dealer.

'Lucas.' There was more than a hint of annoyance in Kieran's voice.

'What?' Lucas picked up his glass.

'I need a name, remember? You agreed to help me out.'

Swallowing down a large mouthful of whiskey, Lucas groaned. The quicker he got it over with, the quicker the boy would fuck off and leave him alone, he decided. 'Go on then. Tell me what you know.'

Kieran grinned. 'His name, the bloke who might have been topped, is Terrance Matlock. He came from over Barking way.' He took a sip of his drink, oblivious to just how still Lucas had become. 'You and my dad came from over that way. My old nan still lives there. Did you ever hear anything about this bloke?' He gave a slight shrug of his shoulders. 'I mean, what could have happened to him? Apparently, he just disappeared into thin air.'

'What are you dragging that up for?' Realising that he had already said too much, Lucas downed his whiskey and wiped the back of his hand across his lips. The colour slipped from his face, leaving in its place a slight grey tinge. Of all the names young Kieran could have come up with, it had to be that one. 'Speak to your dad, son. I'm not saying anything more.'

Kieran sat back in the seat and narrowed his eyes. It wasn't the reaction he'd been expecting. 'I'm asking you' – his voice had a steely tone to it – 'not my fucking dad.'

'And like I said, I'm saying fuck all.' He made to stand up. 'You wanna know about Matlock, then do us both a favour and ask your old man.'

Taken aback, Kieran clamped his hand over Lucas's wrist, restraining him. 'It was my dad, wasn't it?' He gave a half-laugh, his eyes wide. 'It was him. He topped the bloke.'

'I'm saying fuck all.' Wrenching his hand free, Lucas walked away from the table without a backwards glance. As far as he was concerned, the conversation was closed and his lips would remain firmly sealed.

As the man walked away from him, Kieran slumped back in the seat. Instinctively, he knew he would get no more information from his father's friend, no matter how much he might want it. So, just what was the big secret? It wasn't as though his dad topping someone would have come as a big surprise. He already knew that he'd killed. His dad had told him and Jonah one night after they had all sunk one too many beers.

He thought back on Donna's words. She'd said that Matlock had been married, and that she suspected the wife and her new fella, a supposed face, of his murder. So his dad must have been seeing someone, a married woman, long before he met his mum.

Picking up his pint glass, he downed the lager in one large gulp. Still, it didn't make any sense to him. His parents had been together forever; they had been childhood sweethearts. At least that was the story they had told him and Jonah. So when exactly had he been seeing this married woman? Had he cheated on his mum? Was that the big secret? Was that what Lucas was so afraid of revealing?

He glanced behind him and watched as Lucas stuffed a small package into his pocket. Just what was the big man so afraid of?

206

Whatever it was, it was more than enough to make him keep schtum.

He continued to think back to the very first time he had met Donna, and as her words came back to haunt him, he felt his blood run cold. She'd told him that he looked just like this Terrance Matlock bloke, that he was his double. A sickening wave hit him, and as he sat up straighter, beads of cold sweat broke out across his forehead. Supposing his mum had been the married woman, and his dad... no, he shook his head, pushing the dark thought to the back of his mind. No way. He looked like his dad; his mum had told him that so many times over the years.

An image of Paul and Jonah sprang to his mind. Not only did they look alike, but they were also mirror images of one another – same height, same build, same smile, same dark blue eyes, same mannerisms. He recalled his own eyes. Unlike his brother's, his were dark brown, his hair was a shade darker, too. Standing abruptly, he shoved his cigarettes and lighter into his jacket pocket, and as quickly as he could, he left the pub.

Opening the front door, Angie eyed her eldest grandson with a measure of suspicion. 'Well, look who it is. To what do I owe this pleasure, eh?' She studied the handsome young man before her. 'Why ain't you at work, you lazy little bugger? Are you skiving off again?'

'Cheers for that, Nan, and it's nice to see you and all.' Stepping over the doorstep, Kieran made his way down the narrow passageway towards the kitchen. The familiar scent of lavender furniture polish and stale tobacco assaulted his nostrils. It was somewhat comforting.

'Your dad will skin you alive if he catches you skiving, you know that, boy.' With her hands placed on her hips, a Rothman cigarette dangled from the corner of her mouth. As the smoke drifted upward, she screwed up her face.

'What dad?'

'What do you mean, what dad? Your dad.' As she followed her grandson through the hallway, Angie rolled her eyes to the ceiling in annoyance. 'How many dads have you bleeding well got?'

Kieran turned and, lifting his eyebrows, he looked his grand-mother dead in the eyes. 'That, Nan, is exactly what I would like to know.'

'What the fuck are you talking about?' Angie's heart began to hammer wildly inside her chest, and a prickle of unease gripped the back of her neck. Her daughter, not to mention Paul, would skin her alive if she ever let slip the truth about the boy's true parentage.

'I think you already know the answer to that question.'

Angie looked up at this big handsome grandson of hers and sighed wearily. He was Terrance's double all right, of that much she did know. Deep down, she had often wondered why the boy had never questioned how different he looked to his brother and the man he called dad.

'Come on then, Nan.' Sitting down at the Formica-covered table, Kieran crossed his arms over his chest and grinned amica-bly. 'I think you'd best start talking, and fast.'

Angie sighed. What she would do for a drink or two right now. After all, it wasn't her secret to tell, and God only knew how many times she had told her daughter to tell the boy the truth over the years. Now look at the upshot. The aftermath of Cathy's lies and deceit had been brought to her door. It wasn't even anything to do with her, not really. All she was, was an innocent bystander, wasn't she?

'Well?'

'Speak to your mum and dad, sweetheart.' Stubbing out her cigarette, Angie joined her grandson at the table. The fact that she could barely look him in the eye was not lost on either of them.

'No.' Kieran thumped his fist down on the table, anger clearly evident across his handsome face. 'I'm going to batter the next fucking person who tells me to do that. I need to know, Nan. Please, just tell me the truth.'

Closing her eyes tightly, Angie took a deep breath. 'Your mum will kill me, and as for your dad...' She gave a shake of her head. Who knew what Paul was capable of? Serious bodily harm? Murder? She would put nothing past the long-time partner of her only daughter, and deep down, she still believed that he had killed her Samson. Oh, he could deny it until he was blue in the face, but she knew. She could see it in the arrogant stare he gave her whenever she mentioned the man's name. The very thought was enough to make her blood run cold.

'Is it true?' Kieran sat forward in the chair. 'Is... is Terrance Matlock my father?'

Angie hesitated, then slowly nodded. 'Biological father, yes, but your dad' – she paused momentarily and clutched her grandson's hand – 'I may not be Paul's biggest fan, but he is your real dad, sweetheart. Make no mistake about that, and he's the only dad you've ever known. From day one, he was there for you and your mum. He brought you up, and for that, I can't fault him. Not once has he ever treated you differently to Jonah. In his eyes, you are his son, and it's as plain and simple as that.'

'But I'm not, am I? I'm not his son; I never was.'

He looked so crestfallen that Angie's heart went out to her eldest grandchild. 'Yes you are.' She gave his hand a squeeze and, using her finger, wiped away the lone tear that had slipped onto his cheek. 'You, my boy, have got more Mooney in your little toe than you will ever have Terrance Matlock in your entire body. Take my word for it, sweetheart.'

Kieran shrugged and, sniffing loudly, he looked down at the table. 'What was he like?' He looked up. 'Terrance, I mean?'

As she lit a fresh cigarette, Angie thought the question over. 'Terrance' – she smiled gently – 'was a handsome fucker all right, and you are the image of him, like two peas in a bleeding pod, but that is where the resemblance ends. He was a woman-iser and he treated your poor mum abysmally. He was handy with his fists, too, and more often than not, he treated her like a punching bag.' She sighed deeply. 'Many a black eye or spit lip your mum would have, all thanks to him and his bloody temper. I begged her to leave him, begged her, but by then, she was already pregnant with you, and well' – she shrugged – 'it wasn't so easy for her to up and leave him then, was it?' She watched her grandson screw up his face and her voice became gentle. 'And that, my darling, is why you are nothing like him. In here' – she poked a finger into his chest – 'you've got a good heart.'

Kieran sighed, wondering where his Donna came in to all of this. Just the mere thought that this man, his father, had been with her before he had, made him feel physically sick. 'So, what happened to him? Where did he go?'

'That,' Angie said, pointing the cigarette towards her grand-son, 'is the million-dollar question. The bugger just upped and left one day. Him and your mum had had a bit of a ding-dong. Nothing new there,' she said, 'they were always having some sort of barney, and well, I suppose he wanted a change of scenery, a change of woman. He had tarts all over the place. Bugger should have been a sailor, a woman in every port and all that.'

Raising his eyebrows slightly, Kieran laughed. Until he'd met

Donna, that had been him all over, but he decided to keep that little piece of information to himself.

'So' – getting up from the table, Angie crossed over the kitchen and switched on the kettle – 'does that answer your questions?'

'Yeah.' Leaning back in the chair, Kieran placed his hands behind his head. 'I suppose so.'

Angie smiled and, pouring boiling water into two mugs, she glanced towards her grandson. 'Maybe we should keep this between us.' She placed the kettle down and stirred in a dash of milk. 'I mean, you ain't got to say anything to your mum and dad, have you? Why upset them now after all these years?' It was said craftily. As always, with Angie, she was only looking out for herself.

Groaning, Kieran stood up and, walking across the kitchen, he wrapped his arms around his grandmother's tiny frame. 'Thanks, Nan. You know, for letting me know the score.' He smiled at her. 'And I'm not going to say anything, you're right,' he sighed. 'My dad is my dad, no matter what.' More than anything, he didn't want anything to rock the boat or alter the relationship he had with Paul. They had always been close and even shared the same interests.

'Good boy.' Angie's shoulders slumped with relief, and as she continued to stir the tea, she grinned happily.

18

In Stepney, East London, Lucas's eyes lit up and his hand greedily snaked out to take the wrap of heroin from Marty Hanratty.

'Now what do you say?' Snatching the bag out of the big man's reach, Marty laughed heartily. He loved nothing better than to goad the junkies. It was one of his favourite pastimes, and should be declared as a national sport, in his opinion.

A bully as a child and an even bigger bully as an adult, Marty had a short stocky build, round face, and mousey brown hair. He was no looker, and was the first to hold his hand up and admit that fact, but what he did have in abundance was a cunning that, over the years, had stood him in good stead. He liked to be on the winning team, and right now, he was hedging his bets on Devan Barkley emerging as the victor. It was only this fact that made him so outwardly loyal to the man.

Once again, he dangled the wrap in front of Lucas, and with his large palm wrapped around the tiny, knotted plastic bag, he taunted his latest victim. 'I asked you a question. Now what do you fucking say?'

Eyeing the closed palm that contained his much-needed fix,

Lucas flushed with shame. 'Please?' It was said quietly and with as much dignity as he could physically muster.

'Nah, I can't hear you.' Cupping his ear, Marty chuckled. Oh, he did love winding the scumbags up. It actually made his day that much sweeter to see them beg.

'I said, please.' Lucas's expression was hard, alerting Marty to the fact that there was a bit more to this particular junkie than met the eye.

'All right, keep your fucking hair on. I was only having a laugh.' Bored with the scene before him, Marty dropped the wrap to the pavement, and as the big man scooped down to pick it up, he contemplated kicking him in the head. He would have actually followed it through, if Lucas hadn't been so quick. Before he could even lift his foot off the floor, the big man was stalking away from him. However, he would get him the next time, and he made a mental note to remind himself.

* * *

'Who is he?' Sitting in his car, Paul intently watched the scene that played out before him. His expression was hard and his lips were curled in disgust.

Jason peered through the windscreen. 'That, to me, looks like Marty Hanratty, one of Devan Barkley's so-called crew, better known as his right-hand man.' He nodded. 'Yeah, that's him. I'd bet my fucking knob on it.'

Paul nodded and, starting the ignition, he eased the car forward. It had taken a lot longer than he'd expected for Alek Symanski to open his mouth and talk. Begrudgingly, he had earned Paul's full respect by keeping schtum for as long as he had. In the end, the man had begged for death, screamed for it, in fact. He, being the generous type of bloke he was, had been more than happy to oblige. He had no concerns of a comeback where Alek was concerned. The middle men were ten a penny in their world, and there was always someone eager to take over their business interests. He flicked the indicator and, keeping a reasonable distance, he began to follow on behind Marty's car. 'I think it's about time we introduced ourselves, don't you?'

Jason lit a cigarette, and as he pulled the smoke deep into his lungs, he curled his free hand into a fist. Fucking Devan Barkley. They should have known right from the start that he was involved in Lucas's latest downfall.

* * *

Marty was whistling as he took the concrete steps two at a time up to his small bedsit. Behind him, he heard the communal door slam closed, and with a grin across his face, he turned his head. Within moments, the smile was gone and he narrowed his eyes until they were two mere slits in his pale bloated face.

'What do you want?' A coward through and through, there was a tremor in his voice, and he wiped his sweaty palms down the front of his jeans.

'That's not very nice, is it?' Paul's voice was jovial as he ascended the staircase.

Jutting out his chin, Marty reworded the question. 'What are you doing here?'

'We' – Paul gestured behind him to Jason – 'just want a little chat, that's all.' With the smile still firmly held in place, Paul had reached the top of the staircase. 'Shall we?' He gestured towards the front door.

Reluctantly, Marty dug his fingers into the denim pocket of his jeans and pulled out his door key. 'Can't we talk out here?' His voice had a whine to it and his hands ever so slightly shook. The last thing he wanted was to be trapped inside his bedsit with Mooney and the heavy-set man beside him.

'No, Marty, we can't.' Despite the smile across his face, the tone to Paul's voice was hard. 'So do us all a favour and open the fucking door.'

* * *

The inside of the bedsit resembled a pigsty, and as he was frog-marched through to the kitchenette area, Marty watched the men wrinkle their noses at the stale stench that permeated his home. He'd never been one for doing housework. He fully believed it to be a woman's domain, and as a result, his belongings were flung haphazardly around the room and piled up in the sink. Across the grimy scum-encrusted draining board, were dirty dishes covered over with dried remnants of mouldy food. Carelessly scattered amongst the dishes were discarded greasy takeaway containers. The congealed fat that had dripped down and across the plates resembled large white shiny orbs. Buzzing overhead, were several large black flies.

'Bit of a shithole this place, eh, Marty?' Paul raised his eyebrows in mock surprise. 'Not that I'm surprised really. I can't quite see you with a can of furniture polish in one hand and a feather duster in the other.'

'It's a good job he hasn't got any mates then, isn't it?' Jason added as he slammed Marty none too gently onto a wooden chair. 'I mean, as if you'd willingly bring anyone back to this shit tip?'

'Nah, you're right. Who would want to bring anyone here?' Shaking his head, Paul sighed theatrically as he looked around him. 'How about a cup of tea?'

'Really?' Glancing towards the plates and chipped, tea-stained mugs piled up in the sink, Jason recoiled slightly. 'We'll end up with a fucking disease if we drink out of those cups.'

'Yeah, why not,' Paul said, grinning. 'I'll tell you what' – he winked – 'I'll even make it.' He moved across the small kitchen, lifted the plastic kettle off the stand then, stepping across to the sink, he pushed the dirty dishes out of his way and twisted open the cold water tap. 'Do you take sugar, Marty?' he asked with a grin.

Marty looked between the two men and, stunned by this turn of events, nodded. 'Yeah, five, please.'

'Five?' Paul's eyes widened and he shook his head once more. 'Fuck me, no wonder you're so fucking fat, mate. You need to cut down on the sugar.'

'Yeah, I plan to.' Marty's cheeks flamed bright pink at the slur, not that he was going to argue the case. He was fat and there was no denying or hiding that fact. He'd been meaning to lose a bit of weight, and had even contemplated joining a gym, but as his old mum had often stated to anyone who cared enough to listen, he was big boned, and no amount of exercise was going to change that fact.

With the kettle now filled to the brim with water, Paul replaced it onto the holder and flicked the switch for it to boil. Leaning casually against the worktop, he smiled. 'You see the thing is, Marty' – he paused for a moment to light a cigarette – 'you don't mind if I call you Marty, do you?'

Marty shook his head; it was his name after all.

'You see, the pubs' – he took a deep drag on the cigarette, then blew the smoke out noisily – 'by rights, belong to me, well, to me and Jason over there.'

Marty looked up at Jason for confirmation, who nodded down at him in return.

'Legally, they don't belong to Lucas.' He held open his arms.

'It's an easy mistake to make, I know, and well, your good pal, Devan, he must have caught the wrong end of the stick, because for some strange reason, he seems to think that he can barge his way into my boozer and shout the odds.'

Sweating profusely, Marty nodded. 'That's right, and like you said' – his voice was thick with fear and he spoke fast – 'it was an easy mistake to make. We didn't know.' He looked between the two men. 'We didn't have a clue, in fact. How could we have?'

'That's right.' Paul grinned good naturedly as he continued to smoke his cigarette. 'Now, the little mistake that the two of you made, I could swallow, but to come into my boozer' – he stabbed his finger into his chest to hammer home his point – 'and then to terrorise my staff...' Screwing up his face, he flicked the cigarette butt into the sink and as it landed on a glob of fat, the burning embers hissed loudly. 'Well your pal, Devan, he just made the situation personal.'

On the kitchen worktop, the kettle had reached boiling point and a thick hot trail of steam billowed out of the spout.

'And then...' Paul sighed theatrically and shook his head as though Marty had thoroughly disappointed him. 'Then to top it all off, you know, just to make my day that little bit more fucking abysmal, I watch you, yes you, Marty' – he stabbed a stiff finger forcibly into Marty's chest – 'I watch you treating one of closest pals like he's a fucking no mark, like he's some kind of fucking cunt.'

Marty opened his mouth to speak, only to be stopped by Paul raising his hand in the air.

'And that, Marty,' he said with a low menacing growl, 'I can't and I won't fucking swallow.'

Calmly, he turned back to the kettle, lifted it off the stand, and then peeled open the plastic lid. The boiling water spat over the worktop and the hot steam billowed up into the air. Without saying another word, he turned his body and threw the steaming contents full-pelt into Marty's face.

The action resulted in carnage. Holding his face between his hands, Marty slid from the chair onto the floor, screaming and howling, whilst Jason, whose ankles had been splashed in the process, was hopping from one foot to the other.

'For fuck's sake, Paul, you could have fucking scalded me,' Jason yelled. 'A bit of a heads up on the situation wouldn't have gone amiss.'

Paul shrugged apologetically and, stalking forward, he stood over Marty's prostate form. Steam continued to radiate from his body, whilst his skin melted into the thin cotton. It was going to sting like fuck when it came to removing the garment. He guessed correctly. On the floor, Marty continued to scream a high-pitched wail, all the while, his head, face, neck, and chest, had turned a deep crimson. Already, large white plasma-filled blisters were beginning to break out across the scalded, nerve-damaged skin. He'd need several skin grafts if he survived, Paul surmised, not that he gave one iota about his survival. In fact, he hoped the slimy little fucker did die. In fact, if Paul had his way, it would be a real slow and painful death. As far as he was concerned, it was exactly what the bastard deserved.

'Stop screaming like a fucking tart and listen.' Paul kicked his foot out with the maximum brute force, his heavy boot connecting with Marty's kidney area with a sickening thud. The man would be pissing blood for weeks, and the thought made Paul want to smile. 'Now, I could have beaten you to a fucking pulp.' He clenched his fists into tight balls, all the while, battling within himself to keep his temper in check. Once upon a time, he would have thought nothing about steaming in and kicking Marty to death, but today, he wanted a message relayed and it was imperative that Marty was still alive for the time being, at least, to pass it on. 'I could have slit your fucking throat, but I didn't, and every time you look into the mirror, that's if you survive first, of course, you are going to see exactly what happens when you upset me.' He kicked out once more for good measure, his steel toe-capped boot connecting with a hard thud against Marty's soft flesh. 'And you have fucking upset me, Marty, make no mistake about that.'

He crouched down and breathed heavily through his flared nostrils. As he studied the blisters that had begun to break out across Marty's upper body, he felt no remorse, and why should he? The ponce had taken liberties and this was his comeuppance. 'You'll most probably pass out from the pain at some point,' he stated matter-of-factly, 'but when you come around, you're going to get onto the blower to your old pal, Devan, and you are going to relay a message, and tell him that he can consider this a fucking war.' He grasped Marty's jaw tightly in his fist, ignoring the shriek of pain that came from the man. 'A war that I will win. So let that sink in before you even think about coming near me or mine, trying to cause aggro in the future.' He straightened up, his voice taking on a cheerful sing-song tone. 'Have I made myself clear enough for you, Marty?'

Despite the agony that ravaged through Marty's body, he ever so slowly and painfully nodded. It was clear to see that he'd made a mistake by throwing all of his eggs into the wrong basket – a very big mistake.

Devan had been cruising along the Romford Road when the call came through. He slammed his foot down on the brake and did a three-point turn, all the while, screaming out a tirade of obscenities. 'The fucking bastard, the fucking cunt.' He punched his fist down on the dashboard, barely able to contain his anger. So Mooney wanted a war, did he? Well, he'd come to the right place. A war was exactly what the smug bastard was going to get.

The fact that Marty had taken a hit should have meant absolutely nothing to him. After all, his number two meant fuck all to him, and even more than that, he was replaceable, as was everything and everyone else in Devan's life. Yet, he saw the attack as a personal affront, a piss take, a slur on his own reputation.

Pushing his foot down on the accelerator, anger continued to build throughout Devan's body. Mooney, Paul fucking Mooney, the no good slag. At the back of his mind, a little voice niggled away at him. Wasn't this exactly what he'd wanted, for Mooney to feel the full force of his wrath, to know that there was a vendetta against him, to make him feel fear, to have him know how it felt to lose something or someone he cared for?

Reaching across to the glovebox, he yanked it open and took out a zoot. Placing the joint between his lips, he lit up and inhaled the grass deep into his lungs. He wished now that he'd taken Mooney clean out, that he'd crept up behind the bastard and shot him in the back of the head, instead of playing games and toying with him, and more importantly, allowing him the chance to retaliate and fight back.

19

Jonah was helping himself to a bottle of beer from behind the bar when Kieran walked into The Jolly Fisherman.

'Do you want one?' Jonah gestured to the bottle in his hand.

Kieran raised his eyebrows. 'Are you paying then, bruv?' he asked, taking a seat on a barstool.

'Leave it out.' Jonah rolled his eyes. 'What's the point of owning a pub if we can't have a beer on the house every now and then?' he asked in a low voice so their father couldn't hear.

'Yeah, I suppose so.' Taking the bottle, Kieran took a deep swig. 'Is he here? Dad, I mean.'

'Yeah, he's up in the office.' Jonah lifted the beer bottle towards the ceiling.

For a few moments, Kieran was thoughtful and, studying his brother, he cleared his throat. 'Have you ever' – he paused and began again – 'have you ever noticed how different me and you look?'

'What?' Jonah screwed up his face.

'Me and you' – Kieran swallowed deeply – 'how different we look.'

'Well, we ain't fucking twins, are we?' Jonah laughed off his brother's words.

'Nah, I know that.' He swallowed again. 'You look like Dad, and I look like...'

'Mum?' Jonah volunteered.

'Yeah, I suppose so,' he answered, his voice flat. He was quiet for a moment and began peeling off the label from his beer bottle. 'You're right,' he sighed deeply, 'I look like Mum, I suppose.'

'Are you all right?' Jonah tilted his head to one side. His eyes narrowed with concern.

'Course I am.' Slipping off the bar stool, Kieran forced a grin across his face. 'I'm gonna go up and see Dad.'

'Okay.' Jonah watched his brother make his way around the bar. 'Are you sure that you're all right?' he called after him.

'Yeah, why wouldn't I be?' Kieran answered as cheerfully as he could.

* * *

'What did I tell you?' Sitting behind his desk, a smug grin was plastered across Paul's face. 'I told you, Barkley was fuck all for us to worry about. Two weeks, and the snide cunt hasn't even had the bottle to show his face.'

'I already knew that,' Jason answered dismissively. 'He was nothing as a kid and is still fuck all now.' He chuckled lightly. 'Do you remember that night in the car park? You smashed the windows of his car and the little fucker pissed himself.'

Paul laughed. 'Yeah, I vaguely remember.'

'Who pissed themselves?' Walking into the office, Kieran smiled a greeting.

'Barkley.' Lounging on the sofa, Jason chuckled. 'Him and

your dad had a bit of a confrontation one night, and Barkley, the useless prick that he is, pissed himself.'

The smile left Kieran's face and he cleared his throat. 'Actually, Dad, can I have a word?' He glanced towards his uncle. 'In private?'

'Sounds ominous.' Paul frowned, then leaning back in the chair, nodded. 'Your uncle was just leaving anyway.'

Kieran smiled his thanks, and as his uncle stood up, he took his vacated seat.

'Well, come on, out with it. What's this all about?' Once Jason had closed the office door behind him, Paul picked up his cigarette packet, took two cigarettes out, and passed one across to his son. Lighting up, he squinted through the curling smoke. 'What have you done now?'

'I haven't done anything.' Kieran laughed off the accusation.

'Thank fuck for that.' Relaxing, Paul smiled and studied the boy in front of him. 'Come on then, son, what's on your mind?'

Hearing those words trip so easily off Paul's tongue, Kieran sighed and looked down at his feet. When he raised his head, he looked Paul in the eyes. He and Jonah looked so much alike that it amazed him how he had never questioned his parentage until now.

'Well?' Paul opened out his arms. 'I'm a busy man; I haven't got all day.'

Kieran chewed on his thumbnail. His nan was right; Paul was his father, no matter what. If he opened his mouth, confronted him, and told him he knew the truth, then nothing would ever be the same again. 'It's nothing.'

'Are you sure?' Paul narrowed his eyes, studying his eldest son. If he hadn't known better, he'd have bet his last pound that something was troubling the boy. 'You've not got something on your mind, have you?' He cocked his eyebrow. 'Has someone been causing you hag?'

'Nah, I'm sweet, Dad.' Smoking his cigarette, Kieran dismissed his father's words.

Relaxing into his seat, Paul smiled. 'I want you and Jonah to work the door at the Fiddlers tonight. We've got one of those celebrity deejays coming in. Should pull in a big crowd. By all accounts, they have a big following.'

'Yeah, all right, Dad.' Stretching out his legs, Kieran made to stand up. 'I'll give Jaden a bell and get him on board.'

Paul nodded and, standing up, he moved around the desk and pulled his son into a bear hug. It was unexpected and, unbeknownst to him, exactly what Kieran had needed. 'Are you sure that you're all right?'

'Yeah, course I am.' Pulling away, Kieran smiled widely and left the office. He looked down at his watch. He still had a few hours to go before he needed to be at the Fiddlers. He'd go and see his Donna, he decided. A sliver of shame crept over him. Ever since he'd discovered the truth about her and Terrance, he'd tried to distance himself, but even he had to admit the pull of her was too great. They had something good, something he'd never experienced before, and he was pretty certain that he loved her – a first for him.

Still smiling, he climbed behind the wheel of his car and, glancing up at the upper windows of the pub, he saw his dad was looking down at him. He gave him a cheerful wave and started the ignition. As he pulled away from the kerb, he failed to notice a nondescript navy blue Ford Sierra pull out behind him.

* * *

Devan was deep in conversation. Sitting across the far side of the room, Marty watched both him and his companion intently. Shifting his weight to ease the tightness across his shoulders and neck, he sneered. From his position, he couldn't hear what was being said, and absentmindedly, he ran his hand across his close-cropped head – the taut, rough, flaking skin that resembled yellowing fish scales still felt alien to him.

Plasma-filled blisters the size of his fist had broken out across his head and upper body. The pain from the third degree burns had been excruciating, and one of the larger blisters that ran from his temple to cheek bone had become infected. Day and night it oozed foul smelling yellow-coloured pus. The smell was as horrendous as the pain. The scent of paraffin ointment permeated from him. He stank of the stuff, yet it did nothing to mask the odour of the infection. It was enough to make him want to gag, and as a result, he kept his distance from people, conscious that they, too, could smell the foul stench that followed him around.

Two weeks had passed since his injuries had occurred, and in that time, he'd only once found the courage to view his reflection. During his hospital stay, curiosity had finally got the better of him and he had reached out for the hand mirror that had been left on the bedside cabinet. Just one quick glance was enough to show him the extent of the damage caused, and he had no desire to take a second look.

Mooney had been right about one thing. He would forever be scarred, a permanent reminder of his wrongdoing. A part of him wished that Mooney had slit his throat that night. It had to be better than being forced to live disfigured. His new horrifying appearance had even made a small child cry before being hastily bustled away by his mother. He looked like a monster and he felt like a monster, too.

'Marty.'

Marty looked up. In a world of his own, he hadn't heard any of the conversation that had taken place between Devan and his companion, Sean Matthews. He didn't like Matthews. Ex-military, he still walked the streets wearing Army green combats, and a permanent scowl was written across his face. In his early forties, he looked a lot older than he actually was. With short mousey brown hair and cold blue eyes that were constantly narrowed, a thick white puckered scar ran down the length of his cheek. He had a natural aggression about him that made Marty wary.

'We're on.' Devan rubbed his hands together and, sitting forward in the chair, he grinned happily. 'Ta-ra, Mooney, you fucking cunt,' he joked, mimicking Sean Matthews's broad York-shire accent.

Marty nodded. He should have felt happy, exuberant even, but he didn't, not really. The revenge Devan had planned out would make no difference. The circumstances would never change. He would still be disfigured; he would still look like a monster, and it was as simple as that.

* * *

Kissing the top of Donna's head, Kieran rolled onto his side, pushed the duvet away from him, and swung his legs over the side of the bed.

'Hey.' Beside him, Donna stirred and reached out to caress his bare back. 'Are you leaving already?'

Kieran nodded and turned back to her, giving her a wide smile. 'I've got work tonight.'

Donna frowned. 'Work? Since when did plumbers work at night?'

'I'm on call.' The lie tripped easily off Kieran's tongue. After their initial meeting, he'd not only told her he was a plumber, but also that his surname was Smith. Not for one single second had he assumed they would share anything other than a one night stand, or at the very most a quick fling. Now, all these weeks later, he supposed that if she was going to become a permanent fixture in his life, then it was about time he came clean, told her the truth, and more importantly, told her who he really was. He glanced at the bedside clock. 'And you have to collect the boys from your mum, remember?'

'Oh shit.' Noting the time, Donna leapt out of bed and shrugged on a flimsy dressing gown. 'I didn't realise it was so late.'

It was so typical of Donna. She'd be late for her own funeral. Shaking his head at her, Kieran smiled as he began to dress. 'I can come back tonight after work, if you'd like?'

Donna paused. 'I'd like that.' She flashed a grin and then continued to dress. 'The boys will be happy to see you in the morning. They keep asking me where you are. They like you.'

The knowledge made Kieran's heart leap. He liked the boys, too. They were good kids, well-behaved and respectful. Donna had done a blinding job raising them.

Once dressed, Donna dragged a hairbrush through her dark locks and spritzed a generous amount of body spray down the length of her body. It was a cheap scent and Kieran made a mental note to buy her some decent perfume when he had the time.

'Give us a kiss then.' Moving around the bed, Donna puckered her lips before leaning in for a kiss. Smiling, she used her finger to wipe away the sticky lip gloss that had transferred to his mouth. 'Suits you.' She grinned.

'Leave it out.' Laughing, Kieran used the back of his hand to double check the lip gloss had been wiped clean. 'Right' – he raised his eyebrows – 'I'll see you tonight.'

'And I'll be waiting.' She blew him a kiss and then was gone from the room.

As the front door slammed behind her, Kieran smiled to himself. The bedroom looked as though a tornado had passed through it. He pulled the tangled duvet up from the floor and haphazardly threw it across the bed before following suit and leaving the house.

* * *

Standing outside the entrance door to The Merry Fiddlers, Jonah was in high spirits. As a group of women passed through the doors, he nudged Jaden in the ribs. 'Wouldn't say no to her.' He gestured to the young woman in question, a leggy blonde wearing gold-coloured hot pants and a matching crop top that barely concealed her large firm breasts.

Jaden raised his eyebrows in return. Once upon a time, he would have agreed and enjoyed the banter, but seeing as he had saddled himself into getting married to Katie, he decided to keep schtum on the matter. Under the circumstances, it had to be a lot safer than the alternative.

'Where the fuck have you been?' Looking down at his watch, Jonah's forehead furrowed.

'What?' As he approached his brother, Kieran shrugged. It had only just gone half past seven and the main attraction didn't start until at least nine.

'We've been here for over an hour.' He jerked his thumb towards Jaden. 'You're lucky the old man didn't turn up. You know what he's like; he would have torn you to pieces.'

Kieran shrugged a second time. He was getting sick and tired of his brother's attitude of late. He was always whining, always having a pop about something or other. 'What the fuck is with you lately?'

'Me?' Jonah stabbed his thumb into his chest and chuckled incredulously. 'What's wrong with me? You're the one who was late.'

'Yeah, you heard me right, what's with you?' He poked his head around the pub door, caught Big Bernie's attention, and motioned for a pint of cola to be brought over to him. 'Well?' He turned back to his brother. 'You're starting to sound like an old woman.' He used his fingers to mimic a mouth opening and closing. 'Always fucking moaning.'

Jonah laughed even harder, and stepping aside so a large group of women could enter the pub, his blue eyes twinkled as he nodded after them. 'Bit of all right, them, ain't they?'

'If they ain't careful, they'll have someone's eye out with them knockers.' Wrapping his arm around his brother's shoulders, Kieran grinned good-naturedly. 'You know what your problem is, don't you? You need to get yourself laid, bruv' – he sighed theatrically – 'and the sooner the fucking better it'll be for all of us.'

'Yeah, all right.' Detangling himself from his brother's embrace, Jonah winked at the women cheekily. 'Have a good night, girls.'

'See, I told you.' Winking across to Jaden, Kieran grinned widely. 'He's like a dog on heat.'

* * *

If there was one thing that Cathy loved more than anything else, it was entertaining. Topping up Stella's wine glass, she replaced the bottle into the polished silver ice bucket, then moved across the kitchen to where the large American fridge was housed. Opening the glossy black and chrome door, she took out a carton of fresh orange juice and poured out a glass for Katie.

'I'm starving.' With her legs tucked underneath her, Katie sat at the table.

'You're always starving.' Passing across the filled glass, Cathy laughed lightly. 'How about I order in a couple of pizzas?' She glanced down at her watch. If she ordered them now, they should arrive roughly the same time as when Paul was due home.

'Can I have pineapple on mine?'

Stella rolled her eyes. 'Pineapple doesn't belong on pizza.'

'Yes, it does. Please, Auntie Cath?' Ignoring her mother's comment, Katie smiled sweetly at her aunt.

'Course you can.' Cathy answered with a wink as she placed a selection of takeaway menus on the kitchen table. 'Choose whatever you want, darling.'

'You spoil her,' Stella grumbled.

Still smiling, Cathy shrugged. What was the point of having children if you couldn't spoil them?

Twenty minutes later, the pizzas had been ordered and, sitting down at the table, Cathy happily listened to her niece chattering away about her upcoming nuptials.

'And so we are going to have a horse-drawn carriage, and I want rose petals scattered down the aisle. And then at the reception, we are going to have one of those big balloon arches. I was thinking of having rose gold for the colour theme, but Mum thinks pink or peach would be better.'

Cathy couldn't help but smile. Katie's enthusiasm was contagious and she found her mind wandering to her own wedding. On her finger was a square cut diamond ring. It was beautiful and she knew it had cost Paul a small fortune, but as he had told her when she protested over the price, he had waited more than twenty years to be able to propose.

'So what do you think, Auntie Cath? Rose gold or one of the colours Mum suggested?'

Cathy smiled gently, and squeezing her niece's hand, she answered, 'It's your wedding, darling. You choose whatever you want.'

'Rose gold it is then.' Katie beamed, much to her mother's annoyance.

* * *

By the time evening had descended, as was expected, The Merry Fiddlers was packed to the rafters. As a result, a queue of customers snaked around the side of the building awaiting entry. The atmosphere was jovial, and a ripple of excitement filled the air.

Bypassing the queue, a group of six men headed towards the door, and holding up his hand, Kieran shook his head. It wasn't unheard of for customers to push their luck and try to bypass the queues, and in truth, if they had been women, he may have just let them sneak in.

'Not tonight, lads.' He raised his voice to be heard above the music.

The words had barely left his mouth, when from underneath one of the long leather trench coats the men favoured, he saw a flash of steel. As if in slow motion, he motioned for his brother to move out of the way, but it was too late. As Jonah turned to face him with a familiar grin plastered across his face, a steel machete crashed down across his head, splitting his skull in two. As he fell to the ground with a surprised expression still emblazoned across his face, pandemonium broke out.

Without even pausing for breath, the men swung the

weapons forward in what could only be described as a planned and frenzied attack.

As they too went down underneath the blows, Kieran and Jaden had no chance whatsoever to defend themselves. Within seconds, it was all over, and as they lay bleeding out their life's blood supply on the dirty pub floor amid screams and chaos, the assailants had already left the scene.

* * *

Oblivious to what had just taken place in Dagenham, Paul walked behind the bar of The Jolly Fisherman and, taking two glasses from the shelf, he filled them with brandy. It was the good stuff they kept behind the bar, rather than the cheaper watered down version contained in the optics. Passing a glass across to Jason, he nodded towards the back of the property. 'I've just got a couple of things to finish up, and then we'll shoot off. Cath's just text me; she's ordered in some food.'

'Good.' Rubbing at his stomach, Jason grinned happily. He was so hungry that he could eat a scabby horse.

Together, they made their way up the stairs to where the office was situated, and as they ascended the steps, they chatted easily.

'Paul, phone call for you.' From the bottom of the stairs, Sue called up to him.

'Who is it?'

'What am I, your fucking secretary?' With a damp cloth in her hand, Sue bristled at his words.

Paul chuckled. 'You, Sue, are my godsend. What would I do without you, eh?'

Basking in his praise, Sue patted her silvery grey hair before passing the telephone across. A wide smile was etched across her face. If only she was twenty years younger... The thought was enough to make her giggle. 'It's Bernie.'

'Bern.' Still smiling, Paul spoke into the telephone receiver. Within moments, the smile froze upon his face and his skin had paled. 'How bad are we talking?'

He listened intently to what Bernie had to say and, forgetting that Bernie couldn't actually see him, he silently nodded.

'What's going on?' Joining Paul in the hallway, Jason mouthed the words.

Replacing the telephone, the hairs on the back of Paul's neck stood up on end. He wiped his palm across his cold clammy face.

'Well?'

'There's been an incident.' He looked around him, barely able to comprehend what Bernie had just told him. 'It's the boys.' He shook his head and dragged his palm once more across his face. His stomach churned, and as his mouth watered, bile rose up in his throat. 'There was an incident and the boys...' He could barely get the words out without wanting to wretch.

'What?' Jason asked. 'For fuck's sake, Paul, spit it out, will you? Are they okay?'

Paul shook his head and, slumping back against the wall, he gazed out unseeingly towards the bar. The sound of customers laughing and in high spirits was suddenly loud to his ears. 'It's not good.' He pushed his hand into his trousers pocket and took out his car keys with a trembling hand. 'It's not fucking good.'

Snatching the car keys out of his brother-in-law's hand, Jason dragged Paul towards the side door. 'I'll drive,' he stated. 'You're in no fit state.'

With the car keys held tightly in his fist, Jason hastily unlocked the doors and climbed behind the wheel.

'Cathy.' Paul closed his eyes tightly and his voice faltered. 'I have to tell Cathy; she needs to know.'

Jason shook his head. Placing the key into the ignition, he glanced sideways. 'Find out how bad it is first, mate, then you can let her know, once you know the full score.'

The bomb detonating could be heard throughout Barking. The explosion that took place was ferocious enough to rock the neighbouring properties to their very foundations. Engulfed in a raging fireball, there was virtually nothing left of Paul's car.

In the aftermath, and amidst the smoke and rubble that littered the pavement, in a daze, the customers of The Jolly Fisherman warily made their way outside onto the pavement.

Taking in the wreckage before her, Sue became hysterical. Instinctively, she knew that her bosses were gone. Just one glance at the tangled, twisted, burning wreckage that had once been Paul's car was more than enough to tell her that.

20

The sound of the doorbell chimed throughout the house and, leaping up from her seat, Cathy called out to her niece and sister-in-law.

'The food's here.'

With the money held in her hand, she pulled open the front door. The sight that met her made her frown.

'Can I help you?' As she said the words, fear clutched at her heart. It wasn't every day that the police turned up on the doorstep. Her Paul must have had a capture, a day she had always secretly dreaded. Instinctively, she knew there was nothing incriminating in the house. Paul may have been a lot of things, but he wasn't stupid enough to leave evidence lying around.

'Mrs Matlock?'

Willing herself to calm down, Cathy nodded slowly. She watched the officer remove his peaked hat and place it underneath his arm, and narrowed her eyes even further. No one had called her by her married name in years. 'Is there a problem?'

Police Constable Steven Brent gave a gentle smile. 'May we come in?'

Nodding, Cathy pulled open the door and looked between the two officers. 'What's this about?' she asked. Behind her, Stella and Katie had joined her in the hallway.

Looking past her to where Stella and Katie were standing, Steven took a deep breath. 'Maybe you should sit down.'

Cathy let out a strangled sob and, placing her hand across her throat, panic began to set in. 'Something's happened,' she shrieked. 'Is it Paul? Has he been in a car accident?'

Beyond where the police officers were standing, she saw through the open front door the bright headlights of a vehicle pulling up outside the house. For a brief moment, her heart surged, thinking it was Paul. Until that was, she remembered the pizza delivery. The second police officer walked onto the drive and sent the driver away. In that moment, she knew, she knew the police were there to tell her not only something unimaginable, but something that would shatter her whole world to pieces.

'No,' she cried. 'Please no.' She felt Stella's arms wrap around her, and as the enormity of the situation hit home, and the police officer began to speak, she sunk to her knees. 'No,' she screamed, 'not the boys, not my boys.'

Placing a joint between his lips, Devan Barkley was in the mood for a party. In his hand was a glass of spiced rum, and on his lap, a naked woman with short spikey blonde hair, whose name for the life of him he was unable to remember, gyrated her hips in time to the music.

'To us.' He lifted the glass in the air and nodded across to both Sean and Marty. On the sound system, Bob Marley blared out and he stifled the urge to laugh out loud. 'And to the demise of Mooney.' He took a long sip of his drink, rinsing it around his mouth before swallowing down the sweet caramel flavoured liquor. 'Fucking cunt that he was.'

Sean sat forward in his chair. In his hand, he held a bottle of brown ale. His sly, ferret-like eyes observed everything around him, a habit he'd acquired from his days of serving in the army. The bomb had been his idea, his masterplan, and the knowledge that it had been a success brought a sadistic twisted grin to his face. It wasn't often he smiled, but what the hell, he was celebrating. In fact, he couldn't wait to read the newspaper headlines, couldn't wait to read all about how clever he was for building the bomb that had ripped Paul Mooney and his passenger to pieces.

He swallowed down a mouthful of brown ale. The army would be sorry for kicking him out. Medical discharge, they called it, on the grounds of his mental health. They seemed to think he was unhinged, that he was some kind of a looney tune. No, they would be sorry. After all, they had let slip through their fingers a fucking genius.

* * *

Days later, the doorbell chimed once more, and as she wearily opened the front door, Cathy's mouth fell open. She blinked rapidly at the woman on her doorstep. Talk about blast from the past; she could barely believe her eyes.

'I never knew who he was.' Donna Cassidy smiled; it was a gentle smile that made her look a lot younger than she actually was. 'To me, he was just my Kieran. If I'd have known...'

'What are you talking about?' Cathy shrieked out the words and, narrowing her eyes, she looked the woman up and down. In the twenty years since she had last seen her, Donna had barely changed at all. Only the slight crow's feet around her eyes portrayed her true age. 'Your Kieran? Your fucking Kieran? He was my son, not yours.' Tears pricked at her eyes, and it took all of her strength not to break down in front of this woman, the very same woman she had loathed for the majority of her life.

'I saw it on the news. I saw his photograph.' Donna bowed her head for a moment to gather her thoughts before looking Cathy in the eyes. 'I didn't know who he was, I swear to you. How could I have?' she repeated. 'And, I don't want to cause trouble, honestly I don't, but...' She placed her hand upon her tummy.

'What?' Staring down at the woman's hand, and more importantly, where it was placed, Cathy's heart began to beat faster. No, please no. She wanted to scream. This could not be happening, not now, not when her son was unable to even defend himself, and more importantly, deny he had been anywhere near this woman.

'Cathy, I'm pregnant with his child.'

'I don't believe you.' Cathy gasped out loud and gripped onto the wooden door frame, feeling suddenly light-headed. 'My son would never.' She stopped herself. The fact that her boy, her Kieran, was more like his father than she had ever given him credit for was forced from her mind. 'No, he wouldn't.' Tears sprang to her eyes. 'No, not with you. With anyone, but you.'

Donna's cheeks flamed bright red, and she gave a slight shrug of her shoulders. 'Like I said, I didn't know who he was, I swear to you. If I'd have known...'

'What?' Cathy sneered. 'You would have steered clear of him? You wouldn't have tried to steal my baby away from me like you did his father?' She knew she was being irrational. Her boy had been his own man. He could be a stubborn bugger, too, when the mood took him. If he'd wanted Donna, then nothing she or Paul could have said would have changed that fact.

'It's the funeral, you see.' Donna gave her a gentle smile. 'And well, I'd like to go. I'd like to pay my respects, and more than that,

I just want the chance to say goodbye.' Her hand travelled to her tummy once again, and it took all of Cathy's strength not to lash out, to beat this woman to a pulp. It was only the fact that a lingering part of her son could very well be growing inside of Donna that she kept her clenched fists firmly at her sides.

'Please, it would mean the world to me. I loved him, you see. He just never knew that, at least I don't think he did.' She gave a shy smile. 'I never actually told him, and that will always, until the day I die, be my biggest regret.'

The sincerity of Donna's words threw her for a moment. To know this woman had loved her son so much that she had turned up on her doorstep, despite knowing full well the reception she would receive, was her undoing and the tears began to roll down her cheeks. They were never far away, always threatening to spill from her eyes, and she berated herself for that fact. She wanted to be strong, strong for both Paul and the boys.

She knew she must look a state. She had barely even pulled a comb through her hair since the night the police had turned up on the doorstep and told her that her whole world had been turned upside down, that they were gone. Her perfect family was gone, and with it, her perfect life. She couldn't even speak to Paul's mother, nor her sister-in-law. She couldn't bear to see the grief she herself felt written across their faces. And little Katie, she, too, had lost not only her father, but also the father of her unborn child, just like this woman on her doorstep had. She felt Donna's arms wrap around her slim frame and, clinging to the woman, she sobbed her heart out. Her babies and her Paul were gone, really gone, forever.

Twenty minutes later, the two women were sitting at the breakfast bar in Cathy's large spacious kitchen. In front of them were cups of steaming coffee. If truth were told, Cathy would have preferred a glass of wine, or even the whole bottle, but seeing as Donna's predicament meant that she shouldn't drink, she had automatically switched on the coffee percolator.

'Do they know what happened? Why it happened, or who was responsible?' Donna sipped at her coffee.

Cathy shook her head and turned to look through the patio doors and the sprawling garden beyond. She seemed to do that a lot lately, just stare into space. Before she knew it, hours had passed without her even having any recollection of the morning or afternoon she had missed.

'Maybe, once those responsible have been brought to justice...'

The words broke Cathy's reverie and she lifted her shoulders in a shrug. Deep down, she wondered if the police were even taking much of an interest. As far as they were concerned, it was a gangland killing, thugs wiping out thugs. So long as no innocent bystanders were injured in the crossfire, then what did they care?

'How could you have not known who he was?' It was said in an accusing manner.

Donna shrugged. 'He told me his surname was Smith. I thought he was a plumber. He even fixed my mum's leaking tap in the bathroom.'

Despite herself, Cathy laughed. 'He did a short plumbing course back in school.' She took a sip of her coffee. 'He was the image of Terrance though.'

'He was, but' – Donna paused before continuing – 'he was different, nicer I suppose. He didn't have Terrance's spiteful streak. He was just a really nice bloke.' She smiled gently. 'I'm not saying that there wasn't another side to him, there must have been, seeing who his father was, but with me and my kids, he was just lovely.'

Cathy nodded. It was nothing new to her; she already knew

her son had been one of the good guys, that he'd been lovely, as Donna had so rightly pointed out. 'Will you keep the baby?'

A wide smile creased Donna's face and her hand fluttered towards her tummy once more. 'Of course I will. This baby is the only thing of Kieran's that I have left.'

Cathy nodded and sighed gently. It was exactly what she had expected Donna to say.

'It's bound to be a boy.' Seeing Cathy's eyebrows rise, Donna laughed gaily and she pushed a lock of dark hair off her face. The action was both dainty and feminine, and for the first time since opening her front door, Cathy could see her son's attraction to the woman. 'I only seem to have boys, me.' She picked up her coffee cup and took another sip. 'This'll be baby number five. My eldest, Adam, is eight, the next one, Darren, is six, then, Connor, is five, and then there's the baby, Daryl, he just turned two last month.' She took another sip of her drink, her cheeks blushing. 'I expect you're wondering about the fathers?'

'It did cross my mind.' Cathy smiled. As much as she hated to admit it, there was something endearing about Donna. She was up front, and there were no hidden agendas. It was refreshing, and she liked that about her.

'Well, the elder three, they share the same dad, useless ponce he was. In the end, I couldn't wait to get rid of him. He even raided the kids' piggy bank once,' she said in a scandalised tone. 'There wasn't much in there, mind, only a few quid I suppose, but that wasn't the point. It was my boys' money. I knew then that I had to get shot of him once and for all, and the baby' – she sighed deeply – 'let's just say that his sperm donor was an even bigger ponce. I never seemed to have much luck with men.'

Laughing, Cathy wrapped her hands around the cup, savouring the warmth. 'And then there was my Kieran.'

Donna's face lit up. 'He was my keeper,' she said. 'He was

going to be the one, the one who I could depend on, if you know what I mean. I know he would never have let me down.' She raised her eyebrows theatrically. 'He would have never raided the kids' piggy bank for starters.'

'No.' Cathy laughed harder. It was a laugh she wouldn't have even believed she had inside of her. 'That is one thing he would never have done. Put money in, yes, but he would never have taken it out.'

Finishing her drink, Donna set the china cup down on the breakfast bar. 'I suppose I should get going. I left the kids with my mum and they'll be wanting their tea soon. My boys are a fussy lot. They'll only eat the finest chicken nuggets I'll have you know. None of that cheap crap me mum buys for them from the supermarket.' It was said lightly and Cathy wanted to thank this woman for bringing some light relief to her life. For just a few short moments, she'd pushed the misery that had become her existence to the back of her mind.

'Will you visit again? Maybe next time you could bring the boys with you. I'd like to meet my grandchild's brothers.'

'Course I will.' Donna gripped hold of Cathy's hand and, looking into her eyes, her cheeks blushed bright pink. 'I'm sorry, you know, about what happened before. I was just a kid. I didn't realise, I didn't even understand what it was like to love a man, and to be loved back by him.'

Cathy flapped her hand dismissively. 'You did me a favour in the end. I didn't realise it at the time, but because of you, I had my Paul, and through him, my Jonah.' She sighed sadly and placed her hand above her heart. 'And I wouldn't change that for the world.'

She felt Donna's arms reach around her, and she instinctively hugged her petite frame back with meaning.

'See you soon then.' Donna made her way towards the front

door, and as she turned back to face Cathy, she gestured around the grand hallway. 'The little sod,' she said, grinning, 'came from this, but never once let on. He seemed to love my little flat. Even the mismatched furniture and chaos didn't seem to faze him.'

Smiling gently, Cathy looked around her. She'd loved the house, too, once. It had been a real family home, but with her Paul and the boys gone, it was nothing but bricks and mortar, an empty shell.

'Well' – Donna opened the front door – 'bye, and I'll see you soon.'

Cathy watched Donna leave, and as she neared the end of the driveway, she called out to her. 'It's on Monday.' She watched Donna cock her head to one side, her forehead furrowed. 'The funeral; it's on Monday.'

'Thank you.' Donna's face lit up. 'I'll be there. I'll do him proud.'

Left standing on the doorstep, Cathy was deep in thought. She looked down at her dressing gown and ran her hand through her matted hair. To see her looking like this, so bedraggled and unkempt, would have broken her Paul's heart. Taking a deep breath, she closed the door, leaned against it for a short moment, then made her way towards the staircase. A hot bath, hair wash, and fresh clothes were very much needed, and if nothing else, Donna's visit had given her the push she needed to sort herself out.

Her mind wandered to the impending funeral. Just like Donna, she, too, would do her boys proud. She would make sure of that, even if it was the last thing she ever did. Forcing a smile across her face, she walked sedately up the staircase. Once the funeral was concluded, once she had laid her family to rest, she would get down to the business of finding the bastard who was behind the murder of her babies, and make them pay, she fucking would.

* * *

Standing in front of the full-length mirror in her bedroom, Cathy smoothed down her sleeveless dress. The black designer garment skimmed over her curves, and as she moved her body from side to side, for the first time in her adult life, she couldn't care less if the outfit showed off any lumps or bumps. Next, she slid her arms into a matching bolero jacket, and then, slipping on her black high-heeled shoes, she stood back to inspect the final ensemble. Her hair had been freshly washed and blow dried, and her makeup she kept to the minimum – just a touch of foundation and some mascara.

From downstairs, the faint lull of conversations filtered up to her room. She wanted to tell them to go away, but she wouldn't, not today of all days, not on the day she was going to say goodbye to her Paul and her two sons, her babies.

As she descended the staircase, her hand gripped tightly onto the rail, her knuckles turning a deathly shade of white. Reaching the bottom step, she took a deep breath then made her way towards the lounge. Pushing open the door, her gaze settled on Lucas. He looked broken, his eyes red rimmed, his face pale and pinched. She turned her face away, unable to feel any pity for him. Over and over again, she had wondered why his life had been spared. Why take Paul, Jason and the boys and leave Lucas behind? Still, it made no sense to her.

'Auntie Cath.'

Cathy turned her head and, seeing the tears roll down her niece's cheeks in big fat streaks, she held open her arms. 'Come.'

She closed her eyes tightly as Katie walked into her embrace. 'It's going to be okay,' she soothed.

'No.' Katie's voice shook. 'No it isn't, Auntie Cath.'

'I know.' Cathy swallowed down the hard lump in her throat. Of course it wouldn't be okay, nothing would ever be the same again. From across the room, she gave Donna Cassidy a weak smile.

'What the fuck is she doing here?' As she glared at Donna, Angie's booming voice was loud. She'd already been at the brandy and was, as usual, half cut.

'Shut up, Mum.' Gritting her teeth, Cathy looked over her shoulder to where Angie was standing.

'Well?' She looked around her for effect. 'Is someone going to explain to me what the fuck is going on, and tell me what this dirty slapper is doing here?'

Releasing her niece, Cathy spun around and, clasping her mother's elbow, she none too gently dragged her across the lounge.

'Not today, Mum, okay? Donna is here because I invited her, that's all you need to know.'

'You invited her?' Angie's scarlet-stained lips dropped open. 'After what she did to you, you invited that slapper here, today of all days?'

'That's right, Mum.' Keeping her voice light, Cathy hissed out the words.

'Have you gone stark raving bloody mad?'

Cathy nodded. 'Yeah, just maybe I have, Mum.' With those parting words, she walked away and, reaching Donna, she held open her arms. 'Thank you for coming.'

Embracing Donna, Cathy's gaze travelled around the room, her thoughts elsewhere as she wondered for the umpteenth time that morning if she had unknowingly allowed her family's murderer to step foot inside her home. Was the culprit here? She stared around her, scrutinising the faces of the men her husband had done business with. One of them, maybe more than one could have been behind the massacre. Her gaze returned to Lucas. Out of everyone, he had the most to gain; he'd been in partnership with Paul and Jason, and with them out of the way did he think that he had a sole claim to the businesses?

* * *

The funeral was a grand affair, and as the five horse-drawn carriages trailed through the cemetery gates, mourners lined the tree-lined pathway.

Five identical oak coffins were carried into the chapel and, clinging to Cynthia, Cathy could barely breathe, so acute was her grief. Following behind the coffins, she felt her legs buckle. Why? She wanted to scream. Why did they have to take her babies? She barely acknowledged those around her as she took her seat in the front pew, and balling a tissue in her fist, her eyes were automatically drawn to the five portraits that had been placed at the altar.

The first was of her Paul. The photograph had been taken at Katie's engagement party. He looked so happy, so handsome, and a fresh set of tears filled her eyes. There had hardly been anything left of him, once the bomb had detonated, and she hastily pushed the sickening image away from her mind.

Secondly, she looked to the photograph of her brother-in-law, Jason. He'd been a good man who had idolised his wife and daughter. She sucked in a deep breath before looking at the photograph of Kieran, her first born, her big handsome son who had looked so like his father. Tears were rolling down her cheeks. Her heart was breaking all over again by the time she reached the photograph of Jonah, her baby, her Paul's double, a big strapping lad who'd had his whole life ahead of him. Finally, her eyes settled on the photograph of Jaden, the young man she had known since boyhood. The fact that he would never meet his unborn child made her weep that little bit harder.

In a daze, she sat through the service and around her, she could hear the sobs that came not only from Cynthia, Stella, and Katie, but also from Jaden's loved ones. Hers had been a close family and she was proud of that fact. Her boys had been loved, and her Paul had been loved.

She turned her head, searching for Lucas and found him towards the back of the chapel. She watched his shoulders heave as he sobbed. Still, she was unable to find it in her heart to feel pity for him. Why was he still alive and her family dead? She wanted to scream out the words, to demand he tell her why his life had been spared, and as she began to rise from her seat, she felt a tug on her arm pulling her back. It was Donna. Smiling sadly at her, she shook her head.

'Now is not the time,' she whispered.

Cathy closed her eyes. Of course Donna was right. To cause a scene now would have been so very wrong of her. She glanced back over her shoulder. It would keep, and more importantly, Lucas would keep.

21

'Are you okay, Auntie Cath?'

It was early evening, and with the funeral concluded, the women had gathered at Cathy's home. Looking towards her mother, Katie raised her eyebrows. There was a tension in the room and the ticking time bomb that was Cathy stood at the patio doors with her back to them as she stared out across the manicured lawn. She and Paul had loved to sit in the garden with a glass of wine on an evening, the solar lights placed strategically around the garden, making it look both pretty and welcoming.

'Cathy?' Stella's voice was both loud and impatient.

Standing with her arms crossed over her chest, Cathy inwardly sighed as she slowly turned around and studied the three women sitting at her kitchen table. Still dressed in their funeral attire, Cathy had placed several bottles of wine and a carton or fresh orange juice on the table in front of them. It had been a long day, and as weary as Cathy felt, she highly doubted that she would be able to sleep any time soon. At least not without a glass of wine or two first.

'Was he here?'

'Who?' Swallowing down a mouthful of orange juice, Donna cocked her head to one side.

'The man responsible.' Cathy's eyes flashed dangerously, and walking forward, she held onto the back of the wooden chair for support. 'Was he here, in my home?'

The three women shrugged.

'We don't even know how many people were involved, Auntie Cath. It could have been ten, or it could have been one lone man, for all we know.'

Cathy flapped her hand dismissively. Turning back to the patio doors, she stared out across the garden.

'I want him dead. I want to see every single one of them dead.'

The three women turned to look at one another.

'Someone knows.' Cathy turned around again. 'Our men are dead, and someone knows why.' She stabbed her finger forward. 'Someone knows who they are, who was responsible. This would have taken planning, careful planning. It was no lone wolf. More than one person was involved, I'm sure of it, but behind them would have been the mastermind. I want to make him pay; I want to see him dead.'

White-faced, Katie shook her head. 'You don't mean that, Auntie Cath. Even if we did find out who was responsible' – she looked towards her mother and Donna for confirmation – 'you, of all people, could never hurt someone. It isn't in your nature.'

As she locked eyes with Stella, Cathy's voice was clipped as she answered, 'I wouldn't be so sure about that, Katie, if I were you.' She picked up the wine glass and chugged back the contents. 'Once that baby of yours is born, then maybe you'll understand how it feels to love someone unconditionally. My babies are dead, and as their mother, I cannot rest until the bastards responsible have been dealt with. It eats away at me.' She thumped her fist against her chest and screwed up her face.

'In here, it eats away at me like a cancer. My boys are gone.' Her voice cracked. 'It's driving me out of my mind. It's all I can think about. I want justice, I want vengeance.'

'I'm with you on that one.' Picking up her own glass, Donna raised it in the air. 'My kids' – she took a sip of the orange juice – 'even this little one growing inside of me, are my whole world and I would kill for them.' She made a slicing action across her throat. 'I wouldn't even give it so much as a second thought.'

Cathy turned back to face the garden. 'So are you with me then?' When she turned back around, her expression was hard. 'Each of us have lost someone, someone we loved, and I won't – I can't,' she corrected, 'let that go.'

'I'm with you.' Sitting up a little straighter, Donna looked around her and, noting the two horrified faces staring back at her, she threw up her arms. 'What? Cathy's right, our men are dead. We can't just sit back and do nothing.'

'Our men?' Stella snapped, her voice hard. 'This has absolutely nothing to do with you, and while we are on the subject, Donna, maybe you can explain to me what you are even doing here. You're not family; you're not involved in any of this.' She spat the words out with venom, her eyes flashing dangerously.

'She is family.' Cathy stabbed her finger in Stella's direction. 'Donna is pregnant with Kieran's child.' She ignored the expressions of shock that fell across both her sister-in-law's and niece's faces. 'And that makes her as much involved as we are.'

Reeling from the news, Stella's eyes widened. 'Have you gone stark raving mad? After what she did, are you willing to believe her lies? I doubt she even knew—'

'I don't want to hear it.' Cathy held up her hand, cutting her sister-in-law off. 'We both know what happened in the past,' she said, referring to Terrance and Donna's affair. 'It's old history, so please, just leave it at that.'

Stella raised her eyebrows. Her cheeks pink with indignation, she wasn't stupid. She knew when to keep her own counsel. Cathy, in her opinion, had clearly lost her marbles. She poured herself a large glass of wine and, lifting the glass to her lips, she swallowed down a mouthful, more for something to do than anything else.

'Someone has to pay. Are you with me on this?' Cathy asked, swiftly returning to the subject at hand.

'Someone has to pay? Have you heard yourself? You sound like a bloody gangster's moll.' Not one to mince her words, Stella's voice was loaded with sarcasm.

'Well,' Cathy returned the sarcasm, 'let's face it, I've lived as a gangster's moll for more than twenty years; we both have. This way of life is all we know; it's ingrained up here.' She tapped her temple to emphasise her point. 'It's what we are.'

'Well, you were obviously privy to more information than I ever was,' Stella snorted. Noting the seriousness that had settled across her sister-in-law's face, she went on to close her eyes wearily. 'Even if we said yes' – she traced her thumb down the length of the wine glass, stalling for time – 'I wouldn't know where to begin. How are we supposed to do what the police haven't been able to?'

A smile spread across Cathy's face and she snaked her tongue across her teeth. 'The police haven't looked in the right places. They can't see what's in front of their noses.'

'And we can do better?' Stella rolled her eyes. 'This is madness, Cath, and deep down, you know that as well as I do.' She jutted her chin in the air. 'Where would we even start, eh? Come on, you seem to have all of the answers.' She spread open her arms. 'So come on, I'm all ears. Tell me, where do we start?'

'We start with the one person who was spared.' She sat down

in Paul's usual seat at the head of the table and placed her palms down on the black granite. 'We start with Lucas.'

* * *

As far as Devan was concerned, Lucas had served his purpose. Earlier that afternoon, he'd mixed together a lethal cocktail of heroin and an opiate commonly known on the street as pink. He grinned to himself happily as he inspected the muddy-coloured liquid. He'd even given the deadly concoction a nickname: pink champagne.

'Got a little prize for you.' His manner was friendly as he waved the hypodermic syringe in front of Lucas's face.

Eyeing the syringe greedily, Lucas licked at his dry lips. He was pleased that the squat was empty, that it was devoid of the usual inhabitants. He wasn't in the mood to share – this was his fix, and his alone. His fingers itched to reach out, grab the narcotic-filled syringe and then plunge the needle deep into his bulging vein. He needed this hit more than he'd ever needed anything else in his life. It was only then that oblivion would come; only then would he find a much needed escape from the daily nightmares that plagued him, each and every time he closed his eyes.

'You did well,' Devan continued, his tone cajoling. 'You pulled off a fucking blinder, so think of this' – he flicked the syringe with his forefinger and gave a menacing wink – 'as a little reward.'

'Reward? What are you talking about?' Lucas tore his gaze away from the syringe and, cocking his head to one side, his fore-head furrowed. 'A reward for doing what?'

Devan laughed nastily. 'You served Mooney up on a plate. You see, I had to get his attention somehow, and you were the bait.' He watched the big man frown and dangled the syringe in front of him a second time. 'All I had to do was introduce you to this' – he nodded down at the cloudy liquid – 'and you, my friend, did the rest.'

'No.' Lucas swallowed deeply. Underneath his arms, beads of hot clammy sweat began to pool. 'No,' he repeated. 'That was nothing to do with me...' His voice trailed off and he closed his eyes tight, but he was unable to drown out Devan's words. It wasn't true; it couldn't be true. 'It was you, you killed them,' he spat. 'The boys, they were only kids, and you had them butchered.'

'Nah, man.' Devan grinned widely and once again, he toyed with the syringe held between his fingers. 'It was you who killed them. You'd do anything for a hit. You would sell out your own fucking granny for this.' He pulled a thin length of rubber tubing from his jacket pocket and threw it across. 'It was you, Lucas.'

Even as Lucas continued to shake his head, he was dropping to the floor and thrusting out his arm. He wanted oblivion, needed it in fact, now more than ever. In front of his eyes, he could see the faces of his friends, and then the boys, kids he had known since birth. He would never have willingly harmed them, never, even if they were what he'd considered to be a proverbial pain in his arse the majority of the time.

The tourniquet was tight. Somewhere in the back of his mind, he was aware of Devan backing away from him, and his heart began to beat faster. The anticipation was more than enough to send him over the edge, and his tongue snaked out to lick at the beads of sweat across his top lip whilst he waited for the familiar sharp scratch of the needle, the one that would tell him the oblivion he craved was close by, that it was near. He wanted to fly, fly so high that nothing would ever hurt him again.

Holding the needle just centimetres away from his bulging vein, Lucas screwed up his face in concentration. Sweat mingled with tears blinded his vision and he used his free hand to wipe his eyes dry. His breath came fast and his heart was heavy, as an image of Paul and Jason flooded his vision. They had been friends since boyhood, brothers-in-arms, and in his mind's eye, he could see the disappointment for what he was about to do spread across their features.

'You served your pals up on a plate,' Devan continued to goad.

Lucas blocked out the words and plunged the needle deep into his vein, and there it was, the sharp scratch he craved. All he had to do was push down on the plunger, and he would have the oblivion he so desperately craved.

'That's good, man.' Devan backed away even farther, his voice becoming distant. 'That's really good.'

'Are you sure about this?' Donna warily looked up at the decrepit building. If she hadn't known better, she would have fully believed the property was due to be demolished. As it was, it looked like a death trap, and that was just the outside. She had a horrible feeling that the inside would look even worse.

Pulling her hair up into a high ponytail, Cathy nodded. Paul had once told her that Lucas liked to frequent the squats around East Ham and the surrounding areas. After staking the property out, it had seemed as good as any a place to start their search for the man in question. Gingerly, she used her foot to propel the front door open. The splintered door had been patched up with plywood and as it swung ajar, the light from the streetlamp shone through to the hallway, revealing dusty, littered, wooden floorboards and graffiti-covered walls.

'I don't like this.' Pressed against Cathy's back, Donna whispered the words.

Cathy ignored her and, stepping over the threshold, she pulled a small torch from her pocket, switched it on and shone it around the darkened hall. 'This way.' She jerked her head towards the end of the hallway, and as she slowly moved forward, every inch of her being was on high alert.

'What's that noise?' Donna gripped Cathy's arm tightly, her eyes wide with terror.

'For fuck's sake, Donna.' Gently pushing the other woman away from her, Cathy hissed out the words. 'Get a grip. What's the worst that could happen, eh?'

'What's the worst that could happen?' Donna's voice rose a decibel. 'We could end up bloody murdered, that's what could happen, and I am pregnant, you know.'

Rolling her eyes, Cathy shone the torch around the hallway. 'Come on.' She jerked her head a second time and took two steps forward. In front of a wooden door they came to a halt. She looked over her shoulder. 'Are you ready?'

Donna swallowed deeply. She looked behind, checking that the coast was clear, then nodded.

Ever so slowly, Cathy eased down the door handle. The squeak of the rusting hinges as the door opened was as loud as a gunshot in the otherwise eerily quiet house. As she moved forward, Cathy held her breath, and for the first time since she had entered the property, she realised just how stupid her idea had been. No one even knew they were here. What if Donna was right and they walked in on an addict who was ready and waiting to pounce with the intent of robbing them for his or her next fix?

A strong odour of mould and dust hit their nostrils as they entered the room, and across the window, blocking out the moonlight, a threadbare woollen moth-eaten blanket had been hung. Cathy's shoulders slumped downward. The room, much to her relief, was empty.

'He's not here,' she said, stating the obvious.

With one last look around the room, they made to walk forward when the sound of heavy footsteps crashing down the wooden staircase stopped them in their tracks.

As Donna opened her mouth to scream, Cathy slammed the palm of her hand across her lips, her eyes beseeching her to stay quiet. Moments later, they heard the front door swing closed.

'Oh my God, oh my God.' Donna was practically hopping up and down, so acute was her terror. 'I thought I was gonna piss myself for a minute there.'

Holding her finger up to her own lips in a bid to quieten Donna down, Cathy ever so gently pulled open the door and peered around the wooden frame. 'They're gone.' She turned to look at Donna and burst out laughing. It was a real belly laugh, tinged with hysteria. Wiping the tears from underneath her eyes, she leaned back against the wall as she tried to catch her breath. 'Donna,' she cried, 'your face, you look like you've seen a bloody ghost. You're as white as a sheet.'

'Yeah, and?' Pushing past Cathy, Donna's back was up. 'Your boat didn't look too clever either, I'll have you know.'

Once Cathy's laughter had subsided, they made their way back out to the hallway.

'Do you think that could have been him, you know, Lucas?'

Cathy shrugged. 'Could have been, I suppose.' She looked towards the staircase and cocked her eyebrow. 'Only one way to find out for sure though, eh?'

'What? No.' Donna grasped Cathy's hand. 'No way, I'm not going up there.'

'Then wait here for me.' Shrugging Donna away from her, she slowly ascended the staircase, the torch lighting the way. On the upper landing, she came across four closed doors and, unsure of which one to open first, she gingerly reached out to turn a door handle. Over the years, the metal had been painted over and it felt chipped and rough to her touch.

The first room she entered was in the same state of disrepair as the main room downstairs. It was also empty. Slowly, she crept across the hallway and placed her hand upon the door to the second bedroom. The sound of a faint mewling stopped her in her tracks, and for a brief moment, she cocked her head to one side, listening before gently pushing open the door.

'Hello?' Her voice was barely a whisper. In the torchlight, she made out the shape of a bed and what looked like a bundle of blankets thrown haphazardly across it. She inched closer, her eyes straining to adjust to the darkness. The faint mewling she'd heard from the hallway had grown louder. It was a heartfelt cry, reminding her of a wounded animal. She took a step closer, fully expecting to stumble across a wounded cat or maybe even a fox.

The torchlight settled on a large form at the foot of the bed, far too large to be an animal, and she rocked back on her heels, in readiness to run from the room. In her haste to escape, she spun around, and as she did so, the torchlight picked up on a flash of distinctive blonde hair that rooted her to the spot. Within a matter of moments, she had taken in the scene before her – the sobbing, the tourniquet, the syringe. Her hand flew to her mouth, and as her heart began to hammer a tattoo inside her chest, the colour drained from her face. She would recognise him anywhere. It was Lucas.

As quietly as she had entered, Cathy backed out of the room and, looking over the banister rail, she called out for Donna to join her.

On hearing Cathy's voice, Donna turned her face upward. 'Is he up there?'

Cathy didn't answer. Instead, she ran down the steps, grabbed Donna's arm and dragged her up the staircase.

'Bleeding hell, Cath, have a day off, will ya?' As she paused to catch her breath, Donna's chest heaved. 'You're scaring me half to death.'

'In here.' She shone the torch forward and motioned for Donna to follow.

The room was in darkness, just as Cathy had left it moments earlier. Shining the torch on the large form at the foot of the bed, she inched closer.

'Lucas.' Her voice was gentle. She could see the fear in his tear-filled eyes, mingled with something else Cathy noted... shame. Turning to look over her shoulder, she raised her eyebrows. 'Lucas, it's me, Cathy, Paul's wife.'

His fingers were poised around the syringe and it took all of Cathy's strength not to run from the room. She'd always known that he was a user, an addict, but to suddenly be faced with his demons was downright terrifying.

'You don't want to do that, mate.' It was Donna who spoke, and in that instant, Cathy could have kissed her. 'What's it going to solve, eh?' Her voice was beguiling as she knelt on the floor in front of him. 'It's not going to make your troubles disappear, is it?' She shook her head sadly at him. 'The demons will still be there' – she tapped at the side of her temple – 'up here. It never goes away, does it?'

He was shaking his head and when he finally spoke, his voice was gruff and wavering. 'I didn't kill them.'

'Of course you didn't,' Donna answered, glancing up at Cathy with wide eyes, 'but I think you know who did.'

The tears came then, big fat tears that left him gasping for air. 'I didn't kill them,' he repeated, over and over again, like a mantra.

* * *

'Incapacitated?' Stella threw her arms up in the air. 'What the hell is that supposed to mean?'

'Exactly what I said,' Cathy answered. 'He's incapacitated. In other words, he's incapable of telling us anything.'

'Well, that's bleedin' great, that is. So how are we supposed to find out who was responsible now?'

The four women were sitting in Cathy's kitchen. In the background, the faint chords of 'Anyone Who Had a Heart' by Cilla Black were playing on the stereo, and all eyes turned towards her, waiting for a response. She had no answers for them. With Lucas incapable of giving them the answers they so desperately needed, Cathy's plans for revenge had taken a nose dive.

Over and over again, she had revisited the scene in her mind's eye – from the tears, to the tourniquet, to the syringe. He'd obviously known a lot more than he'd been prepared to let on, and after spending just over an hour in his company begging him not to jack up, they had finally left the squat with heavy hearts.

'He was scared,' Donna stated matter-of-factly. 'That man is so fucked up in the head that it's actually painful to watch him.' She paused for a moment. 'I've seen it before, you see. My elder boys' dad, well, he was a user, an addict. The bugger would swallow, snort, inject whatever shit he could lay his hands on. It got so bad that in the end, I couldn't even leave a bottle of aspirin lying around. I had to keep the kids' medicines in the washing machine. It was the only place I knew the bastard wouldn't look.'

'What?' Stella's mouth dropped open at the revelation.

'On my life,' Donna reiterated, 'it was an absolute living nightmare. Here Cath,' she said, turning her head, 'did you notice that the rubber tubing was tied around his left arm.'

Cathy nodded. If she was being honest, it was a scene she didn't think she would ever erase from her mind.

'And what the hell does that have to do with anything?' Stella snapped.

'He was left-handed.' Cathy swallowed down a mouthful of wine as she looked across to Donna. 'Just like Kieran was. We always joked about it in the past, you know, what a coincidence it was.'

'Exactly.' Donna agreed. 'Kieran was left-handed.' She mimicked the action of trying to tie something around the opposite arm she wrote with. 'Why would he have chosen to use his weaker arm to jack up?'

Cathy shrugged. 'He wouldn't, unless, of course, it wasn't him who tied the tourniquet.' She sat up straighter in the chair. 'Whoever helped him tie that rubber tubing wouldn't have known that, would they?'

'Oh my God.' Donna wrapped her arms around her slim frame and involuntarily shuddered. 'You know what this means, don't you? It must have been him.' She looked to Stella and Katie. 'We were in the house and heard someone come down the stairs. It had to be him.'

Stella thought this over and, playing with the stem of her wine glass, she looked around the table. 'Well, that's that then, I suppose. There's no way of finding out who was responsible, now is there?'

Sighing deeply, Cathy downed her wine. No matter how much she hated to admit it, her sister-in-law was right. Without Lucas's input, they would forever be none the wiser. The knowledge did nothing to erase the ball of anger that had settled in the pit of her stomach.

22

Manoeuvring little Chanel's buggy through the entrance door of a busy café, Keisha swore underneath her breath as the plastic shopping bags she had placed over the handles, became caught in the frame.

'Do you need some help?' Donna smiled warmly. She instantly recognised the woman. They had been friends at school, but over the years, had lost touch.

Keisha looked up. 'Donna?' she exclaimed. 'Bloody hell, I've not seen you in years. How are you keeping, mate?'

Despite the smile that remained plastered across her face, Donna's heart sank. How was she? How on earth was she supposed to answer that question? She felt dog rough most days and her heart ached for Kieran, so much so that she still cried herself to sleep at night.

'I'm good,' she lied.

Keisha placed little Chanel's buggy beside Donna's and sat at the table next to hers. 'How old is he?' She nodded down at Daryl.

'Just turned two.' Donna sipped at her tea and glanced

towards the door as it opened, bringing with it a blast of cold air. She shivered even though it wasn't particularly cold in the café. It was the anticipation, the hope that it could be Kieran walking through the door, larger than life. As daft as it sounded, she still looked out for him, hoping against hope that the past few weeks had all been a terrible nightmare, a mistake, and that somehow, he had survived the attack.

'Is he your only one?'

There was genuine interest in Keisha's voice and Donna shook her head. 'I've got three older boys.' She didn't tell her about the baby. Her tummy was still flat, and even as she rested her hand upon her abdomen, she wanted to keep her news quiet. In that moment, she wondered if Kieran was looking down on her, or if he was happy that she was growing their child inside of her. She hoped so. 'And how about you?' She forced herself to ask the question and nodded down at little Chanel.

Keisha sighed. 'She's the only one, and will probably be my last, if her father has his way.'

Sipping at her tea, Donna grinned. 'Like that, is it?'

Keisha nodded and, after giving her order over for a cooked breakfast, she turned in the seat. 'He didn't even want her; told me to get rid of it when he found out I was pregnant.'

Donna raised her eyebrows and glanced at the little girl. With light brown hair and deep blue eyes, she was a pretty little thing. How could anyone not want her?

'He reckoned becoming a father would ruin his bad man reputation.' Keisha lowered her voice and sighed. 'He's such a wanker.'

Donna didn't answer. She was actually at a loss for words. She'd always assumed that Keisha would have more sense than to get lumbered with a man who only thought of himself. Out of the two of them, Keisha had seemed to have a bit more nous about her. She'd even had a Saturday job in a trendy hairdressers when they were younger, which was much more than she herself had ever done.

'And like I said to Devan,' she said, 'if you didn't want kids, then you should have put something on the end of it, simple as that.'

'Devan?' Donna instantly recognised the name and she lifted her eyebrows in a quizzical fashion. 'Devan Barkley?'

'That's him,' Keisha replied as the waitress placed a steaming mug of tea in front of her. 'He was in our year at school.'

'I remember him.' Taken aback, Donna sipped once more at her own tea. What on earth had Keisha ever seen in the likes of Devan Barkley? He'd been a timid, acne prone, scrawny, scruffy kid, who as a result, had been mercilessly bullied throughout his school life. He certainly hadn't come across the way Keisha described him. In fact, it was quite the opposite. The Devan she knew wouldn't have said boo to a goose.

'He even chucked me and our Chanel out of the house,' she said in a hushed tone. 'We had to go and stay at his mother's house for a while, until the council gave us a flat over on Gascoigne estate. He's a bad one all right, the fucking ponce. The tight bastard owns a string of brothels over Stepney way. He's raking it in and can't even pay me a bit of maintenance for our Chanel.' She slurped at her tea and, glancing around her, she lowered her voice even further. 'Did you hear about that bombing over in Barking?' It was said with a hint of excitement, and her cheeks were flushed pink as she surveyed Donna over the rim of her mug.

The breath caught in Donna's throat, and as she nodded, she swallowed deeply, not trusting herself to answer.

'Well, that was him.' Keisha paused. 'I heard him planning it all out, you know, before he chucked me out of the house. I didn't actually think he would follow it through, though.' She took a sip of her tea. 'Just goes to show you, eh? You never really know someone, or know what they are capable of, come to that.'

Abruptly, Donna stood up. A sliver of panic spread through her veins, and gathering her up belongings, she could barely look her old friend in the eye. The way she spoke about the bomb, as if it was nothing, as though the murders were nothing, repulsed her. Her man was dead and the way Keisha was carrying on, anyone would think she was discussing something as mundane as the weather.

With the mug of tea held up to her open lips, Keisha sat up straighter. 'Was it something I said?' she asked with concern.

Donna shook her head. 'I've got to go.' She choked out the words and, rummaging inside her purse, she fished out some loose coins and placed them on the table. 'Shirl,' she called out to the waitress, 'the money for the tea is on the table.' Hastily, she pulled the wedged buggy out of the tight space where it had been parked. 'See you around, Keish.' She didn't wait for a reply, and as fast as she could, she left the café, her heart thumping wildly inside her chest and her mind still reeling.

* * *

Forty minutes later, Donna was climbing out of a taxi outside Cathy's home in Chigwell, Essex. Placing her son on her hip, she dragged the collapsed buggy behind her. 'Bastard.' Over and over again, she muttered the word to herself.

Within moments, Cathy had opened the front door. She took one look at Donna's face and ushered her inside the house.

'What's happened?' Her gaze strayed to Donna's abdomen. 'Is it the baby?'

Donna shook her head. She watched the older woman's

shoulders slump with relief and felt the first stir of tears glisten her eyes.

'What on earth is wrong?' As she cajoled the younger woman through to the kitchen, concern was etched across Cathy's face.

'It was him.' The words came out in a sob.

'Who?' Taking the child from his mother, Cathy sat him on a chair and absentmindedly opened the kitchen cupboard. She took out the biscuit barrel and placed a biscuit into the little boy's chubby fist as she sat down at the table. 'Who has upset you?'

'I was in the café, and Keisha...' She began to hiccup through her tears. 'Keisha, a girl I went to school with, she was my mate.'

Cathy nodded, trying her utmost to keep up.

'Well, she said her bloke, this Devan' – she hiccupped again – 'it was him, him that planted the bomb.' She cried even harder, her heart breaking all over again. 'It was him, Cath, she said it was him.'

Placing her palms on the table, a jolt of shock resounded throughout Cathy's body. She had all but given up on ever finding the culprit responsible for the murder of her family. 'What did you just say?' Her voice shook with incredulity.

'It was Devan.' Donna used her fingertips to wipe away traces of smudged mascara from underneath her eyes. 'Devan Barkley.'

'I've never heard of him.' Shrugging, she stood up and, moving across the kitchen, she switched on the kettle, purely for something to do while she thought the situation through. 'Who is he?'

'He went to school with me and Keisha.' She wiped once more at her eyes. 'He was a skinny kid, bullied mercilessly most of the time. He used to say he was Samson Ivers' son. I never really believed him at the time, I mean Samson was a face, wasn't he? And Devan, well, he was scared of his own shadow.' She sniffed back her tears. 'I just can't believe he would do something like this.'

'Samson?' Pouring boiling water into two china cups, Cathy frowned. 'We, me and Paul, I mean, we went to his funeral.' She thought back to the day in question. It was so long ago, she could barely remember the details, but as for the man having a son, she couldn't remember seeing one or any family come to that, at the funeral. 'Blimey, Donna, you're going back some years. I was pregnant with Jonah at the time.'

'Keisha said he owns a string of brothels over Stepney way.' She shook her head and took the steaming cup of tea from Cathy. 'What do we do now?' she cried.

Cathy was thoughtful. Looking down at little Daryl, she was reminded of her own sons at the same age. As she spoke her voice hardened. 'First of all, we find him and when we do...' Her voice trailed off.

Donna nodded, understanding the meaning behind Cathy's unspoken words. 'We're going to make the bastard pay.'

23

At a haulage yard in Leytonstone, East London, Devan was watching Sean Matthews intently. For all intents and purposes, and much to his displeasure, it appeared that Sean had loose lips. As his father had often stated, loose lips sank ships – a saying that had stayed with him throughout his lifetime.

Mob-handed, Devan had turned up at the yard where Sean worked as a security guard. That should have been his first warning right there. For all his gangster talk, Sean was nothing other than an employed lackey, albeit a dangerous lackey, with not only the mind of a genius, but also the morals of a complete and utter nutcase.

Sean, for his part, seemed to be unfazed by his sudden appearance, and was as usual full of arrogance. A fact that was beginning to royally piss Devan off.

He allowed the man to carry on speaking, boasting about his life in the army, how he'd killed in the past, and had literally got away with murder, time and time again. Devan almost laughed in his face. Hadn't he, too, murdered and got away with it, with Lucas Vaughn being his latest victim?

'You ever taken a hit?' Devan was grinning as he asked the question.

Sean narrowed his eyes and shrugged. 'Shot at? Yeah, course I have.'

Devan continued to grin. 'So you haven't then? You haven't actually taken a hit?'

'No, not an actual hit.' Sean crossed his arms over his chest, and for the first time since Devan had arrived, he looked around him and felt a ripple of unease settle at the bottom of his gut. 'What's with all the questions?'

Still continuing to grin, Devan pulled a small handgun out from the waistband of his jeans. 'What do you reckon of your chances?' He took aim at Sean's chest. 'If I was to blast you right now?'

Sean shrugged. 'I'd say they were pretty slim.'

'That's right. I'd say your chances were pretty low.' He continued to aim the gun. 'You see, the thing is, Sean' – he scratched absently at the stubble covering his chin – 'I've heard one or two whispers connecting me to that bomb and that's not cool, man. There's only one place those rumours could have come from, and that was you.'

Sean kissed his teeth. 'So what are you going to do, shoot me?' He glanced around him a second time and picked up on a nervous energy. 'Is that what you are planning to do?' he asked, his voice full of arrogance.

'You know a bit too much for my liking.' Curling his finger around the trigger, Devan shook his head sadly. 'And that can never be a good thing.' He smiled once more. 'Ta-ra, Sean,' he said, mimicking Sean's broad Yorkshire accent.

The gunshot was loud, and in the distance, several dogs began to bark.

'What shall we do with him?' Marty's voice shook.

Looking down at Sean as he writhed on the floor groaning in agony, Devan watched with fascination as blood spilled out of a small round hole in the man's chest. He took aim again and fired a second bullet into Sean's gut. 'Leave the loose-lipped bastard where he is,' he sneered.

* * *

Dressed in a black trousers suit, white silk shirt, and black high-heeled shoes, it took all of Cathy's strength to climb out of her car and put one foot in front of the other. Her instincts screamed at her to turn around and run, run far away and never look back. Purposely, she had parked across the street from The Jolly Fisherman, and as she walked across the car park of the public house, her eyes were automatically drawn to a patch of scorched concrete, the only evidence left from the car bomb. The image made her feel sick to her stomach and she swallowed down the familiar sense of grief that hung over her like a thick black blanket.

'Cathy, I'm glad you could make it.'

She tore her gaze away from the scorch marks and gave Darren Mitchell a weak smile before looking up at the building. Other than the windows that were still boarded up with plywood, the forecourt had been cleared of any remnants the devastation had caused. 'How does the inside look?'

Darren chewed on his bottom lip. 'Pretty much how you'd expect. The place has been boarded up for over a month.' He put out his arm and gestured for Cathy to make her way around to the side door. 'You need to get the locks changed, and the sooner the better. This one looked as though it had been tampered with.' He looked over his shoulder and smiled reassuringly. 'More than likely, kids trying to get in.'

The inside of the public house was pretty much how Cathy had expected it to look. Unwashed glasses were lined up on the bar haphazardly, the scent of stale cigarette smoke and beer filtered the air, and fragments of glass still peppered the upholstered seats and tables. She shook her head sadly. It was all such a mess. 'How long do you think before we could be up and running again?'

Darren nodded. 'Within a week or two, maybe.' He paused. 'I've been trying to get a hold of Lucas, you know, what with him being a joint owner...' His voice trailed off.

'Lucas isn't in the right frame of mind at the moment.' She shook her head sadly, knowing full well that Darren would have known of Lucas's drug problems. After all, they were hardly a secret. 'That means, right now, you're stuck with me, I'm afraid.' She smiled to take the edge off her words. 'Do I need to sign anything?'

He produced some paperwork and, glancing over the sheets of paper, Cathy added her signature to authorise the go-ahead for any essential work to be carried out. Once done, she slipped the pen back inside her handbag and tilted her head to one side.

'Oh,' she said casually, 'did Paul ever do business with a Devan Barkley?'

Darren screwed up his face, as if thinking the question over. 'Barkley?' he repeated back. 'Nope, I can't say that I recognise the name.' Of course it was a lie, a lie that Cathy immediately saw through. 'Why?' His voice was strained. 'Is there a problem?'

Cathy flapped her hand dismissively. 'No problem. Stella mentioned him, that was all, and I wondered who he was.'

Darren nodded. He was clearly rattled and it showed. 'Will there be anything else?'

'No.' Cathy smiled and took a second glance around the bar. Her Paul would have been devastated to see the pub looking so dilapidated. She held out her hand for the keys. 'I'll lock up. I still have a few things to do here.'

Darren hesitated before handing over the bunch of keys. He could hardly refuse, after all, she was the majority stake holder now – Paul had left everything to her in his will. 'Any problems, just give me a bell.'

Nodding, she waited for him to leave, then switched off the main lights, sank down onto a bar stool, and held her head in her hands.

Moments later, a heavy footstep across the polished wooden floorboards caused the hairs on the back of Cathy's neck to stand upright, and she snapped her head in the direction of the sound.

'Who's there?' Her voice cracked, and reaching for an empty beer bottle, she clutched it tightly in her fist. 'Darren?' she called out. 'Is that you?'

There was nothing but silence, and as the footsteps edged closer, she wanted to berate herself. Other than a light illuminating the hallway, the bar area was swathed in darkness.

'I said, who's there?' Her heart began to beat faster. 'I'm armed,' she shouted, 'don't come any closer.'

The shadow of a figure danced off the walls, and hopping down from the stool, Cathy braced herself. She raised the glass bottle in the air, ready to crash it down on top of the bar. The jagged edges would make an excellent weapon, one that she wouldn't be afraid to use.

'Cathy, it's me.'

The voice was so quiet that Cathy was unsure she had heard right. Her heart continued to beat a tattoo inside her chest, and she tilted her head to one side, her eyes wide with fear.

'It's me.' Moving out of the shadows, Lucas held up his hands.

Taking a step away from him, Cathy felt as though her heart was in her mouth. 'What do you want, Lucas?' She stumbled backwards, hitting the small of her back against a wooden pillar. 'I don't have any money.'

'I don't want money.' She could hear the hurt in his voice at the accusation. 'I'm clean, I swear to you, Cath, for the first time in years, I'm actually clean. I know it's only been a couple of weeks, but I'm determined to stick it out for Paul and Jay, I owe them that much at least.'

Looking past him, she tried to gauge whether or not she could make it to the door before he was upon her. 'Why are you creeping up on me? What do you want?'

Lucas shrugged and sat down heavily on a barstool, his tall frame large and intimidating. 'Paul and Jay...' He paused and blinked away the tears that threatened to sting his eyes, and across his face, the pain he felt was clear for all to see. 'We were best mates.'

'When it suited you,' Cathy sneered.

'I admit, we had our fair share of fall outs. I blamed him, you see, Paul, for something that happened years ago, but I was equally to blame.' He gave a slight shrug. 'I could have walked, but I chose not to.'

Not having a clue what he was talking about, Cathy gave a curt nod of her head.

'I heard you asking Darren about Barkley.' Lucas glanced around the empty bar, as if remembering the happier times, before fixing his dark brown eyes on her.

Cathy nodded, not trusting herself to speak.

'You need to be careful. He's a slippery bastard.' He gave a hollow laugh. 'Trust me, I better than anyone, know that to be a fact.'

'I'll bear that in mind.' Gathering up her handbag, Cathy could barely look at him. 'I have to go.'

'I mean it, Cath, watch out for Barkley.' Lucas's voice was serious as he caught hold of her wrist.

'If you don't get your hand off me,' Cathy hissed out the words, her expression full of contempt, 'I'll scream.'

Lucas smiled softly. As if anyone would hear her scream, not that he was in the habit of harming women. 'This isn't a game, Cath.' He released his grip slightly. 'Use me instead.'

'I beg your pardon?' Cathy's eyebrows shot up.

'Use me to get to Barkley.' His words were a plea. 'Let me do that for Paul and Jason.'

Screwing up her face, Cathy snatched her hand away. 'I don't need your help.'

'Don't you?'

'No, I do not.' Looking him up and down, Cathy scowled. 'Why on earth would I need your help? I despise you. It should have been you who died, and I wish to God, every day, that it had been you.'

Lucas's eyebrows shot upward.

'I know you, Lucas Vaughn.' Two pink spots appeared on Cathy's cheeks and her eyes flashed with anger. 'I know how much grief you caused my Paul. He loved you like a brother, and you threw the help he gave you back in his face.' She screwed up her face again, her voice hard. 'You had him murdered, you had my boys murdered.'

As his shoulders sagged, Lucas sighed heavily. 'You don't know what you're talking about.'

'Oh, but I do, I know everything.' She pointed her finger towards his face. 'I know what you did and I know why you did it. You want all of this.' She gestured around the bar and took a step closer. 'Well, let me tell you now. Over my dead body, will you get a penny more than what you deserve, not a single penny, and I'll tell you something else for nothing. My Paul was worth ten of you.' She looked down her nose at him. 'He was honest and he was decent, and he would never have betrayed one of his friends.'

Lucas laughed bitterly. 'He was honest? Did you seriously just say that? How the fuck do you think he got all of this in the first place?' He motioned around the bar. 'I'll tell you how. He played the game and won. He murdered and schemed his way to the top. What?' he growled, when he saw her face pale. 'Did you honestly believe that he asked nicely if he could buy the pubs out? No, he steamed in, using brute force and fucking took over, but all of this was only a front.' He held out his arms. 'As you already know, seeing as you think you know everything, a front for the real business, a business that Paul, Jason, and your boys were up to their pretty little necks in.'

Swallowing deeply, Cathy turned her head away. She didn't want to hear the gruesome details, didn't want to hear any slights against her man or her two sons.

'He was honest and decent? Don't make me fucking laugh. I take it he told you all about Mad Dougie and Samson Ivers then? And believe me, they are just two from a very long fucking list of men who he wanted rid of. Did he tell you that he was the mastermind behind their deaths? That he had them murdered in cold blood, just so he could get his hands on their businesses, their drug empires? All of this' – he motioned around him – 'the boozers, that beautiful house you live in, the cars, the holidays to the Caribbean, oh, and let's not forget the Maldives... How many times was it that you holidayed there? Five, six times? Well, they were all bought with blood money, and trust me when I tell you, that by association, your hands are just as bloody.' He shook his head at her. 'You know your trouble, Cath? You remind me of a spoilt child. Everything you ever wanted, you had in abundance. You're not stupid, you must have wondered how Paul could afford to buy the pubs, or didn't it matter, as long as the money kept rolling in?'

Cathy screwed up her face. The disgust she felt at his words was evident across her beautiful face.

'I'll tell you the difference between me and you, darling. I knew the real Paul Mooney, but you, nah, you only saw the man he allowed you to see. It was all a façade, you see, a front, a cover up of who he really was. Of course he could do no wrong in your eyes, because you never knew him, not the real him, but let me tell you something for nothing, Cathy. Grow the fuck up and smell the coffee for what it is. Your golden boy, Paul, was a cheat, a murderer, and a dangerous fuck. He wouldn't have thought twice of killing someone if they stood in his way. That' – he stabbed a stiff finger forward – 'was the real Paul, the Paul I knew and loved.'

Cathy blanched at his words. It couldn't be true, not her Paul. Oh, she knew he was no angel, that he was a rogue, but a murderer? She would never believe it of him. 'I don't believe you,' she cried.

Lucas sighed softly and slipped off the barstool, his large frame towering above her. 'Believe what you want, but I am telling you the truth, and sooner or later, your boys would have followed on in his footsteps.' He gave a slight shrug of his shoulders. 'If they hadn't already, of course. Just like Paul, they were vicious fucks, a real chip off the old block, you could say.' He smiled at her gently, knowing that his words would have stung. 'I'm going to go now, but if you need me, you know where I am. Take care of yourself, darling.'

Cathy didn't answer, and as she watched him leave the bar, she looked around her and exhaled slowly. In the darkness, the bar had taken on an eerie appearance, and she gave an involuntary shudder. All the while, Lucas's words rang loudly in her ears.

Samson Ivers. Had her Paul really murdered him? Her thoughts turned to Devan Barkley. Donna had told her that Samson was his father. Was that what this was all about, a revenge killing? Was her family dead, all because of something Paul had supposedly done over twenty years ago? It was a sobering thought.

* * *

With his feet up on the desk, Charlie leaned back in the chair and placed his hands behind his head. He not only looked bored, he felt bored. Turning to look at Darren, he sighed for the umpteenth time that afternoon. 'What are we waiting around for?'

Darren looked up from the documents he was looking over. They were in the Portakabin at Stratford, which Paul and Jason had often used as an unofficial office.

'What do you think we're waiting for?' Darren growled back.

'Dunno.' Screwing up a sheet of paper, Charlie tossed it in the direction of the waste bin. Much to his annoyance, he missed, which pretty much summed up his day, as far as he was concerned.

Rolling his eyes, Darren shook his head. 'Cathy and Stella...' He gritted his teeth. At times, Charlie reminded him of an insolent child. 'We wait and see what they want done with the businesses.'

'Never knew Mooney's missus was in the drugs game,' Charlie snorted.

'She's not,' Darren snapped back. 'She's not like that. She's got class.'

'Class?' Charlie roared with laughter. 'You after her or something? Wanna slip her the old one-eyed snake, is that it?' He winked.

'Fuck off, you prick,' Darren growled. If you asked him, Charlie, the cocky little bastard, had far too much to say for himself. He cocked his head to one side, his expression the epitome of innocence. 'How's your family?'

It was Charlie's turn to snarl. It was no secret that he was considered an outcast by his family, and was, in fact, the only member of the Wilson clan who hadn't stepped foot inside a prison, let alone served time, and that included the women, too.

'Look lively.' Placing the documents on the chair beside him, Darren got to his feet and jerked his thumb towards the car that had pulled up outside. 'Feet.' He swiped his arm towards Charlie, who still lay back in the chair with his feet up on the desk.

'What?' Crossing his arms over his chest, Charlie resumed his position with a smug smirk emblazoned across his face.

Stepping out of his car, Lucas took a few moments to glance around the vast empty plot of land. For the life of him, he couldn't remember what they had planned for it. Flats perhaps, or maybe Paul had planned to sell it on, who knew. He rubbed at his temples, not for the first time wishing his brain, and more to the point, his memory, hadn't been so fucked up by the drugs he'd taken in copious amounts over the years.

'Darren.' He entered the Portakabin and, glancing in Charlie's direction, took in his arrogant grin. 'Charlie.'

'We were just sorting out a few things, you know...' Darren's voice trailed off as he nodded down at the paperwork, before moving across the cabin and swatting Charlie's boots down from the desk. There was a nervousness about him that Lucas immediately picked up on, and he took a wild guess that his sudden appearance was the cause.

'Actually, we were wondering if we were out of a job like.' Stretching out on the chair, Charlie grinned. 'Taffy Robinson has already been sniffing around looking to hire muscle.'

'Taffy Robinson?' Lucas looked between the two men. 'You mean to tell me that bastard was here, that he actually came here?'

'Nah, not here as such.' Shaking his head at Charlie, Darren glared. 'What Charlie meant was that Taffy has made it known that he's looking to hire muscle, nothing more than that.'

Lucas visibly relaxed. He looked down at the scars across his knuckles and swallowed deeply. 'What does Cathy Mooney know about Barkley?'

Darren shrugged. 'Nothing as far as I'm aware.'

'She knows something. I heard her asking you about him.'

Taken aback, Darren opened his mouth to speak.

'I was in the boozer. I heard what was said.' He smiled sheepishly and held up his hands. 'Guilty as charged. It was me who broke in. I wanted to see for myself the damage caused. So, what does Cathy know?'

'What? You couldn't have used a key?' Shaking his head, Darren screwed up his face. 'I thought it was kids.'

Lucas held open his arms and laughed lightly. 'You think Paul would have actually trusted me with a key? We both know that wouldn't have ended well.' He looked away, ashamed by his past behaviour. 'What does Cathy know?'

'She said Stella mentioned him, that was about the crux of it, as you yourself heard.'

Lucas shook his head. 'She knows something is up.' He tapped the side of his nose. 'That's how women work. She was fishing for information.' He looked down at his knuckles once again. 'Problem is, she doesn't know what she is getting herself involved in. We're gonna need to watch her back. Barkley is a ruthless bastard and she'll be easy pickings for someone like him.'

'I'm not working for a fucking woman.' Taking his feet down from the desk, Charlie was incredulous. 'And I'm not working for a fucking skag...' Realising he'd already said too much, Charlie trailed off.

Snapping his head towards the younger man, Lucas snarled, 'I'm clean, have been for fourteen days.'

Charlie rolled his eyes. It was an arrogant gesture that immediately had Lucas's back up.

'I said that I'm fucking clean.'

An awkward silence fell over the Portakabin.

'Look, Luke,' Darren finally broke the silence, 'you can't blame us for being wary.' He opened up his arms in an apologetic gesture. 'You've got a track record, mate. Even Paul struggled to handle you when you were buzzing off your head, and that's saying something. So what hope do we have?'

Lucas nodded. He, better than anyone, knew the truth of that statement. 'That was before Paul and Jason were blown to pieces, before the boys, three kids, were hacked to death, butchered like fucking animals.' He looked at both of them in turn, his expression hard. 'That was before Barkley took fucking liberties and killed my pals. Now I've got a score to settle with him.' He leaned forward. 'But first, I have to make sure that Cathy stays out of his way, that she's kept safe. I owe that to Paul.'

Darren and Charlie exchanged a glance; it wasn't the first time that they'd heard Barkley's name mentioned in relation to the murders, only they'd wrongly assumed it was nothing more than a rumour, or idle gossip doing the rounds.

'Look' – Lucas opened out his arms – 'I don't expect you to trust me. If the boot was on the other foot, I probably wouldn't trust me either, but I have to watch out for her. I have to do that for Paul and the boys. Fourteen days,' he reaffirmed, 'even when I went to rehab, I didn't make it this far.' He looked between the two men, his face open. 'I haven't touched anything, not even a beer, which believe me, says a lot.'

Darren nodded. He had to admit that Lucas looked well. In fact, he looked better than he'd done in years.

'You're really clean?'

'As clean as a fucking whistle.' Lucas grinned.

'Okay.' Darren gave a long sigh. 'What do you want us to do?'

'Woah, hold up a minute.' Charlie held up his hand. 'How much are you paying us first? Because we don't come cheap.'

'You'll be paid.' Lucas chuckled. 'Same rate as Paul paid you.'

'Yeah, all right then.' Looking to Darren, Charlie nodded. 'But you had better stay fucking clean.'

Lucas kissed his teeth. 'And you, Charlie, had better remember who you are talking to.'

Charlie had the sense to look down at the floor. 'Noted,' he begrudgingly grumbled.

* * *

Stella sat back on the kitchen chair and shook her head. 'She's not doing it.'

'Mum...'

'No, Kate.' Stella put up her hand. 'You're not doing it, and that's the end of it.'

Leaning back in the chair, Cathy momentarily closed her eyes. 'She'll be safe.' She wiped away an imaginary crumb from the granite table. 'What's the worst that could happen to her? It'll be daylight, and there will be other people around.'

'I said no.' Stella blew out her cheeks. 'This vendetta of yours is getting out of hand.' She looked around the table. 'I'm sorry, but it is, and someone has to say it.'

Cathy's cheeks flushed pink. 'That's easy for you to say, Stella. You still have your daughter.' She raised her eyebrows. 'What about my boys, eh?'

'I'll do it.'

All eyes turned towards Donna and she shrugged. 'I know Devan; it'll be easier for me to get in and see him.'

Cathy shook her head. 'You can't, you're pregnant.'

'And so is Katie,' Stella reminded her sister-in-law as she nodded down at her daughter's ever-growing bump.

'I know.' Grasping her niece's hand, Cathy gave Katie a sad smile. 'I'm sorry, Katie.' She rubbed at her temples. 'I'm not thinking straight. Every time I close my eyes, all I can see is Paul and the boys' faces.' Her voice broke, and for a brief moment, she closed her eyes tightly. 'I need to do this. I want revenge, and I won't rest until I get it.'

'Let me do this, Cath.' Donna glided her palm over her tummy; only a slight curve was visible. 'I'm not showing yet. Devan doesn't even need to know that I'm pregnant. To be perfectly honest, I doubt it would even cross his mind.'

Nodding, Cathy used her free hand to reach out and grasp Donna's hand. 'Just be careful.' She glanced towards Stella. 'We'll be waiting with the car. Any problems, you scream that building down, and we'll be there like a shot.'

Donna giggled. 'It'll be Devan screaming. If that bastard so much as lays a finger on me, I'll kick him in the gonads.'

24

With purpose, Devan swaggered through his massage parlour in Stepney, East London. Underneath his feet, the outdated yellow and orange patterned carpet that looked more like a sixties throwback was sticky, and the stench of unwashed bodies and sex permeated the air. With a face like thunder, he made his way out to the back office.

He'd lost count of how many times he'd asked his manager to have a tidy around, or at least to get the vacuum cleaner out and run it over the carpets, but no, the carpet cleaner still sat in the hallway, untouched and covered in cobwebs. He scratched at an itch on his arm. Every time he entered the building, he started itching. He had a nasty feeling that they had an infestation of something or other, lice would be his main guess. The very thought made him want to scratch even harder.

'Monica.' He screamed out the name of his so-called manager, although the word manager was a term he used loosely.

Monica Jones was brunette, tall, slim and busty. Despite having nondescript features, she drew in a lot of punters. Why,

Devan had no idea most days. She stank to high heaven and that was saying something. For all her faults, though, she was popular amongst the other girls – a fair and natural leader. She took no nonsense from the punters, and when the shit hit the fan, she wasn't afraid to have a fist fight with a man twice her size. Brought up in the care system, she was a dirty fighter, and more often than not, came out on top.

'What?' Chewing on a piece of gum, Monica's scarlet painted lips opened and closed. Her teeth, which in his opinion had never been her strong point, were tobacco stained and crooked.

Looking her over, Devan shook his head. 'You fucking stink, I can smell you from over here.'

'Well, that's charming, that is.' From underneath the desk, she pulled out a pack of wet wipes and wiped underneath her armpits before taking out a second wipe and rubbing it between her thighs. 'Happy now?' she smirked.

Devan screwed up his face. 'You're like an animal, Mon.'

Monica grinned. She tossed the used wipes into an over-flowing waste basket and pointed a nicotine-stained finger towards him. 'An animal who makes you a lot of money, let's not forget that little fact, Devan.'

Together, they smiled, and as he took a seat, Monica perched her backside on the edge of the desk and lit a cigarette.

'That heavy you sent here last week' – she exhaled a cloud of smoke above her head – 'get rid of him.'

'And why would I do that?' Raising his eyebrows, Devan placed a zoot between his lips.

'He's causing hell with the girls. I've had to break up two fights this week alone over him. He's a handsome fucker, and you know what the toms are like. They're territorial; they see him as theirs. The stupid bitches can't even get it through their thick skulls that he climbs out of their beds and goes home to his wife and kids at the end of every shift.'

'See it as done.' Devan shrugged. It was no skin off his nose. In fact, he'd get Marty in for a couple of weeks. Just one glance at his scarred boat race would send the girls scurrying to their rooms without so much as a murmur.

Hopping down from the desk, Monica stubbed out her cigarette. 'Oh, by the way, there is someone here to see you. I put her in the back room.'

'Who?' Lounging back in the chair, Devan's interest was piqued. It wasn't often that women came to the parlour to see him, unless of course, it was a tom looking for work. He stared at her with hard eyes. 'It's not Keisha, is it?'

Monica shook her head. 'Nah, I dunno who she is, but she asked for you personally, by name like.'

'Well, go and get her then,' Devan snapped as he poured himself out a spiced rum and cola. Monica may have been a good earner, but she certainly wasn't at the top of the tree when it came to intelligence.

A few moments later, he heard her high-heeled shoes clip-clop back across the wooden floorboards.

'This is her.'

About to swallow down his drink, Devan almost choked on the liquid, and forcing the alcohol down, he rubbed his hand across his fleshy lips. He could barely believe his eyes. Standing in the doorway was Donna Cassidy. Despite her cruel treatment of him, he'd fancied her back in school, as did all of the boys. He could recall many a time that he'd wanked off to a grainy photograph of her. He gestured for Donna to take a seat, and then motioned for Monica to fuck off and take the wastebasket with her. It stank of stale fish and cum-filled condoms, and he'd already seen Donna, much to his humiliation, wrinkle her nose at the stale stench permeating the room.

He waited for Monica to close the office door, then grinned. 'Donna Cassidy, in the flesh. Long time no see.'

Donna smiled in return and opened out her arms to reveal a black lacy strappy top that showed off her ample cleavage. 'That's me.'

He continued to look her over. 'And what can I do for you, Donna?'

Lounging back on the chair, Donna crossed one shapely leg over the over. 'I would have thought that was quite obvious.' She licked her glossed lips and looked around her at the room, which held a desk, three chairs and piles and piles of paperwork stacked up untidily. Every available surface was covered in a layer of dust. It was more than obvious that a good clean was needed. In fact, the whole parlour needed a deep clean. Her shoes had stuck to the carpet, and she shuddered to think about what could have been the cause of the sticky white residue that covered the sofa in the room she'd been placed while awaiting his arrival. 'I'm looking for work, and I have it on good authority that this is the place to come.'

'Whose authority?' Dragging his gaze away from her bare thigh, Devan cocked an eyebrow upward.

'Oh' – Donna flapped her hand – 'you know how girls talk. It's always Devan this, Devan that. You have quite the reputation amongst the ladies.'

Satisfied with her answer, Devan grinned. He wasn't surprised. Let's face it, he'd shagged his way across half of London and he was good in the sack. He knew that for a fact and had never had any complaints in that department. He licked his lips as he looked her over. 'Why don't you get your kit off and come and sit over here.'

Donna's eyes widened. 'Excuse me?'

'Get your kit off and come over here.' Laughing, Devan patted his knee. 'We both know that you ain't shy, Donna, and I need to see the goods before I decide whether or not to take you on.'

'I don't think you quite understand.' Donna gave a weary smile. 'I was looking for more of an office position, you know, filing, typing' – she looked around her at the clutter and wrinkled her nose – 'that type of thing.'

Devan roared with laughter. 'What the fuck would I want with a secretary? This is a brothel, love, not a fucking office.' He relaxed back into the chair and laced his fingers across his chest. 'A secretary won't earn me money, Donna. But' – he licked his lips again and nodded down at the flash of thigh on show – 'what's between your legs will, and let's face it, we all know that you've been around the block more than once. You're already a pro' – he winked – 'might as well get paid for it, girl.'

Donna's cheeks flamed bright pink. 'As I said,' she repeated desperately, trying to keep her temper in check, 'I'm looking for more of a secretarial role.'

Devan picked up his glass. 'And like I just said, I have no need for a secretary.' He sipped at his drink, observing her over the rim of the glass through hard eyes. 'Did that cunt Keisha send you?'

'Keisha?' Donna's voice was high. 'Why on earth would Keisha send me here? I haven't seen her in years.'

He shrugged. 'Are you going to get your kit off or not?' He glanced at his watch. 'I'm a busy man and don't like having my time wasted by some stupid little bitch who doesn't want to put out.'

Donna began to stand up. 'My mistake' – she flapped her hand – 'I thought you might have need of a secretary.' She looked around the small space that she took a wild guess coupled as an office, come sex room, if the stacks of wrapped condoms thrown carelessly across the desk were anything to go by. 'But I can see I was wrong. See you around, Devan.'

Devan jumped up from his seat and, blocking the doorway with his hard body, he narrowed his eyes at her. 'What's your game, Donna?' He traced a calloused finger down the length of her cheek and spoke in his usual mockney Jamaican accent. She cowered away from him, as if afraid, and the knowledge was like a balm to him. After all these years, he finally had Donna Cassidy, who'd ridiculed him throughout their childhood, exactly where he wanted her. In the back of his mind, he recalled the cruel taunts that had been thrown at him on a daily basis, stig of the dump, being a particular favourite of hers.

'No game,' she said in a tight voice. 'Like I said, I thought you might have need of a secretary.'

Taking a deep toke on his joint, he blew the smoke noisily into her face. 'I'm not the kind of man to mess with, Donna.' Gone was the smile he'd afforded her when she'd first arrived. 'Now what the fuck are you really doing here?'

Donna licked at her lips. Resisting the urge to gag at the pungent scent of the cannabis, she swallowed deeply. 'I'm looking for work, that's all.' He was so close that Donna could see the tiny threaded veins in the whites of his eyes. 'Why else would I be here?'

Still staring at her, Devan wrapped a lock of her dark hair around his forefinger. 'Are you sure you don't want to get your kit off? I've got men who'd pay a lot of money for a woman like you.'

'No.' Shaking her head vigorously, she took the opportunity to slip underneath his arm and practically ran towards the exit. 'See you around, Devan,' she called out as cheerfully as she could.

With his eyes still narrowed, Devan watched her go. He'd bet his life on it that there was more to the sudden appearance of

Donna Cassidy than met the eye, or his name wasn't Devan Barkley.

Her hands still shaking, Donna climbed into Cathy's car.

'Well?' Turning in her seat, Cathy looked the younger woman over.

'It's him all right.' She held up her hand to reveal the tremor there. 'I don't know how I managed to stay so calm.' She screwed up her face. 'That bastard killed my Kieran, I know it was him, and I won't, I can't, forgive or forget something like that.'

'What if it wasn't him though?' Katie's voice was small and, clutching her mother's hand, her face was white and pinched. 'What if we kill an innocent man?'

Cathy thought this through. She knew for a fact that if what Lucas had told her was true about him being Samson's son, then Devan had a motive, and looking towards Donna, she raised her eyebrows expectantly.

'It was him.' Donna's face was hard. 'When Keisha first told me, I admit I found it hard to believe. The Devan I knew was a scrawny, scruffy little kid, but him' – she nodded towards the brothel and screwed up her face again – 'there's something about him. You can see it in his eyes, in his demeaner. He's bad to the bone; he did this. He killed our men; I know he did.'

Turning in her seat, Cathy studied the building and took note of the entry and exit points. 'How many are in there?'

Donna pursed her lips. 'I saw at least seven toms and then there's the manager, Monica something or other, a right hard-nosed bitch, she was an' all.' She nodded. 'She's the one we have to watch out for.'

'In that case, we take her out first.' Cathy continued to watch the brothel. 'Any cameras in there?'

'Not that I could see. It's a brothel. He wouldn't be that stupid and put up cameras, would he? I mean, it's hardly legal, is it?'

Cathy shrugged. 'I doubt he cares very much about that.' She looked up at the nearby street lamps. It stood to reason there would be CCTV in operation, cameras were everywhere these days. 'We need to make sure that we won't be identified – dark clothing, something to cover our faces.'

From the back seat, Stella shook her head. 'Cover our faces? You're taking this a bit too far now, aren't you, Cath? I mean' – she looked around her – 'we're not really going to go through with this, are we?'

'What is your problem, Stella?' Cathy turned in the seat, her expression thunderous. 'Your man is dead. Jason, remember him? Your husband, the man you supposedly' – she lifted her fingers, using them as quotation marks – 'loved.'

'Of course I loved him,' Stella spat back.

'Well then, grow a fucking back bone.' She turned back to face the windscreen and pointed towards the brothel, her voice a lot softer than it had been previously. 'The man who killed our family is in there. Are you going to sit idly by and do nothing?'

'We could always phone the police,' Katie volunteered.

Cathy laughed. It was a nasty cackle that resounded around the car. 'What, and let him get away with a slap on the wrist? No, I don't think so.'

Katie shrugged and, placing her hand on her bump, she looked at her mother with frightened eyes.

'Thanks to him' – Cathy jerked her thumb towards the building – 'your baby will never know his or her father. Where's your loyalty, Katie? You were so close to your cousins and you caused fucking ructions to be with Jaden, and what, now that they're gone, dead, it's a case of out of sight out of mind?'

As Katie shook her head, tears slipped down her cheeks. 'Of course not.'

'Well then, you know as well as I do that we have to do this.' Resuming her position, Cathy gave the brothel one final long look, before starting the ignition. 'With or without you, he is going to pay,' she muttered to no one in particular.

Leaning back in the seat, Charlie rested one hand on the steering wheel, while his free hand held a mobile phone to his ear. Having watched the little brunette climb into Cathy Mooney's car, he relayed the women's movements back to Lucas and Darren. Even he could see that they were in over their heads, and as Lucas had stated, Devan Barkley was a slippery bastard with the morals of a complete and utter cunt, and that was putting it mildly.

Ending the call, he tossed the phone onto the passenger's seat and started the ignition. From a safe distance, he trailed Cathy's car, just as he'd done every day this week.

Slamming down the telephone, Lucas was incensed.

'Just what the fuck is she playing at?'

'Fuck knows.' Darren shook his head, incredulous. 'Surely, she can't be in cahoots with Barkley.'

Lucas raised his eyebrows at the slur. 'Of course she fucking isn't.' He stood up, walked the length of the Portakabin, and placed his hands on the far wall, his strong arms taking his weight while he thought the situation through. 'She's going after him.' He spun around, his dark brown eyes wide with disbelief. 'She's actually going after Barkley.'

Darren screwed up his face. The very thought of a woman taking on a man like Barkley, and coming out on top, was laughable. It just didn't happen in their world. 'He'll crush her and laugh while doing it.'

'The stupid, stupid mare.' Slumping down on a chair, Lucas laughed in disbelief. 'She can't be fucking serious. She can't think that she can take him on and win.'

Shrugging, Darren blew out his cheeks. 'You need to warn her off. You have to stop her, mate.'

Lucas raised his eyebrows. That was a lot easier said than done. Darren didn't know Cathy like he did, and it was safe to say that there was no love lost on her part.

Marty was sulking. Once upon a time, he would have rubbed his hands together with glee at the opportunity to work the brothels, but that was before – before Mooney had turned him into the monster that he was today.

After safely manoeuvring his way into the back office with only the bare minimum of girls seeing his scarred face, he closed the door behind him, sat down heavily behind the desk, held his head in his hands, and wept at the unfairness of his life.

A scream resonated throughout the house. Gripping onto the desk so tight that his fingertips turned deathly white, Marty froze. He couldn't deal with the problem, couldn't leave the office, couldn't let anyone see his disfigurement.

'Marty.' Out of breath, Monica slammed open the door to the office. 'That's your cue to get off your fat arse and see what the problem is.' She jerked her thumb behind her to where the scream had originated from.

Still, he didn't move and, throwing up her hands, she stormed through the house. 'Jesus fucking wept,' she shouted out at the top of her voice. 'So much for a fucking heavy. You just wait until I tell Devan about this.'

Marty wept even harder.

25

Angie eyed the wad of money that had been placed on her kitchen table wearily.

'There's five hundred nicker there, and once you've been to see Cathy, there's another fifteen hundred waiting for you.' Lucas pulled a large bundle of cash from his jacket pocket.

'And why can't you go and see Cathy yourself?' Tearing her gaze away from the money, Angie raised an eyebrow.

Slipping the money back into his pocket, Lucas shrugged. 'I doubt she would see me, to be honest, but you being her mother, you shouldn't have any trouble getting into the house.'

Still eyeing the money, Angie sighed. 'She won't listen to me. Nothing I say to her will cloud her judgement when it comes to Paul. The girl was besotted with the man, you know that as well as I do.'

'Have you heard of a man named Devan Barkley?' Lucas leaned across the table.

'Can't say that I have.' Pursing her lips, Angie looked away.

'How about his mother, Cristiana Barkley? She was a friend of Samson's, and I use that term loosely.'

Angie snapped her head towards him. 'Of course I've heard of her,' she snarled, 'the slut. I had to sit back and watch that woman throw herself at him, night after night.'

'Then you will know that Devan is her and Samson's son?'

'Can't say that I knew.' Angie swallowed deeply. It was a lie, and they were both well aware of that fact.

'Well, Cathy has managed to get herself involved with him.'

'What on earth for?' Sitting upright, Angie was aghast. 'Why would she have anything to do with Devan?' She paused and her eyes widened. 'You don't mean romantically, do you? I mean, her and him?' She pressed her forefingers together to emphasise her point.

'Would make my job a lot easier if she was,' Lucas muttered underneath his breath. He rubbed at his temples. 'She believes that Devan killed Paul and the boys.'

Angie recoiled. 'And did he?'

Lucas shrugged. 'The point is, Devan believes that Paul killed his father, Samson.' He spread open his arms. 'An eye for an eye springs to mind. Why the fuck he waited this long to act out his revenge fuck only knows; Samson's been dead for over twenty years. Maybe,' he sighed, 'it was the ultimate way to hurt Paul by taking out the boys first.'

'Huh,' Angie snorted. 'I should have known that Paul would be at the root of all this upset.' She eyed Lucas across the table. 'I always knew it was him, that he was involved in my Samson's murder.'

Lucas nodded. 'And I also know that Samson was Cathy's father. Paul told me, and apparently Samson had told him.'

'And the only person who doesn't know is Cathy,' Angie sighed.

'And that, Angie, is where you come in.' He tapped the bundle of cash. 'I want you to tell her.'

'Me?' She poked herself in the chest. 'Why would I do that?'

'Because if you don't, Cathy is going to find herself in a lot of trouble. Her life is in danger and I can't allow anything to happen to her. She'll listen to you. All you have to do is tell her that Devan is her half-brother; it might be enough to stop her from making the biggest mistake of her life.' His voice became hard. 'Five hundred now,' he reminded her, 'and another fifteen hundred once you've told her.'

Angie eyed up the money. She could do a lot with two thousand pounds – endless bingo trips, nights out at the pub, and for once in her life, she would actually be flush. 'Go on then,' she said, 'I'll do it.'

Lucas smiled. 'I had a feeling you would say that.'

The quip was not lost on Angie.

26

Angie was put out and it showed. She had decided to pay a visit to her daughter and was shocked to discover that she already had a house full of guests. Well, since Cathy was now in the right frame of mind to see visitors, where was her invite? Surely, she should have had some sort of precedence over her daughter's in-laws. After all, she was her mother.

'Mum.' Cathy hastily kissed her mother's powdery cheek and ushered her out to the garden.

Looking around her, Angie nodded at the women. 'I'm not intruding, am I?' she asked innocently.

Cathy laughed; it sounded flat to Angie's ears. 'Don't be daft, Mum. Take a seat.'

Angie did as she was asked, although it didn't escape her notice that the women had become unusually quiet. She'd bet her last penny that she had interrupted something. What that was though, she didn't have a clue.

'Are you my nan?' A little boy of about five tugged at the hem of her leather skirt.

Both Cathy and Donna sniggered.

'Come away, Connor.' Still laughing, Donna dragged her son away. 'Angie isn't your nan, and you know full well she isn't.'

'She looks like my nan,' Connor answered, with only the innocence children have. 'She's old like Nanny Von.'

Angie bristled at the remark. To be called old was one thing, but to be told she looked like Yvonne Cassidy was a downright insult, and she poked her tongue out at the child.

'Take no notice, Mum.' Winking across to Donna, Cathy stifled the urge to laugh; Angie wasn't the type of woman to grow old gracefully. 'You don't look a day over sixty.'

Angie looked up at her daughter with a steely glint in her eyes. 'Well, that's charming, that is,' she spat.

Thrusting a glass of wine into her mother's hands, Cathy smiled. 'It was a joke,' she said, 'that's all.' She nodded at the women. 'You know everyone here, don't you?'

'I do.' Angie's answer was crisp as her eyes settled on Donna. 'Some better than others.'

Cathy raised her eyebrows. 'Not today, Mum, please.'

Sipping at her wine, Angie sighed. Her daughter was one touchy so and so, and she wondered briefly where she had inherited that particular trait from, because it sure as hell wasn't from her.

'Who would like a top up?' Collecting the empty wine bottle from the patio table, Cathy smiled at the women.

'I would.' Holding out her empty wine glass, Stella stretched out her slim body on a sun lounger. 'This is the life, eh, Ange?'

Nodding, Angie followed her daughter into the kitchen and, leaning back against the worktop, she looked around her. No wonder the kitchen was her daughter's pride and joy. It was beautiful, all black granite and chrome, truly stunning.

'You know, Cath, you're a good girl, and I'm proud of how you turned out.'

Cathy laughed lightly. 'Leave it out, Mum,' she said as she collected a chilled bottle of wine from the American fridge.

'No, I'm being serious. I'm proud of you.' Angie clasped her daughter's hand in hers. 'I wasn't there for you when you were growing up.' She looked down at the floor. 'Not like a real mum should be.'

Eyeing her mother suspiciously, Cathy lowered her voice. 'What's brought this on, Mum? You're not ill, are you?'

'No, of course I'm bleeding well not.' She flapped her hand dismissively and reached out for her wine glass. 'It's just, well... your dad.'

Cathy's breath caught in her chest. 'What about him?' It was the first time Angie had ever mentioned her father, and a ripple of unease flowed through her body. 'I don't want to see him, Mum, not now, not after all these years.'

Angie laughed softly. 'Would be a bit bleeding hard, love. The poor bugger has been dead for twenty years.'

'Then why bring him up now?' Cathy screwed up her face. 'I've done all right this far, not knowing who he is.'

'It's the thought of those kiddies' – she nodded towards the garden to where Donna and Katie were sitting – 'two innocent fatherless babies, and well, it made me realise you had been fatherless, too.'

Cathy narrowed her eyes, watching as Angie gulped at her wine.

'I should have told you who he was.' She shook her head. 'I don't even know why I didn't, really. He didn't want me to, I suppose. He didn't want it made common knowledge, but I should have insisted, I can see that now.' She shrugged. 'I can see the error of my ways.'

'Mum.'

'No.' Angie held up her hand. 'I need to get it off my chest. I need you to know where you came from, darling.'

'Go on then.' Cathy swallowed deeply. All of a sudden, her throat felt dry and she wished she'd had the sense to pour herself out a tumbler of alcohol. She had a sinking feeling that she was going to need a stiff drink of some sort.

'I loved him, just know that; it's important, Cath. I really loved him, and I like to think that he loved me, too, in his own way.' She shrugged again. It was a lie she had told herself so many times over the years. Deep down, she knew that Samson had never had any real feelings for her, not really. She sucked in her bottom lip. 'He was murdered, and—'

'Murdered?' Cathy's mind reeled. 'How? Why?'

Angie shook her head dismissively. The why's weren't important. 'I think it was your Paul.' She clutched Cathy's hand. 'I think that he killed him.'

Snatching her hand away, Cathy recoiled away from her mother. 'What did you just say?'

'Paul.' Angie sighed. 'I think he killed him. Why, I don't know. Maybe he guessed the truth, guessed he was your father.' She shook her head sadly.

'Why are you telling me this, Mum?' Cathy's voice was high, and her breath caught in the back of her throat. 'Why are you doing this to me now?'

'Because you need to know the truth, darling.' She recalled the speech Lucas had insisted she deliver. 'You need to know what he was capable of, and you need to stop seeing him through rose-tinted glasses. I know that you are planning something. I'm not a fool, Cath. I've heard the whispered conversations, I've seen the signs, and I want you to know that Paul isn't worth you going to prison for. He was a vicious thug and he would have moulded those boys into miniature replicas of himself as time went on.'

Cathy's fingertips turned white as she gripped onto the butler sink. 'And what about my boys? Are they not worth me seeking revenge?' She turned her head to look at her mother. 'Are they not worth going to prison for?'

Angie sighed. Since she hadn't been blessed with natural maternal instincts, she was unable to answer. Would she have gone to prison for her daughter? Of course she wouldn't. The very notion would never have even occurred to her.

'My boys...' Straightening up, Cathy began to wash the glasses in the sink. Her movements were rigid as she slammed the washed glasses down onto the draining board. 'Unlike you, Mum, my boys were my life. I would have killed for them. I would have died for them.'

'And is that what you're planning?' Angie grasped her daughter's wrist and spun her around to face her. 'Is that what you're planning to do, kill someone?'

Cathy didn't answer.

'My God, you are, aren't you?' She shook her head sadly. 'You're your father's daughter all right.' She lit a cigarette and blew out a cloud of smoke, all the while, studying her daughter. 'Samson, Samson Ivers, was your father, darling.'

'No.' Cathy's head began to swim and she dug her fingernails into the palm of her hand. No, it couldn't be true, and as the realisation of her mother's words finally hit home, she looked across to Angie, her face a mask of hatred. 'You're lying,' she spat.

'It's the truth, darling. Samson was your father and I can see him in you; you look alike.' It was said with a sense of pride. 'You have a half-brother, too, Devan Barkley. He's a few years younger than you, grew up on the estate. Maybe you knew him?'

Cathy blanched at the words and, closing her eyes tight, a wave of sickness washed over her. If what Angie said was true, then the past could so easily have been avoided. Her Paul and her boys would still have been alive if they'd all known the truth, if they could have embraced Devan into the family. If they could have acknowledged his existence, then surely, it would have swayed the course of events that had stolen her family from her.

Curling her hands into fists, Cathy screamed at her mother, 'You vicious bitch.' Using her considerable strength, she pushed Angie in the chest, causing her to crash heavily against the worktop. 'This was all your doing. If it wasn't for you, my boys would still be here.'

Angie's mouth dropped open. Never had her daughter physically lashed out at her before. In fact, she'd always considered her to be meek and mild, weak even.

'Now get out.' None too gently, Cathy dragged her mother towards the front door. 'Get out and don't you ever show your face at my door again. This was all your doing. You killed them; you killed my babies.'

In shock, Angie fell to her knees. 'Cathy,' she cried.

'No.' Standing over her mother, Cathy looked down at the woman she had loved and loathed in equal measures for the majority of her life. 'All my life, I've made excuses for you. I told myself that you loved me, even when you put yourself first, put your mates first. Even the pub came before me. As long as you were all right, then fuck everyone else, and that included me. Well, mother,' she snarled, 'that isn't how I live my life. My sons were my world, they were the air I lived and breathed. Everything I did was for them and they knew it, too. Not once did my boys ever have to wonder if I loved them, which is more than can ever be said about you.'

Tears glistened in Angie's eyes. No amount of money was worth losing her daughter for. Only it was too late to take back what was already done. 'Of course I love you, Cath; you're my daughter for Christ's sake.'

Cathy shook her head. 'I'm done, Mum, done with you.' She looked to the sky and sighed. 'I should have got shot of you years ago. Paul asked me to, many a time, but me being me, I put up with you. I thought you'd change. Well, Mum, this just about takes the biscuit, and as for Samson Ivers, he is not and never will be my father.' With those parting words, she slammed the front door closed.

'Are you okay, Cath?'

Cathy took a deep breath before turning around. 'Course I am,' she said, fixing a smile upon her face.

'Really?' Stella cocked her head to one side. 'I heard what Angie said about Samson Ivers.' She gave an embarrassed smile. 'I'm sorry. I walked in and overheard. I wasn't purposely eavesdropping on the conversation.'

'I don't want to hear it.' With her back positioned against the front door, Cathy's face was white. 'How could she, Stell? How could my own mother keep something like that from me?'

Stella raised her eyebrows. She had no answers for her sister-in-law. Hadn't they all told Kieran the exact same lie over the years? 'And what do we do, now that you know about Barkley?'

'Barkley?' Cathy's voice became instantly hard. 'This changes nothing. That bastard is still going to pay.' Her voice was high and tinged with hysteria. 'In fact, I think I will enjoy bringing him down that little bit more now.'

As she watched her sister-in-law walk away from her, Stella's face was ashen. God help them all, and more to the point, God help Devan Barkley.

27

'You have got to be fucking kidding me,' Devan roared at the top of his voice as he stared at the scene before him in abject horror.

Spread out on the double bed was a potbellied naked man in his late fifties. A shard of glass was protruding from his neck. The tangled bedsheets, headboard, walls and ceiling were coated in a film of blood.

Monica stood with her hands on her hips and her breath came out in short little bursts. 'He was a fucking nonce; wanted Sheryl to dress up as a little girl and call him daddy. When she refused, he tried to beat her black and blue.'

Devan turned to look at the girl in question. Crouched in the corner of the room, Sheryl shook uncontrollably. Her startling green eyes were staring into space, and her skin was as deathly pale as the corpse laid out on the bed. Her blood-splattered blonde hair was pulled up into pigtails and she was dressed in a school uniform, the pleated skirt barely skimming past her backside. He shook his head in consternation, his dreadlocks whipping across his face from the force of the action. 'Where the fuck is Marty?'

Monica sneered. 'The ponce is still in the office, refused to come out. Where the fuck did you find him? I thought he was supposed to be a heavy?'

Devan's face hardened. Marty, he would deal with later. 'Did he pay with cash?' he asked, referring to the body.

Monica nodded. The majority of punters did. The last thing they would want was a paper trail for their wives or girlfriends to find that would lead them back to the brothel.

'Then turn out his pockets and get rid of him,' Devan growled. 'And as for her' – he jerked his head towards Sheryl, his expression one of distaste, as though her very presence offended him – 'she's out.'

Monica's mouth dropped open and, looking from the body, to Sheryl, to Devan, her body bristled. 'You can't do that.'

'I just fucking did.' He curled his hand into a fist, daring the slapper to answer him back.

Monica rolled her eyes. Clicking her fingers, she gestured for the girls standing in the doorway, watching the spectacle unfold with interest, to help move the body. Finally, she moved towards Sheryl. 'Come on, darlin',' she cajoled, 'let's get you out of here, eh?'

Devan watched her lead the shaking young woman from the room. 'Oh, and, Mon,' he called after her, 'make sure she doesn't talk.'

Monica inwardly sighed. That went without saying.

* * *

Marty was terrified, and rightly so. Hearing a set of heavy foot-steps thunder down the staircase, he braced himself for what was to come. The office door almost came off its hinges as it crashed against the wall, and standing in the doorway snarling like a rabid dog, was Devan.

'You fucking ponce.' Devan charged around the desk and ploughed his fist into Marty's face. 'You no good, fucking ponce.' He punched his fist forward a second and third time. 'Made yourself comfortable, did you?' Snatching up the chocolate biscuits Marty had left out on the desk, he slammed them into Marty's face. 'Is that all you think about?' he bellowed in Marty's ear. 'Stuffing your fat face?'

Cowering, Marty held his arms over his head and cried. How could he even begin to tell the man that it was his scars that had kept him holed up in the office, not fear. Before he could answer, Devan had grasped him around the back of the neck, and was dragging him from around the desk, towards the door.

'Get up them fucking stairs,' Devan roared, as he half-dragged and half-kicked Marty up the staircase towards the bedrooms. 'And do what I fucking pay you to do, and sort this shit out.'

At the top of the staircase, the girls turned their heads at the commotion. The repulsion they felt at seeing his scarred, chocolate-smeared face was evident across their faces, reinforcing Marty's belief that he looked hideous, that he was, in fact, a monster.

The only person who didn't look at him like that, however, was Monica. Marty's scars may have made him look intimidating, but deep down, she thought of him as a sweetheart. Oh, he may have had his moments, and she knew that he could be a bully when the mood took him, but even so, he wasn't cold-hearted like Devan, that was if Devan even had a heart to begin with.

* * *

Snatching the money out of Lucas's hand, Angie scowled at him. Two thousand lousy quid, that was all it had taken to break the bond that she and her only daughter had shared. Admittedly, that bond had only been held together by a thin thread, but still, all thanks to her greed, her need to have a bit of bunce in her purse, the relationship was well and truly severed. Not for the first time in her lifetime, did she wish that she could cut out her own wicked tongue.

'How did she take the news?' As he leant his forearms across the steering wheel, there was genuine concern in Lucas's voice, and it was then that Angie turned on him.

'How do you think?' she spat. 'She was hardly performing cartwheels at the prospect of Samson being her father.' Her face crumpled and big fat tears rolled down her cheeks. 'She chucked me out of the house, accused me of killing the boys. Me,' she cried, 'me, killing them.' She took a tissue out of her handbag and dabbed at her watery eyes. 'I mean, what a wicked thing to say. I loved those boys, loved them. I idolised the ground they walked on.'

Lucas rolled his eyes. Despite her words, Angie would be hard pushed to rattle off her grandsons' birthdates without having to think it through first. 'And what about Devan Barkley? You warned her off him?'

'I did my bit,' Angie growled. 'For all the thanks it got me. She's a hardnosed cow, that girl, always has been. Even as a tot, she always had something to say for herself.' It was a lie, of course.

'Still' – Lucas nodded across to The Jolly Fisherman and said tongue-in-cheek – 'the pub will be back up and running soon. That will give you something to look forward to.'

'Me, step foot in there?' Pursing her lips, she stuffed the money into her handbag and yanked across the zip. 'Me, spend my money in there? Line her pockets? You've got to be kidding me.'

Lucas watched as she flung open the car door. Instinctively, he knew that, come opening night, Angie would be there. She wouldn't be able to help herself.

He waited for her to slam the door closed, without so much as a goodbye, and then sped away from the kerb. As he drove off the estate, he could only hope and pray that Angie had, in fact, got through to her daughter.

In a cloud of fresh flowery perfume, a wide smile was plastered across Cathy's face as she made her way inside the Portakabin in Stratford.

The three men inside rose from their seats and, sensing their discomfort, she raised her hand in the air. 'No need to stand to attention,' she said.

Sharing a knowing look between themselves, they sat back down.

'It's the pub.' As always, she looked immaculate, and as she smiled, she flicked a long lock of blonde hair over her shoulder. 'As you know, we are reopening again tonight, and I would like to invite you all personally.' She rested her gaze on Lucas, forcing the smile to stay on her face. 'All of you are welcome.'

Lucas raised his eyebrows. 'You do realise that I own a stake in the pubs,' he told her in a gruff voice. 'I don't need your invitation to step foot inside my own boozer, Cathy.'

'Cheers for that,' Charlie hastily interrupted. 'Wouldn't miss the grand reopening for anything.'

'Yeah, thanks, Mrs Mooney,' Darren joined in. 'It'd be an honour.'

'Good.' Ignoring Lucas's remark, Cathy looked around the cabin. 'Well,' she said, 'that was all I came for.' She nodded at them. 'I'll see the three of you tonight then.' She smiled widely and turned to leave. 'Oh, and by the way, the first drink is on the house.'

Lucas raised his eyebrows a second time. 'Giving away free booze? Are you trying to put us out of business already?'

Halting beside the open door, Cathy arched her own eyebrows. 'After the first drink, they'll come back for more, don't you worry about that.' The smile left her face. 'I'm not a complete imbecile, you know. I do know how to run a business, and your pockets will still be lined come the end of the night.'

As quickly as she'd arrived, she was gone again. The only evidence that she had even been there was the lingering scent of her perfume.

Lounging back on the chair, Lucas looked to Charlie and Darren. 'What the fuck was that all about?'

Darren shrugged. 'Dunno, but I think it's safe to say that you're not her favourite person, mate.'

Lucas sighed in a dejected manner. Tell him something he didn't already know.

* * *

Walking back across the forecourt towards her car, a devious smile was etched across Cathy's face. The grand reopening was the perfect alibi she needed. Anyone who was anyone would be in attendance to witness her playing the perfect host. In a strange way, it was fitting that she had chosen this night to end Devan Barkley's life – a true tribute to both Paul and the boys, and one that she was very much looking forward to.

By seven thirty that evening, The Jolly Fisherman was packed to the rafters, and after being closed for a couple of months, the regulars all breathed a sigh of relief at its reopening.

Dressed to kill, Cathy stood behind the bar. Stopping to chat to those customers who she had known since childhood, she played the game, and afforded them her brightest smile.

The clang of the tills opening and closing was like music to her ears, and with a queue at the bar that was at least four bodies deep, she knew that this night was a long time coming, and much anticipated by all and sundry.

'Hello, darling.' Angie, despite her initial refusal to come along to the opening night, stood in line at the bar, waiting to get served. 'Get me a dry white wine will you, Cath? I'm bloody parched.'

Cathy looked her mother over and, giving a slight nod of her head, shouted out, 'Sue, serve Angie, would you?' With those parting words, she walked away without a backwards glance, leaving an open-mothed Angie in her wake. Oh, she would let her mother back into the fold at some point, but not before she had stewed in her own juices first. As far as she was concerned, it was exactly what Angie deserved.

* * *

Lucas sipped at a pint of cola, silently observing Cathy. Her movements were both easy and carefree. She looked well, happy even, and he smiled softly to himself. It was good to see that she had come out the other side stronger than ever. From across the other side of the public bar, he took note of Stella, Katie, and Donna. There was a nervousness about them that was at odds with the majority of the punters, and he sighed sadly.

'Good night, eh?' Darren broke his thoughts. 'It's good to see the old place up and running again. Paul would have been fucking proud of her.' He nodded towards Cathy. 'She's done a blinding job with the place.'

Lucas nodded and, looking around him at the new décor, he couldn't help but agree. He'd been sceptical when he'd first been told of her plans for the pub, but even he had to admit, she'd pulled it off. Not only did the bar look fresh, but the newly purchased round polished tables, upholstered chairs, and strategically placed leather sofas gave the pub a modern twist.

He sipped once more at his drink. Taller than the average customer, he had a good view of everything that went on around him. He scanned the bar area over the heads of the crowd. Where was she? His forehead furrowed as he observed the length of the bar. Just seconds, that was all it had taken for her to disappear from his eye line. He snapped his head to where Stella had been standing, and noting that she, too, had disappeared, along with Katie and Donna, his gut began to churn.

* * *

With her hair pulled up into a high ponytail, Cathy kicked off her high-heeled shoes and shoved her feet into a pair of dark coloured trainers. Already, she had discarded the sequined dress she had been wearing for a pair of black jeans and a dark-coloured hoodie jacket. She threw the car keys towards Donna and urged her to unlock the doors, all the while, looking over her shoulder. Her face was partially obscured by the hood that she had pulled down over her head.

'Move,' she hissed, 'we need to get out of here, and fast.'

Dressed head to toe in black, Donna did as she was bade. Urging Stella and Katie into the car, she slipped behind the wheel and pushed the key into the ignition.

'Go,' Cathy cried. In the rear-view mirror, she checked to see that they hadn't been followed, and as the car purred to life, she relaxed into the seat.

'Are you sure about this, Cath?' Stella asked, in between biting on her thumb nail.

'I've never been surer.' She pulled a rucksack up from the footwell and placed it on her lap. Unzipping the bag, she took out several kitchen knives and passed them across.

'What are we supposed to do with these?' Turning the kitchen knife over in her hand, Stella was genuinely perplexed.

'If that bastard so much as looks at you the wrong way, slice him up.' Ignoring the look of shock that passed across the women's faces, Cathy turned back in her seat and, carefully lifting out a hand towel, she placed it in her lap and then proceeded to unwrap it.

'Fucking hell, Cath.' Glancing at Cathy's lap, and more importantly, what she had there, Donna veered across the lanes, narrowly missing the oncoming traffic. 'Jesus Christ, where did you get that from?'

Cathy laughed. Holding up a hand gun, she turned it around, inspecting it as she did so. 'It's not loaded,' she lied, before smiling at Donna's obvious shock. 'Paul may have been a lot of things, but he wasn't stupid. He would never have left a loaded gun lying around.'

'Where did you get it from, Auntie Cath?' Sitting forward, Katie's eyes were equally as wide.

'I found it in a shoe box at the bottom of Paul's wardrobe.' She placed the gun in her lap and caressed the hard metal.

'Jesus fucking wept,' Stella muttered from the back seat.

Cathy smiled once more. 'Like I've already said, it isn't loaded, so stop your worrying. All I'm going to do is use it to scare them into doing what we want.'

Locking eyes with Donna in the rear-view mirror, Stella shook her head. They were in over their heads, and with Cathy the driving force behind them, it could only be a recipe for disaster.

* * *

Racing towards his car with Darren and Charlie behind him, Lucas was incensed. Just seconds, that was all it had taken for him to lose her.

'Why weren't you watching her?' Charlie growled.

'And why the fuck weren't you?' Lucas answered back, shooting Charlie a hard stare.

They jumped into the car and, starting the ignition, Lucas sped out of the car park, leaving behind him a cloud of dust and exhaust fumes. By his reckoning, they were only a few minutes behind her, fifteen at the very most. Surely, she couldn't get herself into too much trouble in that short space of time.

28

Donna parked the car and climbed out. She eyed the high street wearily. 'I just had a thought.'

The three women looked at her.

'What if he isn't in there?'

Cathy smiled. Tapping the outline of the gun that she had slipped inside her jacket pocket, she said, 'Then we make sure that someone gets him here. We've not come here to play games, Donna, and the sooner they realise that, the better it will be for everyone concerned.'

Keeping their heads down low, they walked along the busy high street. Bright lights from nearby shop fronts, takeaways and bars illuminated the pavement. Around them, people bustled along the street. Some were eager to get home from a hard day at work, more concerned with what they were going to cook for tea, than to take notice of four women dressed head to toe in black. Others were making their way to meet up with friends for the evening, their excited chatter loud to the women's ears.

Finally, they reached their destination. This end of the street was much more dilapidated than the former end, with buildings boarded up and brightly-coloured graffiti sprayed across shuttered shop fronts that had long since gone out of business.

Taking a deep breath, Cathy looked at each of the women in turn, then pulled the gun out from her jacket pocket.

'I don't like this,' Donna whispered, nodding down at the weapon. 'You never said anything about bringing a gun, Cath.'

Cathy rolled her eyes. 'How many times do I have to say it? It's not loaded.' She then proceeded to rap her knuckles upon the wooden door.

It seemed to take an age for the door to open, and with their hearts beating wildly inside their chests, the four women braced themselves. No matter what, Cathy was determined that she would get inside the building, even if that resulted in her steaming in and using brute force.

'Yeah, who is it?' The door opened to reveal a young woman dressed in a sheer black body stocking that left little to the imagination. On her feet, she wore six-inch high-heeled open-toed stilettos. All the better, as far as Cathy was concerned. At least she wouldn't be able to easily escape their clutches wearing those heels.

'Where is Devan?' Hissing out the words, Cathy was upon the woman within nanoseconds. She twisted the terrified girl's arm up behind her back and shoved the gun into her side, before she'd even had the chance to open her mouth to answer them, and more importantly, alert anyone else to their arrival.

Frog-marching the girl down the hallway, she twisted the girl's arm up even further. 'Tell me where he is, otherwise I'll break your fucking arm,' she growled into the terrified girl's ear.

'He's not here.' Marcella was close to tears. 'He hasn't been here all day.'

'What's going on down there?'

Cathy snapped her head towards the staircase. A thin

brunette woman wearing nothing but a short red satin kimono that was tied loosely around her waist, exposing her full breasts, walked down the carpeted steps.

Still holding the girl's arm in a vice-like grip, Cathy pointed the gun out in front of her. 'I take it that you're Monica?' She saw the woman's back ever so slightly stiffen. 'Well, Monica, do yourself a favour and get Devan here, now.' She twisted hard on the girl's arm until she was gasping with pain and practically bent over in two. 'I'm not playing games. I want that bastard here. Do that, and no one will get hurt.'

Monica held up her hands and, reaching the bottom step, she gestured towards a door that led off the hallway. 'The telephone is through there.'

Cathy licked at her dry lips and nodded.

Following closely behind Monica, they came to a halt outside a door at the far end of a dimly lit corridor.

'Wait' – Cathy aimed the gun at Monica's chest – 'no funny business, I'm warning you. I'm not scared to use this, lady, and the mood I'm in, I'd shoot you dead and laugh while doing it.'

The hint of a smirk played out across Monica's lips. 'And from where I come from, darling, I wouldn't need a gun to tear your fucking head off.'

Cathy took the warning on board. Curling her lips into a snarl, she jerked her head towards the door. 'Move it.'

* * *

Marty was having a nap when the office door crashed open. Blinking his eyes rapidly, he gripped onto the desk and reeled backwards in shock at the scene in front of him.

'What's going on?' Swallowing down the urge to cover his scars, his voice was thick from both shock and fear.

'These ladies would like to see Devan.' Monica's eyes were full of meaning as she nodded down at the phone. 'Be a love, would you, Marty? Get him on the blower. Tell him' – she looked across to Cathy and cocked her head to one side – 'who are you exactly?'

Cathy gave a nasty chuckle. 'I'm his worst nightmare come true, darling.' She yanked Marcella's arm up an inch higher, causing the girl to let out a strangled sob. 'Tell him that Cathy Mooney is here to see him.'

On hearing the name, Marty's eyes widened and he scrambled to reach for his mobile phone. In his haste, he knocked a packet of chocolate digestives, a full mug of tea, and a pile of paperwork to the floor.

By the time he'd located his phone, his breathing had become shallow, and tapping out a series of digits, he didn't take his gaze off the gun as he relayed the situation across to Devan. The man's response was enough to make him break out in a cold sweat. Switching off the call, he cautiously placed the device on the desk. Aware that any sudden movements could easily result in a bullet careening in his direction, he blurted out, 'He's on his way.' He caught Monica's eyes and raised his eyebrows slightly. 'He said to clear out the building.'

'She stays where she is,' Cathy growled and, flicking her head towards an empty chair, she motioned for Monica to sit down.

Monica rolled her eyes. Sighing deeply, she shook her head. 'He'll kill you for this.'

'Maybe,' Cathy sneered, thrusting the gun forward, 'maybe not.'

'They've got a point, Cath, the less witnesses the better,' Donna whispered from behind her.

Taking a moment to think the situation through, Cathy nodded. 'You' – she yanked the scantily clad girl towards her and growled in her ear – 'get everyone out.' She yanked on her arm a second time, ignoring her yelp of pain. 'If you so much as utter a word about what is going down, I'll kill you, you got that?'

Marcella vigorously nodded, and as Cathy pushed her none too gently towards the door, she rubbed at her injured arm. She was clearly terrified and it showed. She didn't even look back in Marty's or Monica's direction as she fled from the room as fast as her high-heeled shoes would allow her to.

'Well, this is much better, isn't it?' Cathy grinned. 'All we need now is for the bastard who murdered my family to make an appearance.' Her gaze fell upon Marty and her forehead furrowed. 'You.'

Marty swallowed deeply.

'Were you involved? Were you there when my boys were butchered?'

Marty shook his head so fast that his heavy jowls wobbled. 'It wasn't me,' he cried.

Cathy's expression became hard. 'But you knew.' She turned the gun on him. 'You knew what he was going to do? What he'd planned?'

'No.' He continued to shake his head, his throat suddenly dry. 'I swear to you, I didn't know.'

'He's lying.' From behind her, Katie's cheeks burned red as she spat out the words. 'He's lying, Auntie Cath.' She charged forward and her hands flew out in all directions as she punched and slapped Marty's scarred head and large cumbersome body. 'My baby,' she screamed, 'will never know their father, because of you.'

'Enough.' Nodding, Cathy indicated for Stella to pull her daughter back. 'Save your energy for that bastard Barkley,' she told her niece dryly.

* * *

Devan was a man on a mission. Racing through a number of red lights, it took him just eight minutes to reach the brothel. He climbed out of his car – a gleaming brand spanking new black BMW – slammed the door closed, and without even bothering to lock up behind him, he charged across the pavement towards the front door.

With flared nostrils and eyes that appeared both wide and manic, he could taste the anger that flowed through his veins. 'The bitch,' he growled, 'the fucking bitch.'

The door almost came off its hinges as he kicked it wide open and proceeded to tear down the hallway.

The front door slamming against the wall made the occupants of the room jump out of their skins, and hearing heavy footsteps make their way along the hallway, Stella, Donna and Katie nestled against Cathy's back, with the kitchen knives she had provided thrust out in front of them.

'What the fuck is this?' Standing in the doorway, Devan was practically frothing at the mouth.

Cathy looked up at the man responsible for the deaths of her family and sneered. There and then, she was thankful that she could see no resemblance between them, nothing to indicate that he was her half-brother. Had she seen the faces of her sons in the man she was determined to annihilate, deep down, she knew she would have faltered. How could she have not? It would have been the equivalent of killing her boys all over again.

Taking this as their cue to move, both Monica and Marty jumped up from their seats.

'Sit down,' Cathy screamed, and as she waved the gun

between them, her hand shook. 'We're here for him.' She trained the gun on Devan. 'You killed my family.'

The laugh that spilled from Devan's lips only served to increase Cathy's rage even further.

From the corner of her eye, she noted a movement, and spinning around, she aimed the gun at Monica. 'I told you to sit the fuck down.'

It was Marty who charged out of his seat, and in a state of fear, Cathy involuntarily squeezed the trigger. The gunshot was deafening in the small room.

Amidst Marty's screams that he'd been hit, in a blind panic, she dropped the gun to the floor. Shock that she had actually shot someone spread across her face.

Within seconds, Devan was upon her. He punched her full pelt in the side of her face, blurring her vision, and then slamming her up against the wall so hard that her head thudded painfully against the concrete, his fingers curled around her throat.

Gasping for air, Cathy clawed at his hands. Around her, she could hear the bloodcurdling screams that came from Stella, Donna and Katie. She could hear the blind panic in their voices. Still, she continued to try and fight him off, but he was too strong for her, far too strong, and as darkness edged into her vision, she could only hope and pray that it wouldn't be long until she saw Paul and her boys once more.

* * *

Amidst the chaos in the room, Devan squeezed his fingers around the little blonde's throat even harder. Sensing her life begin to ebb away, he dropped her unceremoniously to the floor, and turning his head at the sudden movement in the doorway, his eyes widened. Standing as large as life, as if he was some kind of avenging angel, was Lucas Vaughn. He blinked rapidly. No. No way could he have survived the deadly heroin and opiate cocktail that he himself had prepared.

He opened his mouth to speak, but before he could even utter a word, the man's fist began to rain blows down on top of him.

For the first time in his life, Lucas understood the red mist that had often descended over Paul. Years and years of pent up rage and anger was unleashed as he kicked and punched the living daylights out of Devan Barkley. He had a score to settle and knew instinctively that he would never rest easy again until he had dished out his own form of retribution.

After what seemed an age, he could feel himself being roughly dragged away. Somewhere in the back of his mind, even as he continued to kick his feet out, he could hear the screams for him to stop, could hear the concern in the women's voices as they tried to get Cathy to her feet. He looked down at the bloodied mess that had been Devan Barkley, and hawking deep into his throat, he spat on the man's lifeless form.

Breathing heavily, he swatted Darren's and Charlie's arms away from him, and making a beeline for Cathy, he pulled her gently up from the floor and into his arms.

'Are you okay, darling?' he asked softly.

She collapsed into his chest, coughing uncontrollably and gasping for air. Already, he could see a large swelling across her cheek that made her beautiful face look grotesque, and he had a sneaky suspicion that her cheek bone was fractured, if not broken. Littered around her slender neck were the vivid red marks Barkley's fingers had left. They would soon turn to purple and black bruises, a reminder of the fact that she could so easily have lost her life.

Although it had so far remained unspoken between them, they were both well aware that if he hadn't arrived in the nick of time, then Barkley would have killed her. It was as plain and as simple as that. Gently stroking her hair as he held her tiny frame tight, he whispered in her ear, 'It's over, darling. It's finally all over.'

* * *

Darren and Charlie, also known as the aptly named clean-up crew, set to work. Ushering the women out of the room, they looked down at Marty Hanratty. The denim jeans he wore were stained with dark crimson blood, and in his thigh, a bullet that had narrowly missed an artery was lodged.

There were to be no witnesses left behind, and after dumping Barkley's body into the boot of Lucas's car, they dragged a clearly terrified, screaming, and crying Monica and Marty from the room and into the cold night air.

Once their night's work was done, there would only be one last task left to be executed, and that was to torch the building. Using enough petrol to fill a fleet of cars, the brothel would subsequently erupt into flames, leaving nothing but charred beams and ash remnants in its wake. All fingerprints, all knowledge that Cathy, Lucas, the women, and of course themselves, were ever in close proximity was to be destroyed forever, along with the brothel and its deadly secrets.

EPILOGUE

Cathy could barely keep the smile from her face as she watched her tiny grandson take his first breath. Screwing up his face, Kieran Junior screamed and hollered loudly, as if letting the world know of his safe arrival.

She took the tiny, wrapped bundle from the midwife and peered into the infant's face. It was like history repeating itself all over again. The child was the image of his father, and his father before him.

'He's beautiful.' Tears glistened in her eyes and, turning to look at Donna, she half-smiled and half-cried. 'I can't believe it,' she said, studying her grandson's face. 'I'm actually a grandmother.'

From the hospital bed, Donna beamed with delight. 'Let's have a hold then.' She opened up her arms and as Cathy gently placed the tiny bundle into them, silent tears slipped down her cheeks. This baby, this little boy, was a gift from Kieran himself, she was certain of it.

Together, the two women laughed and cried as they marvelled over the miracle that was childbirth.

* * *

Two days later, Cathy busied herself making a pot of tea. It had seemed only fitting that her son's child should spend his first weeks, or if she had her way, his first few months, in his father's home.

From the kitchen window, she watched her new grandson's brothers charging around the garden and she smiled to herself. As time had gone on, she had grown to love each and every one of Donna's children. They even called her Nanny Cath, much to her delight.

A knocking at the front door broke Cathy's reverie and, wiping her hands on a tea towel, she made her way out into the hallway and opened the door.

Standing on the doorstep was Lucas. In his hands, he held a blue teddy bear and he smiled at her shyly. 'For the baby,' he said, thrusting the bear towards her.

Cathy flapped her hand. 'Get yourself inside,' she said gently. 'If you're lucky, you might even be able to pry the baby from my mother's arms.'

'Oi, I heard that,' Angie called out from the lounge.

Smiling widely, Cathy pulled the front door open even wider. Gone was any animosity that she had once regarded Lucas with. The man had always been a big part of Paul's life. He'd loved him like a brother, and finally, she was able to understand why. When she'd needed him the most, Lucas had been there for her, and more than anything, she knew that without him, she would never have seen her grandson's face, would never have held him in her arms, and more importantly, she would never have truly known peace.

Months earlier, they had come to a joint decision to sell the public houses and business, and other than her home, there was nothing left to remind her of the past. Finally, it was all over. Kieran Junior would never follow on in his father's or grandfather's footsteps. Never would they have to await a knock at the front door to tell them his life had been cruelly taken away from them.

With the tea made, Cathy carried the tray into the lounge and, setting it down onto the coffee table, she gazed into the wicker Moses basket. Her grandson was fast asleep. She smiled down at him, noting how peaceful, how innocent he was. She closed her eyes momentarily. No, Donna would never receive that same knock on the door that she once had.

Finally, she was ready to lock away the hurt and the pain that had engulfed her entire being. Not that she would ever forget Paul or her sons. How could she? They were her everything, they always would be, but with her new family around her, it was finally time to begin living life again. Finally, the nightmare was over.

MORE FROM KERRY KAYA

We hope you enjoyed reading *Reprisal*. If you did, please leave a review.

If you'd like to gift a copy, this book is also available as an ebook, digital audio download and audiobook CD.

Sign up to Kerry Kaya's mailing list for news, competitions and updates on future books.

http://bit.ly/KerryKayaNewsletter

Another gripping gangland read from Kerry Kaya, *The Price*, is available now.

ABOUT THE AUTHOR

Kerry Kaya is the hugely popular author of Essex based gritty gangland thrillers with strong family dynamics. She grew up on one of the largest council estates in the UK, where she sets her novels. She also works full-time in a busy maternity department for the NHS.

Follow Kerry on social media:

 twitter.com/KerryKayaWriter

 instagram.com/kerry_kaya_writer

facebook.com/kerry.bryant.58

ABOUT BOLDWOOD BOOKS

Boldwood Books is a fiction publishing company seeking out the best stories from around the world.

Find out more at www.boldwoodbooks.com

Sign up to the Book and Tonic newsletter for news, offers and competitions from Boldwood Books!

http://www.bit.ly/bookandtonic

We'd love to hear from you, follow us on social media:

facebook.com/BookandTonic

twitter.com/BoldwoodBooks

instagram.com/BookandTonic